THE DARKENING ARCHIPELAGO

NeWest Press

theDARKENING ARCHIPELAGO

A COLE BLACKWATER MYSTERY

STEPHEN LEGAULT

Library and Archives Canada Cataloguing in Publication

Legault, Stephen, 1971–
        The darkening archipelago [electronic resource] / Stephen Legault.

ISBN 978-1-897126-66-0

        I. Title.

PS8623.E46633D37 2010   C813'.6   C2009-906233-X

Editor for the Board: Don Kerr
Cover and interior design: Natalie Olsen, Kisscut Design
Cover image: Alexandra Morton, Raincoast Research Society
Author photo: Dan Anthon
Copy editing: NJ Brown

The lyrics on page 101 are from the Blue Rodeo song "Fools Like You," written by Greg Keelor and Jim Cuddy, and were reprinted with the kind permission of Thunder Hawk Music.

NeWest Press acknowledges the support of the Canada Council for the Arts, the Alberta Foundation for the Arts, and the Edmonton Arts Council for our publishing program. We also acknowledge the financial support of the Government of Canada through the Book Publishing Industry Development Program (BPIDP).

201, 8540–109 Street
Edmonton, Alberta T6G 1E6
780-432-9427
NeWest Press www.newestpress.com

No bison were harmed in the making of this book.
We are committed to protecting the environment and to the responsible use of natural resources. This book was printed on 100% post-consumer recycled paper.

1 2 3 4 5 13 12 11 10
printed and bound in Canada

This book, like everything else in my life, is for Jenn, Rio, and Silas.
And with love and gratitude to Bob, Sharon, and Mabel.

1 The rain began suddenly. From the west, skipping like a flat stone over the broad waters separating Vancouver Island from the convoluted knot of smaller islands at the mouth of Knight Inlet, the storm raced toward the steep slopes of the Coast Mountains. When it reached them, it ricocheted up their flanks and back and forth across the narrow passage at the mouth of the fjord. With the rain came wind that moulded the water into small waves, churning it into ten-foot swells within an hour. The sky pressed down and pounded the water with machine gun volleys of driving rain. The tops of the densely forested mountains rising from the inlet disappeared as a tattered blackness settled against the sea.

Archie Ravenwing felt the storm approaching before he saw it, before it soaked him through. He could feel it coming on for most of the day. Maybe someone had done the weather dance last night, their blankets twisting as they moved back and forth to the chorus of voices, to the beating of drums. Maybe he should have paid closer attention to that morning's marine weather forecast.

He felt the storm in his hands. Twisted and corded like the ropes he had spent his sixty years working with, his joints always ached when a storm loomed. From November to March, and sometimes well into April, his hands always seemed to ache. There was no denying it — he was well past his prime. But he still had work to do.

Ravenwing had set off from Port Lostcoast on the *Inlet Dancer* before dawn. On the north shore of Parish Island, Port Lostcoast was where he was born and where he had spent most of his life working as a fisherman. But he wasn't fishing today. The salmon season wasn't set to open for another two months, if it opened at all. For thousands of years, people along the wild, ragged coast of British Columbia had guided their boats through the heaving waters of the Pacific, harvesting the fish for food and ceremony. Among the tribes of the West Coast, salmon was the most important animal in the world. Life turned on salmon seasons. But in the last twenty years, so much had changed. Ravenwing thought of this as he powered up the inlet that morning, intent on his destination but aware of the shifting weather around him.

Salmon smolts had been running for nearly two weeks, and Ravenwing had spent every day on the water since they started. These silvery darts spent as many as three years living in the tiny headwater tributaries of Knight Inlet. Most of the salmon born there were eaten or died of natural causes. Only ten percent survived to grow large enough to migrate down river and out into the salty water at the mouth of the creeks and then into the Inlet itself.

The morning had been bright enough, with nothing more menacing than a few clouds hanging over the mountains of Vancouver Island, far to the west. But now Ravenwing suspected that by day's end there would be rain. He flexed his thick, burled hands as he lightly played the wheel of his thirty-two-foot troller, heading east up the inlet.

By the time the day started to warm, Ravenwing had reached Minstrel Island and the narrow mouth to Clio Channel, the ideal place for a couple hours of dip-net sampling before he turned his attention to the small bays and coves that marked the jigsaw puzzle shore. Archie shut down the *Inlet Dancer*'s powerful Cummins 130-horsepower inboard motor and let the silence of the morning wash over him. He stepped from the wheelhouse onto the aft deck with a Thermos of coffee, stretching and yawning. Thermos in hand, he deftly walked the high, narrow gunwale and sat on the raised fish box, which doubled as a table. He unscrewed the cap of the Thermos and closed his eyes to savour the scent of hot, rich coffee. The smell mingled with the tang of the ocean, salty and spiced with the yin and yang of coastal life and decay, and the pungent fragrance of the thick Sitka spruce and red cedar forest rising up along the towering cliffs just a hundred metres off his port side. Archie Ravenwing smiled broadly as he drew these fragrances deeply into his lungs.

He poured coffee into the Thermos cap and blew on it gently, squinting at the steam that swirled up and disappeared on the breeze. Later, Archie guessed, that breeze would turn into a squall. But for the moment the morning was warm and gentle, and he savoured it. He sipped his coffee and looked around him.

Born into the Lostcoast band of the North Salish First Nation, Archie Ravenwing had been fishing, guiding, hunting, and exploring the coastal estuaries, inlets, reaches, and straits from as far away as Puget Sound to the Queen Charlotte Islands since he was old enough to manage a bowlegged stance in a boat. As he let his eyes roll over the massive sweep of land and water and sky before him that morning, he was happy that this reach of the Broughton Archipelago had remained unchanged for generations. The hills jutted steeply from the rich waters, their shoulders cloaked in spruce and fir. Beneath those giant trees, tangles of salmonberries and alders gripped the soil. And between them walked another totem species for the Lostcoast people — the grizzly bear. Bears and salmon and the ancient forests that surrounded them were a holy trinity for Archie and his people. Grizzly bears fed on the salmon as the fish bashed their way up through the ankle-deep waters of the tiny tributaries to their spawning grounds each fall. The grizzly bears grew fat, often eating only the fish brains, rich in the nutrients they would need for their winter hibernation. The dead fish, left to rot in the woods, nourished the stalwart trees, which in turn held the entire ecosystem together with their wide, spreading roots. The trees sheltered and cooled the salmon rivers and fed the many smaller creatures that made their homes among them. When the trees fell into the streams, downed logs created places for the spawning salmon to hide and rest as, exhausted and crazed, they struggled back to their source of life.

Archie sipped his coffee, thinking about this cycle of existence. He pushed back the sadness that approached whenever he thought this way. There was some question as to whether there would be enough wild salmon in this year's run to allow for a commercial fishery. Talk in Victoria, the provincial capital, and among senior federal officials responsible for the fishery, suggested that a complete ban might be necessary to allow decimated salmon runs to recover.

The people of the Lostcoast band had been fishing there for thousands of years, but they had never contributed to the decimation of salmon the way the modern industrial fishery had. Now Archie Ravenwing's people would pay the price incurred by the greed and short-sightedness of the commercial fishing industry and its proponents in government. In the years since British Columbia's current Liberal government had lifted the moratorium on new salmon farms in the province, there had been an explosion of interest in new aquaculture developments along BC's knotted west coast. In the Broughton Archipelago, where Archie Ravenwing fished and lived, there were nearly thirty salmon farms in operation. Many of these open-net farms were located on the migration routes of native wild salmon. And though industry advocates argued that the two were unrelated, along with the development of salmon farms came a corresponding decline in the number of wild salmon. Archie knew that, in a recent count, only one hundred and fifty thousand wild salmon returned to the Broughton, down from the historical three and a half million. In 2002 the wild pink salmon stock collapsed, with only five percent of the native wild fish returning to spawn. Archie knew the numbers by heart.

For Ravenwing, it was as if part of his own body, his own soul, had vanished. The part of his heart that swam through the waters of Tribune Channel and up the mouth of Knight Inlet was gone, lost like the spirit of the once-great salmon.

Archie tried to keep his darkening sadness at bay. How could it have come to this? he wondered. After a thousand years of tradition, his family wouldn't be allowed to fish their ancestral waters? He turned his face toward the sky. A throaty call greeted him, and he opened his eyes to see a jet-black shape cruise overhead. He heard the husky chortle again. Archie raised a hand in greeting. "Good morning, Grandpa," he said quietly, waving at the raven, a smile creasing his face. "U'melth, Raven, who brought us the moon, fire, salmon, sun, and the tides," he recited. "Trickster, grandfather of a thousand pranks. Okay! I'll lighten up!" He drained his mug and slung the dregs into the water. "Time to get to work," he added.

Archie rose, stretched out the stiffness that had accumulated in his joints, and walked back to the wheelhouse, where he opened a large bin and removed the tools he would need for his morning work. He put the long, flexible net together on its pole and readied half a dozen plastic sample jars. These he put on the fish box on the deck of the boat. Without ceremony he began his sampling, drawing forth the tiny salmon fry to be funnelled into the jars. So few, so few. Ravenwing shook his head as he dipped again into the waters.

By noon he had filled the jars with juvenile salmon, whose tiny, finger-sized bodies were being consumed by sea lice. This was what Archie Ravenwing was seeking—irrefutable evidence that the wild salmon stocks of Knight Inlet and the Broughton Archipelago were being parasitized by sea lice.

Archie held a jar up to the light and counted the lice clinging to the salmon. On one smolt he counted four parasites from two different species. Adults might succumb when they had six or seven sea lice on their fins, gills, or skin. Smolts like those in Archie's sampling jars would die with only a few sea lice feeding on them. Archie regarded his unfortunate catch. "Not doing so good, are you, little friends?" He kept finding more and more smolts with more and more sea lice on them, and he had yet to reach his day's destination: Jeopardy Rock. There he expected to find the epicentre of sea lice contamination.

"Not so good...." he repeated, his voice trailing off.

Ravenwing knew that sea lice were a natural parasite that preyed on wild salmon along British Columbia's wild coast and elsewhere across North America. But in the last ten years there had been a shocking rise in the number of lice infesting wild salmon. Where before the numbers had been low, and very few salmon actually died as a result of playing host to the lice, now entire runs of wild pink and other salmon were being devastated by them. Despite protests from the salmon farming industry, irrefutable evidence pointed to the rash of farmed Atlantic salmon as the source of the outbreak. The Atlantic salmon could survive with many more sea lice than the native pink, chum, and coho.

Archie took a black felt pen from his shirt pocket and labelled the jars. He would return these to Dr. Cassandra Petrel for her study.

Archie flexed his big hands and looked at the sky. "Starting to crowd in," he said aloud to nobody in particular. "Fixing to churn up pretty good, I think."

He knew he should head back down the inlet toward Port Lost-coast before the storm set upon him, but he had one more thing to do that day. Something was eating Archie Ravenwing, and he had to set it straight. So instead of turning the *Inlet Dancer* for home, he powered across the inlet toward the mouth of Tribune Channel, skipping the heavy boat across the small waves already being formed by the wind.

■ Now the rain fell in torrents, churning the waves like knives thrust into the sea. The *Inlet Dancer* bounced and rocked, nose into the waves, powering past the fish farms at Doctor Islets and into the main body of Knight Inlet, making for home. Archie stood in the pilothouse near the stern of the boat, one hand locked on the wheel, the other clenching the throttle. This blow was bigger than he had foreseen and, though he was prepared to moor and wait out the storm, this stretch of water had few safe harbours.

After what he had seen at Jeopardy Rock, a new urgency filled Archie Ravenwing and made him push for home against what seemed prudent for the weather.

A wave crashed over the bow of the *Inlet Dancer,* and the boat dipped into the trough behind it, rising up the side of another stack of water. The swells now topped fifteen feet and came in irregular patterns, every fourth, fifth, or sixth wave taller than the rest, coming on faster than the others. Ravenwing firmly held the wheel, keeping the boat head-on to the storm, not wanting the narrow vessel to get punched side-to by one of the rogue waves.

He had suspected for some time that what was happening at Jeopardy Rock was more than just simple salmon farming. He had suspected for some time that the company was doing more than just breeding Atlantic salmon. Now he was certain. He would make his calls when he reached Port Lostcoast and begin to set the record straight. He would begin to make amends. Did Archie Ravenwing believe in redemption? He believed in justice, even if his own actions hadn't always seemed just. He believed that a man's motivation sometimes propelled behaviour that appeared inconsistent with his espoused values. But we are complex creatures, reasoned Ravenwing.

Another wave rocked the *Inlet Dancer,* and Archie pitched forward. He patted the wheel and remembered that she had survived worse.

It was growing dark. The day was slipping from the sky, and the clouds pressed down so low that the tops of the trees on mighty Gilford Island were hardly visible. Ravenwing switched on his running lights — not so he could see, but so he could be seen. Sonar and radar would guide him down the inlet, through the darkness and the storm, but he worried about small pleasure crafts caught in the weather with no such second sight.

Ravenwing counted the waves, counted the minutes. A half hour passed and the hulk of Gilford Island started to recede. The waves still crashed on the *Inlet Dancer*'s bow, and now he was moving across the channel toward the eastern tip of Turnour Island. At his pace of seven or eight knots per hour, it would be another two hours or more before he would be abreast of Parish Island, and home.

The VHF marine radio in the pilothouse crackled and, intuitively, Ravenwing set it to scan. Static filled the wheelhouse, the white noise engulfed by the sound of the storm that darkened the archipelago around Ravenwing. Then there was a voice, clear as a bell: "Any craft in the vicinity of Deep Water Cove, this is *Rising Moon.* I've lost my primary and am taking on water."

Ravenwing snatched up the handset and spoke over the howl of the storm. "*Rising Moon,* this is *Inlet Dancer.* I'm passing Ship Rock now, about to make the crossing. What is your position?"

"Glad to hear your voice, *Inlet Dancer.* I'm about one mile west of Deep Water, but I'm getting pushed toward the rocks on Deep Water Bluff."

"Do you have secondary?"

"I'm running on my little Evinrude 25, *Inlet Dancer.*"

"Okay, hold on, I'll circle back for you."

"I'm glad to find you out here," came the static-filled response.

"I'm not," Ravenwing said over the VHF and returned the handset to the radio.

For a moment he would be side-to the brunt of the storm, so

Ravenwing determined to make that quick. He throttled up, pushing over the breaking waves, and counted. The big waves pushed a wall of water over the boat's bow onto the deck, momentarily flooding it until the water drained away through the breaks in the gunwales. He counted. A wave crested, ebbed, and Ravenwing throttled back, spun the wheel, and turned to lee, then powered back up again as the stern of the boat was engulfed in the next white breaker. The ocean flooded into the wheelhouse, washing Ravenwing to his ankles in icy water.

In ten minutes he was adjacent to Deep Water Cove, the massive bluffs that guarded the opening black through the shadowless night.

Ravenwing spoke calmly into the handset. "*Rising Moon*, this is *Inlet Dancer*. Can you see my running lights?"

There was no response. He peered at his sonar and radar, watching the rocky coast weave its white line along the left side of the screen, searching for rocks and logs in his path, scanning for the tell-tale shape of a boat. "*Rising Moon*, this is *Inlet Dancer*...."

"I see you, Archie," came the voice, clear through the radio.

"What's your location?"

"I'm right behind you."

Archie turned in the pilothouse and saw the *Rising Moon*'s running lights emerge from the cove.

"I found some shelter to wait in. Can you come alongside me?"

"Yup," Archie said, turning again in the roiling waters. Another wave broke over his boat, and he was slammed hard into the fibreglass wall of the pilothouse. He stayed standing, his fingers locked on the wheel and the throttle.

The *Rising Moon* was a small pleasure craft that had seen better days. Archie cut his throttle as much as he dared so close to the shore and eased toward the smaller boat. The canopy was up, the pilot eclipsed by the windshield and the rain that drove down on the inlet like an angry fist.

"Do you want me to tow you into the cove, *Rising Moon*?" Archie asked into the handset.

"Can you come alongside, and we'll talk it through?"

Archie cursed. It was always the same with this guy it seemed. "Sure, but let's make it quick, as it's fixing to blow pretty good and I don't want to be out longer than need be." He put the handset down and guided the *Inlet Dancer* alongside the drifting *Rising Moon*.

When the two boats were just ten feet apart, Archie killed his motor and stepped out from the pilothouse, grabbing a gaff hook from the wall. He stepped onto the narrow deck of the boat and peered through the storm, holding onto the gunwale for support. "Jesus Christ, man, come on deck and let's get this over with," Archie cursed into the howling night.

Finally a shape emerged from beneath the canopy of the *Rising Moon*. The man waved and moved to the stern of his vessel, holding on for dear life. Over the clamour of the storm he yelled, "Imagine *me* needing help from *you*."

"Imagine," mocked Ravenwing. "So what exactly are you doing out on a night like this? And in that little tub?"

"I could ask you the same question," replied the man, who was using a gaff of his own to hook the stern gunwale of Ravenwing's boat. Ravenwing used his tool to reach for the *Rising Moon*'s fore cleats. The boats rose and fell, waves surging against them, and they came together with a crash of the *Inlet Dancer*'s sturdy, fibreglass-covered wood against the *Rising Moon*'s aging hull.

"Your boat is going to be crushed if we stay out like this," Ravenwing yelled. "Let's hook a line and I'll tow you into the cove. We can find a place to secure this tub and we'll motor back to Lostcoast on the *Dancer*."

The man on the *Rising Moon* gave a thumbs up and manoeuvred himself to the bow of his boat on hands and knees, clinging to the craft. He tossed his bowline to Archie. Ravenwing secured the line from the *Rising Moon* to a cleat on the port side of the *Inlet Dancer*'s stern. The man on the *Rising Moon* held on to his line with his left hand, the three-foot gaff in his right, made a knot fast on the bow cleat, then turned and clambered for the safety of the stern of his boat.

"Permission to come aboard, *Captain*," he barked to Ravenwing, who had stepped back into the pilothouse to crank up the boat's powerful motors.

"You know the way," Ravenwing yelled, shaking his head.

The man, gaff still clenched in his hands, stepped onto the *Inlet Dancer* and grabbed the handrail on the side of the pilothouse for stability. Ravenwing engaged the throttle and the boats began to cut into the cresting waves again.

"What the hell were you doing out on a night like this?" Ravenwing asked, his voice disappearing into the storm.

"I have my reasons."

"They must have been good ones. Only a fool would venture out on a night like this."

"Well, you're out."

"I am. But everyone around here knows I'm a fool."

The two men stood side by side as the *Inlet Dancer* began west toward the mouth of Deep Water Cove.

"You said you took shelter. Where?"

"I just set the throttle to keep abreast of the cove and waited for you."

"I didn't see you."

"I was there."

"What happened to that nice E-Tec 115 you bought last year?"

"Don't know. Think I took on too much water. Washed it out. Maybe water in the fuel line. I couldn't get that thing going."

Ravenwing looked at the man, who looked straight ahead, his face hidden by the bill of his cap, his body snug in an orange float coat.

"But you could use the 25 to keep abreast of this storm?"

"You're not the only one in this country who can pilot a boat, Archie."

"Who's towing who?" Ravenwing spat. Then he sighed and said, "Okay, let's see if we can't find a place to leave this tub for the night and make for home." He looked at his sonar for the depth of the water beneath him, and then at his radar to search the shore for a safe harbour.

"You're still pissed at me," the man said through the pelting rain.

"You done anything that would change my mind otherwise?"

"That's the thing with you, Archie. You hold everybody to such a high standard, no one can ever live up to your expectations."

"That isn't true and you know it. But I do expect some common sense. And what you've done is beyond the pale. You know it, so don't play dumb with me. I know you got plenty of brains in that thick head of yours. You've got a responsibility."

"You can be a real jackass, Archie."

"Don't I know it. But at least I know when I've done something wrong. I aim to fix it. You? I just never figured this sort of thing from you. But then I should have guessed this was coming."

The man turned to regard Archie Ravenwing, who was watching his sonar, the VHF still crackling. He said, "Don't you think that your people deserve better? Don't you think that I deserve better?"

"Of course we do. Of course you do!" Archie's voice was coarse over the din. "So act that way. Act like you deserve better. Stop waiting around for someone to hand you things. Go out and get what you want."

The man stepped back a few feet from Archie. "I'm goin' to."

"Well, I'm glad to hear you say it...."

But Archie didn't finish the sentence. The gaff hook caught him in the side of his head, just above the ear, behind the softness of the temple. The blow made no sound over the clamour of the storm. The curved hook pierced Ravenwing's skull and he fell sideways and down, hard, onto the pilothouse floor. There he lay as the water washed into the pilothouse. In the darkness, the deep pool of blood from where the gaff pierced Ravenwing's skull was indiscernible from the dark water that sluiced across the deck of the *Inlet Dancer*.

The assailant dropped the gaff on top of the body and took control of the fishing boat. He pulled back on the throttle, easing the boat's speed, and turned off its running lights so it could not be seen. He set the wheel to veer the boat into the inlet, toward open water. He flipped open the seat top in the pilothouse and found what he was looking for — a short, stout bungee cord. He used it to secure the wheel of the boat so that it maintained its current course. There was no time to set the boat's autopilot.

The killer dropped to one knee and looked at the body of Archie Ravenwing on the deck of the boat. His eyes open, lifeless. He then dragged Ravenwing from the pilothouse onto the narrow aft deck, pulling him to the lee side gunwales and heaving him into the ocean. He threw the gaff hook overboard.

The man took hold of the rope that connected the *Inlet Dancer* to the *Rising Moon* and reeled in the smaller craft. When the pleasure boat was close enough, he tied a clove hitch in the rope and fastened it to the aft cleat. Then he lowered himself onto the bow of his own craft, holding on to the boat's safety rail. He turned and tried to untie the ropes from the cleat on the stern of the *Inlet Dancer*. His clove hitch came loose, but the second knot wouldn't come free with the weight of both boats on it.

He slid on his belly down the length of the bow of the *Rising Moon* and scrambled under the canopy. Moments later he emerged with a hatchet in his right hand and felt his way back toward the bow. As he reached the tip of his boat, he pulled again so that the two boats were bow to stern, and began to chop where Archie had made the rope fast around a metal cleat. A giant wave broke over the bow of the *Inlet Dancer* and then the *Rising Moon*, sending a wall of white foam and black ocean into the man's face, washing him down the slick nose of his boat. He managed to grab the safety rail with his left hand, his right hand still clinging to the hatchet. The water streamed from the bow of the pleasure craft, pushing the man's legs over the port side as he scrambled to hold on to the boat. Eyes wild with panic, he heaved himself back on to the bow and slid back to the fore of the craft. He pulled the boats together again, raised his right hand, and hacked at the rope on the stern cleat — once, twice, three times — and then he was free. He threw the remnant tatters of the rope into the ocean and slid back to the cockpit, under the canopy. Then he fired up the boat's 115 outboard motor, switched on the craft's running lights, and made for home.

2 Through the greasy light, Cole Blackwater eyed Frankie "Fingers" Delarosa. Circling his opponent, Cole shuffled sideways, bouncing, always trying to keep his feet moving. Hands up in front of him, he tracked the glistening form of the man in front of him, who travelled the perimeter of the ring, bouncing lightly. They traded punches, each absorbing the force of the blows in his gloves as they circled. Fingers threw a left-right combination that caught Cole on the chin, and he stepped back heavily but kept moving. Sweat poured from Cole's curly brow into his eyes, and he winced, his vision blurring. Waiting for the bell again.

Fingers feignted left, and as Blackwater stepped to the right, he caught a solid blow to the cheek. A spray of sweat leaped from his face and speckled the dingy canvas as Blackwater stumbled toward the mat.

Fingers dropped his hands but remained vigilant as Cole caught himself on the ropes, his arms behind him. Frankie stepped side to side, waiting. Breathing heavily, Cole shook off the sting from the solid right-hand blow, his hair wet against his forehead, his eyes dark and focused.

He raised his gloves and motioned for Fingers to begin again.

The men circled in the pool of light from four lamps that hung from the low ceiling, its shadows accentuated by the network of pipes and ducts that crossed it. The long, squat room was filled with the sounds of fists on heavy bags and speed bags and bodies shuffling, moving, colliding. In the corners, the shapes of men glistening with sweat could be seen jumping rope and doing push-ups and sit-ups, holding up punch mitts while their training partners worked through a combination. The sound of a tinny radio rattled in a far corner, where no one listened to it.

Cole Blackwater stepped in, gloves up, and Frankie Fingers began to circle again. They traded punches, Cole landing a blow to Frankie's belly, which didn't move the man at all. Their shoulders touched and the two men stepped back. More punches. Fingers tried to feint again, but this time Cole saw it and, instead of stepping to the right, stepped forward and caught Fingers with a left-right combination. But he still took Fingers' roundhouse on the cheek.

The bell sounded and both men retreated.

"Pretty good, pretty good," came a voice from the darkness beyond the ring. "Grab a seat." Cole stepped back into his corner. Frankie Fingers did the same, his smile exaggerated by the mouthguard he pushed out of his teeth.

A small black man, not more than five-foot-six, hoisted himself onto the ring. "You're doing okay there, Cole," he said, wiping Cole's face with a towel. "You're learning. You're learning. You didn't step into that right hook that Frankie likes to throw. Good for you. Good for you. But you've still got to stop thinking about what to do after you avoid that sort of set up. Got to just let your body respond. Don't think. There's no time for that. Just let your body do what it knows how to do. Respond."

The man made a jab with his small hand. "Let your body get the information from your eyes without *you* getting in the way." He tapped Cole's head. "I see you hesitate for just a second, and that's why you're not landing that left-right combination." The man picked up a water bottle and squirted some water on Cole's face and in his hair, then wiped him down again. He pushed the bent straw from the bottle between Cole's teeth and let him drink.

"I'm feeling old, Jessie," Cole said, spitting a mouthful of water into a bucket.

The man grinned. He wore a pork-pie hat at a rakish angle over his tight black curls. "You *are* old, Cole. But don't let that stop you from having some fun in there. Okay?"

"Thanks, Jessie," Cole said sardonically, still breathing hard. He fit his mouthguard back in place.

Jessie turned to the shadows and said, "Okay, Denny, let 'em have it."

The bell rang and Cole moved in quickly with a series of punches, all of which Fingers blocked with arms and shoulders. The men circled each other, looking for openings with quick punches.

Somewhere in the room a cellphone chimed, and for a moment Cole's attention was diverted. He paid for it as Fingers landed a quick left jab, but Cole managed to step away from the right that followed. The phone rang again.

"You want me to get that, Cole?" came a voice from the shadows.

"Busy right now," Cole mumbled through his mouthguard.

He could hear Denman Scott rummaging through his bag next to the ring. The ringing stopped.

Cole stepped forward with two left jabs and a right hook, but Fingers absorbed the blows and hit Cole with an uppercut that set him back on his feet. His stomach was his weak spot. Cole stepped in with a punch to Frankie's gut and the two men locked for a moment.

"Knock it off!" came Jessie's voice from the side, followed by laughter.

"Cole, it's Mary," Denman said.

Cole stepped away and Frankie stepped in.

"Cole, it's important."

Cole and Frankie circled, eyes low, brows streaked with sweat, panting.

"Cole!"

Cole Blackwater's attention slipped off Frankie Fingers like a wet bar of soap off the side of a bathtub. Fingers saw the opening, feinted left, and landed a solid right. Cole didn't even see it. His left cheek took the whole force of the blow, and he dropped to the canvas. Frankie stepped back. Cole pushed himself to a sitting position and shook his head. A trickle of blood seeped from his mouth.

"Cole," said Denman, standing at the ropes with the cellphone in his hands.

"What in the name of God's green earth is it?" said Cole, spitting his mouthguard into his gloved hand, a string of saliva and blood coming along for the ride.

"Cole, that was Mary. Archie Ravenwing is dead."

■ Cole stuffed his gloves into his gym bag and pulled on his leather jacket over his sweater.

"Cole, I'm real sorry to hear about your friend," said Frankie Fingers from behind him.

"It's okay, Frankie. I appreciate that. Hey, good fight." Cole straightened, felt the stiffness in his neck and shoulders, and picked up his bag with his left hand. He extended his right toward Frankie.

"Yeah, good fight, Cole. You've really come a long way, man." Frankie extended his hand.

"Pop any fingers this time around?" Frankie got his nickname because he dislocated a finger or two during nearly every fight — loose ligaments, his trainer told him — and it kept him from turning pro a few years back.

"Two," he said, smiling. "But it ain't no-thing." He stepped toward the mirror and combed his hair into a point in the front. "And hey, I'm sorry about that last cheap shot."

"My fault," said Cole. "For twenty-five years people have been telling me to stay focused, not to let my guard down. Seems I've still got a ways to go."

"Well, you're looking good out there, man," said Frankie. "See you next week." Frankie exited the dim locker room, and Cole took his place in front of the mirror. He straightened as he peered at himself. Not so bad, he thought. He'd dropped almost ten kilos since he'd been back in the ring. He was still a little soft in the middle, still carried fifteen pounds more than he liked, but progress was progress and he shouldn't complain. He was aiming to be super middleweight by summer. Maybe then he'd actually take his shirt off when he fought.

He examined his face. The twisted white scar that cut across his right eyebrow was still visible after ten months, and likely always would be. The disfigurement on his left cheek was also plainly evident. They were ugly reminders of his time in Oracle, Alberta last spring, when he had come face to face with a killer and had nearly become a victim himself. It was hard to believe it had been almost a year.

He pushed back the memory and studied the most recent round of bruising. His left cheek was red and a little puffy. Maybe he'd put some ice on it when he got home. Or he might find a cheap cut of steak in his fridge and slap it on like they did in the movies. Either way, by morning he'd have a good bruise. He pushed his hair into some semblance of order and stepped out of the locker room.

"How you doing, Cole?" asked Denman Scott. Scott was seated on a plastic orange chair in the dim lobby of the East Hastings Boxing Club. He wore a jean jacket over a hooded sweatshirt and sported a tan flat cap on his closely shaved head.

"I'm all right," Cole said.

"Sorry about that. About distracting you."

Cole smiled at him. "I'll never learn, it seems."

"Aw, come on now," said Denman, rising and moving toward the flimsy doors that opened into the night. "You're looking really good in the ring. Really."

Cole smiled again. "I actually feel pretty good. Lighter, you know? I feel like my movement is coming back. Like I'm actually moving like a fighter again. But I'm slow with my hands, and when I fight a guy like Fingers, who's what, half my age? Man, it's tough going."

"I'm proud of you, Cole."

"Thanks, Denny."

They stepped into the night. The air was damp but mild.

"Where to?" asked Denman.

"I've got to head downtown. Go to the office. Make a few stops."

"You want to catch a bite to eat and a pint?"

Cole sighed. "Can't say no. Could use a few jars right now."

They walked west along Hastings, past Main Street and the crowd of drug dealers, prostitutes, vagrants, homeless people, and frightened tourists in front of the Carnegie Centre. People nodded to Denman, a few said his name, and three or four stopped him to chat briefly. All Cole warranted was, "Up, down, or rock?" A query about his preferred narcotic. He smiled and said he was just passing through, and nodded toward Denman. "You're quite the celebrity these days," Cole said.

"Depends on who you ask."

"Those folks think you're a hero. A modern-day Robin Hood."

Scott smiled. "That would make the mayor Prince John, wouldn't it?"

Cole looked serious. "And the chief of police the Sheriff of Nottingham."

Denman smiled even wider. "Guess you're Little John then?"

"Who you calling Little John?" Cole tried to punch Scott in the arm, but his friend simply shifted his weight and Cole slipped past him and down onto the street. Scott pulled him back by the sleeve of his jacket. "Easy there, slugger."

"You're a slippery little bugger. "

"Not so much slippery as sleek."

"One of these days you're going to have to teach me how to do that."

"Anytime. The offer stands. But you've got to leave your boxing gloves at home."

"One step at a time. It took a near-death experience to get me back in the ring. I don't know what it's going to take to get me to dress up in those pyjamas you wear and prance around your dojo."

"How about a near-life experience?" asked Scott.

"Don't start on me tonight, Denny."

Scott simply smiled. "As you wish, grasshopper," he said with an accent more practiced than real. Cole couldn't keep the grin off his face, though it did hurt to smile.

They arrived at the corner of Hastings and Cambie and waited for the light, while the working poor and the desperate did business in the Quick Cash store on the corner, making criminally large interest payments to cash a cheque without an address. The light changed and they crossed the street to the Dominion Building, an ancient office tower that was home to Cole's Blackwater Strategies and another dozen lost causes. The building had been the tallest in the British Empire in its day, but it was now dwarfed by dozens of office towers, condominiums, and the phallic Harbour Centre a few blocks away.

"Stairs?" asked Denman, turning to start the climb to the eighth floor.

"Not tonight," said Blackwater, pushing the elevator button.

"Come on, you promised."

"And I take them every morning, I swear it, Denman. But Mary is waiting."

Denman chuckled and positioned himself next to his friend.

"I mean it. Every morning."

"I didn't say a word," said Scott, looking up at the floor indicator above the elevator.

Blackwater Strategies had been on the eighth floor of the Dominion Building for nearly four years. When Cole Blackwater had signed the lease on the two-room office, he had promised himself that he would take the stairs up in the morning and down at night, but soon he had abandoned that pledge, slipping into a self-imposed sloth. His arrival in Vancouver, in pursuit of his estranged daughter and in deference to the will of his ex-wife, Jennifer Paulson, had marked the nadir in his short life. The lethargy it induced was a vicious cycle, thought Cole, waiting for the elevator. You stop exercising, and your body starts to go to pot. You start to go to pot and you get depressed. You get depressed and you want to eat more. You eat more and you get more depressed. You get more depressed and it gets harder to exercise. So you lie around and watch television and feel sorry for yourself. Okay, Cole admitted to himself, *he* felt sorry for himself. But Oracle had delivered the much-needed slap on the side of the head that Cole needed to get off the couch and back into action. When he'd returned from Oracle, he'd started visiting the gym and taking the stairs again.

It hadn't solved all his problems, not by a long shot. But it had helped.

The elevator chimed and the two friends waited for the door to open.

"Last chance," said Denman.

Cole shot him a look and stepped into the waiting elevator.

Another thing had changed since his return from Alberta. Cole had begun spending more time with Denman Scott. He had considered the compact aikido master his best friend since moving to Vancouver four years ago, but when Cole came unravelled the previous spring, it was Denman who had helped him pull himself back together.

The door to Blackwater Strategies was ajar when the two men stepped onto the eighth floor.

As they entered the brightly lit room, Mary Patterson was seated behind her desk, talking on the phone. Cole looked at his watch. It was seven-thirty on a Friday night. Denman sat in a club chair opposite Mary's desk, while Cole opened the door to his own office and entered to turn on the desk lamp. When Mary hung up the phone, she greeted Denman. Cole emerged and said hello.

"Grace Ravenwing is hoping for a call, Cole. And I've looked into tickets to Port Hardy as you asked."

"Thanks, Mary, you're amazing. What's it going to set me back?"

"About five hundred round trip, with taxes."

Cole sighed. Five bills was still big money for the financially challenged Cole Blackwater. "Okay," he said. "Go ahead and book the flights. But just one-way. I have no idea when this thing is going to happen. I can book the return myself when I'm there."

"When do you want to leave?"

"What did Grace say?"

"She was pretty upset. I think she could use your support."

"Okay, book it for tomorrow afternoon. I'll clear it with Jennifer. And I guess we'll have to postpone the Nexus Energy thing."

"I'll take care of it, Cole," said Mary.

He didn't like putting off a paying client, especially one like Nexus Energy, who held the distinction of being his first business client who paid him a monthly retainer. And all he had to do for them was join a weekly conference call to discuss communications and government relations. It was easy money.

"What are you doing for Nexus?" asked Denman, leaning against the door frame.

"Going to get all the company brass in a room next week and talk them through the government-relations angle of this big tidal power project they want to do. See if we can't pry some cash out of the feds for something other than the tar sands. Maybe get some diversification happening in our national energy policy."

"Can I tell them that you can be available by phone if they need you?" asked Mary.

"Sure, that's great. Please," said Cole. "You'll have to give them Archie's — Grace's number," he said, his face growing pale. "I never can seem to get a strong cell signal up there. And no internet on Parish Island."

Cole busied himself in his office. Denman stepped inside. "Jesus, Cole, this place is a shithouse. When are you going to let Mary get this place organized?"

Cole was seated at his desk, which was buried beneath papers. His laptop was open on a stack of newspapers nearly a foot high. He held a wireless keyboard on his lap. "It's all good in here, Denman. I know where everything is."

"This place is a fire hazard is all I'm saying."

"Out," he said, not turning to look at his friend.

▄ They crossed Cambie between traffic and threaded their way between college kids smoking outside the doors of the Cambie Hotel. Always the same every Friday night, the Cambie was a raucous riot of sound and sight and smells. Televisions playing a hockey game blared from every corner. The dozen round and rectangular tables were crowded with young men and women from the surrounding campuses, along with a rougher assortment of mostly men, but some women, from the eastside neighbourhood. Cole and Denman pushed their way to the bar, Cole performing his perfunctory scan of the joint for friend or foe. He'd been doing this for so long that it was second nature. And though he'd had the snot beaten out of him in a bar in Oracle when he failed to notice three thugs lying in wait for him, he felt he could let his guard down a little when he drank with Denman. Not only was Denman a black belt, but he was universally respected in East Vancouver. College kids didn't pick fights with the stout Cole or the solid Denman, and the locals knew that Denman was on their side, watching their backs.

The men ordered pints of Kick-Ass from the bar, and Denman paid for the beer with a ten-dollar bill. They touched glasses and drank deeply.

Cole sighed appreciatively. Denman licked a bit of foam from his lips and looked around the room. Denman nodded toward the far corner of the bar, past the pool tables. "Over there," he said, distracting Cole from the twenty-year-old college girl he was admiring. "Marty and Dusty." Cole looked up to see Dusty Stevens waving.

"I don't want to get into it with those guys tonight, Denman."

"Then don't," said Denman, deftly slipping between bodies to make his way toward the waving arm.

The four men sat at a long rectangular table occupied by half a dozen other drinkers, only a few of which had retained all their teeth. The further you got from the door, thought Cole, the older and rougher the clientele got. But Cole didn't care. He had finished his second pint and was well into his third, and dinner in the form of a greasy hamburger and fries had just arrived. Cole bit into the burger and felt relieved. It had been two hours since he had left the East Hastings Boxing Club, and he was famished.

"Sorry to hear about Archie," said Dusty Stevens, looking over his spectacles at Cole. "From everything you've told us, he was a stand-up guy. A good man."

"He was," said Cole, wiping his mouth with a paper napkin and taking a gulp of Kick-Ass. "He was one of the good guys."

"How'd he die, if you don't mind my asking?" said Martin Middlemarch, sipping his orange juice. Cole had chided him upon joining the table, saying he didn't even know they served OJ at the Cambie. "They call it mix," grinned Middlemarch as he raised his glass, explaining that he had stopped drinking altogether and was training for an ultramarathon that would take place in June. That had taken the wind out of Cole Blackwater's sails, given that Middlemarch was ten years his senior.

Cole regarded his friends across the table. He had known Martin and Dusty long before he had scuttled across the country from Ottawa four years ago. Now they managed to meet at least once a week at the Cambie to hoist a few and swap war stories.

"Are you okay, Cole?" asked Martin.

"Yeah, I'm fine."

"Not going to ride us about the latest green-washing from the forestry or mining sector?" asked Dusty, almost sheepishly.

"Not tonight," he said, shoving french fries into his mouth and chasing them with the last of his third pint.

"Don't get him started," said Martin, smiling.

"Oh, I still think you're both sellouts. Hell, if Archie was here he'd probably tie you into the whole salmon farming thing he's been working on. Likely pin the death of wild salmon stocks on logging in old-growth forests that the two of you used to fight for when you were with Greenpeace, and now try to spin for the forestry giants." Cole spoke low and fast.

"Cole," said Denman.

"Well, so long as you're not getting into it...." said Martin, finishing his juice, still smiling.

"You know, you guys really —"

"Cole," Denman said more forcefully. The sound of his voice stopped Cole's train in its tracks.

Blackwater looked up. "What?"

"Cole, not tonight," Denman said more quietly.

Cole searched the bar for a waitress and further refreshment. Distracted, he said, "Yeah, yeah, sorry." He caught the waitress' eye and made a circling motion with his hand to indicate that they wanted another round.

Dusty caught Cole's attention. "So, you're heading up to Lostcoast. When is the service?"

Cole drank deeply from his pint glass. "Don't know," he said, eating another fry. "Grace tells me they still haven't recovered his body."

"How do they know he's dead?" asked Dusty.

"He's dead. Archie Ravenwing isn't the kind of guy to just wander off. It's been a week since he went out in his boat to do some sea lice survey work for that researcher, Cassandra Petrel, and he hasn't been seen since. Gracie tells me there was a hell of a storm that night, and that he didn't come home. The Coast Guard has been up and down Knight Inlet, where he said he was heading, along with Tribune Channel, Nickol Pass, and as far south as the Johnstone Strait. At first they thought that maybe he'd had some kind of trouble, lost power, couldn't motor or even call for help, but Grace says they've searched every cove and there's no sign of him. The sea called Archie Ravenwing home."

The waitress brought their drinks, and Martin paid for the round.

"When did you last see him?" asked Martin, knocking back another OJ.

"A little while ago," said Cole, reflecting. "Archie hadn't been a client since, well, since last June, I guess. Right around the time I got back from Alberta, he lost an election and was no longer the band councillor for Port Lostcoast. He was just a private citizen. The new councillor, a fellow named Greg White Eagle, asked Archie to stay on as the North Salish First Nation representative on the Aquaculture Advisory Task Force, but that didn't last long. I guess the last time I talked to Archie was in August. He called to tell me he'd just been booted from the Task Force. Said he and White Eagle didn't see eye to eye, and that Greg had shown him the door. He seemed pretty pissed, but I was in the middle of things on the Spotted Owl file, and I guess I didn't give him much of my time. I meant to call him back but never did. You know how it goes," said Cole, looking at his friends.

"Anyway, it had been awhile. I know Archie always felt guilty about not paying me and all, but I wrote that debt off long ago. I really had put that out of my mind. I guess Archie never did. The little Lostcoast band didn't have any money. Those people are as poor as most of Denny's clients here. Difference is *they* don't have anybody watching their six. They live in the middle of nowhere. An island off an island off an island at the edge of Canada, and nobody could care less if unemployment is seventy percent or if nobody finishes grade six in that little God-forgotten town. The only people who seem to pay them any attention are the logging companies who want access to their timber and the salmon farmers who want access to the Broughton Archipelago."

Cole stopped and took a hearty swallow from his beer. He looked around at Dusty and Martin. "Sorry, Denny made me promise not to get into all that tonight."

"It's nothing. Neither of us has anything to do with salmon farming."

Cole looked down at his hands, as they gripped the pint glass. "I did what I could for Archie, but it never seemed like we could drive a wedge between the so-called Liberal government and salmon farming. When the moratorium was lifted in 2002 those buggers flooded the Broughton with dozens of permit applications. There must be thirty new salmon farms just in that little group of islands. Archie told me that the salmon runs were decimated. Sea lice, he said. Imagine that." Cole swilled the beer in his glass, his head down, his eyes dark and distant. "Sea lice. The size of your pinky nail." He held up his little finger, looking at it closely. "Something that tiny is wiping out a salmon population that is as old as time itself." The fever pitch of the bar suddenly seemed very distant.

"What do you know about this new band councillor?" asked Denman.

"Nothing but what Archie told me. He's originally from Alert Bay, but moved to Parish Island and Port Lostcoast maybe twenty years ago to fish. I think he's a booster of salmon farming, but I really haven't been following it. Archie wondered if White Eagle was on the pad with the salmon farmers, but I didn't take it too seriously. Archie could find a conspiracy under every bush and shrub in the forest."

Martin chuckled. "No wonder the two of you got on so well."

Cole finished his beer and searched for a waitress.

"So, you're going up?" asked Martin seriously.

Cole was still looking for a waitress. "Yeah, tomorrow."

"Anything you need?"

"I need another beer," he said, distracted.

"Cole." Martin put his hand on Cole's arm and Cole turned to him. "Is there anything you need from us?"

Cole looked at his three friends.

"I don't know. I don't know what I need. This is new for me."

"Cole, you've been to funerals before," said Dusty.

"This is different."

"How?" asked Dusty, looking at Cole over his glasses.

"This isn't a funeral. It's a potlatch."

3 One thing Edmonton and Ottawa had in common was cold, hard winters, winters that seemed to stretch from November right through to April, even May in a bad year. But if Nancy Webber was honest with herself, she would admit that Edmonton's winters were even worse than Ottawa's. They were longer and the city was bleaker, lacking the romance of skating on the Rideau Canal and the quick escape to the pretty Gatineau Hills. Sure, you could drive to Jasper, but it took about four hours if the roads were clear. And from November until well into spring, you couldn't count on bare roads.

March in the nation's capital meant that tulips were just around the corner. It meant Saturday mornings in ByWard Market, shopping for that night's dinner, buying fresh flowers, and stopping for a coffee to read her own reporting in the *Globe and Mail*. March in Edmonton meant grey skies and sleet. Sometimes Edmonton would catch the northern edge of a chinook and the snow would melt, but a hard freeze would still turn the city into an ice rink the next day, and not the kind where Beaver Tail shops were just around the next frozen bend.

Nancy sat at her favourite table in the window of the Starbucks at the corner of Jasper Avenue and 100A Street, just a dash through traffic to the editorial offices of the *Edmonton Journal*. She sipped a latte — nothing fancy, just a latte, thank you — and read the Saturday papers.

Outside, the sky hung like a tattered grey tapestry over the city. The temperature hovered around freezing, but the wind off the Saskatchewan River made it feel much colder. If it would only warm up a little, thought Webber while sipping her coffee, she might be motivated to go for a run along the river valley that afternoon. But as it was, she was more likely to end up at her office, working on a feature about homeless people in the capital.

She finished the front section of the *National Post* and began to leaf through the *Globe and Mail*. The paper still held a strong allure for Nancy Webber, though it had been more than four years since she had penned a story for it. She read an article about the country's new prime minister, who was doing what every prime minister since Pierre Elliot Trudeau had done — concentrating power in the Prime Minister's Office. Nothing new. No news. She read a story about the everlasting conflict between Israel and every other country in the Middle East, and about the war in Iraq. It seemed to Nancy that there was no *news* anymore. Just *olds*. The same old stories told again and again and again. Maybe that was why she felt like her job was becoming harder and harder.

She sipped her coffee and flipped the page. She scanned the "Canada in Brief" section. Three stories down, she stopped and read a short blurb.

"Fuck," she said out loud, and a woman reading a novel at the next table looked up. Nancy smiled apologetically and dug out her cellphone.

She held the phone for a full minute before flipping it open and activating the search function, scrolling for the number. Finding it, she hesitated so long that the phone turned itself off again.

"What the hell," she said, eliciting another curious look. She turned on the phone and dialled the number.

He answered as he always did. "Blackwater."

"Cole, it's Nancy."

There was a momentary silence. Then, "Hey, Nancy."

"Cole, I just read that Archie Ravenwing is presumed dead. I'm so sorry."

"Yeah, it's some pretty bad news. I'm sorry, too."

"When did you talk with him last?"

Cole told her. "It's been a while."

"Don't be hard on yourself, Cole. That's the way the world is. Some people we talk to all the time, some we don't."

She heard him draw a long breath. Exhaling, he said, "It's a bad habit with me, Nancy. I let things slip. Let people slip."

Nancy drew a breath. "How is Sarah?" she asked, knowing that Cole was sensitive about staying connected with his daughter. "How old is she now? Like ten?"

"She's nine, going on nineteen. And she's good, thanks for asking. She's actually here right now, cooking me breakfast as usual."

Nancy laughed. "I hope she didn't have to drag your sorry ass out of bed again, Blackwater."

"My butt isn't so sorry these days, Webber. I'll have you know I came this close to winning a fight last night."

"Another Friday night at the Cambie, Cole?"

"In the ring, wise guy. I almost had Frankie Fingers on the mat when I got the call about Archie."

"Frankie Fingers? You're kidding me."

"No, really. I had him on the ropes, and, well...."

"The fights just haven't been the same since they let you guys take your cellphones into the ring, have they?"

Cole laughed. "You know what I mean. Anyway, I'm feeling pretty good."

"That's saying something for you."

"It is."

A silence hung there for a moment. Then Nancy said, "Well, I just wanted to call and tell you how sorry I am. He was a good man."

"You met him when he was at the AFN?"

"That's right. I covered a couple meetings he attended when he was on the Assembly of First Nations. Back in the bad old days."

"Right," said Cole, not wanting to delve too deeply into just how bad the old days had been.

"He was a stand-up guy as I recall. Always high class. Eloquent. Really cared about his people."

"He was also a pompous prick who got under the skin of nearly everybody who knew him," said Cole.

"Well, there's a lot of that out there," quipped Nancy. "I know a few pompous pricks myself." She took a breath as Cole didn't respond. "Are you going up? The paper said there would be a traditional ceremony this week."

"I am. I'm actually flying as far as Port Hardy tonight, then catching a charter to Parish Island and Port Lostcoast in the morning. I guess some muckety-mucks arranged for a few flights straight into Lostcoast, so I lucked out. Maybe I'll be sitting next to the minister or some other big cheese. You're not covering this by any chance, are you?"

"No. I don't know if the chain is going to have someone there or if they'll just make something up and file from Vancouver."

"Okay," said Cole, distracted.

"Why?" she asked.

"No reason. Just asking."

"You sure?" she pressed.

"Of course I'm sure. I was just making conversation," he said, sounding testy.

Talk about pompous jackasses, she thought. "Sorry. Forget I asked."

Silence again. Finally Cole broke it. "Look, I'm sorry. I'm just still in shock about Archie. I need to get my things together, hang here with Sarah for a little while, and then head for the airport. I'll call you from Lostcoast and let you know how things go at the potlatch if you like. Keep you in the loop."

"Only if you want to. Otherwise, give my condolences to his family, will you?"

"I will. I'm staying with his youngest daughter, Grace, at Archie's place. It's going to be a little strange."

"Take care of yourself, Cole," she said. What she wanted to say was, "Don't drink and get in too many fights," but she knew there was no sense trying to change that.

"Okay, Nancy. Thanks for calling." The line went dead.

The man was a mystery to her.

She finished her latte and stepped out onto Jasper Avenue, pulling her coat collar up around her cheeks and hurrying down the street, the wind whipping her long, raven hair all around her. To hell with the run, she thought, crossing the street to her office.

She rode the elevator to the fourth floor and made her way through the maze of cubicles that was the *Journal's* newsroom to find her own little box awaiting her. The room was quiet. Only a few reporters came in on Saturday, since the paper published only a slim edition on Sunday. She sat down in her straight-backed chair and turned on her computer. She knew that Cole would feel guilty about not keeping in touch with Archie Ravenwing. He let that kind of thing get to him. When he was away from Sarah, he got pretty agitated if he didn't talk with her every other day. And God help those around him if he forgot to call for more than a few days in row.

Nancy Webber wondered if it got to Cole Blackwater when he was out of touch with her.

"Now that's a stupid thought," she said out loud.

Just the same, how long had it been since she had seen him? Since the debacle in Oracle last May, she had found only one excuse to see him — the National Newspaper Awards in Vancouver. She had been nominated for an award in the investigations category for her work on the murder of Mike Barnes and the small-town politics that had swirled around his killing. That murder had brought Cole Blackwater back into her life, and their reunion had been volcanic. The wounds of their time together in Ottawa were reopened and some blood was shed. But in the end they had formed a working truce to get to the bottom of the man's untimely death. And by the time the case was closed, they had actually begun to feel something for one another again. Or so Nancy believed.

So when she had arrived in Vancouver for the awards, she had called Cole. They had met for dinner at the Raincity Grill on Denman Street near her hotel.

"How was your visit to your mother's place?" she had asked as they sampled albacore tuna and honey mussels before their main course.

Cole sat across from her. He still looked like a hoodlum, his dark hair falling in ragged curls over his forehead. That night he had worn a dark patterned shirt that had been pressed for the occasion, and a glint in his eyes that she hadn't seen since their days together in Ottawa. It wasn't exactly light, that glimmer — there was something mischievous, or perhaps sinister, in that flash.

Other things seemed different, changed. His face was leaner, and the dark scars that still crossed his cheek and eyebrow made him look dangerous. They would fade with time, she thought, but now, only five months after those jagged imprints had been made, they told a dark story. And Nancy wondered, looking at him across from her, if the darkness that seemed to have flourished would ever recede. Was it just the Mike Barnes affair, or was it something else?

"It was fine," he said, sampling the beef tataki. "This is good. I wish there was more than just one spoonful." He drank from his bottle of Heineken.

"That's all I get? It was *fine*?"

"What's there to tell? The old ranch is just as it's always been. Nothing to report."

"Did you see Walter?"

"Yup, he was there for most of Sarah's and my stay. We rode together a few times, which was great. I'll tell you, keeping up with my older brother, be it in the saddle or on foot, is a heck of an incentive to get back in shape."

"You look good, Cole."

"You do too."

She thought she did. She'd been running and going to the gym, and she'd had her hair done that afternoon at a place on Robson Street in preparation for the awards ceremony the next night.

"You know, I really don't know anything about your family," she said, sipping her red wine. He topped up her glass from the bottle of Ravenswood Zinfandel on the table.

"Not much to tell, really." He shifted uncomfortably in his seat. "My mom is pushing seventy now, but is still hale and hardy. Walter is forty going on twenty-five. Still working for the Parks Service in Waterton Lakes. Puts the cows out each spring, rounds them up every fall. Keeps the ranch a working proposition, though it's really just to maintain our grazing lease. We don't make any money on the operation. Hardly ever did. Even when Dad was running it...." His voice trailed off, and he filled the space with a long pull from his bottle of beer.

Nancy sat and watched him. A beautiful young woman with blonde hair and emerald eyes took away the plate of appetizer spoons. Nancy looked up at the server and then back at Cole. "You were saying?"

Cole had been looking at the woman, too. He pursed his lips. "Only that the ranch is still a working outfit, but only for show."

"You were saying that your father could never make a go of it."

"I don't really want to talk about my father," said Cole, looking sideways and shifting in his seat.

"You are an enigma to me, Cole Blackwater."

"Yeah, well, to me too," he said, returning her gaze.

The blonde served their dinners. Cole ate grilled venison tenderloin with a black trumpet mushroom and lentil ragout, with turnips and brandy jus. He had had to ask the waitress what a ragout was, and then what a jus was, but it was mostly to flirt, Nancy figured. She watched him wash his food down with another bottle of Heineken.

Nancy dined on wild coho salmon with yam purée, sherry-glazed radish, and daikon. She enjoyed her Zin. They ate in silence, in part to savour the meal, in part to let the awkwardness pass.

After dessert they made their way out onto Denman Street and strolled toward Burrard Inlet. It was warm, and the street was busy with tourists and locals enjoying the temperate evening and the light before the cold grey of winter set in. They walked along the seawall toward Stanley Park and sat on a bench as the sun sank low.

Nancy didn't know where the nerve came to ask, but she did. "What happened to your father, Cole?"

He sat implacably beside her, looking across the inlet at the North Shore Mountains, the fading light touching the houses and high-rises that swarmed the slopes of the lower hills. He sat that way for a long time, his face in shadow as the sun slipped below the horizon.

She touched his arm. "Cole?"

He turned his head toward her as if awakening from a dream. His eyes were vacant.

"Cole, what happened to your father?"

"It's really none of your business, Nancy. It's a family thing." His tone was flat, expressionless.

"You need to talk about—"

"I don't need to do anything, Nancy." He stood. "I'll walk you to your hotel."

■ Nancy Webber sat at her desk and let her fingers trail across the National Newspaper Award she had won that evening. Did Nancy Webber believe in redemption? Not as others might. But she did believe in resurrection, and winning the award had certainly contributed to her own slow-but-sure phoenix-like rise from the ashes of defeat. The irony was that Cole Blackwater had led her to the story that led to the award, and that disturbed her. Had he not been responsible for her precipitous fall from grace? It had been his fabrication about a major government environmental initiative that had got her fired when she printed the false story. Of course, it was more than that, Nancy admitted to herself. Pillow talk with a married man and the scandal it produced on the Hill has also contributed to her being fired from her dream job.

Nancy reluctantly admitted to herself that she would never have dug into the story of Mike Barnes' murder if Cole hadn't encouraged her to do so. She sighed at the thought. In the years since her estrangement from Ottawa, she'd grown lazy and complacent. But something happened in Oracle that rekindled her excitement for investigative journalism. Her three-part series that chronicled the swirl of intrigue, deception, corruption, and politics that surrounded Barnes' death won her the award. It had opened doors, too. The *Journal* gave her better assignments, and she was free to write her own ticket again, and to follow her re-awakened instincts more and more.

Something else had been rekindled in Oracle, but when she and Cole had been together in Vancouver last fall, it had seemed more dormant than alive. And she had plunged in with her reporter's zeal, probing him about his father, knowing he wore that wound openly on his sleeve. Nice move, Webber, she thought.

Nancy turned on her computer and checked her email. She scanned a few newswires for anything about Archie Ravenwing and found nothing. She looked at the *North Island Advocate* website, which served the tiny communities hunched together on the northeastern edge of Vancouver Island. There she found a feature on the life of Archie Ravenwing.

She read that he had been born into a family of seven children, that his father was a salmon fisherman, and his mother worked at odd jobs in Alert Bay and Port McNeill when she wasn't busy with her four boys and three girls. Archie himself had been a salmon fisherman for his entire adult life, first taking over his father's boat and then buying his own small vessel about a decade ago. In the last six years he had started to operate salmon fishing tours from that boat for tourists, taking them into Knight Inlet and Tribune Channel to fish for pink salmon. Neither the boat nor Archie Ravenwing's body had been recovered yet. There would be a traditional potlach ceremony on Tuesday. Gary Kwakana, the band chief of the North Salish First Nation, would lead the ceremony. Greg First Eagle, the representative on the band council for Parish Island and Port Lostcoast, would also be in attendance, as would representatives of the provincial government.

And so would Cole Blackwater. Nancy felt Cole's loss. Archie had been more than a client to Cole. He had been a friend.

She closed the browser for the *North Island Advocate* and opened the website for the *High River Tribune*. She quickly found the archive section and was pleased to see that she could search for stories as far back as 2001; Cole had travelled west in 2002. She knew that he had stopped at the family ranch in the Porcupine Hills, south and west of High River, and that his father had passed away while he was visiting.

She searched for "Henry Blackwater" and found an obituary. What she read unnerved her.

No wonder Cole didn't want to talk about his father. His obit revealed that he had taken his own life with a shotgun. Suicide was "the likely cause of death," the story said. He had used a branding iron to pull the trigger. And the story left the distinct impression that Cole had found the body.

"You must have been one miserable old fuck," said Nancy, looking for follow-up stories that confirmed the medical examiner's initial impression of suicide. "To kill yourself and leave your body for your family to find. No wonder Cole hates you." She searched through several other stories about the death of Henry Blackwater but found no further reference to the cause of death. Nancy went to the staff kitchen for a cup of coffee. The cream curdled at first but she stirred it in and sipped. Not too bad.

Back at her desk she found the number for the *High River Tribune*. She picked up the phone.

"Casey Brown," a man answered on the first ring.

"Hi, it's Nancy Webber calling from the *Edmonton Journal*. How are things down south today?"

"Good, thanks. Actually a really nice day. Pretty clear. Supposed to get some rain or wet snow tonight. What can I do for you, Ms. Webber?"

"It's Nancy, thanks. Well, I'm just curious about a story in the *Tribune* from a few years back. It's about the suicide of a man named Henry Blackwater. Do you remember that story?"

"I know it happened, but I wasn't reporting here then. I was still in college."

"Well, I found a few stories about it in your online archives, but I wonder if there is more to the story than what was online?"

"Could be. The paper hasn't put everything online. Just some features."

"So there might be more?"

"Sure, I guess. I mean, if there was an update on the story, like a sidebar or something, it might not make it online."

"Can I find out?"

"Can't see why not. But that would be a job for Betty Oberg. She's our receptionist. She does all the research and library requests. She'll be in on Tuesday."

"You can't have a look?"

"I'd love to, Nancy, but I'm here alone today, and I've got four stories to write for our Monday paper. I'm really jammed."

Nancy tapped the rim of her mug. "What if I came down? Could I look myself?"

"Can't see why not. We have all the past editions on microfiche. You could have a look."

"Are you there tomorrow?"

"Boy, you're really interested in something, aren't you? Care to share?"

"It's more a personal interest than professional. I'll tell you about it tomorrow."

"I'll be in around nine. Then I've got an auction to cover at noon, but I should be back around two PM."

"Great. If this clear weather holds I can be down there by two."

She hung up. Something ate at her. The key to understanding Cole Blackwater might be understanding Henry Blackwater. A good place to start might be the man's death.

4 "You're through, Archie. Politically speaking, you're done." Greg White Eagle was a broad man, his grey hair pulled back and tied neatly in a ponytail, his eyes hidden by aviator sunglasses.

It would be eight months before Archie would make his fateful voyage into the storm. He sat on the deck of the *Inlet Dancer* sorting and repairing fishing gear, a steaming cup of coffee at his elbow on the large fish box that dominated the force of the boat. "Your grace in victory is a great comfort to me, Greg."

Greg White Eagle stood on the dock next to the *Inlet Dancer's* slip. His hands were in his pockets. "I'm not without compassion, Archie. I'm a reasonable man. The chief says he wants you to stay on as the band's representative on the aquaculture committee, at least for the time being. I think the continuity would be a good thing for the band. But you've got to understand something: you're not a councillor anymore. You'll be reporting to me. And to the chief."

Archie Ravenwing focused on his tackle.

"Look, I know you feel hard done by, losing your seat on the band council after all these years. But you have to see that the people just wanted some change. They wanted someone new. With new ideas. New ways of doing things. And your outspoken opposition to salmon farming simply doesn't resonate anymore."

"I don't feel hard done by at all, Councillor. You can have the seat. I was getting tired of the trips to Alert Bay anyway. But don't try and tell me that the people of Lostcoast elected you because I'm opposed to salmon farming." Archie smiled broadly at White Eagle.

"Well, you're against it, I'm for it. I won the election fair and square, Archie. Folks will be turning to me for leadership now."

"You really think that folks around here understand the long-term consequences of salmon farming?"

"You think your people are fools, Archie? That what you're saying?"

"I'm not saying that, Councillor. What I am saying is that you and your pals at Stoboltz Aquaculture have pulled the wool over people's eyes. You've sold them a bill of goods. Told them that fish farming is the only way they can make money, maybe buy a new boat. Don't think I didn't hear what you were telling people during the election."

Greg White Eagle looked at the sea beyond the small port. Without looking at Ravenwing he said, "The chief said he still wants you on the aquaculture committee. I would think that would give you some comfort that we're not changing direction."

"It's really only a matter of time, Greg."

"Matter of time before what?"

"Before you weasel your way onto that committee, too. Another month, maybe two, and you'll have the band council convinced that letting more fish farms into the Broughton is the way to lift our people up out of poverty."

"It is! It is a way to lift us out of poverty. Look around you, Archie. Not everybody can afford to live in a fancy house up on the hill like you do. Look around you!" Greg White Eagle pointed at the cluster of shacks that lined the shore of the harbour.

"Oh, it will lift a *few* folks out of poverty. People like you working really close-like with the company will do well. If you know what I mean. But the rest of 'em, well, they'll have seasonal work just like always, and we'll be left with nothing. No wild salmon —"

"I'm not sure I like your tone, Archie."

Archie shrugged. "I don't really give a damn, Councillor." He stood up, arching his back and stretching his arms over his head.

Greg White Eagle turned and looked down at him. "You know what your problem is, Archie?"

"I got lots of problems, Greg. Which one are *you* referring to?" He laughed.

White Eagle didn't share the humour. "Your problem is that you think you're better than everyone else. That somehow everybody's got to live up to the standard that Archie Ravenwing sets for them. Well that boat has sailed. The people of Lostcoast have said they've had enough, and frankly, I've had enough. Enough of your holy-roller, better-than-thou attitude." He looked down at the man, hands on his hips.

Archie Ravenwing looked up at him, grinning. "That's a good speech. Good speech. You practising for band council meetings there, Greg? Or for the newspapers? How long 'til you run for chief? Then what, the Assembly of First Nations?"

Greg made a dismissive gesture.

Archie stowed the tackle in a metal chest on the bow of the *Inlet Dancer.* He wiped his hands together after he finished. "How deep does Stoboltz have its hooks into you, Greg?"

"Bah, there you go again, Archie."

"No, really, how deep?"

The big man on the dock turned his back and began to walk away, then stopped. "Don't tell me you're clean as a whistle, Ravenwing. We both know you're not. And don't forget who's in the band office now. That's my people who are there now. My people doing the numbers. My people who can look back over the past decade and see where the money's gone. You better hope there's no skeletons in your closet."

"We all got skeletons, Greg. It's just that yours are paying your freight. How long 'til you try and convince the council that more salmon farming is inevitable, and we might as well get on the gravy train? Isn't that what Stoboltz paid for your election for?"

"Watch yourself, Archie," said Greg White Eagle, his hands clenched at his sides. "Watch yourself."

A ring-billed gull watching the confrontation from a lamp standard screamed and took flight, joining others over the open water. The sky was clear and the sun beat down on the two men. It was unseasonably warm for May, and Archie was in shirt-sleeves as he worked on the deck of his Radon fishing boat. This weather is a gift, Archie Ravenwing thought, tidying the deck of the *Inlet Dancer,* ignoring Greg White Eagle's threats. He looked up in time to see his daughter Grace walk down the dock, her long, purposeful stride reminding him of his wife, dead eleven years now.

"Hi, Greg," she said, her voice high and sweet.

"Hey, Grace."

"Congratulations on the election. Now I get to see my old man a little more." She smiled and held out her hand.

"Thanks," he said, uncurling his fist and shaking her small, strong hand. "I had better be getting on."

"See you around, Councillor," said Archie, waving as Greg White Eagle made his way up the dock to the parking lot. "Come by for a chat anytime."

"What was that all about?" Grace asked, stepping onto the bow of the *Inlet Dancer*. She carried a small plastic ice box.

"Oh, you know, just Greg being a sore winner."

"You're not being a sore loser, are you, Dad?"

"Who, me?" Archie made a generous gesture, opening his arms. "I'm a team player. Greg tells me the chief has asked me to stay in the Aquaculture Advisory Task Force on behalf of the band. Why would I be sore?"

Grace sat at the table and put the ice box down, flipping it open. "I brought you some lunch. I noticed you left without it this morning."

"Hey, that's great! You like some coffee?"

"No thanks, I'm not going to stay. I've got to run over to the school and finish up a few things."

"But it's Saturday."

"Yeah, but I've got a few things to deal with before Monday morning."

"You work too hard," said Ravenwing, taking a wax paper-wrapped sandwich in his hands and folding back the paper before taking a bite.

"Look who's talking." She watched him eat. He looked toward Knight Inlet. "Are you and Darren heading out again this afternoon?" she asked.

"If he ever shows up."

"He always does."

"Yeah, eventually."

"You fishing today or snooping?"

He smiled at her over the sandwich. "A little of both."

"How's it looking out there, Dad?" Her voice was low now, more serious.

"Not so good, Gracie. Not so good. Our catch is okay, but so many of the pinks are covered in lice." He chewed his sandwich and looked out at the inlet thoughtfully. "You know, I think Stoboltz and the others are still trying to convince the government and the public that sea lice aren't dangerous."

"Dad, don't start."

"Come on, Gracie, I know you understand this. The lice, they don't hurt the adults too bad. But it's the juveniles that are getting hit pretty hard. They can't survive with the current infestation. And that infestation is a direct result of lice infested Atlantic salmon mixing with the wild West Coast species. There's no doubt in my mind, or in Cassandra Petrel's, for that matter, what is going on out there." He looked east toward the mouth of Knight Inlet. "It just keeps getting worse. I think we could be in for serious trouble."

"You looking for trouble again, Arch?" Darren First Moon walked down the dock toward the *Inlet Dancer*.

"I don't need to look for it, Moon, it finds me." Ravenwing finished his sandwich and balled up the paper, putting it back into the ice box.

"How you doing, Gracie?" Darren First Moon asked, stepping onto the gunwale of the Radon and down onto its deck.

"I'm good, Darren. You good?"

"I was born good," he said.

"Well, I'm going to school. Let you guys get out into the inlet."

"Okay, sweetheart," said Archie, kissing his daughter on the forehead.

"Bye, Darren," she said, stepping onto the dock.

"See you, sweetie."

Archie shot him a look.

"Just being friendly-like," he said, his face reddening.

"Be friendly with someone else," said Archie, but he was smiling. "Let's get ready to hit the water."

They prepared the boat quickly, moving around as two men who have worked side by side for many years, each aware of what the other is doing and what his own tasks are.

"Greg White Eagle was by today," said Archie as the two men passed one another.

"What did he have to say?"

"About what he always says. Absolutely nothing. I can see his mouth moving, but nothing ever comes out. It's the most amazing thing."

"You sore?"

"Why does everybody think I'm sore?"

"Well, you lost."

"If you ask *me*, I won."

Darren First Moon was a thickly built man, about forty, whose hair was cropped short and covered with a greasy ball cap. He wore an orange float coat on and off the boat, and had crewed with Archie for the last decade, guiding with him for the last half dozen. "I guess if it means spending more time on the water, I'm all for it."

"I want to get to the bottom of some things. I've got the time to do it now."

"Bottom of some things. That doesn't sound good."

"No, not good. But we got to get to the bottom of them just the same."

"We, eh? Okay, partner, let's go and make our catch, and then we can get to the bottom of whatever you like."

They were about to untie from their mooring when Archie's cellphone rang. If the wind blew lightly from the west and the tide was high, Port Lostcoast got cell reception. He flipped it open. "This is Archie."

"Archie, this is Lance Grey." The voice crackled.

Ravenwing straightened up, looking at the sky. "Hi, Lance. Listen, I'm just about to head out into the inlet."

"This won't take long, Archie. The minister has received your most recent letter about salmon farms and asked me to call you and assure you he is considering all the options about the future of aquaculture."

"That's what you told me the last time, Lance. That's why I wrote you *another* letter. I don't want him to consider *all* the options. We need you to fund closed containment pens. These open pens in the Broughton and elsewhere are disease factories and they're killing the wild salmon. I'm looking for the government to commit funding so that Stoboltz and the others can move their stocks out of the migration routes of juvenile pinks, coho, sockeye, and chum, and onto land, where the fish can't escape, shit in the ocean, or pass on parasites to what's left of the wild fish."

"Take it easy, Archie. This is just a courtesy call."

"Look, Lance, I don't need a courtesy call. I need action. Why don't you ask the minister to come and see for himself?"

"He's been up recently."

"Yeah, to tour Stoboltz farms."

"He met with the band council. You were there, as I recall."

"He invited us to an hour-long meeting and spent fifty minutes of it talking. He didn't listen to a word we had to say."

"Archie, I'm not getting into this with you right now."

"Then when, Lance?"

"Are you going to be at the next Aquaculture Advisory Task Force meeting?"

"Damn right."

"Well, I guess we'll see you then."

Archie hung up the phone without saying goodbye. "Pecker head," he said, smiling.

"Who was that?" asked First Moon, starting the *Inlet Dancer*'s motors.

"Lance Grey from the minister's office."

"You were pretty hard on him."

"A kid. They hire a kid to do the political dirty work. He can't be more than twenty-five."

"Still, you were pretty rough. Why are you always talking that way to people, Archie?"

"Come on, Moon, don't play dumb. Sometimes it's the only way people will listen."

"Oh yeah, how's that working for you so far?"

Ravenwing looked straight ahead. Darren piloted the boat from the slip and moved out of the harbour dead slow.

"I guess the thing is, Archie," said First Moon, pushing forward on the throttle as they cleared the breakwater of the harbour and entered Knight Inlet's open water. "You can be an advocate for wild salmon without making everybody you talk to want wring your neck."

5 When the plane banked and circled, starting its precipitous decline into Port Lostcoast, Cole Blackwater's lunch sluiced in his stomach and threatened to decorate the interior of the tiny fuselage. He gripped the armrest and closed his eyes.

"Don't like flying?" the man next to him asked.

Cole, eyes pressed shut, didn't say a word, fearing that opening his mouth might provide the opportunity his breakfast was looking for to vacate his stomach. The plane dropped like a stone out of the sky toward the pan-flat ocean at the mouth of the harbour. What had only a moment before looked like a village of sticks and stones took the form of a real community huddled around a small bay, the fingers of the harbour slips pointing at the breakwater. The most recognizable building was the community centre, perched on a small bluff overlooking the bay, its stalwart totem pole visible from high above, adorned with the images of bear, otter, and raven. Around the centre, spread out on ill-defined streets, were small, colourful wooden homes, and near the water stood a row of storefronts and businesses: a grocery and hardware store, a gas station, a restaurant, and a bar called The Strait.

Cole had flown from Vancouver to Port Hardy the night before and spent the evening in a cheap motel on the waterfront, watching a hockey game in a bar across the road. He drank too much beer and walked the streets of the tiny fishing and lumbering town until after two AM, thinking about his friend Archie Ravenwing. Then he finally crashed into his bed, fully dressed, to be awakened a few hours later by Mary Patterson, who called to tell him she'd booked a charter flight to Lostcoast.

He couldn't have been happier.

"The trick with these little planes is to keep your eyes on the horizon. That's why I always take the window."

Cole took a deep breath and looked at the man sitting next to him — a kid, really. He tried to focus on the horizon over the man's shoulder, but all he could see out the window was water, the harbour, and the tiny settlement as the plane banked again.

His travelling companion had introduced himself when Cole

had shuffled onto the plane and taken the last seat available in the ten-seater. Lance Grey, special assistant to the provincial minister of Agriculture and Lands for Fisheries and Aquaculture. Cole asked him how he knew Archie.

"We worked together on the provincial Aquaculture Advisory Task Force," said Grey, looking out the window.

"I think Archie might have told me about you," said Black-water.

"Don't believe everything you hear," said Lance Grey, a broad smile on his face.

"I don't. The truth is usually far worse," Cole said, buckling his seat belt.

Now the plane levelled then skipped once, twice on the flat water. The engines whined, and Cole's body pressed into the seat belt, putting uncomfortable pressure on his churning gut. When the motion came to a stop, Cole breathed out heavily through his mouth.

"You never did say how it is that *you* knew Archie," said Grey, unbuckling his seat belt and straightening his sports coat.

Cole pressed his palms against his thighs. "I was helping him shut down fish farms," he said.

They disembarked from the plane, the latest arrivals to Port Lostcoast. Cole sucked the moist ocean air into his lungs, feeling his legs wobble under him as he made his way down the dock. It had been two years since he'd been on Parish Island. The last time he was here was to serve the band council in its effort to keep the Broughton Archipelago off-limits to new fish farms. The BC Liberal government had reversed a policy by the previous government that kept these salmon-rich waters off-limits, and dozens of new farms were springing up along the migration routes of wild pink salmon. He had stayed for nearly two weeks, working with local band council member Archie Ravenwing, biologist Cassandra Petrel, and other members of the community to cobble together a defense against the corporate onslaught of open-net Atlantic salmon farms. They had joined with others along the coast—First Nations and environmental activists—to plot a joint strategy, and dug in for a long fight.

The days were punctuated by time spent on the water, when Cole would ride out into the inlet with Archie and Grace Ravenwing. In the short time that Cole was in Port Lostcoast, he came to respect and admire Archie Ravenwing for his courage and vision. And he came to care for Grace and the rest of Archie's family, who seemed to come and go from Parish Island on a nearly daily basis. Cole had left them with a four-pronged plan: take on the provincial government regarding its retrograde policy; target the public with messages about public health; take on the federal government about federal fisheries laws that were supposed to protect wild salmon; and go nose to nose with the fish farmers with an aggressive media campaign in Europe and across the United States.

Cole knew it was not a spectacular plan. He knew it then and he knew it now. He'd been new to consulting, new to the job of stitching together other people's ideas. He'd been distracted. Two years into his life on the West Coast, the events that had propelled him across the country still festered in a shadowy, hidden corner. He spent more time than he should have in the strait. He drank with Archie's friend Darren First Moon and tried to steer clear of the inevitable loose cannons that a remote place beyond the reach of the police tended to attract.

Cole woke with a hangover each morning only to start all over again. That was the extent of his experience in Port Lostcoast.

The provincial government's response to the strategy had been to create the Aquaculture Advisory Task Force to "study" fish farming's future, while continuing to expand the industry at breakneck speed.

Where Archie had passion and determination in spades, he lacked administrative skills, and Cole Blackwater's invoices went unpaid, further supporting Cole's precipitous downward spiral. Lacking new clients and mired in his own inadequacies, Cole couldn't keep doing pro bono work, and he had to close the salmon farming file. He hated to do it, but what choice did he have? He certainly felt like he was abandoning Archie Ravenwing, his proud family, and the wild salmon that Archie defended.

Now he was back in Port Lostcoast, only one day before the

spring equinox. The salty air was still and warm. He walked to the end of the dock, the voice of Lance Grey still ringing in his ears like an annoying car alarm. He stole a look back over his shoulder to see Grey chatting with another band councillor who had greeted the plane.

"Cole!" The voice brought his attention back to the dock, and Blackwater saw Grace Ravenwing running toward him. "Cole, I'm so glad you made it!"

"I wouldn't have missed it, Grace," said Cole sombrely. He dropped his flight bag and embraced the young woman. She hugged him tightly, her small body disappearing in Cole's leather jacket. He could smell her hair, like flowers, and the feel of her against him made him dizzy.

"I'm so sorry about your dad."

"Me too," she said, lifting her gaze, her eyes red.

They stood looking at each other for a moment. Finally she said, "So, how was the flight?"

"To be honest, pretty awful. I've been in lots of these puddle jumpers, but I never really enjoy them. The Queen Charlotte Strait was lovely, but I could do without the splash down."

"Come on, let's get you settled." She took him by the arm to lead him down the dock.

"I appreciate you asking me to stay at your place. Are you sure it's okay?"

"Why not? It's big enough, and it feels pretty empty now with Dad gone," she said, a tear sliding down her cheek.

She hooked her arm into his while he slung his bag over his shoulder and steadied himself after the flight and the night of drinking. With Grace leading, he trudged toward the tiny town.

"I'll see you around, Cole," said Lance Grey striding past them, his flight bag and computer on tiny wheels bumping along the uneven dock. "Oh, hi Grace," he said, looking back. "I'm sorry about your dad."

"Thank you, Lance," she said, not turning to face him.

"Well, see you." Lance reached the end of the dock before them and continued down the hard-packed dirt street toward Port

Lostcoast's only accommodation, a six-room bed and breakfast next to the gas station.

"You know Lance?" Cole said as they reached the end of the dock. Grace led them to a grey 1988 Ford Ranger pickup.

"Oh, sure. He's here all the time, schmoozing the band council, schmoozing the business folks in Port McNeill and Alert Bay, schmoozing everything with a pulse." She laughed, and Cole thought she sounded just like her father when she did. "He's a dirt bag. I think he means well, but there is something about the way he does things that's just, well—"

"Slimy?"

"Yeah," she said, opening Cole's door as he hoisted his bag into the cluttered bed of the truck. The box was strewn with fishing nets, broken paddles, floats, assorted tackle, a dented and rusty tool box, and an assortment of beer cans and soda bottles.

"Dad's truck," said Grace, seeing Cole take inventory. "Bit of a pig. I only drive it once in a while. I thought you might have had more luggage, or I would have walked."

"I like to keep stealthy. You know, slip in and out of town without any fuss." Cole grinned.

"I remember...." Grace said, not smiling.

Red faced, Cole got in the cab and kicked a space on the floor for his feet. Grace slid in behind the wheel. "The only part of his life that wasn't a junk heap was his boat. I've managed to keep the house in one piece since Mom died, but it's been a Herculean task." The truck rattled to life and Grace piloted it up the hill and between houses whose colourful paint jobs were weathered and chipped from the winter gales that howled down the Queen Charlotte Strait and over tiny Parish Island. Grace piloted the truck up a steep hill, past an exposed cliff face, and onto a hillock where seagrass blew in the light breeze.

They parked in front of a ramshackled home that looked as though it was a perpetual work in progress. The original house was squat and sturdy, and two new wings jutted out on either side, one built into the rocky hillside devoid of trees and scoured by the ocean winds, the other built on stilts on the side of the cliff where it plunged down to the harbour. A broad deck, lacking a railing, circled that addition, twenty feet above the rocks below.

"Dad called it the Bluff House," she said, shutting off the engine.

"I remember," Cole smiled. "Is that addition new since I was here last?" Cole asked, pointing to the precarious wing on stilts.

"Dad was never content to do just five or six things at once, you know," Grace said, leading Cole up the oyster-shell pathway to the front door. "He was never satisfied to leave well enough alone. Always tinkering, finding fault, finding something more to do."

Cole nodded, and knew that Grace Ravenwing was talking about more than the house.

They entered the main home, where the aroma of seafood stew greeted them. The front door led to a mud room, where slickers and boots and float coats were hung on pegs, and a broad deacon's bench was open, exposing hats and gloves and assorted fishing paraphernalia. Cole pulled off his shoes and dropped his bags, looking around the sprawling home. A wide, open kitchen with broad windows providing a view out over the harbour and the strait beyond opened off the mud room. There were no cupboards above the counter to spoil the view, and Cole recalled many meals prepared in this kitchen while watching pods of orca or humpback whales swimming up and down the watery west coast highway.

"It smells great in here, Grace."

Grace swept into the kitchen and checked on the stew. "You hungry?"

Cole felt his stomach rumble, and he hoped it was from hunger and not his airsick hangover. "I could eat," he decided.

They sat at the dining room table, floor-to-ceiling windows providing a panoramic view over the Queen Charlotte Strait to the north and the mouth of Knight Inlet to the east. To the west were the humpbacked shapes made by the clutter of islands scattered up the southwestern side of the Broughton Archipelago.

"Good grief, it's beautiful here," said Cole, swabbing his bowl with freshly baked bread.

Grace nearly spit out a mouthful of stew, not quite able to suppress a laugh. She dabbed at her mouth and smiled. "I see you're maintaining your promise to Sarah, Cole. You sound more like Charlie Brown than a brooding hoodlum."

He scowled at her. "Who's a hoodlum?"

"You are. You look like the guy who stands at the back of the room in gangster movies — you know, in the shadows. And when the guy can't pay the money he owes, the boss says something like —" Grace improvised an Italian accent — "my man Guido here's goin' a breaka' you knees."

Cole laughed. "That's pretty good, Grace. I know this Italian guy named Frankie Fingers who does a pretty good Salish accent. You should hear him!" Then he added, "Truth is, I slip up every now and again, but I'm trying. I'm really trying."

"You're a good father, you know."

"Thanks, but it doesn't always feel like it. We've had our ups and downs."

"Every father and daughter does. My God, my dad and I fought like badger and bear, but we loved each other and there was always respect."

Cole stood and brought their empty bowls to the sink. He sat back down.

"So Grace, can you tell me what happened?"

She drew a sharp breath. "I don't really know, Cole. The RCMP and the local search teams haven't recovered Dad's body yet, and they haven't found the *Dancer*. They haven't officially declared him dead," she said, tears spilling from the corners of her eyes, creating glistening tracks over her face. Cole reached out and took her hand, and she squeezed his fingers. Even in her grief she was beautiful, with her high, round cheeks, almond eyes, and thick, black hair that fell halfway down her back. She was full bodied, but by no means heavy. Voluptuous, the kind of body Rembrandt loved to paint. She was in her late twenties and looked youthful. Natural. Her beauty had stopped Cole in his tracks more than once.

"Our people think it's important to send the spirit on to the next world quickly, so we're not willing to wait for the official medical examiner's report." She stopped a moment and looked out the window. Cole let the silence sit between them.

After a few minutes she spoke again. "The RCMP and the people from the Joint Rescue Centre down in Victoria figure that Dad was trying to make it home through a big gale that blew up. He had been out nosing around the mouth of Tribune Channel, looking for trouble as usual. They figure he must have misread the storm and pushed for home after dark. He didn't make it. The Coast Guard, the RCMP, and even the Navy had boats, helicopters, and those big airplanes from Comox in the inlet looking for the *Dancer*. My brother Jacob and Darren First Moon have been out on Jacob's boat all week. So have many other men, from all over the place. There were boats here from as far away as Victoria. But no sign of him...." Her voice trailed off. Cole grasped her hand tightly.

Grace held her face upright, wiping her tears with the back of her free hand.

"You said he was looking for trouble. You think he was being reckless?"

"Dad was never reckless when it came to the sea. He was pretty cautious. No, I think he was nosing around that farm at Jeopardy Rock, or further up Tribune Channel. He told me that he was onto something. Something that just wasn't right, but he didn't say exactly what."

Cole looked out the window as a glaucous winged gull landed on the patio of the new addition.

"We had a bit of a tussle recently, and, well, he stopped telling me what he was doing then."

"What did you fight about, Grace?"

"God, it seems so stupid now," she said, fresh tears forming in her red eyes. "Dad could be such a conspiracy theorist sometimes. He was going on about how Stoboltz was doing research at one of their farming operations, where the old DFO labs are up at Jeopardy Rock. He thought they were doing genetic engineering or something, breeding super salmon. I guess I didn't take him seriously enough. But you know how he was. He really rubbed people the wrong way when he thought he was right and everybody else was wrong."

"Your dad could be pretty persistent."

"Yeah, well, I guess I know where I get it from. But the thing is, Cole, he was really rattling people's cages lately. Since he lost the election to Greg, he was impossible to get along with. Always fighting with someone. If it wasn't Greg, it was Darren. If it wasn't Darren, it was one of the rednecks from the bar. That bigot Dan Campbell. And Lance Grey, and the minister, too. He seemed to be on their cases constantly. People would cross the street when they saw him coming. They just didn't want to deal with him. Even Darren First Moon and he were at each other's throats."

"Seems like he was really upset about something. You don't know anything more about what he was onto at the DFO station? Maybe there's something I can help with, you know...."

"No idea." Grace shook her head. "But you're welcome to have a look through his papers and his computer, Cole. Maybe you can figure it out. I really don't know much. He just shut everybody out, at least when he wasn't picking a fight. He still talked with Cassandra, but not often. He was off on his own most of the time."

"That doesn't really seem like Archie's style, does it?"

"He was always a bit prickly, but the way he was provoking people the last few months was a bit much, even for him."

Cole found himself very curious about Archie's preoccupation.

"Cole," said Grace thoughtfully. "There's something else."

"What is it?" he asked, distracted by his own ruminations.

"Well, it seems pretty strange, timing wise."

Cole looked at her, listening.

"The day before he went up Knight Inlet and didn't come back, he dug his will out of a file and left it on his desk."

Cole felt a shiver clamber up his vertebrae.

Grace shook her head. "I didn't even know he had a will. He sure never talked about it. But when he didn't come back, I went to his office to see if there was anything that might be helpful to the Coast Guard and I found it on top of his usual clutter. What do you think about that?"

Cole broke eye contact with Grace. "I don't know," he lied, looking out the window at Knight Inlet. But it seemed obvious; for whatever reason, Archie Ravenwing believed that his life might soon end.

6 What usually got Nancy Webber into trouble was too much thinking, too much reflection. Her first impression was most often correct, her first impulse the one she should follow. But given sufficient time to brood, she could find a hundred reasons to second-guess her intuition and jump to all manner of erroneous conclusions.

The drive from Edmonton to High River takes about four hours if Calgary's main highway, Deerfoot Trail, isn't backed up with commuter traffic. Intuition told her to let the proverbial sleeping dogs lie. Cole Blackwater was a dog that should just be left to doze through his life — as he did so well, Nancy thought. Before clearing Edmonton's city limits, she had twice almost turned around. But the longer she drove the more she second-guessed her intuition, and by Airdrie, hundreds of kilometres south of Edmonton, she had convinced herself of a massive cover-up of Henry Blackwater's death, and also that she was the one to get to the bottom of it.

That morning the lack of traffic on the Deerfoot allowed Nancy Webber to sail down to High River at a nice prairie coast of one hundred and twenty kilometres per hour. She arrived just after noon on Sunday, March 20. She tried to remember when she had last been in High River but couldn't recall, and decided that this must be, in fact, her inaugural visit. She parked near the newspaper office and searched for lunch.

What began as a service centre for the ranching community, and had later served the region's short-lived coal mining operations and then the oil and gas developments that pocked the foothills, was now a bedroom community for burgeoning Calgary. Like many foothills towns, High River maintained a small, rustic, though not antiquated, downtown with the usual assortment of curios shops, a quilt store, a genuine First Nation's jewellery and artwork boutique, and a bookstore that doubled as a coffee shop. But High River's current energy sprang from the sprawling developments that ringed the downtown centre of the community, threatening to suck the life out of the historic downtown core.

Nancy found a place that served milkshakes and ate a salad

for the sake of achieving balance, and then walked back to the *High River Tribune*'s office to look for Casey Brown.

As she walked to the newspaper's front doors in a circa 1970s strip mall, she heard a voice call from behind her. "Ms. Webber?"

She turned to see a man pedalling his bike up onto the sidewalk. He wore a helmet with a blinking red light on top and an orange safety vest, and his pant leg was safely tucked into one woolen sock. She waited for him to dismount and offered her hand. "It's Nancy." She smiled at him.

"Hi," said the man, catching his breath. "I'm Casey Brown. Sorry to be late. The auction went a little longer than I expected. I hope I haven't kept you waiting?"

"Not at all. Just got here myself."

Casey opened the door to the newspaper office and pushed his bike inside. "Come on in."

He wheeled his way between the desks to the back, and when he re-emerged he had doffed his cycling attire and was dressed in jeans and a plaid shirt.

"I bet you fit in around here better when you're dressed like this, rather than with the bicycle road-warrior get-up on," said Nancy, looking around the cluttered space.

"You can say that again. I grew up in Toronto. I rode my bike everywhere. When I graduated from Ryerson, I didn't just want to go to work for some leftie Toronto magazine filled with ads for gay dating services, you know what I mean? Not that I have anything against gays. God, listen to me, now I'm starting to sound like an Albertan. Anyway, I applied for positions at a bunch of little papers in the Rockies, and this is where I landed. The folks around here are actually pretty used to seeing cyclists now. Lots of the Calgary commuters ride the trails in Kananaskis on the weekends. The old-timers still have a tough time with it. But they give me a wide berth. I guess it's like passing a horse on the road."

"Sure," said Nancy. "Except I doubt you'll kick a headlight out if you get spooked."

"You never know," said Brown, sitting on the edge of a desk. "So what was so important that you had to drive all the way down here on a Sunday?"

Nancy considered this question herself. What was so important? She'd spent four hours on the road devising cockamamie stories about a cover-up of Henry Blackwater's suicide, convincing herself it was the reason that Cole kept her at a distance now. But she couldn't very well share this with Casey Brown. "Well," she began, "I don't know if it's anything at all. I just want to look through your coverage on Henry Blackwater's suicide."

"Like I said on the phone, I wasn't here then. But it's all on file. I'll show you the way."

Casey led Nancy to the back of the office to a microfiche scanner and filing cabinets filled with reels of stories filed by date. "You said it was around the spring of 2002?"

"Yeah, around then. I don't know the exact date."

Brown flipped through the files. "Well, here you go. This is the first story. You should be able to easily scan through the files that follow."

"Thanks," said Nancy, sitting down on a small stool to begin her research.

"No trouble. Holler if you need anything."

Nancy Webber didn't need to holler. It took her a little over an hour to scan everything the *High River Tribune* had written on the death of Henry Blackwater. In that time she learned little that she didn't already know: Henry Blackwater had presumably used a branding iron to engage the trigger of a Remington 12-gauge shotgun, shooting himself under the chin. According to the medical examiner, he died instantly. The suicide had occurred in the middle of a boxing ring in the barn on the Blackwater Ranch in the southeastern side of the Porcupine Hills. The youngest of two sons — Cole — had discovered his father after hearing the shotgun blast. Walter Blackwater had been on the ranch at the time as well and had arrived at the barn shortly after Cole.

There had been no RCMP investigation of the shooting, as the ME had determined that the death was consistent with that of a suicide.

There it was again, thought Nancy. That ambiguity. Consistent with that of a suicide.

Nancy couldn't get over that ambiguity. It kept coming up in relation to the death of Henry Blackwater.

She rubbed her eyes. Too much time to think, she thought.

She filed the fiche, found Casey Brown, and thanked him for his time.

"Anytime," he said, looking up from his computer and stretching. "You find what you were looking for?"

"Afraid not," she said, and headed out the door into the afternoon sunshine.

Now what? Drive back to Edmonton and put this silliness behind you, she heard a voice say in her head. Give the man a break, she heard herself think. He's obviously been through a lot. The last thing he needs is Nancy Webber poking around in his past. Let sleeping dogs lie, she repeated. But that was the problem, wasn't it? That was always the problem with Cole Blackwater. He lied. But something else kept getting in the way.

Nancy Webber was reasonably certain that what kept getting in the way right now was the nagging questions about how Henry Blackwater died.

She started to walk back downtown and snatched her phone out of her pocket. She dialled directory assistance, found the number she was looking for, and called it.

"Fort Macleod RCMP, how can I direct your call?"

"Is Sergeant Reimer in today?"

"Hold a moment."

"Reimer."

"Sergeant, it's Nancy Webber calling from the *Edmonton Journal*."

"Tracked me down, did you? What can I do for you, Ms. Webber?"

"Well, frankly, Sergeant, it's a bit of a long shot, I know, but I'm looking for some information on a suspicious death and I really don't know where to turn right now."

"Whose death?"

"Well, you're going to laugh when I tell you. Henry Blackwater."

Reimer didn't laugh. "Is this a relation of Cole Blackwater?"

"It's his father."

Nancy heard the RCMP officer take a breath on the other end of the line.

"Look," Nancy said, "I know the whole thing in Oracle probably left you feeling a little sore. Cole has a way of doing that. I'm just looking into something for my own personal edification. This isn't for a story. I've been digging into the archives of the local paper about the suicide of Cole's father, and, well, there are some missing pieces."

"Like what?"

"Well, the paper reports that the coroner says that the likely cause of death was suicide, but there was no RCMP investigation into the death. Just a medical examiner's report. Nobody seems to have considered any other possibility."

The line was silent a moment. Then Reimer said, "Have you read the ME's report?"

"No," said Webber.

"Neither have I, but I bet it would be a good place to start."

"Do you have access to it?"

"It's a different district."

"Can you get it though?" Nancy was almost at her car.

"I'll find a copy and give it a read. I owe you."

"That you do, Sergeant."

"Where should I send it?"

"I'm in High River right now. Maybe I'll come to you."

"Okay. How about first thing tomorrow?"

"That sounds great," Nancy said.

Then Reimer asked, "What is this all about, Nancy?"

Nancy Webber unlocked her car door. "I don't really want to speak out of turn."

"You've got to be thinking something. You don't drive from Edmonton to Fort Macleod on a Sunday just to visit the historic North West Mounted Police fort."

"You're right about that," said Webber.

"So what is it?"

"Off the record?"

"You know that nothing is off the record," said Reimer, repeating what she knew all too well about police and reporters.

Nancy sighed. "Well, it's probably nothing. Just my imagination, you know? But I think the circumstances of Henry Blackwater's death are suspicious. Nobody seems to be a hundred percent certain that his death was a suicide. At least nobody who has put anything down in print. The newspaper reports say things like 'likely' and 'consistent with.' That's just not good enough for me."

"That's often the way suicides get filed. We say 'consistent with' when there may be some chance of accidental death. Do you think it may have been accidental, like a hunting accident?"

Nancy cut her off. "Sergeant, I don't think it was an accident. Anyway, why would anybody choose to report it as suicide rather than an accident? It's usually the other way around."

"I don't know. People are funny when it comes to suicide."

"Don't I know it. But Henry Blackwater didn't trip on a rock while hunting and shoot himself in the face. He was found in the centre of a boxing ring, his blood splattered across the bales of hay ten feet away, and Cole was the person who found him."

7 Cassandra Petrel sat on the deck of her boat moored next to seining and trolling boats at Port Lostcoast on Parish Island. It was nine PM on the longest day of the year, and the sun still lingered in the western sky over the fractured archipelago. The day had been warm and sunny, but as the sun dipped it grew cooler, and Petrel had pulled on a wool sweater after finishing dinner. The *Queen Charlotte Challenger* was a forty-two-foot Whitby ketch that Petrel had bought at auction for just shy of eighty thousand dollars four years ago after selling her house in Victoria. It was the perfect boat to call home, with a comfortable galley, a spacious forward berth, and all the amenities she needed. The previous owner had taken meticulous care of the boat's interior, and Cassandra loved the look and feel of the handcrafted wood finishing.

Petrel had bought the boat after she had quit her teaching and research job at the university, opting to live full-time on British Columbia's jagged coast. The politics of the university, the distaste that some of the more conservative members of faculty left in her mouth, and the looming proximity of her retirement had forced her hand. Did she want to sit on the sidelines for the remainder of her academic career and merely point out what was so blatantly obvious — that the ocean was dying? Or did she want to roll up her sleeves and lend a hand, however modest, to help fix the problem? The sleek, three-sailed vessel was now her home, her office, and her floating research station. And though she wasn't yet confident enough to pilot it solo through the most rugged waters of the Johnstone Strait, she foresaw the day when she would be. Cassandra Petrel considered herself a fast learner.

Gulls wheeled overhead, and the stillness of the evening was pierced only occasionally by the whine of a four-wheel drive truck or ATV negotiating the steep dirt roads of the community or by the protests of a raven or gull in the harbour. She sipped a cup of tea, holding it in both hands, watching the sun's final hour on the western sky as it painted the slopes of forested hills and the distant undulation of mountains on the big island.

From where she sat she could see Archie Ravenwing's battered grey Ford Ranger roll to a stop at the entrance to the docks. She put her cup to her lips and then stood to step down into the galley of the boat to put on a kettle. By the time she had returned, Ravenwing was making his way down the docks to her slip, hands in his pockets.

"Evening, Archie," she said, sitting back down.

"Good evening, Cassandra."

"It's a beautiful night. Care for a cup of tea?"

"I'd love a cup of tea," he said, taking the invitation to step aboard.

"Longest day of the year," she said, looking west.

He turned, hands still in his pockets, to gaze at the spectacular sunset. His smile broadened. "We've been blessed," he finally said.

The kettle whistled and Cassandra rose and went into the galley of the boat, returning a few minutes later with a fresh pot of tea and a mug for Archie. She gestured at the wooden bench that lined the cockpit and invited him to sit.

She poured them tea. The vapour from their cups danced into the night, and they both sat holding the heat of their mugs close to them.

"How have things been up the inlet?" she asked, taking a tentative sip.

He turned to look east, toward the darkening shapes of hills that rose and fell like the backs of bears bent over a salmon stream.

"First Moon and I have been up there pretty much every day since the season opened. It's okay. We're making a fair catch, but it's not like — well, it's not like before. The pink run is very, very low. There's a lot of sea lice."

They drank their tea.

"In the three years since the government opened these waters for more salmon farming," said Petrel, "we've seen a sharp rise in the number of sea lice, both on adult fish and juvies. The adults can take it. The little ones can't. This whole thing is going to collapse if we don't get those farms off the migration route, period. Full stop."

Archie nodded. "I've been pleading that case to the Aquaculture

Advisory Task Force for more than a year, but my days are limited there. I don't know how much longer the chief will keep me on the team now that Greg is the councillor for Lostcoast."

Cassandra squinted at the setting sun. She recited what they both already knew: "I'm afraid that the sun is going down on an ecosystem that has been here since before your people, Archie. It's a delicate balance. The salmon is at the very centre of the whole thing. Everything else depends on it. Other fish, bears, eagles, killer whales, even the forests. Everything feeds everything else. Sometimes I feel that we're just yelling into the wind here. And Stoboltz has more farms planned. More open-net pens planned for all through the Broughton. And that can only mean more accidents, more Atlantic salmon escaping, destroying the habitat for native fish species. More disease. You keep, what, half a million, a million salmon all penned up together, and no amount of antibiotics is going to keep them from passing disease on to the wild salmon that swim past them. Not to mention that we're eating all that crap," she said, her voice growing frustrated.

"Cassandra, I think it's worse than that."

"What do you mean?"

"Well, I think something is going on up at Jeopardy Rock. Something bad."

Cassandra looked at Archie over her mug of tea.

"First Moon and I were up there the other day, guiding some tourists, showing them around, and we stopped in at the salmon farm, you know, to show folks what it was doing to the environment. Show them the scale. The old DFO station that's there, you know, the research station? Well, Stoboltz has taken it over to use as some sort of regional base for its operations. They've got a dozen farms within a day's motoring of that site, so I guess it makes sense. But I think there's more to it than that. I just don't know what."

"I think I do. At least, I can guess," said Petrel.

"What?"

"I'm going to tell you something that I don't want you repeating, Archie. Not to Grace. Not to Darren. It's just a nagging suspicion that I've got, and I think you may have found one of the missing pieces. I think that Stoboltz is doing genetic engineering on Atlantic salmon, or at least they're doing the research."

"What do you mean?"

"I think they are trying to breed a more disease-resistant fish. Or fish that can somehow resist the impact that sea lice have on them. Maybe ones that can survive some of the superbugs that might lead to massive die-offs."

"On the face of it, not such a bad idea," said Ravenwing grimly.

"No, not on the face of it. The whole question of genetic engineering and food isn't really my area of knowledge. I know lots of people don't like the idea of tampering with the food chain, but what worries me is the impact it might have on wild salmon. Imagine this." She set down her teacup on the bench beside her and held her hands out in front of her. "You build a super species of Atlantic salmon, one that can resist certain diseases, and then *they* escape into the wild population, which is what happens all the time, and it could be disastrous. It could be absolutely devastating to the entire food chain."

"What makes you think that's what they're doing?"

"Nothing concrete. Nothing at all, really. Just history."

"What history?"

"Let's just say that I have a history with someone at Stoboltz. From my university days. If I know this person like I think I do, whatever he is supposed to be doing for the company is almost certainly going to devolve into genetic engineering and tampering with the ecosystem in a most disastrous way."

"Sounds like a bad dude," said Archie.

"I don't think he intends to be bad. He even comes off as being sincere. I just don't think he can help himself. He actually believes what he's doing is right, you know? But his view of the world is just so fundamentally different from yours or mine, Archie. And there is no love lost between him and the environmentalists."

They watched the last of the colour fade from the western sky while the sun sank on another solstice. The days would seem long for a few more weeks into July, but there was no denying that the crest of the season of light would now slip into the past. Soon the myth of summer would start to unravel, and autumn was always closer than anybody in the remote village cared to admit.

"What should we do?" asked Ravenwing.

"We need to find out what Stoboltz is up to. We need to find out what is happening at Jeopardy Rock."

8 The wind battered the community of Port Lost-coast. It barrelled down the Queen Charlotte Strait as if fleeing the far north, paying little regard to the broken islands that lay in its path. It whipped the waters of George Sound and Salmon Channel into a convoluted frenzy of eight-foot swells and deep troughs punctuated by breaking waves whose spray felt like ice. The sky above was clear, but the temperature had plunged, and the mourners who filed from the Big House clutched their coats around themselves to ward off the needled chill. Drummers and singers led the group, which marched in solemn union toward the sea.

Above the procession, ravens wheeled on the wind. They rose, wings extended, high above, riding the turbulent pockets of air that were tossed onto the shore and against the bluffs that the town was built around. When the wind eased to near-gale force, the birds tucked their wings and dropped like torpedoes into the harbour, only to extend their wings again and rise on the blustery air.

The mourners followed Grace Ravenwing away from the docks and the harbour to a rocky promenade at the ocean's side. There they gathered around her while she drew the carving of a raven from a bundle of cloth. Speaking a few inaudible words into the wind, she flung the bird into the breaking waves, where it was instantly consigned to the sea.

She, her two sisters, and one brother stood together for a few moments on the shore and then turned to make their way back toward town, the others forming a ragged line behind them. Cole Blackwater fell in behind Grace and her siblings, silent as they made their way back to the Big House. He had received no relief from the potlatch ceremony celebrating Archie Ravenwing. Despite a day of feasting, singing, dancing, and trading gifts, Cole felt restless. He pulled the collar of his coat up against the wind, his curly hair blowing around his face. He turned his eyes to the caterwauling ravens overhead, their black forms contrasting starkly with the almost-white sky. When the procession reached the Big House, Cole opted to stay apart from the others and stood on a small rise of stone from which he could see the harbour, the empty slip where the *Inlet Dancer* should rest, and across the passage to the hulk of Gilford Island. He buried his hands into his pockets and ruminated on the nature of loss.

His thoughts ranged far beyond the frayed archipelago of islands, over the rugged Coast Range, and across the belly of inland British Columbia to another range of mountains — the Rockies. They stretched two thousand miles from stem to stern, marking the border of Alberta and British Columbia for much of their distance. He had crossed the Great Divide last year for the first time since leaving Alberta in 2002. He had crossed the divide that separated the watersheds east and west, and he had crossed the divide that separated him from the anguish he felt at the losses in his own life. Now, thirty-eight years old and somewhat worse for wear, Cole Blackwater was cutting his way through the inevitable scar tissue that had formed over some of his darker wounds. He touched the real scars on his face. These physical markings were, though always visible when he looked in the mirror, easier to put out of his mind.

The scars he faced with unwelcome candour were far beneath the skin.

Like the red stain on the boxing ring in the barn on the Blackwater ranch. That stain dug into Cole like a dull blade.

After Oracle, Cole went to the ranch with Sarah to ride horses and find peace with the place. But confronting the broad splatter of blood on the mat of the boxing ring brought no peace whatsoever. It opened the wounds, and Cole Blackwater seemed powerless to suture them again. Standing in the dim light of the barn, Walter had told him that people would understand if they knew what had really happened in that barn in the spring of 2002 when their father had died. They would understand, and nobody would blame him for what had happened.

Cole remembered their conversation as if it had happened yesterday.

"I doubt it," Cole had said derisively. They would blame *him* and they *wouldn't* understand. "People might talk like they wouldn't blame a boy for the sins of his father. They talk that way, but deep down inside, they'd be wondering what it was I had done to deserve the old man's treatment. And they would look at this red stain on the mat, and at what he had done to me, and they would wonder if I hadn't just about had enough. And they'd be right, Walter. They would be right." Cole had turned in the half light of evening in the Porcupine Hills. "I had enough. I don't know why I came here. I swore I never would again. But leaving Ottawa, my life one big fucked-up mess of my own making, I thought that it couldn't get any worse. But then I show up here and it was like he had been waiting for twenty years, storing up all that anger for me. When I arrived, it was like he felt relief because he would be able to empty out that anger on me one more time.

"He didn't come at me at first. He just waited, and then that day —" Cole pointed to the red stain — "I was out riding and he pounced, and in his own way was able to put the knife in and twist it. He didn't come at me with his fists this time, Walt. Just a few words was all it took. It felt like I was a kid again. I was powerless to stop him."

He and Walter stood shoulder to shoulder, Cole a few inches taller but Walter broad and strong, his stained Stetson in his hands, his wispy hair matted with sweat.

"Mom told me that Dad had taken it out on her, too. She told me that day when the old man and I got back from riding. She told me that when I left home to go to Calgary, then Toronto, he took it out on her! Did you know that?" said Cole, his voice cracking with anger.

Walter nodded. "I know that he had some pretty harsh words for her."

"More than that, Walter. More than words. He hit her! He hit our mother! Did you know about that?" Cole turned accusingly to face his brother, his eyes wild and bright with tears that he would not shed.

"I didn't know about that," said Walter, looking down at his boots.

"How could you not? You were still around in those days."

"I didn't know, Cole." Walter turned and looked at him gently.

"I was a boy, too. Older, yes, but just a boy. I was afraid of him, too. He never hit me. I don't know why. That's not my fault. But he never did. And I didn't know about Mom."

"She told me that very day." Cole pointed again at the stain. "I came in from my ride, and I told her what the old man had said, and she told me what he had done. I don't think she meant to. It just came out. She said it only happened twice and that she had threatened to call the police, that he promised never to do it again and kept that word. Can you believe it?" said Cole, exasperated. He shook his head, stepped onto the red mark, and hunched down. "Maybe the old bastard got what he deserved. There was nothing I could do. Part of me wished it had happened sooner, so that fewer of us would have suffered."

"It's a tough thing to talk about your father like that," said Walter.

"I don't feel any pity for him. I don't see his death as a loss."

They could smell supper emanating from the house as they stood in the barn, looking at the boxing ring for the last time. The next day they had torn it down and burned it in the yard. Sarah stood with Cole, hand in hand, and watched the huge bonfire send sparks high into the sky over the foothills.

Now Cole faced the sea. Another passage. Another ending. He didn't think of his father's death as a loss. But what he did regard with bereavement was the time his father had stolen from him. Time, and the possibility of himself as a man without the ragged scars that marked his life.

"I've never been to a potlatch before." A voice with a European accent interrupted Cole's self pity, and he turned to see a man in a heavy Gore-Tex coat beside him, also looking at the ocean. "That was quite the ceremony."

Cole looked at the man, wishing he didn't have to engage with anybody at that very moment. But the man went on. "It's hard to believe that your country banned the potlatch tradition for more than seventy years."

"Have we met?" Cole asked.

"I'm sorry, let me introduce myself. I'm Erik Nilsson," The man held out a hand.

Cole removed a hand from his pocket and shook. "Cole Black-water," he said.

"So you're Cole Blackwater," said Nilsson. "I should have guessed." He smiled. "Archie told me so much about you. How you were helping him shut us down, how you were going to stop us in our tracks." He laughed in good nature. "I would have thought you were ten feet tall to listen to Archie."

"You're Erik Nilsson of Stoboltz?"

"I am."

Cole turned back to the sea. "Didn't expect to see anybody from your company here today."

"Why not? I've known Archie for many years. He was a worthy opponent. He kept us honest," Nilsson laughed. "Sure, he could be a pain in the ass, but—"

"We don't speak ill of the dead," said Cole, not looking at Nilsson.

"Please," he said, "excuse me. I don't know all the traditions here."

"Here or any place else," said Cole.

"Of course," said Nilsson, opening his hands to indicate his acceptance. "Of course, you couldn't resist the opportunity the ceremony provided to speak ill of us." He smiled when he said it.

"I spoke my mind. I only spoke the truth."

"Come now, Mr. Blackwater, we all know that truth is just a matter of perspective. You say that salmon farms are destroy-ing the wild salmon runs in the Broughton and elsewhere. You accuse us of increasing disease and parasites in this ecosystem. You claim our product harms human health. But I know many who disagree. I know many who say that our operations provide much-needed employment for a people stricken with poverty. I know people who are glad to have a healthy food choice that is affordable and that tastes good."

Cole regarded him from behind the hair that threatened to cover his eyes. "It's not really the time and place for this, Mr. Nilsson."

Nilsson gestured with his hands again. "I can appreciate that. This community has lost a great man. I respect that. I would like to introduce you to someone. I hope you will talk to him before you accuse our company of some egregious wrongs, Mr. Blackwater. Come, may I ask you to meet someone?"

Cole said nothing, but stepped from the rock. Nilsson guided him to a small group of people chatting outside the hall. Cole recognized Greg White Eagle and two other men from the Lostcoast community. Nilsson said something in Swedish and a third man stepped toward him. "This is Dr. Darvin Thurlow. He's our senior staff scientist. He has been working here in the Broughton for the last year as we set up our operations, helping to ensure we have no impact on the ecosystem. He's also leading our research into minimizing the impact of sea lice on wild salmon. Doctor, this is Cole Blackwater."

Thurlow extended his hand. Cole took it. It was icy from the bracing wind, the fingers long and thin but strong. Cole shook. "Good to meet you, Doctor."

"Sorry that it's under such difficult circumstances," said Thurlow, his face looking baleful.

"Where are you based?" Cole asked.

"Well, I'm adjunct at UVic, but I'm based in Alert Bay. I really don't spend much time in either these days. All my time is spent at our operations in the archipelago."

"I was just asking Cole if he would find the time to talk with you about our operations so that he can at least hear our side of things," said Nilsson. "Learn from you all that we are doing to improve the environment and the working conditions at our operations. "

"I'd be pleased to talk anytime."

Cole felt dizzy, and an immediate need to get away from both Thurlow and Nilsson overcame him. He was aware of Greg White Eagle watching him. "I'm sure we'll find a time," he said. "Now, please excuse me." As he made his way toward the dirt road that wound its way up the hill to Archie Ravenwing's home, he was aware of eyes on him, and their inaudible words pierced him as he walked.

Cole was halfway up the hill when he heard someone calling from behind him. If it's Nilsson, Thurlow, or White Eagle, he thought, I'm going to have to punch someone in the mouth. Turning, the wind slapped him in the face. He had to squint into the late afternoon sun, low on the horizon, to see who had hailed him. He felt as though God herself was against him that day.

"Hey, Cole, wait up!"

Cole watched a man in a heavy orange float coat labour up the hill. He was broad in the shoulders and heavy in the chest, and wore a ball cap pulled down low over his forehead. As he half-walked, half-ran up the hill, he looked more like a child than the forty-year-old man that he was.

"Hey, Darren, glad to see you," Cole said, finding that he was genuinely pleased to see Archie's former fishing partner. "I saw you there at the community centre, but we didn't have a chance to talk." Cole reached out his hand as the big man caught up to him.

"Hey-ya, Cole. Good to see you, too. What's it been? Two years?"

"Something like that, man. Time flies."

"When you're having fun," finished Darren.

"Well, even when you're not, actually," said Cole. "I'm heading up to the house. Walk with me?"

"I got to get back, Cole," said Darren First Moon. "I just wanted to say hey."

"I'm glad you did. I was surprised when I didn't see you around town the last couple of days. I got in on Sunday."

"Yeah, I've been out with the Joint Rescue boys looking. And I've been, well, you know ..." Darren looked down and kicked at some dirt on the road with his work boots.

"I know. The two of you were like father and son."

"Yeah, we did some time together," said Darren, looking out over the harbour.

"What are you going to do now, Darren? Can you keep on fishing and guiding?"

"I don't know, Cole. I suppose if I could get my hands on a decent boat I could, but mine isn't built for commercial fishing or guiding. It's plenty fast, but there's no room onboard for tourists or for a catch. Something will come up. Always does. Maybe I'll go back to logging on the big island."

"You could do worse," said Cole, filling the silence.

"Yeah, I could end up working for a fish farm," said Darren. He let out a half-hearted laugh and looked back at the strait.

Cole looked at him. "Things are pretty tough around here, Darren. Nobody would blame you if you did, you know."

"Archie would," he said, looking at the horizon, his face buffeted by the wind.

"Well, Archie is free from worldly concerns now, Darren. A man has to take care of himself and his family. That reminds me, how is your family?"

"Good. We got two on the street and one in the oven," he said, his face lightening, becoming childlike again.

"That's great news, Darren. You look out for them."

"I will, Cole. Hey, how long you staying?"

"Just a few more days, and then back to the city."

"Why don't you come by The Strait tonight? A bunch of us are going to hoist a few in honour of Archie."

"I might do that."

"Okay, Cole. Well, be seeing you." Darren First Moon stuck out his big hand and Cole Blackwater shook it.

■ By the time Cole Blackwater reached the empty home of Archie Ravenwing, the squall had passed, leaving the ocean bobbing in its wake, the sky calm and dark green. Cole let himself into the house and found a bottle of beer in the fridge. He drank from the bottle as he looked across the tiny town, the harbour, and out at the Queen Charlotte Strait. With the wind down, the temperature was tolerable, so he pulled a chair from Archie's office out onto the deck and sat in the sun, his eyes closed, the warm rays penetrating him.

He pushed the disturbing image of the Blackwater ranch and barn from his brain, chasing it with beer that sluiced over his thirsty pallet. How long he sat there he didn't know, somewhat comforted by the sounds of the ocean, the fading wind, and the calls of ravens circling above the town. He must have fallen asleep, because when Grace spoke to him he was startled awake.

"I'm sorry to disturb you, Cole, but there's a message on Dad's phone for you."

Cole felt his body creak as he stood and moved ponderously across the deck and into the house.

"Thanks, Grace. Guess I dozed off. Didn't sleep very well last night."

She smiled and handed him the portable phone, restarting the message as she did.

"Hi Cole, it's Mary. I tried to reach you on your cell, but you must have it off, or maybe there's no coverage where you are. At any rate, call me when you get a chance. There's a package here that I think you should know about. It's from Archie Ravenwing."

Cole switched off the phone. He watched Grace moving about the kitchen. He sat at Archie's desk and dialled his office.

"Blackwater Strategies."

"Mary, it's Cole."

"I'm sorry to disturb you today, Cole. Do you want me to open this package that arrived this morning? It's from Archie."

"When was it posted?"

"March thirteenth."

"Day before Archie went missing."

"It was posted by courier, but it can take some time to get anywhere when it's coming from one of the tiny islands. Do you want me to open it?"

"Please," said Cole, his heart beating hard in his ears.

"It's quite a big package, Cole." He could hear her ripping the envelope. "Okay, there's a large sheath of papers held together with a big clip, and a cover letter. I'll read you the cover letter."

Cole closed his eyes.

> *Dear Cole,*
> *It's been a while since you and I have spoken. Too long, old friend. I'm sorry for letting our friendship and our business relationship go cold. I've been feeling pretty foolish for not insisting the band pay your account in full, and I guess I felt guilty enough to let that keep*

me from calling you. To make amends I've attached a personal cheque to this letter. It's not the full amount we owe you, but it's a start. Now that Greg White Eagle is councillor for the Port Lostcoast band, I doubt that you'll ever see any money from the band, so I'll do what I can to pay your old invoices myself.

The main reason for writing you, Cole, is to fill you in on new information that I dug up with Cassandra Petrel. What started as an investigation into an Atlantic salmon breeding program last fall has taken a crazy turn. I think I've uncovered evidence that points to genetic engineering being undertaken by Stoboltz Aquaculture, the company with the vast majority of fish farms in the Broughton area. At first I thought they were only doing engineering on Atlantic salmon, trying to build resistances to disease and to the impacts of sea lice. But I've learned that they are working on sea lice themselves. I just don't know how, or why.

Enclosed is a package of information that I have compiled, in part through my own research and in part through "brown envelopes" passed to me by provincial employees. These should help you start building a file on this matter. I have some maps that might interest you, too, but I haven't made copies yet.

I need your help, Cole. I can't trust anybody in Port Lostcoast, with the exception of Gracie. Cassandra is above reproach, but she's got a history with one of the people from Stoboltz that's getting to her. Most others in town don't care about the ravings of an old man. They've heard it all before! And Greg is on the pad with Stoboltz. There's some email documentation here that proves it. I think they may have even rigged the election last fall to get him on council to influence how the band deals with future salmon-farming applications.

I know this sounds like one of my conspiracy theories, Cole, but you know me well enough by now to realize that I've got good reason for my suspicions. I'm asking you to help me find out the truth about what Stoboltz is up to, and why. Then I need you to help me stop it.

I'm going to head out to Jeopardy Rock tomorrow to look into what is going on there. I believe that Stoboltz is using the old Department of Fisheries research station as a base for their genetic engineering work. I'm going to case the joint, confront Dr. Darvin Thurlow, and try to get to the bottom of this. I'll call you if I learn anything. In the meantime, have a look at the enclosed documents and see what you can make of it all.

It will be good to work together again, Cole. I haven't forgotten our friendship.

Hi-ee'chka....

"It's just signed Ravenwing," said Mary, finishing.

Cole closed his eyes.

"What do you want me to do with this, Cole?"

He was silent a moment. Mary Patterson knew Cole well enough not to interrupt.

Finally he said, "Make a copy and get that package back up to Port Lostcoast as soon as you can. I'll look around Archie's office for the original file. He wouldn't have sent that."

"Okay, Cole. What about this cheque?"

"Don't cash it. Not yet."

When he finished the call he finally opened his eyes. Genetic engineering of Atlantic salmon to make them more disease resistant? And what about sea lice? Why would anybody want to mess with them?

And what exactly had Archie learned when he had visited Jeopardy Rock on the day he had gone missing?

9 They met at the Port Hardy Motor Inn. It was the only accommodation in the northern Vancouver Island town with a conference room, but even so they were crammed one on top of the other. The minister of agriculture had arrived the day before and spent the day meeting with representatives of the salmon-farming industry. Stoboltz Aquaculture had made a boat available, and, together with the heads of three of the largest salmon farming companies, the minister had spent the afternoon on the water, motoring between several of the fish farms in Hardy Bay and around the southern tip of Nigei Island. A television crew, alerted to the possibility of an announcement on the future of fish farms, captured an image of the minister dressed casually, a broad smile on his face as he rode on the flying bridge of the Stoboltz boat flanked by industry representatives.

The mood the following morning was more sombre. In the morning, the minister had invited representatives from industry from the Chamber of Commerce, the North Salish First Nation, and environmental groups in the area to attend a briefing session.

Archie Ravenwing and Cassandra Petrel weren't on the invite list, but they were there anyway. As the media was ever alert to potential conflict, Archie had received calls from CBC radio and television, Global TV, the *Vancouver Sun*, and the *Globe and Mail* less than an hour after the minister's voyage. Everyone wanted to know if he was going to be at the meeting. Everybody wanted his opinion.

Archie and Cassandra had taken the *Inlet Dancer* to Port Mc-Neill, then caught a ride up the island with Carrie Bright, the locally based leader of the Save Our Seas coalition. Ravenwing called Lance Grey as they drove north to let him know that he would be attending the meeting, and that if Grey or the minister had any trouble with that, they had better call the RCMP.

"No trouble at all, Archie," Grey had said.

"And the media, you can expect calls from the media too if you don't let us in." Archie was nearly belligerent.

"Take it easy, Archie. The minister will be happy to see you again. Simple oversight, I assure you."

When they arrived to find places on the sticky vinyl chairs, there were a dozen other people in the cramped room. The meeting started poorly and went downhill fast.

"It's bloody hot in here," complained Lance Grey, heaving on a window that refused to open. "I thought it was supposed to be cool up here, even in August." Disgusted, he peeled off his suit jacket and hung it on the back of a chair. "The minister is on a call with some of his cabinet colleagues right now, but he'll be down in a minute. Are we waiting for anybody else?" He looked around the crowded table.

"Nobody that I can see," said Jerry Cooper, who was sitting at the far end of the table. He was a giant of a man whose bulk threatened to make matchsticks of his chair. "But then there's some here that weren't invited in the first place."

"Why is Archie here, Lance?" asked Dan Campbell. Seated next to Cooper beside the open door, Campbell wore jeans, a plaid shirt, and a ball cap sporting the BC Wildlife Federation logo. "And what about her?" said Campbell, nodding toward Cassandra Petrel.

"Why don't you ask them yourself, Dan?" said Grey, not bothering to hide his annoyance.

Both Dan and Jerry looked across the table. "Well, Archie?"

Archie smiled. "I've missed your charming disposition, Dan. I don't see you nearly enough around Lostcoast, so I figured I'd come to the big island to bask in the warmth of your adoration."

"Come off it, Archie. You're not on the AATF anymore. You've been replaced. The band found someone who wasn't so openly hostile to industry. It's bad enough we've got to put up with the enviros getting in our way here, but to have you throwing up roadblock after roadblock — you've been replaced, Archie," said Dan Campbell, looking over at Greg White Eagle. "Don't you know when you're not welcome?"

Archie maintained his smile and shrugged. "I guess I don't, Dan."

"I don't think it's right for Archie to be in this room," said Jerry Cooper, who was sweating profusely in the summer heat. "He's going to leak what goes on here to the media."

"Really, Jerry," said Carrie Bright. "Do you really think the media doesn't already know what's going on here? You think the minister was just out for a pleasure cruise yesterday? I watched the news out of Victoria. The ministry has already leaked their announcement, softening up the public. I got half a dozen calls last night. This is just a formality, Jerry, and you know it. I don't like the tone you guys are taking here. Save Our Seas isn't about roadblocks. We're about protecting wild salmon."

"Save the sermon," said Dan, taking off his hat and running a hand through his sweaty hair. "We're not on camera now, Carrie. We're behind closed doors. Your group will not be happy until you shut down every single fish farm on the BC coast. Don't try to deny it."

"Who's denying it?" said Carrie, leaning back in her chair. "It's on our website. It's our policy. No open-pen salmon farming. We're not trying to hide our position. We don't like open-pen aquaculture. It's killing salmon. It's killing the ecosystem. And frankly, I don't think the fish are all that healthy for human consumption. What I don't get is, what is your agenda, Dan? If anybody has a hidden agenda, it seems to be you."

"I'm here as a voice of reason," said Dan.

"Reason?" blurted Archie Ravenwing. "Reason? You're here to protect your own ass, Dan. That's the only reason you're here."

Dan looked at Archie sideways, his face twisted into a vile knot. "Look who's talking about protecting his own interests. Look who's talking about protecting his own ass. The noble savage speaks about protecting interests. Whose interest are you protecting by building that fancy addition to your house on the bluff, Archie?"

Archie grinned, but his words didn't match the smile on his face. "You know, Dan, my people have had to put up with trash like you coming onto the islands that we've called home since the beginning of time, taking what you want and leaving your filth in your wake. Cutting our trees, killing all the wildlife. Now you're killing the salmon. We welcome you into our community, and still you hate us. If you loathe us so much, why stick around?"

"Okay, folks, this is getting a little personal," said Lance Grey. "Let's remember our ground rules for our meetings. Hard on the issues, easy on the people."

Dan Campbell shook his head. "Jesus Christ, why are Jerry and I sitting in this room listening to this? I'm a guide outfitter and he's a logger, and we're arguing with Archie and Carrie about fish farming. Aren't you guys going to say anything?" He looked at Erik Nilsson and Darvin Thurlow.

Nilsson was standing, looking out the window. "You know," he said, "in Sweden, we have air conditioning for when it gets this hot. Don't you have that here?" He turned and smiled and walked to his chair next to Darvin Thurlow.

"Why are the logger and the hunter fighting with the Indian and the fish-kisser about salmon farming?" Dan edged forward in his chair.

"Because you like to argue?" suggested Nilsson.

Dan sat back heavily, shook his head, and blew air out between his lips.

"We don't need to argue, Dan," said Darvin Thurlow, his face cool, his hands pressed together as if in prayer.

"Why's that?" Dan Campbell shot back.

"We won," said Thurlow, without a hint of guile.

The minister walked into the room just then. He was a tall, stately man, his pressed dark suit showing no sign of the heat that hung in the tiny room. "I'm sorry to keep you all waiting," he said, shaking hands with Dan and Jerry, who were closest to the door, then making his way around the room. His smile was wide and genuine, and he spoke a few words to each of the people gathered in the room.

"Archie, it's good to see you again," he said, taking the man's hand and holding it a second. "You understand we didn't invite you because your colleague Greg White Eagle is now on the committee, but as far as I'm concerned, you're welcome here."

When he got to Cassandra Petrel, she rose and he took her hand. "Dr. Petrel, I've heard a lot about you, and read many of your reports. Thank you for coming." She smiled thinly.

"Please, let's get started," the minister said, taking his seat.

"I trust Lance has been entertaining you while I was being sedated by my cabinet colleagues. You know, I think they call it the cabinet because it's big and awkward and when it falls on you, it's really hard to get out from under it." A ripple of laughter went around the room. The minister turned to Lance Grey. "It's pretty hot in here, Lance, could you see about getting some air in here, please?"

The assistant nodded and left the room in search of help.

"First," said the minister, "I want to acknowledge that our meeting today is on North Salish traditional territory. I want to give our colleagues Greg and Archie special greetings and thanks." The minister stopped a moment to acknowledge the two men. "As you know, we're here to talk about salmon farming. Over the last two years, you folks have met a few times down in Victoria, up here, and, as I understand it, over on the mainland in Bella Bella. I want to thank you all for your time and the energy and thoughtfulness that you have provided during this process. I know this hasn't been easy. And I know that some of you will be disappointed with what I am going to announce tomorrow morning back in Victoria. But I want you to know that regardless of which side of the coin you are on, your input has been carefully considered, and I value your contribution."

Lance Grey returned at that moment, followed by a man with a screwdriver, who proceeded to pry the painted windows open. They creaked and groaned in protest as he did. Otherwise, the room was silent. The minister sat quietly, reviewing notes on a piece of paper in front of him. Archie looked around the room. His eyes caught Dan Campbell's. Dan lived on Parish Island most of the year. He used the island as a base for his own guiding operations. During hunting season, Dan shuttled Americans and the occasional Canadian up Knight Inlet in search of their quarry. In the fall, he and his clients hunted grizzly bears along Knight Inlet's many salmon streams. Dan made no effort to hide the contempt he felt toward the North Salish people he lived among. He reminded Archie of the men who, a century before, had banned the potlatch ceremony, referring to the North Salish as savages. How a man with such obvious disdain, even outright bigotry, could live in a community that was more than 90 percent First Nations was deeply perplexing to Archie.

The window was finally convinced to open, and refreshing air rushed into the room. The man from the hotel smiled and departed, and the minister said, "Well, that's a little better."

"So," he said, resuming, "as you know, our government made a commitment to consult with the people of BC, and to take under advisement all the opinions that we heard, and all the research that we have conducted and compiled. Our determination is that, if done properly with strong environmental regulations in place, salmon farming can be expanded in the Broughton Archipelago without adversely affecting wild-salmon populations.

"We're going to be implementing some stringent regulations on how this can happen," he said, looking first at Archie, then at Carrie and Cassandra. "This isn't the wild west." He smiled. "But we are going to have more salmon farming. The demand is high, the economics of the operations are good, and we believe that any negative impacts can be mitigated with regulations."

"Minister," said Carrie Bright, "did you consider closed-containment aquaculture, where the fish are kept on land in large man-made ponds?"

"We did, Carrie," he said. "We looked at all the options. While closed containment would largely eliminate any of the negative impacts of farming, we felt that it was unnecessary. The output from the farms—I guess there's no way of skirting it—the fish poop—" he smiled and so did Lance, Jerry, and Dan—"is localized in its impact. The area directly below the farms do suffer some, but it's a tiny, tiny area."

"Minister—" Cassandra Petrel raised her hand tentatively.

"Yes, Dr. Petrel," the minister said, though Lance Grey frowned.

"Minister, closed containment certainly addresses the pollution issue, but more importantly, it keeps the Atlantic salmon, their diseases, and their parasites from coming into contact with the migrating pink, chum, and sockeye. Sea lice are becoming a huge issue, as you know. More salmon farming on the migration routes of the wild populations could be disastrous."

"Thank you for bringing that up, Doctor," said the minister. "Tomorrow, together with making the formal announcement, our government is also going to announce a research project, to be funded in part by my ministry and in part by industry, that will look more closely at the impacts of sea lice and how we can mitigate for those impacts. We'll be funding this research at the University of Victoria."

"Due respect, Minister," said Petrel, "but we already know enough about the life cycle and impacts of sea lice to say pretty clearly that fallowing these farms during migration periods — taking the fish and their pens right out of the water — is necessary to prevent the transfer of disease and of deadly levels of sea lice from the farmed Atlantic to the wild Pacific salmon. We don't need another study."

The minister was silent a moment. "You know," he said finally, "politics is the art of the possible. We have many interests to balance as we're making these decisions, many points of view to consider. The world has a growing appetite for our salmon. The health benefits of eating salmon are well known. Our friends in the industry, and in health promotion, have done a wonderful job telling people how good salmon is for us. The level of demand is far greater than our wild stocks could ever endure. I've got people telling me that there should be no harvest of wild salmon whatsoever. That the number of wild salmon left on our coast is at an all-time low, and that we should close the season entirely. The federal minister of fisheries and oceans was on the phone this morning saying that this year's harvest could be the smallest in a generation, if it happens at all." He poked his index finger on the table with each of his words. "If it happens at all. Those were *his* words.

"And yet the world wants our salmon. So, we need a solution. We're going to need to feed those people somehow. They can't all go out with Archie and catch their own." He smiled. "They can't all afford wild salmon. Not if stocks continue to decline. So, we've got to have a solution. We're going to have more farmed salmon to meet demand. It's going to bring a lot more wealth and prosperity and employment to the coast. The North Salish

First Nation and other bands up and down the coast are all going to benefit from that prosperity. People will find work on the farms. We'll do our best to address your concerns, Dr. Petrel, and yours, Archie and Carrie. We'll take everybody's ideas into account. You know that you can always contact Lance with any concerns." Lance nodded, his eyes on the doodle he was drawing on a pad in his planner.

"Minister," said Archie, smiling, "I don't have to tell you that you have a responsibility to protect those wild salmon. It's a legal responsibility. The Fisheries Act lays it out."

The minister smiled warmly. "No, you don't have to tell me. The federal minister and I were just discussing it this morning. We're doing all we can —"

"Hear me out, Minister," said Archie. "I'm not oblivious to the various demands, the pressures on our salmon population, and I'm aware of the argument that more salmon farms should mean less pressure on wild stocks. But the correlation doesn't exist. Demand for both wild and farmed salmon is on the rise, despite our best efforts to talk people out of buying the farmed stuff. You're going to have to do a whole lot more than you are right now if wild salmon are going to survive."

"I agree, Archie. I really do. Between us and the feds we're starting to develop recovery strategies for pink, coho, chum, even steelhead. It takes time, and there's a lot of politics involved, I don't need to tell you that. We're working toward a solution."

The minister stood. "I'm afraid I have a plane to catch. I really appreciate your time, all of you. Thank you." He walked around the table again, shaking a few hands, and left the room in silence.

"Well, there you have it," said Jerry Cooper.

"Yes, there you have it," said Archie, standing to leave.

10

"What's this all about?" asked Sergeant Reimer. She and Nancy Webber sat in a coffee shop near the RCMP detachment in Fort Macleod.

Nancy sipped her coffee. "I'm not really sure," she sighed.

"You drove all the way here from Edmonton and you're not sure?"

"It might just be stupid. I feel a little foolish pursuing this — it's about Cole Blackwater."

Reimer stiffened. "What about him?"

"Look, I know that whole business in Oracle was bad news for you. I don't blame you if you're sore at both Cole and I."

"I'm a professional," said Reimer, drinking her coffee. She was in plain clothes, her hair down and framing a young and pretty face. She didn't look anything like what a small-town RCMP staff sergeant looked like in Nancy Webber's memory.

Nancy smiled. "Okay, well, from one professional to another, I'm looking into the death of Cole's father, Henry."

Reimer sipped her coffee. "You said that on the phone. I dug up the medical examiner's report and read it."

"Did you bring a copy?"

"You know I can't do that. If you want it there are official channels. I *can* tell you that the death was ruled a suicide, and that's that."

"It was reported as a being *consistent* with suicide. Another report used the world 'likely.'"

"What are you getting at?"

"Cole never talked about his old man with me. Even when we were in Ottawa, you know, together, he never said a word about him. Then he left Ottawa for the west coast, stopped off for a month at the family ranch, and while he was there his father killed himself."

"Do you think — ?"

"I don't think anything."

"But you do. You're wondering if Cole popped his old man."

Nancy looked around the room. Nobody was within earshot.

"I'm just saying that it all seems a little fishy. Why wouldn't the local RCMP investigate?"

"I'm just going by what's in the file. It said that Cole heard a shotgun blast around dinnertime on a Sunday night, and when he went to the barn, he found his father lying on his back with a gaping wound under his chin. The shotgun was at his side, as was a branding iron. Apparently the old man used that to push down the trigger. It was a full-length barrel. You can't reach the trigger and still have the muzzle against your chin. Too long. Cole called it in. The ambulance arrived first, then the RCMP."

"So why call it 'likely?'"

"You tell me. I can't figure out why journalists write anything they do about police procedure."

They finished their coffee.

"Do you mind me asking you a personal question?" Sergeant Reimer levelled her gaze at Nancy.

"Go ahead."

"Why are you doing this? I thought that you and Cole were, you know, close."

Nancy smiled. "We have been in the past."

"Not anymore? You spent a week at his bedside when he was recovering in Oracle."

"Yeah, well, he needed someone to look out for him."

Reimer just looked at her.

"The truth is, I thought that maybe we were going to get back together. But he's aloof. Distant. Distracted by something. Sometimes when we're talking he just disappears into his head. And a few times, when we've been talking, he has said things that seem funny to me."

"Like?"

"Just little things. Stupid things. About his father, about his family. He never talked about them before. I didn't even know that he had a brother until recently." She laughed. "But when he does talk about his father now, it's really dark. He's got so much anger in him."

"Was he abused?"

"How the hell should I know? Like I said, he never said anything about his family until after his father's death."

"If you don't mind me saying so, I think you're letting the journalist in you get the better part of your judgment."

Nancy turned her face and looked out the window. "Maybe."

"But you're still not satisfied."

"I guess I'm not."

"Okay then. What next?"

"Would you do me one more favour?"

Reimer raised her eyebrows. "Depends."

"Will you call around the Claresholm detachment and see if you can learn anything?"

"No promises, Nancy."

"Okay."

"And what are you going to do?"

Nancy stood up. "It's lovely in the Porcupine Hills at this time of year. Think I'll take a drive."

■ She explained herself to her editor. "I need a little time," she said.

"What are you on to?"

"Maybe nothing. I don't know."

"But you want me to pay you to chase it down?"

"Yup," she said, her cellphone at her ear, steering the car with her knee as she peeled back the top of a cup of Tim Hortons coffee.

"Two days," he said.

She hung up the phone without saying goodbye. Ungrateful bastard, she thought to herself. She had won a national newspaper award after chasing what appeared to every other reporter to be a dead end. She thought about Vancouver. The *Sun* had made her an offer. She hadn't given them an answer. After she had met Cole for dinner all those months ago, she had attended the award banquet and the next day met with the editor-in-chief. They had discussed her career. She had been very forthcoming with him. Her precipitous decline at the *Globe and Mail*'s Ottawa Bureau was well known — there was no sense concealing that from anybody.

"What do you want to do?" Frank Pesh had asked her. He was

a lean man, with long fingers yellowed from a lifelong addiction to cigarettes. His longish hair, greying at the sides, was combed back over his ears. He wore very small, very stylish glasses.

"If I could write my own ticket?" she asked.

"Sure," he said, looking out the window of his office at Burrard Inlet.

Nancy looked, too. Would she go back to Ottawa? she wondered. The place that had been the centre of her professional desire for so long, from where she'd been banished when she had printed Cole Blackwater's lie, no longer seemed to hold any appeal. At least that's what Nancy Webber told herself. "I'd write a combination of politics and human-interest stories. The human dimension behind the politics of a place."

"What do you know about BC?"

"Not much. Never lived here. Don't have a lot of contacts."

"Not much of an incentive to hire you," said Pesh, smiling.

"I can learn all I need to in two months on the job."

He turned and studied her. She had worn a power suit that morning, her most expensive, and her hair fell over her shoulders with the blue-black sheen of a raven's back.

"Let me think about it."

That happened in October. In December, just before Christmas, Pesh had called her. If she wanted to write for the *Vancouver Sun* there would be a job for her. Junior provincial affairs writer. She'd split her time between Victoria and Vancouver.

She spent the holidays examining her life. And it always came back to one thing, one man: Cole Blackwater. Was she now ready to face whatever it was that Cole kept buried? So deep inside that he might not even know what it was? She didn't want to show up in Vancouver until that dark question had been resolved.

The landscape of southern Alberta rolled past. What had he told her before he left the province last spring? Alberta could break your heart. It was spring again, the rolling prairie was brown and wasted, the rough, dry fescue that remained was pressed flat against the earth. The sun, lying low on the western horizon, painted the prairie the colour of burnt umber. Before her, rising from that horizon, mountains appeared like a serrated spine the colour of wild roses. She thought about Cole. The man was like the landscape he had been raised in: stark, prone to extremes. One moment he was warm and kind and tender, and the next minute full of rage, a gale wind blowing snow and sleet and needling rain. It was hard to open up to that. Hard to let that into her life.

Alberta could break your heart, all right.

She spent the night in the Motel 6 on the highway in Claresholm, and in the morning she went to a diner to have coffee and breakfast. She sat at the counter and ate toast and drank coffee from a porcelain cup. When she was done she walked to the newspaper office, but there was nobody there, so she strolled to the library and had to wait for it to open. When it did, she asked if she could look back through their newspaper files, and tried to learn more about the death of Henry Blackwater. Instead, she read about his life, served up in public interest stories dating from the end of World War II. He had returned from England to recover from undisclosed wounds suffered on D-Day, but he never spoke about the role he had played in the landing at Juno Beach.

In the years following the war, Henry Blackwater had won awards for his cattle, sold stock at auction, and maintained a low profile for the better part of a decade. In the 1960s, stories began to paint a different picture of Henry Blackwater. He was arrested once in 1963 and twice in 1964 for being drunk and disorderly in a Claresholm bar. In 1965 he was arrested for his role in a barroom brawl at the Longview Hotel saloon in which he broke the jaw of an oil man who had made a comment about cowboys. In 1967 he was arrested for assaulting the local Reeve from the municipality after a debate about irrigation in the district. None of the arrests resulted in Henry Blackwater being charged, or in his having a criminal record; he had settled both of the assault charges out of court. But it was pretty clear that Henry Blackwater had a reputation in the foothills as a hothead and a scrapper who would just as soon crack a man's head as settle a difference of opinion like a gentleman. Then, after the late 1960s, Henry Blackwater's name didn't appear in the paper again until the 1980s, when his sons boxed at the provincial level.

The final Blackwater stories were about Cole. In 1987 he had fought for the provincial junior welterweight championship, and had lost his final bout in a split decision. There was a picture of Cole, lean, muscled, his face stern and resolute after the loss. She searched for any resemblance to the man she now knew and could detect only vestiges of his old self in the present one.

Like father like son, she thought. Both men solved their problems with their fists. Nancy leaned back in the plastic library chair. She rubbed her eyes. She tried to recall details of her time with Cole in Ottawa. She and Cole hadn't been together in situations that might provoke Cole Blackwater's hair-trigger temper. They hadn't hung out in dark bars where loggers drank. She hadn't witnessed any back alley confrontations with disgruntled miners. Had she seen any evidence of violence? She pressed the fingers of both hands into her temples. No, she didn't remember a violent incident. Cole did always seem paranoid, at least when they entered a bar together, like he was looking for a fight. Or for someone who might start one. Nancy had written this off as the mark of a man cheating on his wife in a town that had no secrets. Maybe there was more to it.

But violence? She hadn't seen it in Ottawa.

But things had come unravelled there, and Cole had skipped town to Vancouver. He had stopped in at the Blackwater ranch for the better part of a month, and while he was there, his father had committed suicide.

Had Cole been abused? That was Sergeant Reimer's question. It seemed entirely possible that loose-lipped oil men in the Longview Saloon weren't the only ones to feel Henry Blackwater's anger and frustration.

What had gone wrong during those few weeks in the spring four years ago? Was it the tragic culmination of a lifetime of abuse?

She stood up, her back sore and her feet numb from being locked around the legs of the flimsy chair for so long. It was time to find out, she thought to herself. It was time to follow this story to its source.

11 "Did you know what your father was up to?" Cole asked Grace Ravenwing. They were sitting together in her father's office. Her brothers and sisters, their families, and some friends were gathered in Archie's home. From the kitchen, over the din of pots and pans and serving utensils, were the raised voices of many cooks preparing a meal. The air was rich with the aroma of supper. Every so often, Cole and Grace were interrupted as a group of laughing children raced into the office, hiding behind various pieces of furniture — desks, chairs, tables, Cole and Grace themselves — and were subsequently discovered in a game of hide-and-seek that had been going on for more than an hour.

"Nobody really ever knew what Dad was up to, Cole. You know how he was. He'd just go off on some foolish crusade. One month it was grizzly bear hunting, the next logging, the next mining."

"But salmon farming had been his cause célèbre for many years."

Grace nodded, tousling the hair of one of her nephews as he slid behind her to hide.

"He didn't tell you about the package he sent to my office?"

"No," she said.

Cole was silent. The youngster who was hiding behind Grace was caught and the game started again.

"He said in the letter that he trusted Cassandra Petrel, but that she was skeptical. What do you think he meant?"

"Cassandra is a scientist. She's really committed to this issue. She truly believes that sea lice are killing wild salmon, and that salmon farming is to blame. I think she might have thought my father went out on a limb sometimes."

"Did he?"

"You know how Dad is — was. He really believed in his heart that what he was doing was right for his people, for our land, for the sea. Sometimes he got carried away." Grace Ravenwing looked down as she said it. Cole took her hand.

"This is hard, I know. I just want to honour what it was your father was fighting for." And I want to make amends for letting him down, thought Cole, tightening his hand around Grace's small but strong fingers.

She looked up. "So do I," she said, wiping a tear with the knuckles of her free hand. "So do I. Let's talk with a few folks. I think we need to talk with Cassandra—I *know* we can trust her—about what Dad was up to. Maybe he told her more than he told me. And I think we should talk with Darren. I know he seems kind of simple sometimes, but Dad really loved him. They worked together for so long that if anybody knew what Dad was doing it would be him."

Cole let go of Grace's hand and looked at her. "You're very brave," he said.

She smiled. "I don't think so. But I love and honour my father, and I want to ensure that whatever he was working on before he died is kept alive somehow."

"Grace, I can't help but wonder about something," Cole said.

"What is it?"

"Well, your father leaving his will somewhere that you could find it. Don't you think that's, well, odd? I mean, the timing...?"

Grace drew in a sharp breath. "I've been thinking about that too," she said. "Dad never told me that he made up a will. He did say once that he should, given all the flying he was doing, going down to Victoria for meetings. He figured he might die in a plane wreck, and said he wanted to make sure this place and his boat went to family and friends. But he never discussed it with me. I don't know why he would have got it out. Though as you can see," she said, looking around the office with its stacks of papers and open file drawers, "Dad wasn't exactly the most organized person in the world. Maybe he just came across it and had meant to file it soon. Or take it with him when he went to Port McNeill to put in a safety deposit box."

"Doesn't really sound like Archie," said Cole, looking around. "Shoebox, maybe. Safety deposit box, not so much." Cole paused and looked at the sheath of papers. "Have you looked at it yet?"

"I'm not ready," she said. Then she thought of something. "Will you do something for me, Cole?"

"Of course," he said.

"Your mentioning a safety deposit box makes me think of something. Dad, like a lot of the older men in our community, had a treasure box. I guess it seems kind of funny to a white person, like maybe it's a hope chest, but it's a very old tradition with our people. Before the potlatch was outlawed, our chiefs and elders would keep a lot of their ceremonial pieces in these boxes. Important possessions would be put in the boxes for safekeeping. The boxes were ornate, beautifully painted.

"Anyway, Dad had such a box. It had been his father's, and his father's before him. I don't think Dad had anything of real value in it anymore. A few years back, when our people were repatriating our sacred potlatch masks, Archie gave what few authentic possessions he had to the U'mista Museum in Alert Bay for display. It was just a drum and a mask, but they had been kept hidden from the Indian agents and were very important to the people of Port Lostcoast. Dad used his box mostly as an extension of his filing cabinet. Cole, I wonder if you'd go through it and see if there is anything in there that might be of help to us?"

"Grace, I'd — are you sure?"

"Yes, I'm sure."

"You don't want to do it?"

Again she pushed tears from her cheeks. "I don't think I can. Not now. But there might be something important in there."

They sat listening to the sounds of the house for a few minutes. Cole watched Grace Ravenwing. She was beautiful and epitomized her name with the way she moved and spoke and acted.

"Of course I'll do it," Cole said finally.

"The box is there under the table, behind all the files," she said, pointing.

"I'll go through it later and let you know what I find."

She stood up. "Maybe we should join the others. We've got a big fish stew on the stove." Cole stood too and stepped toward her. She walked into him and he put his arms around her. She smelled of the wind that had blown across them all day, and of saltwater spray. She placed her face against his chest and he held her close. He felt her body move as she cried, and she wrapped her arms around his back. They stood that way a moment until another gang of children raced into the office, and then she pulled away, wiping the tears that tracked her face.

"Let's eat," she said cheerfully, and herded the children toward the kitchen.

Cole stood in the empty office and looked out the huge windows to the unfinished deck, then down at the treasure box that had survived one of the worst periods in the history of the North Salish. Beyond it all he saw the lights of the village tucked around the harbour, the final glow of the day being absorbed by the pan-flat sea.

■ They ate at the long table in Archie's dining room while the children sat at a low table and watched *Finding Nemo*. Fresh clams, salmon from the previous season, and halibut with a thick, savoury broth was ladled into bowls and eaten with bread. They drank water and tea. When they finished, Cole helped clear the table with Grace's sisters Myrna and Rose, and her sister-in-law, Betty. All three of her siblings lived on Vancouver Island now, and rarely came back to Parish Island except for seasonal celebrations. The women laughed together in the kitchen as Cole dried the dishes and looked out the window. When the kitchen detritus was cleared away, he went to the office and sat alone for a few minutes in the darkness. Then he switched on the desk lamp and maneuvered the treasure box out from under the long table. It was two feet long and nearly as tall, and it was painted with the intricate artwork of the North Salish. A raven adorned the lid, painted black against a red and white background, where a supernatural halibut man stood on one side, and a salmon giving birth to a man graced the other. Cole touched the box with his fingers and, after a moment, opened it. It smelled of earth, and Cole realized that Archie's grandfather must have buried the box and its contents to hide it.

Indeed the box seemed to be full of simple possessions: the title to the *Inlet Dancer*, the title to the Bluff House, some other documents about the status of the Ravenwing family. Cole found documents pertaining to Archie's father's attendance at the residential school in Alert Bay, and then found a certificate of attendance for Archie, too. Cole shook his head at that dark period of time in Canadian history.

There were photos of Archie's wife and children. There was a Hudson's Bay blanket wrapped around a framed photo from Archie's wedding day. Cole studied the man in the picture and felt tears welling inside of him. Archie had been so proud. And then, under the blanket, he found a CD. It had a yellow Post-it note attached to it, and Cole recognized his own handwriting. "For when you are down," the note said.

It was Blue Rodeo's *Lost Together*, one of Cole's favourite albums. It was released during Cole's first year at the University of Toronto. He had seen the band play at the El Mocambo on Spadina and bought the album afterward. He knew the words to every song on the CD. He had sent it to Archie two years ago after spending time with the man, his family, and colleagues devising a strategy to stop fish farming in the Broughton.

Cole switched on Archie's computer. He slipped the CD into the player and sat back in Archie's chair. The music started and Cole closed his eyes. The first track had been the tune that had inspired the gift. It was called "Fools Like You." The song amped up, and Cole found himself drumming on the desk, eyes closed.

I just don't understand
This world of mine
I must be out of touch
Or out of my mind
And will the profits of destruction
Forever make your eyes blind
Do you bow to the corporations
'Cause they pay their bills on time

God bless Elijah
With the feather in his hand
Stop stealing the Indian land
Stop stealing the Indian land
Stop stealing the Indian land

When he opened his eyes, the track was over and he turned off the computer, closed the box, and pushed it back under the table. He stood and, rubbing his eyes, found Grace in the other room and told her he was going for a walk. He put on his leather coat and stepped out into the evening air.

He made his way down the hill to the harbour and stood on the pier, looking at the sea. He could smell the ocean. The air was still, in stark contrast to the hard biting wind of the afternoon. The sky above was clear, and a broad smear of stars roofed the heavens. The temperature had dropped, and Cole could see his breath as he looked out over the sea, toward the mouth of Knight Inlet. Where are you, Archie Ravenwing? he thought. Where have you gone?

He walked back to the dirt road that ran along the harbour and found himself in front of the town's pub. He hadn't had a drink in two days — none of Archie Ravenwing's children drank very much, so he had restrained himself around them. But as he stood in front of the pub, his body yearned for a shot of Irish whiskey and a pint. Then he recalled that Darren First Moon had told him that some of the local townsfolk would raise a glass in Archie's honour tonight, and that was all the excuse Cole Blackwater needed. He stepped through the salt-blasted door and into the warmth of the bar.

He let his eyes adjust to the lights of the room. The Strait was just one large space with scuffed, rough-hewn board floors, a plywood bar along the wall opposite the door, and a dozen mismatched tables arranged on both sides of the bar. The long, raw rafters were festooned with fishing gear: nets, tackle, and floats of all shapes and colours. The lighting in the room came from brass lamps that hung from nautical rigging strung between the pillars. The room was loud, warm, and welcoming. Cole immediately felt at home.

He had begun his precautionary scan of the room when he heard his name ring out. "Hey, Cole," came a voice from a set of tables to the right of the bar. "Good to see you!" It was Darren First Moon, his large, powerful arm waving from a group of men who sat together drinking pints of golden ale. Darren pushed himself to his feet and made his way shakily toward Cole. Cole grinned, watching the big man approach him, his face round and happy like a child's. "Good to see you, brother," Darren said, simultaneously shaking Cole's hand in his huge paw and pounding him on the back, jarring Cole's left shoulder and producing a loud slap against the leather of his jacket. "Come on, let me pour you a pint." Cole let himself be led by Darren First Moon to the table of revellers. "Everybody, this is Cole Blackwater," Darren said loudly. "He was a good friend of Archie's. He's a kick-ass, take-no-prisoners environmentalist," he said, slurring a little. "And he was working with Archie to shut down the salmon farms."

Cole managed to grin at the faces looking up at him, and became aware that others in the room had become more subdued. He felt eyes on his back and realized that, apart from the large group of Archie's friends sitting to the right of the bar, a quieter group of white men sat at a table to the left, not a part of the merrymaking in Archie's honour.

"Good to see you all," Cole managed to say before Darren First Moon found an empty glass, poured draft into it, and handed it to him. "To Archie!" he called out, and the group of twenty or so drinkers sang out together, "To Archie!" Their glasses raised overhead, clinking and sloshing beer onto the tables and the floor. Cole managed to turn a little to his left as he drank, and from the corner of his eye could see five or six men sitting together at a table on the far side of the room, watching him from beneath ball caps.

A chair was found for Cole, and he sat down and listened as the men told stories about Archie. It seemed a general consensus that Archie was a pillar of the community, but also a bit of a prick, something that didn't surprise Cole Blackwater. "Old Ravenwing could burrow under a man's skin like a teredo worm burrowing into a log," said one man, taking a big slug of beer. "We loved him, and we hated him at the same time," said another.

Cole watched it all, finishing two glasses of draft before rising to make his way to the bar, empty jugs in hand, in search of refills. He stepped to the bar and rested his arms on the plywood counter, painted and sealed with a heavy coat of varathane, but worn and scuffed over the years by many arms and full pint glasses. The bartender was a large man, heavy in the middle, who wore his hair back in a ponytail, and who filled the pitchers without being asked. "And a Jameson, neat," said Cole, digging into his pockets for money. He fished a few bills from his pocket, along with half a dozen elastics, a tube of lip balm, a broken pencil, a small collection of paper clips, and a shocking assemblage of multi-coloured lint. The bartender gave him his whiskey and took his money. Cole stuffed the rest of the debris back into place.

"Sounds like you're some kind of white knight," said a voice to Blackwater's left. Cole had seen the man rise from the group on the far side of the bar. Cole watched him settle in next to him without making eye contact. Cole could see that he wore a BC Wildlife Federation baseball cap stained with sweat and grease, and a red-checkered shirt tucked into a belt with a large silver buckle.

Cole ignored him, but watched him from the corner of his eye. Tonight, he reminded himself, was a celebration of Archie's life. He wasn't in the mood to mix it up.

"Sounds like you're some kind of angel avenger," said the man again. Cole paid for the jugs of beer and sipped his whiskey. He wiped his mouth with the back of his hand. He could feel the blood flowing in him, and the heat of the Irish whiskey warmed his throat and stomach.

"You're not going to introduce yourself?" said the man, looking at him intently.

Cole turned and smiled. "You haven't."

"Dan Campbell."

"Cole Blackwater," he said, offering his hand, which Campbell shook.

"You must have been Archie's man in Vancouver."

Cole smiled. Archie liked to advertise.

"He told me that he had some help down in the city. Said he was getting some help when he was trying to shut down the grizzly hunt."

Campbell's name suddenly came back to Cole. Dan Campbell

was part of a vocal group of local guide-outfitters who was often on the radio and in the newspaper trying to keep the grizzly hunt open. When the CBC needed to hear from someone in support of the ongoing hunt, they called up Dan Campbell. He represented BC's version of the Wise Use movement, a collection of industry-financed, kitchen-table, and back-room organizations conceived to paint a thin, green veneer over the ongoing exploitation of natural resources. About two years back Archie had been working to shut down the grizzly hunt in Knight Inlet and along the mid-coast of BC. He had turned to Cole once or twice for advice, and to help broker a relationship with the larger provincial environmental groups who were also working on the issue. "A real motherfucker," had been Archie's blunt description of Dan Campbell.

"See you're drinking with the Indians tonight. Why don't you come and join us over here for a few pints?" said Campbell, grinning under his ball cap.

Cole sized him up. Super middleweight at best, he thought. Strong enough looking, and likely the veteran of many a bar brawl, given his charming disposition and outright bigotry.

"Men are men," said Cole, not looking at Dan Campbell's face.

Campbell laughed. Cole watched as he turned back to his friends and grinned. "I'd think a guy like you, coming from the big city, would know otherwise. Just a bunch of drunks on the street corners in Vancouver, aren't they?"

Cole felt the pulse in his wrists quicken. He threw back the rest of his whiskey. "How's a guy like you live in a place like Port Lostcoast?" Cole asked him, his voice quiet.

Dan laughed. "What do you mean? Live here with all the Indians?"

Cole didn't smile.

"They mind their own business, I mind mine."

"This town is a First Nations town," said Cole, looking around him.

"Half-and-half. They keep to their side. We keep to ours. We meet here in the middle."

"You're the minority here."

"Maybe. Maybe in numbers. But not up here," he said, tapping the side of his head with his forefinger. "Up here, we still call the shots." He grinned.

Cole felt his vision narrowing. It was always like that. He felt his heart beating in his throat and his muscles tense. He tried to breathe, to flood his body with oxygen before his muscles sprang into action.

Dan went on. "You see, the Indians may have some say in what goes on here on Parish Island and at Alert Bay, but the government still listens to *us*. Maybe you Indian lovers want to help them shut down the grizzly hunt and fuck over the fish farmers and stop us from cutting in the so-called Great Bear Rainforest." Dan wobbled his head mockingly. "But the government is not listening to *you*."

"Best government money can buy," said Cole.

"It isn't just the money. Those fucking Indians are just stupid savages," said Dan, spitting the words. "Sure, we closed down the residential schools, but we're still having our way with them — "

It was too much for Cole to take. As Dan pointed his chin, Cole brought his fist up from the bar in a neat, clean uppercut that took Dan Campbell right off his feet. A trail of blood followed him through the air in a graceful parabola. Campbell's hat came off, and, when his feet touched the floor again, he stumbled backward, his left arm grabbing for the bar, knocking over stools and falling back into an empty table. He tumbled over it and onto the floor. It was a spectacular scene. Cole stepped toward him as Dan, mouth leaking blood and spit, picked himself off the floor and hurled himself at Cole, catching him in the mid section and driving him into the bar. Cole managed to get his arms around Dan and, as he collided with the counter, wrenched his body sideways and half pulled him onto the top of the bar. Dan thrashed his head and connected with Cole's sternum, knocking some of the wind from him. From below, Cole quickly landed two right-hand jabs to Dan's face, and another spray of blood leaped across the plywood.

"I'm going to kill you, you motherfucking Indian lover," Dan hissed, spitting blood into Cole's face. Dan kicked himself off the bar, and he and Cole crashed into a second table. Darren First Moon and his friends leapt to their feet, grabbing pint glasses and pitchers as they did. Cole ended up on top of Dan on the floor, but Campbell brought up his knee into Cole's gut and Cole rolled to the side, winded and in pain. Dan threw a flurry of left- and right-hand punches at Cole, who absorbed them with his shoulder and arms as he struggled to his feet. Dan landed a right on Cole's cheek before Cole got his feet under him and stepped in with his own quick left-right combination, sending Campbell into the wall, his nose mangled.

The bar was quiet. Every man in the place was standing. Dan Campbell's five friends had stepped to the middle of the room, but didn't come any closer. Darren First Moon and his friends stood in silence watching the fight, but didn't step toward either of the fighters. The bartender stood at the centre of the room, watching both groups of men. Dan Campbell was hunched over, his back to the wall, his nose twisted and bleeding. Blood ran down his shirt from his mouth. Cole was three arm lengths from him, hands up and ready. His left cheek was glowing red, and a small cut at the corner of his mouth bled. He wore a spray of Dan's blood across his face. The adversaries stared at each other.

"I think that's about enough," said the bartender. "You boys take this outside. You're going to bust up the furniture."

Darren walked over to Cole and put a hand over his left forearm. "Come on, Cole," he said. "Let's buy a round for the house. Keep peace in the village." Cole looked at him, then back at Dan Campbell.

"Why not?" Cole said, breathing hard. "What do you say?" he asked Campbell. Campbell looked at his friends, at the group of men around Darren, and then at Cole.

"Fuck you," he said. He straightened up and walked out the door. Cole caught the words, "You're a dead man," as Campbell exited.

Cole dropped his arms and looked around the room to see if any of Campbell's friends wanted to continue where their buddy had left off. Nobody indicated as much.

Cole walked over and picked up the table that had been knocked over, looking up at the five remaining white men as he did. He righted the table, took one of the empty pitchers to the bar, and, when it was filled with frothy beer, placed it at their table. Then he stepped back to the bar for refills. He bought another whiskey and sat down next to Darren First Moon, his heart still pounding, his cheek and fists sore.

"Okay, who wants to fight Cole next?" Darren said, grinning, and everybody laughed.

■ When he left the bar, it was two AM. He was drunk enough not to feel the pain in his face or hands, but not so drunk that he couldn't walk or be aware of what was happening around him. Darren and two other men walked him home. "Just to be on the safe side," they said. Cole grinned. It was good to have friends to watch your back.

He stumbled in the door, expecting everybody to be asleep at Archie's. But the light was on in the study, so he stepped cautiously to the door and looked in. Grace was sitting at the desk reading a book. She looked up when he entered and frowned.

"What happened to you?" she said.

"Had a disagreement," Cole managed.

"With what? A cruise ship? You look awful."

"Thanks." He grinned, not feeling the tightness in his face that would ache in the morning. "I feel just fine. Why are you up? It's two AM."

Grace put down the book. "The Coast Guard called. Someone found the *Inlet Dancer.*"

12

The heat of August had passed. September ushered in temperate days and cool nights. Archie Ravenwing stood on the deck of the *Inlet Dancer* and sorted through tackle that he and Darren First Moon used on fishing trips with tourists throughout the summer. It had been a busy season, and this was their first day off in more than two weeks. The gear was a mess. Stowed quickly, late each night, and brought out early each morning, some disorder had crept into the workings of the operation. Archie was no stranger to disarray—his office at home was a working experiment in chaos theory. But here on the *Inlet Dancer*, order was required for smooth operations, both during the tourist season and during the salmon runs.

Archie sipped a cup of strong, black coffee from the lid of his thermos as he worked. Every few minutes he paused to look out beyond the harbour to the rounded hills on the nearby islands. A dozen tiny islets dotted the passage between Parish Island and the northern reach of Knight Inlet. The scent of gutted fish and salt water hung in the air. During the hectic summer months it felt to Archie like he had hardly any time to sit and contemplate those hills and the sea that circled them. It had been a busy summer, and he was glad for the work, knowing full well that the commercial salmon season might be a complete bust. The added challenge of the minister's announcement that more fish farming would be allowed in the Broughton made that reality almost unbearable.

After the August meeting in Port Hardy, Archie, Cassandra, and Carrie Bright had driven back to Port McNeill, debating their next move. Bright was clear about her role to hammer Stoboltz and the government in the media and in the markets. "We've got to take the market away from this industry," she said, piloting her Toyota Corolla down the hill to the ferry that would take her across to Sointula. "We've got the campaign all ready to go. It's time to start playing hardball."

"What does that mean?" asked Cassandra Petrel from the passenger seat.

"Newspaper ads in the *Los Angeles Times* and the *San Francisco*

Chronicle, and an on-the-ground campaign to approach restaurant chains and supermarkets to stop selling farmed fish. We'll go on a speaking tour and try to raise the profile of the issue. We'll get supporters to walk into their local stores and upscale restaurants with handbills about the facts of farmed salmon and the alternatives. We've already got an email list of two or three thousand people. We'll start with those folks and recruit more through the tour and the ads," said Bright, her voice sounding confident and determined.

Petrel nodded.

Archie was silent in the back seat, watching the harbour come into view beyond the motels and discount stores, listening. He admired Carrie Bright for her determination and enthusiasm. She had built the SOS coalition with her bare hands, bringing together oftentimes fractious groups like sport fishermen, First Nations, and environmentalists for the common cause of stopping fish farms.

"We need to keep up the pressure on the provincial government," she continued. "They need to be held accountable for this decision. We'll work with the environmental groups in our coalition based here in BC to put pressure on members of the legislature, especially those sitting on the Task Force that is looking at fish farming."

Carrie Bright looked in the rearview mirror at Archie. "You're awfully quiet back there, Archie. You okay?"

Archie took his eyes from the sun-speckled water and looked at the two women in the front seat.

"You okay?" Bright asked again.

"I'm okay."

"You're pretty quiet."

"Just thinking."

"I know it's hard on you," said Petrel, "sitting at that table and not having a say anymore."

"Never did, really." Archie smiled and looked back out the window.

"We were expecting this decision. This government is pro-business. It's ideological for them. We didn't really expect them to say no. We're going to have to fight them all the way on this," said Bright.

"That's not what's bothering me."

"Dan was his usual charming self. Don't pay any attention to him," said Bright.

"That's not what's bothering me, either. He's full of hot air. He's a racist and a bigot, but that's not what's got me thinking."

"What is?"

"Something that Greg White Eagle said — or didn't say, I guess."

"But he didn't say *anything*," Bright said, glancing in the mirror at Archie.

"Exactly. That's what I mean. He didn't say a bloody word the whole time. Not a word. It was like he knew what was coming, and that everything was copacetic. Like he had no worries whatsoever."

"What are you saying, Archie?" asked Petrel, turning toward him.

"Nothing yet."

Petrel looked at him. "You think he's in on the decision?"

Archie shrugged.

"You think that Greg White Eagle is in the pocket of Stoboltz?"

"Or that Stoboltz is in his pocket," said Carrie.

Archie watched the water come back into his view, the sun glinting off the ocean so bright he had to close his eyes.

■ Archie finished sorting his gear and turned his attention to half a dozen jigging rods that were laid out on the deck. He picked up the first one and sat back down to re-thread the line and work on the reel.

"About time we got some cooler weather, hey, Archie?" came a voice from the slip next to the *Inlet Dancer*. Ravenwing looked up to see Greg White Eagle standing next to the boat. Speak of the devil, thought Archie. Greg had his hands in his pocket and wore wraparound sunglasses, jeans, and a long-sleeved canvas shirt.

Archie smiled and went back to his work.

"You're a hard man to track down these days, Archie. Busy season for you, hey?"

Archie nodded and kept at his work.

"Harbourmaster's log says you've been out every day for the last two weeks. A good run for you and First Moon. How is old Darren holding up?"

Archie put down the rod and took a sip of his coffee.

"What is it that you want, Councillor?"

"A chat. Mind if I step aboard?"

"You know the way," said Ravenwing.

Greg White Eagle stepped onto the *Dancer*, his hands in his pockets making him look a little like a duck waddling on the shore. Greg stood near the bow of the boat and looked around him at the other boats. Then he walked to where Archie was seated on the fish box and sat on the gunwale across from him.

"Listen, I know what you've been up to."

"Oh, yeah, what's that?"

"Snooping."

Archie was silent.

"No sense in denying it, Archie. I know you've been poking your nose into everybody's business but your own for a long time. It's your way. It's the way you do things. But now you've been poking your nose into *my* business, into my personal affairs. Just what do you hope to accomplish? What do you want to get out of that, Archie?"

Ravenwing sipped his coffee and turned his attention back to the rod, threading the heavy-gauge deep-sea line through the eyelets and tying off a heavy metal leader.

"That's one down," he said, getting up and selecting a second rod. He sat back down.

"Janice at the band office called me to tell me that you had been there recently. Went all the way to Alert Bay just to poke around. She told me that you were asking to look at the correspondence file. And the financial statements of the band."

"Got a right to do that. Everybody does."

Greg looked at Archie. "Everybody *does*, but *nobody* ever does it, Archie. What are you looking for?"

Archie shrugged. He played out some line from the reel that he had opened.

"Also, I got a call from Lance Grey. He told me that you've filed Access to Information requests with his office. What's that all about?"

"It's a citizen's right," said Archie.

Greg looked away. He took off his glasses and rubbed the bridge of his nose. He stood up. "You're getting under my skin, Archie. You're like some kind of insect, burrowing under and causing an uncomfortable itch. I'm starting to feel like I've got to scratch. You know what I mean?"

Archie smiled. "I don't have the foggiest idea what you mean, Councillor."

Greg put his hands back in his pockets and blew out through pursed lips. "You know, one of the things I get to do now that I'm a band councillor is to review all the past financial transactions for my office. It's very illuminating work, Archie. Very illuminating. Do you catch my drift, Archie?"

"I'm not following you, Greg. Better spell it out."

"Well, I've been digging through some invoices submitted for work done by a contractor from Alert Bay that were paid out from your discretionary account. Bits of work for a few thousand dollars here, and a few thousand dollars there. General repairs and maintenance work. Nothing too unusual. Could be work on the community centre or the school, or maybe down at the docks. But the trouble is, Archie, that there hasn't been any work done at the community centre, or at the docks, not that I can see. Nothing more than fixing the toilet at the centre, and nothing at all on the docks. Nothing that matches those invoices. Not around the dates on the invoices, that's for sure. So I'm starting to wonder — just what was that contractor doing?"

Archie worked on the reel.

"So I called him up. The contractor. Really good guy. Loved coming to Parish Island to work. Said that the office he built and the deck that he worked on was such a nice project to do because the view from the house over the harbour was really lovely. He said he didn't get to finish the deck last spring, but he can come back anytime. Should I give him a call, Archie, and ask him if he's got time?"

Archie didn't say a word. He got up and selected another rod to work on.

White Eagle returned the glasses to the bridge of his nose. "So that really got me interested, Archie. And I kept looking. Seems you signed a bunch of cheques to Cash to pay off a consultant, your buddy Blackwater. Something about needing to pay him in cash because his ex-wife was garnishing his wages and you wanted to pay him under the table. So his ex wouldn't get her hands on the money, I guess. Wonder what was really going on there, Archie."

Archie snorted and put down the rod. Greg White Eagle was still standing, eyes hidden behind his dark glasses, his hands balled into fists inside his pockets.

"Be a real shame, Archie, if the people of Port Lostcoast knew what you were up to. That would be a real shame for you and your family, Archie."

"Okay, Councillor, you've made your point. It's easy to kick a man when he's down. You've done your homework. Sure, I've made my mistakes. But here's the thing, Councillor. I got no-where to go but down. I've had my day. Been to the AFN, been to Ottawa. Got the ear of the minister. Never did me much good." Ravenwing laughed. "Even got my picture in the paper. Did my service for my people. I'm just a fisherman and a tourist guide now. Nowhere to go but down."

"Fraud is a serious offense, Archie."

"Yeah, maybe even do a little time, hey?"

"Maybe."

"Yeah, that wouldn't be too much fun. They might take my house, hey?"

Greg looked away. "Maybe, Archie."

"It's nothing compared to what they would do to you, Greg."

Greg White Eagle looked sharply back at him.

"It's nothing," Archie said, putting a foot up on the gunwale and tying his shoe. "Nothing compared to what they would do to you if they caught you with your hand in the cookie jar."

"What are you talking about?" White Eagle laughed, but there was a tension in his voice that had not been there seconds before.

Archie put his foot down and stood up. He walked over to the fish box, took the cup of coffee, and sat back down. "So I get this file. It's not a big one. It's just a bunch of correspondence. Not band correspondence, you understand. It's printouts of emails. I get it from the Office of the Information and Privacy Commissioner. I didn't even know we kept track of emails, did you?"

Silence.

Archie laughed. "So I start looking through them. All very interesting. Starts back in June, a few months after you took office, Greg. But I got the feeling reading them that it was the continuation of a conversation. That the emails were follow-up, you know? That maybe the conversation had started a few months before. Maybe sooner, I don't know. It was just the way the emails sounded. The emails were all about salmon farming, of course. There was talk of the upcoming announcement by the minister, the one that you and I were at last month. You might remember it, Greg. That was the meeting where you just sat there silently. The meeting where the minister announced more salmon farms in our traditional territory, which may well end our traditional way of life, and you said nothing." Ravenwing was shaking his head.

"But what really caught my attention was when the emails started being cc'ed to a Yahoo! account. Did you know that it's possible to get someone to track down who owns those accounts? I didn't know that. But I found someone who knows how. Probably some kid in his mother's basement. Anyway, it took a little digging, but I found out who the account belongs to. Want to guess?"

Silence.

"Didn't think you'd want to guess," said Archie, smiling. "I'll tell you. Darvin Thurlow. The account belongs to Darvin Thurlow. I just couldn't figure that out at first. Why would our band councillor be copying correspondence to the minister's office to the head scientist at Stoboltz? I guess I'm just kind of slow.

But then it all started to make sense. The three of you talking it up before the announcement last month. I think that's called collusion. I'm not sure, I haven't looked that up," said Archie, taking up another rod from the top of the fish box and playing out some line.

"But it gets better, Greg. Don't leave now. It gets better." Greg White Eagle stood, fists in his pockets, looking toward the mouth of the harbour, barely able to hide his anger. "I think it must have been a slip. Something that nobody should have said. But there it was, in an email from just after the announcement. It was from you to Darvin, with a cc to Lance Grey. It said –" Archie touched his temples as if trying to remember – "'now you've got what you paid for.' I'd say that was pretty stupid putting that in an email, wouldn't you, Councillor? Lance sure did, because he really laid into you after that one."

Greg looked down at Archie. He took a step toward the centre of the boat and placed a meaty palm on the top of the fish box. He leaned in toward Archie. His face was even with Ravenwing's, and only a few feet away. He reached with his free hand to take his sunglasses from his face.

"Just what, exactly, are you saying, Ravenwing?" White Eagle spat, the corners of his mouth flecked with white spittle.

"Sounds to me like someone is on the take, Councillor," said Archie.

The two men stared at each other. Finally Greg stood up and laughed. "You've got nothing on me. Nothing. That email means nothing."

"Maybe. Maybe not. We'll see."

"You listen to me, Archie. You listen. You've got nothing. You think that after what you've done, people would listen to you anyway? After what you've done you'll be lucky not to be in jail, or living in Port McNeill packing groceries at the Super Save. Nobody is going to listen to you, Archie. They'll all be too busy working on the salmon farms and thanking me for finally looking out for their best interests, instead of your own!"

"I suppose they might," said Archie. "But when I get to the bottom of what was paid for, the band council might have something to say about rigging an election. Hey, maybe we could bunk together over in McNeill. Save some money!" Archie grinned.

"You really are a pain in the ass, Ravenwing. You know that? You're getting to be a really big pain in my ass. You're an itch. An irritation. An itch that needs to be scratched. You listen to me Ravenwing—you have no idea who, or what, you're messing with."

13 Nancy Webber drove to where the blacktop wove up toward the height of the south Porcupine Hills, the trees clinging to the lee side of the slopes, the afternoon sun still high in the cloudless blue sky. It was three o'clock when she turned off the pavement, following directions she'd received when she'd called Dorothy Blackwater from the Shell station on the highway in Claresholm.

"Are you sure you don't mind me stopping by?"

"Not at all, dear."

"It's just that Cole has told me so much about the ranch, and I was in the area on a story, and thought I'd just love to come by for a visit," she lied. When Cole found out there would be trouble. She would have to do what she could to prevent him from learning of her visit.

"Come by. I'll fix dinner. I don't get many guests. It will be nice to have some company."

So she turned off the blacktop and drove south and west into the hills, the trees disappearing on the windward slopes of each rise and fall, the rough fescue parkland brown before the heavy spring rain. Two more turns, one missed side road that she had to double back to, and she found Blackwater Ranch. A small, unpretentious sign on the gate told her she was in the right place. She stepped from her car, opened the gate, drove through, and got back out to close the gate behind her. The ranch was laid out in a dale at the base of the drive. The main ranch house was a long, rambling affair with a broad porch in the front and dormer windows on the second floor. Behind the house were the barn and other outbuildings, a drive shed, wood shed, chicken coop, and other wooden buildings. Some of these looked to be well maintained, others leaned eastward, buffeted by the prevailing winds. To one side of the main ranch yard were two ageing and abandoned pickup trucks, one from the 1950s. Otherwise, the yard was orderly and neat. A small kitchen garden was laid out behind the house.

Nancy drove down the hill to the house and shut off the ignition. She rolled up the window and stepped from the car. She could hear cattle and smell the pungent mixture of hay and manure. She guessed that Walter Blackwater, Cole's older brother, would soon trail the cattle into the high country west of Highway 22 on the family's grazing lease. She stood a moment in the yard, letting the smells and sounds of the ranch waft over her. She exhaled and felt herself relax a little after the dusty, bumpy road.

Nancy walked toward the house, casting her eyes at the barn. She longed to walk straight into its darkened spaces and begin to pry at the secrets there, but decorum dictated a visit with Cole's mother was in order first.

From the back porch a border collie bounded toward her, wagging its tail. Nancy bent to pat the dog on the head, scratching behind its ears. She took the steps to the porch, opened the screen door, and knocked on the heavy wood-panelled door beyond. In a moment it opened, and she was greeted by a small, grey-haired woman in a flower-print dress who was wiping her hands on her apron.

"You must be Nancy Webber. Come in, come in. I'm Dorothy Blackwater," she said, extending a hand. Nancy shook it. It was warm and firm.

"It's a pleasure to meet you, Mrs. Blackwater."

She stepped into the house, and the smell of dinner cooking on the stove and something baking in oven welcomed her. "Wow, does it ever smell good in here."

"When you called I put a pie in the oven and made us a little dinner. I'm so glad that you came by." She turned and made her way out of the mud room into the kitchen. Nancy kicked off her shoes and followed. The kitchen was large and bright and warm. Windows opened onto the backyard, facing the sheds, barn, and garden.

"Would you like tea, dear?"

"That would be nice."

"Black tea or something herbal?"

"Black would be fine, thanks."

Dorothy Blackwater set a kettle on the stove and took a teapot from the sideboard, pouring hot water from the tap into it. She sloshed it around before emptying it again.

"Do you take milk or sugar?"

"Both."

Dorothy found a pitcher of milk in the fridge, took a bowl of sugar from the sideboard, and set them on the kitchen table. When the kettle boiled, she put three teabags in the pot and poured the hot water over them. She let them steep, then took them out and dumped them in a bowl filled with vegetable cuttings. "Come, let's sit at the table."

They sat at the kitchen table, Dorothy on the end and Nancy sitting close to her on the side. Dorothy poured tea and produced tea biscuits and homemade Saskatoon berry jam. Nancy sipped her tea and ate the buttery biscuit as they chatted.

"How do you know Cole?"

"He and I met in Ottawa. We met up again when he was in Oracle last year."

"Oh, that was a nasty piece of business, wasn't it?"

"Which?"

"Oh, both, I guess," Dorothy Blackwater said, looking out the window. "But that business in Oracle, my goodness, Cole was a mess after that. I do hope he's more careful now. Do you see him at all?"

"I saw him a few months ago in Vancouver. We had dinner."

"How was he?"

"He seemed just fine," she lied.

"That's good. Have you met Sarah?"

"I haven't."

"She is such a darling, that girl. Just loves horses. She was out at the ranch last spring, and she and Cole rode every day. Wore him out! But she could just go and go and go."

"Cole thinks the world of her," said Nancy.

"As he should. I do hope he's getting on all right."

Nancy sipped her tea.

"So, Cole doesn't talk much about his family, Mrs. Blackwater. I'm really curious to know more about you."

"There's not much to know. I've been here on this ranch most of my life. Raised the boys, always made sure they had good food to eat and that they did their homework. Those boys sure had fun when they were little. They had the run of the place. I'd open the door after breakfast and they'd be off like a shot, running up into those aspens, and I'd have to yell for them at lunch or they'd have starved out there. They'd be gone again after lunch and the same thing after dinner. It just drove Henry crazy, but, my goodness, those boys had a spirit to them."

"It must have been a wonderful place to grow up."

"Well, it wasn't without its hard times. We never had much money. The ranch only just paid its way. We lost money many years when the price for cattle was low, but we got by. I did some work in town, and Henry did odd jobs around the area on other farms. We got by. The boys had to work some. Cole not so much as Walter. Him being older, he got the heavy jobs. But both boys worked. Henry saw to that."

"Cole mentioned boxing."

"I think those boys spent as much time in that blasted boxing ring as they did in school. Every night when they were of age Henry'd have them out there. Poor Cole, he was always getting his nose bloodied. I didn't have the heart to watch. Not once. Never stepped foot in that place." She pointed toward the barn. "Walter being older, I think, got the better of Cole most often, but Cole went on to do well for himself. At least until he went off to college."

Nancy put down her cup of tea. "I'd love to have a look around the place in the daylight," she said.

Dorothy Blackwater stood up, putting her teacup and plate on the counter next to the sink. "Let's go and have a stroll around, and then I'll put the finishing touches on dinner."

The late afternoon was cool and bright. The ground was bare and the earth beneath it hard, full of frozen moisture and frost. Dorothy pointed at the two rusting automobiles. "Walter's been trying to get rid of all the junk that was collected when Henry was alive," she said. "Can't stand to have all those old cars around. Every few months he finds someone to take a few of them away. That used to drive Cole crazy, all those cars that his father bought and stripped and just left there to rust. He said it was fouling up our water. Never seemed to make much difference to me, but Walt says it's better to be rid of them, so ..."

They walked toward the drive shed. "This was built in 1919, when Henry's dad bought his first truck. He'd just come back from Europe and used his soldier pay to buy a Ford automobile. One of the first men in the area to have one." Nancy looked around the shed. A newish Ford Focus was parked there now. They looked in on the chickens and the pigs, Nancy enjoying the sounds and scents of the working farm. They made their way toward the barn. "Over there is a trail that leads up through the aspens to the crest of the hills. From there you can see clear over to the Livingstone Ridge and beyond to the Continental Divide. Cole and Sarah rode up there every day they were here last spring."

"Are they going to come back for a visit this year?"

"Oh, I don't know. Cole loves being here, but it's so hard for him."

"Why is that, Mrs. Blackwater?"

"Oh, goodness, I don't know. He doesn't talk about it much. I think the business with his father really gets to him. I didn't see him for three years after, well, we really don't talk too much about it."

Nancy bit her lip. "Talk about what, Mrs. Blackwater?"

"Here we are. Let's have a look inside the barn." Dorothy led Nancy to the back and showed her where half a dozen cows drank from a trough, and where a few more came and went from the darkened basement of the barn. "I have a boy come from the next ranch over to put some hay out for the herd here every day. Walter comes most weekends to see to some of the heavier work. The cattle get most of what they need to eat on the hills in the summer, but in the winter, well, they need a little help. Walter always says that the open range only exists in the movies, and that our cows would starve or freeze to death if we didn't put up enough hay. I suppose he's right."

They made their way around the barn toward the front doors. "This is where Cole and Walter used to box. Henry built them a ring and strung some lights, and those boys would be out here nearly every night after dinner. They'd come in and I'd have a tub ready for them to clean up in before they went to bed. Henry worked those boys pretty hard." She opened the broad doors.

Nancy felt her heart beating with anticipation. The light slipped between the weathered boards as the door squeaked open and fell across the inside of the barn.

"You see, there's nothing left now," said Dorothy.

And indeed, she was right. The barn was stacked with hay and, in the centre of it, where Nancy imagined seeing the boxing ring with its stories and evidence of Henry Blackwater's end, was parked a riding lawnmower. Nancy stepped inside.

"Walter and Cole took down the old ring last spring when Cole was here. Said it was just taking up space that could otherwise be used for the ranch equipment. They burned most of the wood and even the canvas floor out back. We had a big fire going one day. It was quite the sight."

I bet it was, thought Nancy.

■ They sat at the dinner table and finished their meals. "That was really very good, Mrs. Blackwater," said Nancy.

"Please, call me Dorothy."

"Thanks again for dinner, Dorothy." Nancy smiled.

"Would you like coffee?"

"I think that would be nice. I'll need a little jolt for the drive back to Claresholm."

"You are very welcome to stay here, there's plenty of room."

"I don't know if I can do that, Dorothy."

"I insist," she said, patting Nancy's hand as she stood to clear the table.

"Only if you let me do the dishes," said Nancy.

"That's a deal."

"I don't know if I ever said how sorry I was for your loss," said Nancy, rising to clear the plates away.

Dorothy Blackwater poured water into a drip coffee maker. "Thank you, dear," she said.

"It must have been a terrible blow."

"It really was."

"I hope you don't mind me asking about it."

"What do you want to know?"

"I'm really just worried about Cole is all," said Nancy.

"Is there something wrong with Cole? He does take things very hard, doesn't he?"

"He does. I suppose I'm just worried that maybe he's suffering."

Dorothy took out cups, sugar, and cream and placed them on the table. "How do you mean?"

"He seems to have taken his father's death very hard. I feel that it's changed him."

Dorothy busied herself in the kitchen, piling up the supper things next to the sink and cleaning the stovetop. Nancy stood next to the sink and watched her.

"Can you tell me anything about Cole's relationship with his father that might help me help Cole?"

"I don't really know what I can say," said Dorothy. "They were father and son. Like most, they had good days and bad. There's really nothing more I can say than that."

"Did they, well, get along?"

"They got on okay. Cole and Henry had their differences of opinions. They didn't see eye to eye on how the ranch ought to be run. But Cole knew that Henry ran the show around here. I think much of what came between them was the arrogance of youth. After Cole left for college, he didn't come back very often. We hardly saw him at all until Sarah was born."

Nancy began washing the dishes. She looked out the window over the sink at the hills beyond the barn, aspens moving as the breeze slipped down the hillsides and pooled in the low places for the night.

"Did Mr. Blackwater do most of Cole's training?"

"In boxing? Most of it, yes. When he was seventeen, Cole went to live in Calgary for a year to train in a professional gym. That's when he went to the provincial championships."

"Mr. Blackwater must have been very proud."

"I dare say he was."

"Do you remember if Mr. Blackwater went to see Cole fight?"

Dorothy stopped and looked at nothing. "I believe he must have," she said, smiling. "He was very proud of his boys. He was always talking about what good boxers they were. I think Henry figured Walter would be the one to go on and box for a championship, but when Cole did, Henry was just as proud of him as he was of Walt."

"Mrs. Blackwater, I wonder if you would be able to tell me anything about the time when Cole was here four years ago. When he was heading out to Vancouver."

"I don't know what I can say...."

Nancy piled up the clean dishes and started in on the roasting pan. "It's just that, well, Cole really seemed to change after that. He seemed to, well, get pretty dark after that visit. Can you tell me anything that might help me understand Cole a little better, just so I can help him out?"

"There isn't really anything to tell. It was a very difficult time for us all, Cole and Walter being here and that business with Henry. I really can't say much more." She turned to finish cleaning the counter.

Nancy rinsed the last of the pots and searched the soapy water for any final items that needed cleaning. Then she emptied and cleaned the sink.

"Was Cole here when his father died, Mrs. Blackwater?"

"Oh, Nancy, I just can't talk about that. It was horrible." Dorothy composed herself and then said, "Come, let's sit in the living room and have our coffee. I'll show you some pictures of the boys when they were little." She collected the coffee service and headed for the living room, leaving Nancy to dry her hands and follow behind.

They were seated on the sofa, leafing through a thick album of black-and-white photos, a few colour images toward the end of the book, when Nancy heard a car door slam. For a moment, her heart leaped to her throat. She held her coffee and tried not to stare toward the back entrance, her fingers trembling a little.

"Oh, that must be Walter. He said he might come by this evening."

Nancy sipped her coffee and tried to breathe, but found her chest tightening.

"Hey, Mom," came a voice from the mud room.

"I'm in the living room, Walt."

"Whose car is that, Mom?"

"We've got company. A friend of Cole's."

Nancy heard a man walk into the kitchen.

"Come and have a cup of coffee, Walter, dear."

The sound of heavy feet neared the living room, and at the kitchen doorway a broad man, thick in the chest and arms, appeared. He was wearing the tan shirt and green pants of a park warden and wore a clean Stetson on his head, the brim rolled neatly on either side, his polished badge held fast with a thick brown band of leather. The man removed his hat when he stepped into the room. He reached a large hand toward Nancy. She stood up.

"I'm Walter Blackwater," he said.

She took his hand, which eclipsed her own. "Nancy Webber."

Walter smiled. "It's nice to finally meet you."

14

The wind blew through Cole Blackwater's curls as he stood on the flying bridge of Jacob Ravenwing's boat, the *Salmon Pride*, powering across the mouth of Blackfish Sound toward Cormorant Island and Alert Bay. Jacob owned a 1972 thirty-two-foot Grand Banks cruiser that had seen better days but still maintained some semblance of its original glory. When they had boarded the boat that morning in Port Lostcoast, Jacob told Cole that he had bought it at auction five years ago in Seattle after selling his commercial trawler. Now he lived on the boat, most often moored in Alert Bay, and took tourists fishing for halibut and salmon when it was necessary to earn a little money.

Above, dark clouds scudded on the western horizon, tripping over the low mountains at the north end of Vancouver Island. By the end of the day, Cole guessed, it would be raining again. Cole Blackwater was ready for spring. Or maybe *this* is what passed for spring in this neck of the woods.

Beside Cole was Darren First Moon, and below, next to Jacob at the wheel, was Grace Ravenwing. The four of them had agreed earlier that morning to go have a look at the *Inlet Dancer* in Alert Bay. If it was seaworthy, and the Coast Guard and RCMP were through with it, then Darren would pilot it back to Lostcoast.

The two men stood in silence for much of the trip, the wind pushing at them. Cole felt chilled right through to his bones, even with one of Darren's old slickers worn over a heavy fleece coat. Cole had a black wool longshoreman's cap pulled down over his ears, but a few errant curls escaped. He wore heavy woolen gloves on his hands, and still he shivered.

"Why don't you go down below?" shouted Darren.

"I don't get to do this very often," said Cole.

The truth was, he was embarrassed and didn't want to face Grace Ravenwing. After he had come in from the bar, drunk and bruised, she had given him a frosty reception. When she had asked about the fight, he had been evasive, not wanting the ugly undercurrent of racism that had provoked the bout to further impinge on her already troubled week.

They made the turn at Pearse Island by noon, then entered

Broughton Strait, making for the docks at the north end of Alert Bay. Jacob slowed as they passed the Fisheries and Oceans pier, and the foursome strained to see the *Inlet Dancer*. Grace Ravenwing climbed the ladder to the flying bridge and stood between Darren and Cole. They peered toward the dock, eyes roving over the shapes of the boats for the *Inlet Dancer*. They spotted it next to the *Cape Sutil*, a Canadian Coast Guard search-and-rescue boat from Port Hardy. They motored on beyond the government docks and entered the sheltered waters where Jacob Ravenwing's berth overlooked the cultural centre and museum and the houses of the reserve beyond. Jacob piloted the boat while Darren climbed down to the deck to help guide the *Salmon Pride* into the slip.

"It looks to be all in one piece," said Cole.

Grace nodded. He could see tears in the corners of her eyes. He slipped an arm around her small, solid shoulders and she let herself be pulled into him.

"I'm sorry about last night," he said, looking down. She was silent. "I know you don't like that. You told me before," he said.

Grace Ravenwing breathed heavily.

"Anyway, I'm sorry."

She smiled up at him, pushing a few tears from her cheek with a gloved hand. "Let's go have a look at Dad's boat," she said, and stepped onto the dock. The four of them made their way along the uneven pier toward the road that ran the length of the harbour. Like Port Lostcoast, the town of Alert Bay was divided in two. To the east of the ferry terminal was the white community with its neat houses and storefronts laid out along the water, bulging into a paved road that seemed as if it were an afterthought. To the west, the First Nations reserve, with the U'mista cultural centre, ceremonial Big House, and the world's tallest totem pole.

The four friends stepped from the pier onto the road. Cole stopped. "What the hell is that?" he said, pointing at a four-storey brick building adjacent to the cultural centre and museum. Through the leafless trees the building was imposing, and in many places bricks had become dislodged and fallen from the ageing structure.

"That's the band office," said Jacob.

"It looks like a prison," said Cole.

"It used to be the residential school," said Grace.

Cole nodded. "Figures," he said.

"Come on," said Grace, pulling Cole away from his dark thoughts.

■ The Coast Guard vessel *CCGC Sooke Post* had been on patrol north of the Broughton Archipelago when the overdue report was filed by the Port Lostcoast harbour master. The Joint Rescue Coordination Centre in Esquimalt, BC had notified the RCMP's marine headquarters in Nanaimo, which dispatched boats from its detachments in Alert Bay and Port McNeill. The *Sooke Post*'s crew of four had made for the mouth of Knight Inlet and led the search on the first day, aided by the two RCMP patrol boats and a flotilla of local fishermen. On the second day, they had been joined by the *CCGC Cape Sutil*, under the command of Captain John Bertrand, as it responded to the call from its patrol around the Scott Islands north of Vancouver Island. The RCMP dispatched its Air8 helicopter, and the Comox Canadian Forces base deployed the CC-115 Buffalo airplane and the CH-149 Cormorant helicopter to the region. For two days the region buzzed with activity, but there was no sign of the *Inlet Dancer* or its captain.

After three days, only the *Cape Sutil*, the RCMP, and a dozen local fishermen continued with the sad hunt.

"We found her run aground on Protection Point," said the wiry Captain Bertrand, standing on the dock next to the *Inlet Dancer*. He was a solidly built man in his early forties, with a thick mustache and a slight French-Canadian accent. "As you can see, her port side is a little banged up," he said, pointing to several dents in the fibreglass that covered the boat's sturdy wooden hull. "But as far as we can tell, she's seaworthy. We ran her in under her own power. The *Cape Sutil* accompanied her amidships only for safety sake."

Bertrand paused, then spoke what was on everybody's mind: "There's no sign of Mr. Ravenwing, nor do we have any clues as to what might have happened to him. I'm sorry. We've handed this over to the RCMP. The locals here in Alert Bay will carry on with the investigation. They've assigned a liaison officer. He should be here shortly."

The five of them stood on the dock and regarded the boat.

"I suppose we can all guess what must have happened," Jacob Ravenwing said, looking into the pilothouse.

"I don't think we'll ever be able to say with certainty," said Bertrand, crouching down to put a hand on the hull of the *Inlet Dancer*, his orange float coat bunching up under him. "But I'd say that during the storm, the *Inlet Dancer* was making for home out of the mouth of Tribune Channel, moving through the opening of Knight Inlet, and Archie was swept overboard. The boat appears to have never capsized. There's some water damage to the instruments in the pilothouse, but nothing serious. There's even some fishing gear on the deck, so I think the *Inlet Dancer* stayed upright through the storm." Bertrand pointed to some of the clutter there. "I think we can rule out the boat having gone over. I would say that, at some point, the *Inlet Dancer* must have been taken on the side by a rogue wave — maybe five or ten metres high — and Mr. Ravenwing swept overboard. We had fifty-knot winds that night in the strait, a violent storm rating on the Beaufort scale. It's not outside the realm of possibility to get waves of that height with such high winds. If Mr. Ravenwing was caught on the deck during one of those waves —"

Bertrand cleared his throat. "If one of you can tell me which PFDs are present and accounted for, we might be able to determine if he was wearing one at the time, but it seems academic at this point."

"Our people are continuing to search," said Darren First Moon. It was a statement, but it sounded like a question.

Bertrand nodded solemnly.

"Can we pilot her home?" asked Darren.

"The RCMP will want to go over the boat, but I don't imagine why you wouldn't be able to take her home before the week is out."

"Can we go aboard?" asked Cole.

"Best to wait for the liaison officer to arrive. He was tied up when we brought her into port. He should be here shortly," said Bertrand. And at that Cole and the others turned to see a white Suburban with the RCMP insignia pull up onto the docks. Two uniformed officers stepped from the cab and Cole had a moment of vertigo, thinking about his time in Oracle the previous year.

The officers walked onto the dock and stepped close to the *Inlet Dancer*. The first was tall, lean, and clean shaven, and couldn't be more than thirty years old. He wore a ball cap and looked crisp and efficient in his uniform. He wore long sleeves, and he rested his hand on his overloaded utility belt when he stopped before the group. The second man was older and shorter and wore what had once been the regulation police mustache. His face was wide and red, and his eyes seemed to be in a permanent squint. He brandished sergeant's stripes on his arms.

"Hi, Jacob," said the younger man.

"Hey there, Derek," said Jacob, extending his hand. They shook.

"Derek here is what the cops call a First Nations Community Policing Officer," said Jacob, grinning. "They send him out to deal with us Indians when we get into trouble. We like him, even if he's white," he joked.

Derek Johns introduced himself to the others and to Bertrand, then introduced Sergeant Barry Whiteside. The group chatted for a few minutes about how the *Inlet Dancer* was found, and about the boat's history, with Darren, Jacob, and Grace offering insight into its seaworthiness and Archie's predilection for not wearing his PFD. Finally there was a silence.

"Can we have a look around the boat?" Grace addressed Derek Johns.

The young man looked at his colleague and then back at Grace. "This is still a missing person's investigation unless we find some sign of trauma. We're going to count on you to help us understand what might have happened here. The first thing we need to do here is have a look over the boat ourselves, and then we'll let you come aboard for a look around. Sergeant Whiteside and I will examine the *Inlet Dancer* and its contents, and let you know when it's okay for you to join us on board."

"You said trauma. What do you mean?" asked Darren.

"Only that we're cautious about these things, Mr. First Moon," said Johns.

"Can you tell us more?" asked Cole.

"Not really," grunted the sergeant. "Let us have a look and we'll notify you when we're through."

Grace was standing close to her brother. She looked at the *Inlet Dancer*, its hull dented but otherwise intact. "Okay," she said. "We'll be on the *Salmon Pride*."

It was late in the day when the young constable knocked on the gunwale of the *Salmon Pride* and asked if he could step aboard.

"Be my guest," Jacob Ravenwing called from the bridge. The officer took off his cap.

"Did you find anything?" Grace asked, Cole standing close by her side.

"Nothing yet," he said.

"You're going to continue the investigation?" asked Cole.

"Yes, as a missing person's case."

"Can we have a look?" asked Darren, emerging from the bridge.

"I think we could use your help to tell us if anything is missing," said Derek Johns.

"We'll do what we can," said Darren, stepping onto the dock, pulling on his dirty orange coat. Grace came up beside him and the group made its way back to the *Inlet Dancer*.

When they reached the moored boat, they noted that Winters and Bertrand had left. Derek Johns turned to them and said, "Please, don't take anything off the boat. And touch as little as you can. What I'm asking you to do is tell me if anything is missing. PFDs, gear, and whatnot. I really don't know how this will help, but right now we've got to examine all the possibilities. My sergeant is working with the PEP...."

"What's PEP?" asked Cole.

"Provincial Emergency Program. He's working with them to see if maybe Archie used his cellphone while out on the water. We didn't find a cell aboard the boat and we know he had one.

If he made a call later in the day, we might be able to triangulate where he was before he went overboard...." Derek Johns stopped. "I'm sorry," he said. "I know this is hard. But we've got to exhaust every angle. It might help pinpoint the search."

Grace Ravenwing drew a sharp breath and stepped forward, putting a foot on the heavy gunwale, and then she dropped onto the deck of the boat. The others watched her. Derek Johns stood with his head slightly bowed, his hand resting on his heavy belt.

Grace walked to the stern of the boat and into the open pilothouse. She stood at the helm of the boat and placed her small hand on the wheel. She let her eyes roam around the pilothouse, aware of the eyes of the four men on the dock. She touched the bungee cord hanging from the wheel.

"Darren," said Cole, "you know the boat best. Maybe you could help the constable here with the question of the PFDs."

Darren smiled and said, "Sure. No problem." He stepped onto the boat and moved to the pilothouse.

"What do you make of this?" Grace asked Darren, touching the bungee cord that hung from the wheel.

"That was our autopilot," he said. "Archie and I'd sometimes use one of them to hold a bearing when we were alone on the boat. You know, if we had to deal with nets or gear or take a leak." He smiled weakly.

"I saw that and wondered about it too," said Johns. "My guess was that he had to deal with some kind of emergency and needed to keep her nose into the storm. But we looked over the engines and all the mechanical, and there doesn't seem to be anything ailing her now. Maybe Mr. Ravenwing was able to fix whatever it was quickly."

"I can't imagine what it could have been," said Grace. Then, turning to Constable Johns, she asked, "Do you think that he could have tied the wheel off to check into something and been washed overboard when the boat turned sideways to a wave?"

"It's a possibility."

Grace looked away from the young officer and away from the eyes of Cole and Jacob, and looked out at the wharf beyond the government dock. Darren First Moon put a hand on her shoulder. "You okay?" he asked, smiling.

"Thanks, Darren. Yeah, I'm okay."

Darren continued his search of the boat. "I don't see any PFDs missing. Archie almost never wore one. Lots of old-timers are like that," he said. "It's like seat belts. They know they save lives, but..." He let his thought trail off, aware of Grace Ravenwing nearby. "I'll look around and see what else is missing. Lots of the gear got strewn about in the storm."

Cole and Jacob climbed onto the boat and helped Darren First Moon do an inventory of the equipment. The deck was strewn with fishing tackle, rods, tools, and even a coffee thermos. Cole went below deck, moving through the pilothouse and the companionway, to inspect the crew's quarters. There were a few inches of water in the galley. He sloshed through it and inspected the bunk beds, the small cooking area, and the storage lockers. A few personal effects floated in the water, but otherwise things seemed to be in place. "We'll need to pump this water out," he called up from below, and saw Darren First Moon poke his head through the companionway.

"There's a bilge pump built in. We'll get her fired up," he said.

Cole emerged from below deck to see Darren and Jacob in the pilothouse. Jacob was looking over the instrument panel and had concluded that, though there was a little water damage, it was likely cosmetic and the boat would indeed be seaworthy. Darren fired up the *Inlet Dancer*'s twin Cummings inboard engines and gave a thumbs-up sign to Jacob and Grace before he shut them down again. "Looks like she's good to go," he said to no one in particular. "But we should have a look below just to make sure."

"I'll do that," said Jacob, moving to the stern of the boat.

Darren nodded and began untying a length of rope from the lee-side cleat in the stern.

"What have you got there, Darren?" Cole asked, walking past the fish box to stand beside First Moon, watching the big man's hands pull at the loops of rope and its frayed end.

"Don't know. Looks like Archie got himself tangled up here," he said.

Cole looked at the orange rope that was made fast around the cleat, and then at the rope that was tightly coiled and draped at the bow of the boat. "Looks like he had to hack at this with a machete," said Cole, touching the end of the rope where it was frayed.

"Funny thing," said Darren, finally loosening the rope.

"Wound up pretty tight, hey?" said Cole, looking at Darren.

"I'd say for sure. Like he had tied it off to a tree or something, and the boat had pulled real hard on it. Maybe he had to go ashore for something, you know, maybe snooping around somewhere, and the boat got pulled tight against the line and he had to cut it."

"Did you find a machete on the boat? Did Archie keep one?"

"We always had an axe and a fish gaff on board."

"Are they here?"

"I don't see them," said Darren, coiling the rope. "Must have got washed overboard. Or maybe Archie has them at home."

Cole held out his hand and Darren placed the rope in it. Cole looked to see if Derek Johns was watching and slipped the rope into his coat pocket. "I'm going to hold on to this."

Darren shrugged. "Suit yourself. Just a worthless piece of rope as far as I can see."

Cole walked to the back of the boat. Grace was still in the pilothouse. Jacob had the heavy panel open that gave access to the motor, and had his torso below deck.

Cole looked at Grace. She was sitting on the high seat that her father had used so many times. She was staring straight ahead, through the dirty glass of the pilothouse. In her hand she held the dented aluminum thermos.

"You know, I sat here with him so many times when I was younger. He got this boat when I was maybe twelve or thirteen, and after Mom died he would take me out with him when the salmon were in season, and sometimes when he had tourists, too. He would stand and I would sit here and watch the waves and the shore and the sky. He always had a thermos of coffee with him." She smiled, still looking ahead. "In the morning we'd sit on the fish box and we'd share a cup of coffee." Cole could see her eyes growing moist. He wanted to put his arms around her, to comfort her, but his legs would not budge. "I found this on the deck at the back of the boat," she said, looking down at the cylindrical thermos as if seeing it for the first time.

"For some stupid reason I never believed this sort of thing could happen to Archie," she said, calling him by his first name for the first time Cole could remember. "To Dad." She smiled again. "It seems as if he was more apt to walk on water than drown beneath it. At least that's the impression he wanted everybody to have of him." She slipped down off the seat. Cole watched her intently. His face was pale beneath the black cap, except for the dark bruise on his left cheek.

"You look really silly dressed up like a fisherman," she said, punching him in the arm. Cole grinned.

"How's it coming, Jacob?" she said, turning to Jacob and tugging on his leg.

"Okay, okay, it's all looking good down here. Got a lot of water during the storm, but it's pretty good. We'll run the bilge pump and if that doesn't do it, I'll bring a pump from my boat in the morning and we'll dry this out. Otherwise, it looks pretty good." Jacob reappeared, wiping his hands on a rag. "Cole, help me shut this thing, okay?"

Cole grabbed the heavy door and was about to close it when Grace said, "Wait a minute." Her voice was soft but urgent.

"What is it, Grace?" Cole said.

"What's this here?" she said, putting a finger in the runner where the heavy aluminum door fit into the deck of the boat.

Jacob and Cole came close. Darren First Moon stood at the door of the pilothouse, squinting at them.

"I don't know," said Cole. Grace touched it with a forefinger. It was a thick, reddish-brown substance that seemed to have congealed in the crack where the engine door closed directly behind the pilothouse.

"Could be grease," said Darren, helpfully. "You know Archie, always a little sloppy."

"He was a pig around the house," said Grace. "But you could

eat off the deck of this boat. Constable Johns, could you have a look here?"

Derek Johns stepped onto the boat and moved easily to the stern where he edged past Darren First Moon's bulk. "What's got everybody so interested here?" he asked.

Grace held up a finger.

"Well, well, well," he said, coming closer. "What *have* we here?" He bent and touched the substance.

"Looks like engine oil," said Darren again.

"No, not oil. It's not greasy. It's tacky," said Johns, pressing his fingers together and smelling them.

Cole was beside him. He followed the young constable's eyes from the compartment door to the back of the open pilothouse, the high seat, and then to the gunwales. Derek Johns was thinking the same thing that Cole Blackwater was: when Archie went overboard, he must have hit his head on something pretty good. Hard enough to cause a wound that would bleed heavily. And that wound must have knocked Archie Ravenwing unconscious. Otherwise, how would the blood have found its way back here? A pool of blood must have seeped from the wound where Archie lay unconscious — or worse — on the deck of the *Inlet Dancer,* and crept the distance between his prone body and the compartment for the inboard engines, a distance of four or five feet. That's a lot of blood, thought Cole, especially in a big sea where waves were likely breaking over the bow.

From where he crouched Cole looked up at the gunwales of the boat, more than a foot and a half in height. It would take a powerful wave to lift Archie Ravenwing's body from the deck of the *Inlet Dancer* over those gunwales and into the sea. How would that happen without capsizing the boat, or ridding it of things like fishing tackle or a coffee Thermos?

Constable Johns stood up and unclipped the radio receiver from his shoulder flash and depressed the microphone button. "Alert Bay, this is PC Johns."

"This is Alert Bay, go ahead," crackled the microphone. Cole and Grace stared up at the RCMP officer.

"Tell Sergeant Winters that we've turned up a foreign substance on the boat. Tell him that we're going to need a forensics team in from Campbell River. That we're going to need this boat up and out of the water first thing. We're going to need to lock it down."

15

"What do you think they're up to?" asked Archie Ravenwing. He was sitting in Cassandra Petrel's galley on the *Queen Charlotte Challenger*. The boat rocked slowly back and forth in the quiet harbour.

"I don't know. But as the saying goes, something fishy." Petrel was pouring tea, the steam from the kettle clouding up the portholes in her galley.

"Tell me what you know," Archie said. He was sitting sideways on a bench seat at the table, which doubled as Petrel's desk. Stacked with reports and papers, the makeshift desk was cluttered with vials of sea lice specimens, and on it a laptop hummed. Archie rested his back on an overstuffed cushion, his feet dangling off the end of the bench.

Petrel handed Archie a cup of tea, which he held in both hands for warmth. November had grown cold, and it had rained every day for the last week. Not heavily, but steadily, and the wind had blown down the Queen Charlotte Strait, bringing with it cold air direct from the Alaska panhandle. Archie sipped his tea, blowing on it with closed eyes to savour the warmth. Petrel sat across from him.

"I don't have any proof yet," she said, "so don't go flying off in a rage, Archie. Got it?"

He nodded.

"Okay, here's what I think. We know Stoboltz is expanding. That's certainly no secret. They have, what, twenty-five operations in the Broughton alone?"

Archie nodded again. "Yeah, twenty-five, twenty-six."

"So they have the vast majority of the operations in the Broughton. And more up the coast. And, of course, that's just their BC operations. They've got the market locked up in Scandinavia, off Ireland, and are expanding in the far east. Even into Chile. They're a going concern. Big bucks. Despite the work that Carrie Bright and SOS are doing, the market for farmed salmon is growing. People are more health conscious, they don't want to eat as much red meat. They want their essential fatty acids. It's our own damn fault," said Petrel, putting down her cup and peering through the tiny port window next to the table. "We convinced people that eating fish was good for them. We convinced folks that salmon is a healthy choice. We're now fighting the by-product of our success." She smiled at the irony.

"So salmon sales are booming, and farmed salmon is cheaper, so guess what the American markets are buying? Sure, wild salmon is selling, too, but they've been in free fall over the last ten years, thanks in part to the damage logging does to salmon streams. Because the government has allowed clear cutting right up to the edge of many salmon streams up and down the coast," said Petrel, shaking her head, "those streams can no longer support spawning salmon. No trees mean no shade. No shade means the streams warm up. Salmon are sensitive — they like cool water to spawn in. No trees mean silt and mud in the water. All of this adds up to streams that are no longer suited to spawning salmon. No spawning, no baby salmon."

Petrel sipped her tea and looked at Archie. "And now we add a gauntlet of salmon farms, and the juveniles who *are* born have to run it to make it back out to open ocean. The best waters for the salmon farms, it turns out, are on wild-salmon migration routes. So Stoboltz has done well for themselves. They've managed to put a dozen and a half salmon farms into the Broughton in short order. There are what, another ten, eleven, owned by other smaller players?"

"Yeah," said Archie. "About that. Not insignificant, I might add. A bunch of those belong to one of Canada's biggest food distribution companies."

"So this much we both know. Stoboltz is riding a wave of early success. They are making money hand over fist, and the minister's announcement in August was like a licence to print more of the stuff. They are set up for a big windfall."

Archie put his cup down and stared straight ahead into the galley.

"Here's the part where I'm getting some mixed messages," said Dr. Petrel. "You know that I send some of my samples to the lab at UVic for processing. This is the detailed stuff, the genetics part of the work. They've got state-of-the-art equipment for analyzing my — our — sea lice samples." She smiled. "Comes back in a couple of weeks. Full report. Stacks of paper," she said, patting the piles on her table. "I'm going to need a bigger boat if this keeps up. So a few weeks ago I got a call from the lab saying that they'd had a mix up, and that they had accidentally sent me back the wrong data. I thought it was kind of strange, because as far as I knew I was the only one sending in sea lice samples. The provincial and federal government have washed their hands of it. The minister's so-called commitment to a sea lice study got bumped to next year's budget. So it's just you and me, partner. They asked if I would send the data back, and they would send me the correct stuff. At first I thought that maybe it was salmon data, or black cod, but no, I looked, and it was sea lice data. The strange thing is, the samples were taken from the same area as ours. Mostly in Tribune Channel. So I did something that maybe I shouldn't have, but curiosity got the better of me. I read the reports."

Archie turned and looked at her, raising an eyebrow. "And?"

"Well, it was strange. I don't really understand it. The data on the lice shows levels of veracity that is troubling. First off, there were more lice per fry than I have ever seen. Literally hundreds. They were smaller than what you and I have been finding. That should be good news, but it wasn't, because they were tenacious. The data showed that the lice in question were killing salmon fry at a much higher rate. Almost double what you and I have been finding."

Archie turned on the bench to face Petrel.

"I was pretty curious about this research. Thought that somehow it must be wrong. So I called the lab. I know most of the people there pretty well, so I got someone on the phone and asked them some questions, you know, in confidence. Was this data right? They said it was. So I asked them where it was coming from. It took a little doing but I found out who was submitting the lice for analysis. It was Stoboltz."

Archie shook his head. "Really?"

"Really. Now, don't go jumping to conclusions, Archie. I mean, we've been demanding that they do their own studies for some time. So now they are. But what they are finding is particularly troubling."

Archie rubbed his temples, his eyes pressed shut.

Petrel said, "If Stoboltz is finding sea lice that are that tenacious at taking down migrating salmon fry, then we're going to have to find out exactly where they are taking their samples. We're going to have to demand that the information be made available to decision makers."

"Or skip the middleman and go straight to the media," said Archie, looking up again.

"Eventually, but remember, we're not supposed to have this information, Archie."

"Who cares!" he said, his voice rising an octave. "Who cares," he said more calmly, drawing a deep breath. "This only confirms our worst fears. It could well be that the sea lice that are breeding in the Atlantic-salmon pens up Tribune Channel—likely at that new operation at Jeopardy Rock, where the old DFO station is—are even worse than what we've seen before. Do you know what this could mean come spring? When half a million pink-salmon smolts swim down Knight Inlet? It could be disaster. It could wipe them out!"

Petrel stood and poured them both more tea. "We don't know what this means, Archie. We're going to need more information. We're going to need to verify this ourselves," she said.

"Damn right we're going to."

"Okay, so how?"

"We're going to start taking samples further up the inlet, up around Jeopardy Rock."

"Archie, you know this better than most, I think. Maybe you know this better than I do. Salmon hold this ecosystem together. They hold it together and they give it life. They are the energy that everything else feeds off." She stood up, urgency making her restless. "We're going to lose this animal if we don't do something, and do it soon."

Archie said nothing. He turned his eyes to her. "I don't know what to do anymore. I just don't know what else to do. We've spent the last two years piling reports and papers and evidence on the desk of the minister, and he just doesn't seem to get it. It's not that the information isn't compelling. The scientific evidence is plain as the nose on my face! But he doesn't care. The government doesn't seem to care. The evidence is clear; it's the will on their part to do something, anything, with it that is missing.

"You know," she started again after a brief pause, "that when fishermen bring me these farmed Atlantic salmon, the ones that have escaped from Stoboltz's pens, they practically fall apart in my hands? I can scrape the meat off with my hands and make a snowball out of it, Archie. It's awful. There is no muscle in these fish at all. And cut them open! There is a band of fat that twines around their organs that is completely unnatural. Their guts are just a mess, and where they have been vaccinated against the disease that is rampant in those pens, their guts have actually adhered together, actually bound up into a knot. You can see where the needle has been stuck in them."

"I've seen it, too," said Archie. "We call them 'death with fins.'"

Cassandra nodded. "You know, if I wanted to devise a plan for killing wild salmon, I'd do exactly what Stoboltz and the government are doing. I'd build a series of open-net pens along the most productive migration routes for wild salmon, and I'd stock those farms with disease-riddled fish that are full of sea lice, and then I'd sit back and do nothing. I'd just wait. Because the fry and smolts that are born in the headwater tributaries are going to swim right past those pens. They run the gauntlet when they do. And what we're seeing now is that most of them aren't going to make it. And now, to make it worse, it looks like the sea lice are growing more tenacious. We need to figure out what the hell is going on at Jeopardy Rock."

She sat down, the wind blown out of her sails. "Archie," she said, her face in her hands, "if we lose the salmon, we're going to lose the whole thing. Killer whales. Grizzly bears. The web of life on the land and in the sea is dependent on these animals. We lose the salmon, it's like pulling the plug. It's like pulling the electrical cord that powers this whole ecosystem. The whole place will go dark. This whole archipelago will go dark."

■ Archie Ravenwing sat at his own cluttered desk, his feet propped on a clear corner, his cordless phone in his hands. He looked around the room. Filing cabinets, a club chair, a table piled high with band business. Aquaculture, logging, and grizzly bear hunting files. On the wall was a series of marine charts showing the Broughton Archipelago and Knight Inlet at 1:50,000 scale. Red Xs marked the locations of salmon farms, Blue Xs the locations where he or Cassandra Petrel had taken samples. He would extend those blue Xs further into Tribune Channel and up Knight Inlet itself this winter, towing plankton nets in search of sea lice larvae. He would do everything in his power to stop to proliferation of the red Xs.

He looked out the window at his unfinished deck. He shook his head. A big mistake. One that would cost him, no two ways about it. Greg White Eagle had him over a barrel with that. On the other hand, Ravenwing had information that could put Greg behind bars. Or at least ruin his political career. If a man like Greg White Eagle was allowed to get away with this, it would ruin the good name of the North Salish First Nation. And it would ruin his people's way of life.

How far up the chain of command did the collusion extend? Archie knew that Lance Grey was in on it, though to what extent remained a mystery. Did Lance *and* Stoboltz help Greg steal the election from Archie? He wouldn't put it past them. The political machine in Victoria was hungry for an expansion of salmon farming along the BC coast. Archie believed it was possible that Lance provided the necessary political cover for Stoboltz to finance Greg's election bid. It was possible that the minister's office, through Lance, had actually bankrolled it, but so far Archie had no evidence of that. At this point, Archie didn't know what the complicity between Lance Grey and Stoboltz looked like, but he had his suspicions — a gas rebate incentive, where money was doled out to willing voters to get them to the polling station? Maybe vouchers for materials and supplies? Maybe bribes for votes, plain and simple? Archie would have to dig further to get to the bottom of that debacle. But could he use what he found, given what Greg White Eagle had on Archie himself?

He shook his head and cursed himself. "You really fucked up this time, Ravenwing. Pretty dumb, chum," he said.

He looked at the phone. "To hell with it," he said, and dialled a familiar number.

"Minister of Agriculture's office," came the answer.

"Lance Grey, please."

"Can I tell him who's calling?"

"It's Archie Ravenwing."

"Hold a minute, please."

"Lance Grey."

"Hi Lance, it's Archie."

"What can I do for you, Archie?"

"I've got some questions about sea lice."

"Thought you had the expert right there in little Port Lostcoast."

"Not that sort of question."

"I'm listening."

"What I'm wondering is if Stoboltz Aquaculture has a permit to sample for sea lice in the Broughton Archipelago?"

"That's a funny question coming from you. Haven't you been demanding that they do that for the last four years?"

"Does that mean they have a permit?"

"They do. I recall it coming across the minister's desk from DFO late last year."

"Do you know if the results of their studies are going to be made public?"

"I expect that they will. At least some of them. Anything that doesn't directly relate to business decisions will be, anyway."

"Do you know when?"

"Well, if memory serves me, they are doing a three-year study."

Archie blew out through pursed lips. "Bit of a wait, hey?"

"Good science takes time. You know that."

"Fiddling while Rome burns takes time, too."

"Come on, Archie, enough of the doomsday talk. The minister has made a good decision, one that balances the concerns for wild-salmon populations with the need for new salmon aquaculture in the region. This minister has bent over backwards to accommodate your concerns, and those of the environmentalists and people like Cassandra Petrel — "

Archie cut him off. "Let's not be naive, Lance. The minister is doing the minimum necessary to avoid ending up in court on federal fisheries charges while capitulating with Stoboltz and the other salmon farmers in the slow, silent demise of wild salmon."

"Archie, I have to be going now."

"One more question."

Grey was silent on the other end of the phone. Archie heard typing.

"I wonder what Stoboltz intends to do with all of that data, really?"

"You'd have to ask them. I don't know any of the details of their work, Archie." The sound of typing continued. Was Lance Grey checking his email while talking with him? Archie wondered.

"Do you think it's possible that Stoboltz is going to use the data they get to justify their expansion into other areas of the Broughton?"

"Again, you're asking the wrong guy, Archie. I don't know what they plan on doing with the data."

"But they would have had to specify the purpose of the research on the application for the permit to collect."

"Look, I know that the minister signed it, but it was one of dozens that came across his desk from the department. I didn't even look at them."

"Do I need to go through Access to Information?"

"You seem to know how."

"You never know what I might find, Lance."

"Are we through here, Archie?"

"One more question."

"You said that four questions ago."

"These are multi-part questions, Lance." Archie laughed. "Is it possible that Stoboltz is looking at sea lice so they can figure out a way to breed resistance in their Atlantic stocks?"

"Wow, Archie," said Grey, the typing silenced. "Where did you come up with that theory?"

"Well, they aren't doing it out of the goodness of their hearts. And they aren't doing it to figure out how to restrict the expansion of their operations. They are almost certainly going to use their data to expand, but from what I've seen, the data they've come up with is even worse that what Cassandra and I are finding."

"You've seen the data?"

"Yes."

"Stoboltz gave you access?"

"No."

"Archie, how did you come to see what Stoboltz likely considers a trade secret?"

"I'm not prepared to say, Lance," said Archie, smiling.

"You're playing a dangerous game, my friend."

"You think so?"

"I know so, Archie. I don't know what you and Cassandra Petrel are trying to get at, but I can tell you that Stoboltz is a very serious company. Very serious."

"They should lighten up. So should you, Lance. You're going to have a heart attack before you're thirty."

"Laugh if you want, Archie. You've been warned."

The line went dead.

Archie put down the phone and turned his head to look at the harbour. Ravens circled overhead. Was it a murder of ravens? No, that was crows.

"I'm on a roll," he said out loud. "Why stop now?" He snatched the phone and dialled another familiar number, this time with a Vancouver prefix.

"Stoboltz Aquaculture, how may I direct your call?"

"Erik Nilsson, please."

"Erik Nilsson's office."

"Is Mr. Nilsson available?"

"Who can I tell him is on the line?"

"It's Archie Ravenwing."

There was a momentary pause. Archie pictured the CEO of Stoboltz's Canadian operations contemplating whether to ignore a gadfly named Ravenwing or not.

"Hi, Archie, how's it going? It's been a while."

"Yeah, it's been a few months. I was feeling lonely, thought I'd give you a call, Erik."

"How can I help you?"

"Can you tell me what you're doing collecting sea lice in Tribune Channel?"

There was a moment's pause. "We're monitoring the impact of sea lice on both wild salmon and our penned Atlantic salmon. I would have imagined you'd be happy about that."

"I am happy. Very happy. When were you going to tell us?"

"The Aquaculture Advisory Task Force was told last month, Archie. Greg was there."

"He doesn't pass this sort of thing on to his constituents."

"Maybe he doesn't have as good a relationship with the media as you did, Archie. The thing is, we're not exactly ready to have a public discussion about it. It's early days yet."

"Let's level here, Erik, what gives? Why the sudden interest in sea lice?"

"Same reason you and Dr. Petrel are interested, Archie. We want to be good corporate citizens. Contribute to the body of knowledge. Plus, it's to our advantage to understand more about how the lice affect livestock."

Ravenwing smiled at the use of the word. Livestock. It was jarring to hear a word he usually associated with cattle applied to salmon, even if they were non-native Atlantics. "The lice don't affect your fish, isn't that what you keep saying?"

"So far, but who knows about the future."

"I've seen your data."

There was a pause. "Really? That's interesting."

"Interesting, yeah, if you consider results that show the sea lice you've collected are nearly twice as virulent as the ones Doc Petrel and I have collected. What the hell is happening up in Tribune Channel?"

"I'm not really ready to discuss that, Archie."

"Think that maybe the media would be a good place to have this conversation?"

"I don't appreciate you threatening me, Archie. We've always worked to keep this civil, haven't we?"

"You've got information in your possession that shows that sea lice are getting stronger somehow. That they're having a larger and larger impact on salmon smolts."

"It's isolated, Archie. It's a single capture point."

"I want to see all your data. Cassandra and I need to have access to it."

Erik Nilsson was silent. "Okay. I'll ask Dr. Thurlow to drop in the next time he's heading to McNeill. Okay?"

"I want to see it before the month's out, Erik."

"Archie, you'll see it when Thurlow can get over to present it in person. If I hear anything about this from the media, I'm going to ask the RCMP to investigate how you got the data in the first place, are we clear?"

"Clear." Archie hung up and took a deep breath.

16

Longview, Alberta lay along the banks of the Highwood River where it cut a deep canyon through the layers of sedimentary rock that folded into rounded foothills. South of the town, the river burrowed into the stone and snaked eastward toward High River. Nancy Webber was about to close the circle, in more ways than one, she thought. She drove up the highway from the south, distracted and pushing a hundred kilometres per hour when she saw the lights behind her.

"Fuck," she muttered, slowing as the first buildings of the tiny town swept past. She pulled over to the side of the road as the cruiser parked behind her, and a man who must have weighed three hundred pounds eased himself out of the driver's seat.

Her cellphone rang.

The constable approached her and tapped on the window, which she rolled down.

"Driver's licence and registration, please," he said, breathing hard.

Her phone rang again.

She reached into the glove box and produced the necessary documents, along with her driver's licence from her wallet. She snatched up the phone on the fourth ring.

"Webber."

"It's Sergeant Reimer, Nancy."

"Funny you should call right at this moment. I'm getting a speeding ticket."

"That is funny. Where are you?"

"Town of Longview."

"That's a local. RCMP don't patrol in the town."

"All the same to us chickens," she said.

"Pardon?"

"The fox or the chopping block," said Nancy, looking in her mirror at the patrol car.

"I've got something for you," said Reimer.

"Can I call you after I empty my wallet here?"

"Sure." The line went dead.

Ten minutes later Nancy was seated in the Four Winds Café,

a cup of strong, black coffee and a menu in front of her. She ordered toast from the waitress, picked up her cell, pressed call return, and waited.

"So, what do you have?"

"You understand that this is deep background. You can't print this."

"It's not really for a story anyway, but if I do decide to write this one up, I'll get it through official records."

"Okay. Well, I'm only telling you this because you could have hung me out to dry in Oracle and you didn't. We're even."

"What is it that needs this much lead up?"

"I talked to the staff sergeant in Claresholm yesterday. He told me a tale of sadness and woe."

"Go on," said Nancy, cradling her phone to her ear while she spread peanut butter and jam on her toast.

"It seems that all was not well on the Blackwater ranch."

"Tell me something I don't know."

"If you shut up I will," said Reimer.

"Sorry."

"All was not well. It's not in the official record anywhere, but I guess Cole Blackwater used to show up for school pretty busted up sometimes. I mean, he was a boxer and everybody knew it, but he looked like he took a pretty good beating from time to time. Broken nose, black eyes, that sort of thing. Lost a tooth once. That's not the sort of thing that happens in the ring."

"Mother says it was Walter who laid into him. His older brother."

"You believe her?"

"I don't know."

"I know Walter. I met him at a law enforcement training day in the spring. He's a warden at Waterton Lakes National Park. We do an annual firearms training for them. Unless he's changed a lot since he was a boy, he doesn't strike me as the sort. Oh, he could lay a good beating if he wanted to. The man is still rock solid. But he doesn't have the disposition for it, unless he's a psychopath and is just putting everybody on. But if that was the case, he'd have some arrests on his jacket, you know, for assault and the like, but there's nothing. He's clean as a whistle."

"You checked."

"I'm trying to be thorough. So Cole shows up pretty beaten up at school. Could be boxing matches with other boys, or maybe a little schoolyard roughhouse, right? Well, I can't say this for certain, but my guess is no, it's not. My friend on the desk at Claresholm thinks it was the old man."

"Yeah, that listens," said Nancy, taking a bite of toast.

"Yeah, it lines up. The old man has a record. A pretty long one. No convictions, but lots of arrests. Small-town stuff, you know, some fisticuffs here and there. Settled out of court a couple of times, paid his debt in labour and the like. My friend at the Clarseholm detachment says that Blackwater stayed out of trouble after the sons came along. But Cole started showing up at school pretty beaten up when he was like twelve or thirteen."

"You say that's not on record?"

"It's a small town. Everybody knows everybody else. No secrets."

"Right," said Nancy. It doesn't need to be a small town not to have any secrets, she thought.

"Okay, so that's Cole. So when the old man supposedly pops himself four years back, Cole just happens to be home at the time, first time in years, you understand. Like first time in two decades. People start to ask the same questions you're asking."

"Was there an investigation?"

"God, no. The old man's prints were on the rifle and the branding iron. No latents from Cole. They did look that far. And the old lady confirms that Cole was in the house when they heard the blast."

"She could be lying," said Nancy, lowering her voice, looking around her. "She strikes me as being pretty protective."

"Fat lot of good it did Cole."

"Yeah."

"But," added Reimer, "you know how that sort of thing goes. The old lady likely overlooked the whole thing. She didn't want to get into it. Didn't want to believe that her husband was beating her son right under her nose."

"She said that Walter got the better of Cole while they were training."

"Well, you and I know that's not the case."

"Okay, so you're saying that it's pretty likely that Henry Blackwater was laying a beating on Cole on a pretty regular basis. And that there were pretty strong suspicions when the old bastard blew his brains out that Cole had more than a passing interest in seeing him dead."

"That's right."

"Where does Walter figure in all this?"

"I don't know."

"I met him last night," said Nancy.

"Where?"

"At the ranch."

"You really got balls, don't you?"

"You know it. I went out for dinner and when Mrs. Blackwater and I were having coffee afterward, in walks Walter. He was pretty surprised to see me. I guess Cole had told him about me. Anyway," she said, "we went for a walk this morning and had a chat. He's a real likeable guy."

"Likeable, and unlikely to punch up his brother, it seems to me."

"Yeah, he seems to care about Cole a lot. Maybe that's guilt."

"For what?"

"For letting his father beat the snot out of his little brother and not doing anything to stop it." Nancy looked around the café. She was alone.

"Well, it doesn't help to say this, but I will. Not much a teenager can do to stop a fully grown man from taking out his anger on another boy. Walter's a big lad, but old man Blackwater was a real bruiser. Did you know he fought for the overseas title in 1944?"

Nancy shook her head. "How did you find that out?"

"Got a friend on the base at CFB Suffield with connections."

"I'm impressed. And a little humbled. How did he do?"

"Draw. A black man named Bombshell Bismarck who was in the artillery was the other boxer. He outweighed Blackwater by some forty pounds and towered over him by four inches."

"Jesus. You think that old man Blackwater felt jaded by that and started reliving his glory days back on the ranch?"

"Who knows? I'm no shrink. I did ask about his service record. Apparently Blackwater landed at Juno Beach—"

"On D-Day?"

"Yeah. Pretty impressive. Says that he suffered 'unidentified wounds' and was shipped back to England. Missed all the action."

"What does that mean?"

"Seasick."

"You're kidding."

"That's what my friend at Suffield thinks, anyway. It's not in his military record. He went on to do mop-up work in northern Europe, but missed most of the fun in France and Germany."

"That would piss a guy off, especially if he was a hothead spoiling for a fight."

"Seems consistent with that we've learned."

"That's some good detective work, Sergeant. Thanks."

"No trouble. We're even now."

"That we are."

"So that's pretty much what I know at this point. I don't know if you're any further ahead."

"I don't know that I am either, but this does shed some light on Henry Blackwater," said Nancy. She'd taken her cheque to the counter and paid it with a five-dollar bill. She stepped out onto the gravel in front of the Four Winds. "But, I think in the long run I might be farther behind."

"How so?"

"I think I've got two brothers with good reason to pop their old man instead of just one."

"So long as you know that's your problem, not mine," said Reimer.

"For now," said Webber. "Well, thanks for this. Now I think *I* owe *you* one."

"I'll collect, trust me."

Nancy hung up and went to her car. She opened the door and sat down, but left the door open. The weather was warm, the wind out of the west. It blew dust into little swirls that skipped across the road like tornadoes in training, bouncing their way between the freshly painted walls of the Longview Hotel and the rusted-out auto-repair shop next door. The sky above was streaked with oblong clouds that Nancy thought looked like spaceships. It was warm, nearly fifteen degrees, and the birds sang as if there would never be another snow again.

Walter Blackwater had said it was a chinook.

■ "Chinook. Isn't that just in the winter?"

"Well, technically speaking it still is," said Walter Blackwater. They stood at the top of the ridge above the ranch, the naked branches of aspens bending in the steady wind. Nancy leaned into it a little. "But chinooks can blow year-round. They are just more dramatic in the winter. They melt all the snow. Turn a winter deep-freeze into a thaw over night."

"You really are a park ranger, aren't you?"

"Warden. We call ourselves wardens in Canada."

Nancy nodded, looking west toward the ridges that made up the Whaleback, a thirty-kilometre chain of hills that looked like the spine of a long, beached whale. Below, hidden by the folds of the Porcupine Hills, ran Highway 22. After that, the hills rose and fell until they pressed up against Livingstone Ridge, the front range of the Rocky Mountains. Beyond its jagged back she could see more mountains, blue and grey in the morning light, their crowns and leeward slopes still plastered with spring snow.

"That's the Continental Divide," said Walter, pointing to a triangular shaped peak on the horizon. "That peak is called Tornado Mountain."

Nancy nodded again, pulling the warm, dry air into her lungs. "This is a beautiful place," she said. "It must have been amazing to grow up here."

"The landscape couldn't be beat. Cole and I would sometimes disappear into these hills for a few days — take off when we got off the bus after school on a Friday — and show up for dinner on Sunday, sunburnt and full of bug bites and scrapes and bruises. Scared the hell out of our mother. Caught hell from our father for letting our chores go. It was worth it. Yeah, it was a pretty great place to be a kid."

"You'd catch hell from your dad?"

"Dad was pretty much giving us hell all the time, so it really didn't matter what it was about. I don't think he knew how to deal with us boys."

"How'd you take that?"

"Don't know what you mean."

"I guess I just mean that must have been hard."

"Yup, he was a tough old man. He served, you know? World War II. Before Cole or I were born. But I heard that he had a pretty rough time overseas. He never really talked about it."

"Was he angry about something?"

"Henry Blackwater was angry about everything. Angry and frustrated as hell."

"And did he take it out on you?"

"Cole caught the worst of it. I guess he's told you. The old man liked to use him as a punching bag sometimes."

"Cole told me," Nancy lied.

"I never seemed to get under the old man's skin, you know? Somehow Cole always did."

"He's good at that. It's a skill. Hell, I've slugged him a few times," said Nancy, sitting down and leaning against an aspen.

Walter squatted and plucked a piece of dried grass and put it in his teeth. With his stained Stetson, Wrangler jeans, and canvas coat he looked like someone out of an ad for Alberta beef. Nancy looked at him. Walter was smiling at her joke.

"I'm sorry. That was crass," she said. The sun had crept along its arc and now spilled light like liquid honey across the convoluted folds of earth before them. In the darkness of the dales little could be seen, but along the brightly lit ridges the naked shapes of aspens and the twisted forms of pine trees were easily distinguishable. The whole Livingstone Range was bathed in the radiance.

"There's nothing a little boy could do to deserve what our old man gave us. Gave Cole."

"It was pretty hard on you, wasn't it?"

Walter looked across at Nancy. She was watching the sun on the distant mountains. "It was. Pretty hard. I felt impotent. I couldn't stop him. I couldn't stop him from hurting Cole. And I was stupid enough to believe that he wouldn't hurt our mother, so I didn't even think to try and stop him from doing that."

Nancy kept her focus on the distant peaks. "Did he hit your mom?"

He sighed. "I think so. In the later years. After Cole left he seemed to lose much of his rage. It was like the wind went out of his sails. But as he got older, it seemed to fester again, that anger. I only learned about it by accident. I saw Mom covering up a bruise with some makeup. She said she had fallen. But I've spent enough time reading people's eyes that I know when they're lying," he said. "And I'm pretty sure she was."

"Did you tell Cole?"

Walter sighed again. "No. Not me. I only found out after the old man died. I think our mom let it slip. When Cole was back here."

"How did he take it?"

"How do you think? You know Cole."

"Not well."

"He confronted the old man. The rest is history." Walter stood up, dusted off his Wranglers, and extended a hand to Nancy. "What went on between Cole and our old man that day in the barn is between the old man, Cole, and whatever god he's currently aligned with, if any at all."

Nancy took Walter's hand and stood. "Something is eating away at Cole, Walter. He's shut down. He's put up a wall between whatever it is that's eating him and the rest of us. He's closed down from everybody who cares for him. He's terrified and angry. I'm afraid of what it might do to him, Walter."

Walter looked across to the Livingstone Range in the distance, that space filled with golden light, deep shadows, and only a few places left unknown to a man who had lived his life exploring these hills and valleys. "I'm afraid, too," said Walter when he finally turned to step back onto the trail that led back to the ranch house. "I'm afraid, too."

■ Nancy looked up at the white cinder block wall of the Four Winds Café. Her hands were tightly wrapped around the wheel of her car. Her knuckles white. Cole, you bastard, you need to come clean, she thought to herself, or it's going to kill you. Or someone else.

Now what? she thought. Now where? I'm no farther ahead than I was when Cole called me on Saturday morning. I'm supposed to be back in Edmonton today, or I'm going to lose another reporting job. Whose fault will that be? Cole Blackwater's, she thought, tightening the grip on the wheel. She checked the time on her cellphone. It was ten-thirty in the morning. A long day already. Bloody ranchers getting up before the sun. And her with miles to go before she slept. But miles to go where?

When her cellphone rang, she screamed and jolted her arm violently, knocking it against the driver's side door, dropping the cell to the floor. She bent forward to get it and bumped her head on the steering wheel. "Jesus Christ," she said, blindly retrieving the phone from the floor. "Webber," she said, snapping the phone open.

"Nancy, it's Cole."

Speak of the devil. Her mind raced. "Cole, hi. How are things in Port Lostcoast? How is Archie's family?"

"They're fine, Nancy. Things are fine. Well, not exactly fine. Nancy, I have a problem and I need some help."

17 The night had grown colder still. The sky was clear of clouds. To the north and west, the dim lights of Port McNeill glowed faintly on the horizon. Beyond that intrusion, Cole Blackwater could see stars beyond counting. The smear of the Milky Way was painted across the heavens, a broad tapestry behind which hung a million galaxies. Each star nothing more than a pinprick of light seen from the government dock on an island off an island on the far western shore of North America.

It had been a few hours since Constable Derek Johns had ushered him, Grace, Jacob, and Darren from the *Inlet Dancer.*

"What happens next?" Cole had asked Johns.

Johns looked at the boat from the dock while he spoke. "We bring in the forensic ID section from Campbell River. We'll work with the harbour master to find a dry dock for the boat, and we'll go over it with a fine-toothed comb. The forensics team has a trained serologist on staff—that's someone who specializes in things like blood—and they will do some tests on the boat. If it is blood, we'll first determine if it's human, and then if it's from Mr. Ravenwing. If we get that far, we'll need a DNA sample. A hairbrush or toothbrush."

The four friends were silent.

Cole turned to look from Constable Winters to the *Inlet Dancer.* "Does this mean you're changing the nature of the investigation?"

"No. But it does mean that the boat is off-limits now. Blood indicates trauma, and we'll need to make sure it doesn't come from fish he had on board before he went missing, that it's not a result of any ... foul play."

After leaving the *Inlet Dancer*, Cole, Grace, Jacob, and Darren ate dinner together at a pub, then found accommodation. Grace and Jacob bunked with a cousin who lived on the hilltop near the Big House on the west side of town. Darren opted to sleep on Jacob's boat. Cole found a bed and breakfast near the centre of town.

"Will you be all right?" he asked Grace.

"I'll be fine," she said. "Fine."

But he didn't believe her. The image of Derek Johns' tacky red fingertips kept Cole awake that night. So violent an end for Archie Ravenwing. A man who had made the sea his life should be consigned to it, thought Cole Blackwater, his breath forming vapour clouds before him as he stood at the top of the metal ramp that led to the wooden pier. But why so violently?

He took a deep breath and exhaled, blowing the mist far out into the night. That a life should end with such violence was hard for Cole to accept. But then, he had seen it before, hadn't he?

Hadn't he seen the blood of the man murdered in Oracle? Plenty of it, Cole recalled.

And he had seen his father's blood, too.

He suppressed a wave of anger that started just below his gut and rose up through him, wrapping itself around his heart. That anger flowed like molten magma, down the length of his arms and into his hands, which instinctively balled into fists.

Cole wanted to kill that man the other night. Dan Campbell. The bigoted, inbred, degenerate, redneck hillbilly who had called Cole an "Indian lover," as if that, somehow, was the worst thing Campbell could call Blackwater. While they were fighting, Cole fantasized about punching the man again and again in the face. Mashing his nose and lips and cheeks to a pulp. Cole drew a sharp breath. He flexed his hands. The anger eased a little, slipping from his extended fingers like water might drip from a man standing in the rain. He both loved and hated the feeling it gave him. It was a drug, no doubt about it. It coursed through his veins, and it made him feel powerful and vulnerable at the same time.

Anger was the fuel that Cole Blackwater used to propel himself through his days.

His mind searched for the origin of it. It wasn't hard to find. It was a voice. A face. An odour. A presence, large and looming. A jar of moonshine. A set of balled fists.

Cole walked down the metal ramp and onto the pier, toward where the *Inlet Dancer* was still moored on the docks.

It had been a lot of blood, guessed Cole. Too much blood, he kept thinking to himself. Archie would have had to have hit his head really hard to produce a wound that bled like that, especially with the sea washing over the boat. He would have bled himself dry, thought Cole, his eyes hard on the far end of the pier, where the *Inlet Dancer* bobbed in the moonlight.

It had been a lot of blood. A shotgun at close range is a crude, rudimentary weapon. It produces a combination of devastating, blunt force and the staccato sharpness of a thousand tiny knives. They are tightly clustered. Thousands of tiny ball bearings racing at the speed of sound. Each of them with enough cutting power to inflict a tiny wound, but, when clustered together tightly, they form a steel fist that can reduce a person's body, face, life, to a pasty mess. Cole found it amazing that there are only five pints of blood in the whole human body, because he was certain that he had seen so much more come out of his father when he had been cut down by the blast of the 12-gauge shotgun that night in the barn.

Cole stood before the *Inlet Dancer.* A sawhorse with a Keep Out By Order of RCMP sign stood between him and the boat, but there was no officer present. It might be a matter of a few minutes before an RCMP officer returned to watch over Archie's boat. He looked around for any sign that he was being watched. No one. He stepped around the sign and onto the bow. The boat nodded on the flat water. Cole could see the curving bay that flanked the tiny port town, and he could see the distant lights of Port Mc-Neill. In the narrow channel between Cormorant Island and the Nimpkish River on Vancouver Island, Cole could see the lights of a small cruise ship making its way along the darkened coast.

For all his sight, Cole at times seemed puzzled at the lack of *insight* into the roots of the anger that burned inside of him. But when he considered this under the unflinching glare of moon and stars, he knew this wasn't true. Cole knew that he *had* insight enough, and that he hid behind his own ignorance to keep from facing the truth. Cole knew exactly where his anger came from. It was hereditary. Not passed down through genealogy, but learned. Through behaviour. He took a sharp breath and moved around the boat in the dark, stepped toward the anger that burrowed within him, and the violence that had taken Archie Ravenwing's life.

All souls are one, someone had once told him. He closed his

eyes to recall where he had been when he heard that. Cortes Island. *Of course.* A political strategy session turned group hug. He had been sitting on the beach, drinking out of a bottle of wine, while others in the group danced around a blazing fire to the sound of an African rhythm.

"Our souls are like the Milky Way," a man said, sitting next to him, uninvited, unwelcome. "Seen from a great distance they appear as if they are one great light. It's only close up that individuals appear. All our thoughts, and all our actions, arise from that common place among us all."

Cole had continued to stare across Desolation Sound toward the lights of Powell River. He took a deep pull on the bottle of wine, then another, and indeed the stars did all fade into one.

Now Cole looked up at the sky from the deck of the *Inlet Dancer*. All souls are one, eh, he thought. All thoughts and action arise from that common place between us? All anger, all hatred, all cruelty, all violence, all lust, all greed, all fear is born there and wells up though an individual to come into the world? Why does it pick one man over another? And why does all love, all peace, all joy, all fortune, and all compassion choose differently?

He moved to the stern of the boat, to the pilothouse. The faint glow of the moon left the cabin in dark shadow. Cole sat on the high seat and took the wheel in his hands. He closed his eyes. Imagined the storm. He stood. Archie would have been standing. He took the wheel and played it back and forth. He let his body roll as if he too were on the sea. He turned to look behind him at the engines' hatch engines. Five feet, maybe six, he guessed. He rolled again and imagined a wave breaking against the side of the boat and let his body float sideways, as if thrown by the force of the water crashing onto the deck.

Archie was six inches shorter than Cole, so he crouched a little and rolled again, holding on to the wheel as he imagined Archie would have. What would Archie have hit his head against? Cole pitched again, letting his legs buckle. There was a rib of metal on the casing of the pilothouse that was an inch thick. A heavy handle was welded on either side of the opening to allow a mariner to steady himself moving in or out of the cockpit. Cole let himself press up against that rib of metal, imagining a giant wave catching him from the side and pushing him there. Where would his head connect? He guessed that it would be about four feet above the deck. That is, if Archie had been standing when he hit his head. Cole let his hand trace the cool metal, looking for any sign that this might have been where Archie had suffered the mortal wound that spilt so much of his blood onto the deck of the *Inlet Dancer*.

There was no mark. No indentation. Nothing. The metal was cool and smooth and unmarked.

He did the same on the other side, running his hand softly down the smoothness of the metal, as if caressing the smooth skin of a lover.

Cole stood again. If Archie was making for home, as Bertrand had suggested, and his boat was found on Protection Point, at the mouth of Knight Inlet, the waves would not have taken him on the side, but head on. Cole knew very little about the sea, but he guessed that Archie would have wanted to hit the coming waves with the bow, or risk capsizing.

Cole gripped the wheel and then let himself fall backward, as if a great wave had crashed across the bow of the boat and jarred its very foundation. He caught his back on the seat and let himself fall forward. His head touched the metal below the wheel. He knelt there, searching in the darkness for something that could have caused such a wound on Archie Ravenwing's head. There was a small compartment under the wheel, like the glove box in a car, but rather than being closed, it was open for easy access. Cole felt around it with his fingers. Could this have been where Archie contracted his fatal wound?

Cole's fingers touched something plastic. He took it by the tips of his fingers and pulled. It was a heavy plastic pouch with a zipper that sealed as it was drawn closed. He held it up to the moonlight to see its contents through the opaque plastic, but could not make it out. He looked around the pilothouse for a flashlight, and remembered that Grace had looked under the seat. He popped the seat open and found a heavy flashlight near the top of the contents of the storage container. He looked around the dock again. Still alone, he flicked it on and opened the bag. Inside was a map: it was the marine chart that included parts of Knight Inlet and Tribune Channel, where Archie could well have spent part of his last day on this earth. Also in the pouch were a red and a blue Sharpie marker and a pencil that had been sharpened with a pocket knife. Cole flipped the bench seat down and sat again, unfolding the map on his lap, keeping the light low lest he be seen by a passerby.

The chart had prominent red Xs at Doctor Islets, Sergeant Pass, and Jeopardy Rock. Blue Xs pocked the page, extending up from the mouth of Knight Inlet, beyond Sergeant Pass, and as far up Tribune Channel as Jeopardy Rock. Each blue X had a date beside it. Cole read the dates, following Archie's progress with the blue Xs from late in the fall of last year to March, and the day of the heavy storm believed to have claimed Archie's life. The blue X with the March date was located just a half mile beyond Jeopardy Rock.

Cole knew that the red Xs were salmon farms. He'd seen such a map on the SOS website. But what were the blue Xs? He'd have to ask Cassandra Petrel. Maybe she would know.

Cole studied the chart. He was about the fold it back into its waterproof pouch when he saw, written in the margin, something that caught his eye. It was his name. He held the light closer to see the faint scratch of the pencil. "Call SOS, call Cole, call the media," he read.

"Call Cole," he said under his breath. "Call Cole. You didn't get the chance, Archie. What was it you were going to tell me?" Cole pleaded.

Cole stood and flicked off the flashlight, returning it under the seat and folding the map into its pouch. He was about to slip it back beneath the pilot wheel, but decided that he would keep it instead.

Cole looked back at the deck of the boat, and at the gunwales. A wave large enough to float a bleeding man's body off the floor and over the side of the *Inlet Dancer* would have been large enough to carry everything else on the deck with it — but Jacob, Grace, and Darren had cleaned up fishing gear and floats from the deck. And Archie's thermos. Had a rogue wave caught Archie by surprise and flipped him over the edge?

Or had something else caught him by surprise?

What are you thinking? Cole Blackwater asked himself. What *exactly* are you thinking? The blood didn't lie. You couldn't conceal its meaning, try as you might.

Cole had spent the last four years trying to erase the image of the blood leaping from his father's head. Cole had pushed that memory so far down inside the dark recesses of his mind that he had almost convinced himself it hadn't happened. That he had stopped it. That his old man — that angry, dangerous man who beat his own son, and later turned his fists on his wife, on Cole Blackwater's mother — was somewhere, alive. But blood didn't lie.

Blood didn't lie. He stepped from the *Inlet Dancer*, the crescent moon low on the horizon now, casting a pale shadow of Blackwater along the length of the dock. He saw a man walk up the metal ramp far at the end of the pier, where it met the walkway along the main road through town. Another restless soul who could not, or would, not sleep.

■ Cole awoke late in the morning. Though he hadn't had a drink the night before, he felt hungover with the weight of what had been revealed. He sat up in bed, his face still tender from the blows that Dan Campbell had delivered, his fist still aching from the beating he had given Campbell in return. Two angry men meeting head-on like freight trains in the night. "Still having our way with them" was what Dan had said about the people of Port Lostcoast. His was an attitude leftover from two centuries of abuse, officially expunged but unofficially living on in the bigoted, twisted hearts of a few men who hadn't, and never would, join the rest of Canadian society in the twenty-first century.

Two angry men.

How angry? thought Cole, standing up, stretching. His body felt half decent, a change from years of sluggish decline. He dropped to the floor and did twenty push-ups. He tapped his stomach, which still slumped a little over the elastic of his briefs but was starting to show some definition again.

How angry was Dan Campbell? "Fucked over," he had said. Archie had gone up against Campbell on every major environmental issue to hit the coast of British Columbia. Grizzly bear hunting, logging, fish farming, you name it.

Cole closed his eyes and saw the stern of the *Inlet Dancer*. How angry? Angry enough to step onto Archie Ravenwing's boat, and what? Cole swallowed hard at the image.

He sat down on the bed, suddenly light-headed. He held out his hand and it trembled.

"Get a hold of yourself, man."

But there was no denying it. He looked at the pile of clothes on the floor where he had dumped them the night before. On top was the sealed map pouch. No denying it. Archie was onto something. But he hadn't made it back from Tribune Channel and Jeopardy Rock in time to make his calls.

He needed help sorting through this tangled mess. His thoughts were clouded. Did he dare burden Grace with his suspicions? No. She had suffered too much. And Darren, while affable, was too simple to provide the tough questions that Cole required to unravel and understand what really happened on the *Inlet Dancer* the night Archie Ravenwing went missing. No, there was only one person, and Cole knew it. He picked up the phone on the stand next to his bed and dialled. He waited through four rings and was about to hang up.

"Webber."

"Nancy, it's Cole."

She paused a moment. "Cole, hi. How are things in Port Lostcoast? How is Archie's family?"

"They're fine, Nancy. Things are fine. Well, not exactly fine. Nancy, I have a problem and I need some help."

"What is it, Cole?"

"Where are you?"

There was a pause. "Near Calgary. On a story. What is it? You sound awful."

"Nancy, I need you to come to Port Lostcoast."

"What's going on, Cole?"

"I think Archie Ravenwing was murdered."

18 Another year around the sun, Archie Raven-wing was thinking, walking along Government Street in Victoria. He was headed south, toward James Bay and the provincial legislature. He wore his best town clothes. Clean blue jeans, a pressed white shirt with bolo tie, and a grey tweed sports coat. His hair was combed neatly, in contrast to its usual disarray.

As he crossed the street at the tourism centre, the Capitol rotunda hove into view. He had always loved the legislature buildings, though many of his people did not. They had been built on land claimed by the Esquimalt First Nation, which had caused its share of consternation, but the province was in the process of settling up on that old account. Many of the decisions that came forth from the erratic provincial governments in BC regarding First Nations people had created a deep distrust of nearly all of the province's institutions among many of his people.

But Archie simply loved the architecture of the BC Legislature. He loved the symmetrical elegance of the andesite stone structure. He passed the Empress Hotel's ivy ensconced walls, feeling the hot sun on his face. For more than a month the entire coast had been socked in with rain, sleet, and fog, but this morning the sun had appeared through a crack in the grey canopy overhead, and now, close to noon, the sun burned through the implacable dome of heaven.

Another year around the sun. It had been a raven, the trickster, who had stolen the sun and placed it in the sky to bring light to the earth. He smiled at the children's tale. Today, he thought, *this* raven is going to shed some light on another growing darkness. His marine charts were tucked under an arm, and in a worn and weather-beaten leather shoulder bag he carried reports and printouts that he and Cassandra Petrel had compiled over the winter.

Another year. Today was Archie Ravenwing's sixty-first birthday. Rather than celebrating it on the water, he was in Victoria, pecking away at the conundrum of Jeopardy Rock and the Broughton Archipelago. Pecking, as a raven would, on the barnacled shell of a clam it had dropped from the sky.

All spring he'd been sampling up Knight Inlet, sometimes sleeping on his boat, sometimes arriving home late at night only to turn around and head back out at first light. He'd added dozens of blue Xs to his map, and the picture they painted was bleak.

He waited for the light at Superior, then crossed onto the Legislature grounds.

Before he left, his daughter had told him that she was worried about him.

"You're not sleeping, Dad," she said, sitting with him at the kitchen table early one morning. The sun wasn't painting the eastern horizon yet.

Archie had smiled up at her, his face bright. "There's nothing to worry about, Gracie. Everything is just fine," he said, sipping his coffee and reaching for his toast.

"You're gone up the inlet nearly every day. You look exhausted."

"I'm just fine, really, darling. But thank you for worrying about me. Since your mother passed on, it's good to know I'm making somebody worried sick." He grinned.

Grace looked down.

"I'm sorry. All I meant was that it's nice that you're looking out for your old man, that's all."

"People are talking, Dad."

"So? Let them talk," he said, biting his toast. "They can talk all they like. I'm onto something, something big, and I intend to find out what the hell is going on around here."

Grace smiled. "I love it when you get all fired up, Dad, but I'm just worried. Whatever you and Cassandra are doing seems to have all the folks around here pretty riled up. You know that most of the band doesn't want salmon farming any more than you do, but they have their futures to think of. Greg White Eagle won the election saying he would take the case for more salmon farming to the band council, and that's what he's doing."

"Greg White Eagle is a crook. He's on the take."

Grace was silent. Archie stood and looked out the window at the sheets of rain falling across the harbour below. Finally Grace said, "Do you have proof?"

"Yeah."

"In writing?"

"Yeah. I've got an email. It's enough."

"What are you going to do?"

"Nothing. Not yet."

Grace stood and cleared the dishes from the table. Then she walked over and looked at him.

"What has he got on you, Dad?"

Archie smiled. "What makes you think he's got anything?"

"You're not the type to sit on your hands."

Archie's smile faded. "I just need to build my case against him. I don't want White Eagle and his pals at Stoboltz and in the minister's office to get spooked. Not yet."

"What are you looking for?"

"That's the trouble. I don't know. Stoboltz is up to something, something big. They've been sending samples of sea lice to Victoria for analysis, and what they are finding is way worse than what Cassandra and I are turning up. We keep trying to duplicate their samples — that's why I've been all over Knight Inlet and Tribune Channel this spring, as the smolts start to move, trying to figure out why Stoboltz is coming up with such virulent sea lice samples. More lice, bigger wounds on the fish. But I can't duplicate it. It's driving me crazy."

▬ She hadn't pressed him on what Greg White Eagle held over his own guilty head. He hated to lie to her, but he needed to understand more about the Stoboltz sea lice before he could decide what to do with his information on the band councillor.

He walked up the steps of the Legislature and through the heavy wooden doors. He felt a new mixture of emotions as he passed through the portal: delight that he once again was walking the halls of power, doing his part to influence their direction for his people, and sadness that he no longer held the ear of anybody in this building. He signed in with security, affixed his visitor's pass to the lapel of his sports coat, and proceeded down the hall toward the rotunda. There he turned left and followed the maze of corridors to the familiar office of the minister of agriculture.

He climbed a flight of stairs, turned right at the top, and found the wooden door to the office open.

He stepped into the waiting room and was greeted by a receptionist. "May I help you?" the young man asked.

"It's Archie Ravenwing. I'm here to see the minister."

The young man looked down at a calendar. "Hold on just one minute, Mr. Ravenwing." He picked up the phone and punched in some numbers. "Lance Grey will be right out."

Archie stood a moment, regarding the prints on the wall, looking at the portrait of the premier behind the head of the receptionist.

"Hi, Archie," came a voice from behind him. "Please, step into my office."

Archie turned and saw Lance Grey. He was dressed casually, an orange shirt and black slacks and no coat or tie. He gestured for Archie to follow him.

When they were in Lance's office, he closed the door and asked Archie to sit in one of the leather club chairs across from his desk. "The minister has been called away on business this morning, Archie. I'm sorry. You won't be able to see him today."

Archie felt his heart beating in his chest.

"There has been a case of bird flu discovered on a farm near Port Coquitlam on the mainland. He's gone over to see to the situation himself. I'm sorry, I know we should have called you this morning. He's going to be tied up with this file for a few days. I don't think we'll be able to reschedule," said Grey, his hands folded neatly on his empty desk.

Archie forced a smile. "I understand."

"I spoke with him this morning, and he asked me to meet with you and bring forward anything that you wanted to pass on. I'm happy to do that, Archie."

"Well," said Ravenwing, looking down at this own hands resting on his knees. "Well, I don't know if that will do much good."

"You were here to talk with the minister about salmon farming. He's pretty aware of your concerns, Archie."

Archie took a breath. "Hasn't seemed to help matters."

"Depends on your point of view. We're putting people to work.

I thought you would be happy about that. You've got unemployment rates that are in the high fifties, low sixties in some bands along the coast."

"You don't have to tell me, Lance. I know the numbers. I was on council for a decade. I know the situation."

"So we're putting people to work. Good jobs. Jobs that pay a good wage. It's going to lift people out of poverty."

"My argument with you isn't on job creation. It's the type of job. The North Salish First Nation has been making its living off the sea for thousands of years before Captain Vancouver first laid eyes on this coast."

"Still are, Archie. That's my point."

"But not the way we used to. Not in a way that respects the ecosystem, that is sustainable."

"Times change. Progress, Archie. You're out of step. You're behind the times."

Archie looked down again. "Sure, times change. You see me resisting it? Hell, I've even got a cellphone. I've got email. I've got a GPS on my boat. I'm happy to go along with progress when it's helping me and my people live in a way that respects the nature of things. But the salmon farms are going to put an end to the wild salmon stocks. Slowly, but surely, they will kill off the wild salmon."

Lance Grey sat back in his chair. "That's alarmist talk, Archie. You sound like a raving environmentalist when you talk that way."

"The numbers don't lie, Lance. Less than one hundred thousand pinks in the run in the Broughton last year. There used to be millions. How do you explain that?"

"There's lots of reasons for that. Changes in ocean temperatures, changing currents. And I won't deny that logging has taken a toll on the salmon-spawning streams. But you're trying to blame all of this on salmon farming and I just don't buy it."

"Sea lice will be the death of the wild stocks. The juveniles can't handle the stress it puts on them. And you and your minister and your pals at Stoboltz are sitting on research that confirms our worst fears."

"We're back to this again," said Lance, twisting in his chair to look out the window. Archie couldn't see his eyes.

"I came here to ask the minister for an explanation."

"You're not going to get one from *him*, Archie."

"He won't tell me, or he doesn't know?"

"The minister has the big picture to think about. He leaves the details to his staff, and to his department. We don't trouble him with the minutiae of these matters," said Lance, his gaze focused on Victoria's inner harbour.

"I think it's time you understood something, Lance," said Archie. "What you seem to be treating as a game of cat and mouse is deadly serious. We're talking about the future of a species. A creature that has, for tens of thousands of years, been at the centre of my people's way of life. A creature that is the backbone of an entire ecosystem. No salmon, no bears. No salmon, no eagles. No salmon, no ecosystem. This is deadly serious." Archie started to unfold his marine chart with its red and blue Xs.

"Don't lecture me, Archie, on how serious this is." Lance Grey swivelled in his chair. "I know exactly how serious this is. You're in over your head. Way over your head."

Archie stared at the man. He was less than half his age. He felt a wave of revulsion wash over him, and he choked down the words he wanted to yell. He felt his fingers tremble on the map, and he tried to calm himself. "I've been sampling up Tribune Channel and in the inlet for the last month. We're seeing massive numbers of sea lice on the early migrating juveniles. But nothing like what I saw when I looked at Stoboltz's numbers last fall. How do you explain that, Lance?"

"I don't need to see your props, Archie. Like I said—" Lance Grey smiled thinly, his mouth turning up slightly at one corner—"you're in way over your head."

Archie rolled up the marine chart. "I got your email," Archie Ravenwing finally said.

Lance just looked at him.

"The one that Greg White Eagle sent you and the Stoboltz people after the August meeting. I got a copy of it."

"So what, Archie?"

"Somebody is paying Greg White Eagle to make nice with the salmon farmers. Someone is paying him to push the band council to let more salmon farms into the Broughton."

Lance Grey stood up. "You can't come into a minister's office and make that sort of accusation. You can't sit in *my* office and accuse *me* of bribery, or whatever it is you're doing."

"I've got one piece left to fit into the puzzle, Lance. Then I'm taking this whole thing down."

"You'll go down with it, Archie."

"I'm past caring."

"Think of your family, Archie."

■ Archie walked back toward the entrance of the Legislature. His hands were sweating and his face was flushed. He felt his whole body become weak, and he had to stop and put an arm on a marble column to steady himself. He closed his eyes and took a breath. He saw ravens, their black backs iridescent in the sun. He opened his eyes. One more trick up his sleeve, he thought.

Instead of walking back downtown after leaving the Legislature, he headed south, through the character houses with their four-colour paint jobs, into the neighbourhood of James Bay. In fifteen minutes he was on the seawall. He sucked in the air greedily, its coolness revitalizing him. He found a set of stairs and made his way to the pebble beach below. The winter storms had deposited driftwood and kelp in a hurly-burly fashion there, and he stepped through the tangle and found a place to sit. He let his legs dangle, tucked his hands inside his pockets, and looked across the Strait of Juan de Fuca at Washington state's Cascade Mountains and the Olympic Peninsula. Archie watched gulls wheel overhead. He watched container ships bear down the strait, heading for the open ocean beyond.

Archie felt a momentary sense of envy. How he would love to head out to the open ocean right now. His people were inland water people. Unlike the Nuu-chah-nulth, who had taken to the vast open waters of the Pacific, his heritage rested on the smaller waters of the inland straits. But at that very moment,

Archie Ravenwing wanted nothing more than to feel the vastness of the big water surround him. He thought of salmon, how they are born in tiny creeks deep in the Coast Ranges, and how, when they are still so young, migrate toward the immeasurably vast waters of the Pacific.

The sense of liberation these tiny creatures might feel when at last they break free of comparatively claustrophobic inlets and channels, and, for the first time, join with the incalculably vast ocean, was something Archie Ravenwing dreamed of.

He watched ships pass in the opposite direction, making for the Port of Vancouver, or for Seattle at the head of Puget Sound. Archie could now see that the decisions he had made over the last few years had begun to confine him to smaller and smaller waters. Soon, he knew, he'd be on dry land.

He had been sitting for half an hour when his cellphone chimed.

"Ravenwing here," he said, pressing the phone tightly to his ear.

"Hi, Archie, it's Charles."

Archie's mind raced.

"Charles Knobbles, from The Pacific Salmon Foundation."

"Right, hey, Charles. Sorry, I'm getting old, didn't place the voice."

"You're in town, aren't you?"

"Yeah, how'd you know?"

"Someone at your house told me. Can we have a coffee?"

"Sure, I could use one. What's up?"

"It's better I tell you in person. Half an hour?" They arranged to meet at a James Bay coffee shop that doubled as a bookstore.

"Sounds fine," Ravenwing said, snapping his phone shut.

Archie stood, worked the stiffness from his joints, and walked back into the community. He strolled through the streets admiring the neatly painted houses, and within thirty minutes he found the shop and stepped inside. It was warm and smelled like fresh baking.

"Hi, Archie." A man approached him. Now he remembered. The Pacific Salmon Foundation was part of the SOS coalition, and Charles was their lead person on salmon farming. They shook hands.

"Can I buy you a coffee?"

They sat and drank coffee, and Archie ate a massive apple fritter doughnut. The food and coffee warmed him.

"What brings you to Victoria?"

"Last ditch effort to convince the minister he's making a mistake."

"Minister is out of town today."

"I know. I found out too late. Chickens or something. Somebody caught a cold." Archie laughed. "I met with Lance Grey instead."

"He's a slippery bastard," said Knobbles.

"He sure is," said Ravenwing, finishing his food and wiping his mouth on a napkin.

"I sometimes get the feeling that Grey is running the show on aquaculture. That the minister is just a public face and that Grey does all the thinking on that file. Makes all the decisions."

Archie drank his coffee. "Not so unusual," he said.

"No. But scary. The guy hasn't been elected. We don't know anything about him. He's certainly got no qualifications to be making such decisions. Christ, he's got a degree in economics, not ecology or anything relevant. And he's what? Like twenty years old?"

Archie smiled at Knobbles. "Just listen to us old war horses," he said.

Charles Knobbles returned the smile. They sat for a moment. "So, what is it that you wanted to talk to me about?" Archie asked.

"Right, I almost forgot. Listen, it's good that you're here today. In person. There's going to be an announcement soon, I don't know when. But soon. I just got wind of it from someone in the premier's office. The minister of economic development, the minister for Aboriginal relations, and the minister of agriculture, maybe even the premier himself. They're going to announce a new First Nations training fund. It's designed to help First Nations people transition to resource economy jobs. Mining, forestry, and aquaculture."

"It's been in the works for years," said Archie. "I saw it when I was on council."

"Well, it's about to be announced. And here's the thing I thought you should know: It's got a hefty budget attached to it for industry incentives. Big bucks. There's going to be a bunch of money pushed through for business and First Nations partnerships. I think there's going to be one between the North Salish and Stoboltz."

Archie smiled. "I should have seen that coming. How much?"

"Not sure, but it's going to be in the hundreds of thousands, at least. Likely in the millions. It's a ten-year agreement. It's on the up and up. From a lot of people's perspectives it's a good deal."

"Except that it cements salmon farming as the backbone of our economy."

"It will be pretty hard to argue that salmon farming isn't good for Port Lostcoast. Everybody in town will be driving a new boat."

Archie breathed out and sat back in his chair. It seemed that the trickster had been tricked again.

■ That was how they did it, thought Archie. They didn't need to hide the cash in a paper bag and pass it under the table. They could make an announcement about it on the six o'clock news and get above-the-fold coverage in all the newspapers. They could use the provincial treasury like their own private slush fund to pour taxpayers' money onto the fire that was burning and destroying a culture older than time. And they could get people like Greg White Eagle to stand up and applaud when they did it.

Archie was sitting on the bed in his hotel room at the Traveller's Inn. He had his coat off and his feet up, and he was flicking through the channels. He felt beaten. He had nothing new on what Stoboltz was up to in the Broughton, or why the samples of sea lice being analyzed at UVic were so much more virulent than the samples he and Cassandra were finding. He had been shut out of the minister's agenda. He'd been laughed at by Lance Grey. And threatened. "In way over your head," Grey had told him.

Maybe, worst of all, he was about to be made a fool of by Greg

White Eagle. Here was a man, thought Ravenwing, who had taken money, which he used to win an election. Here was a man who had likely bought the votes of his own people with that money, and who was about to be a hero when the minister announced the agreement between the First Nations, the province, and Stoboltz. Greg would run for chief, and the whole Nation would fall under this thumb.

It made Archie Ravenwing sick to his stomach.

He flicked the channels.

He was about to have a shower when his cellphone rang. Maybe it was Gracie, calling to see how the day had gone. It would be good to hear her voice. Instead it was a voice he didn't know.

"Is this Archie Ravenwing?"

"It is. Who's this?" The caller ID said the number was blocked.

"We haven't met, but I have something for you. Something I think you want."

"What is it? Who is this?"

"Can you meet me?"

"When?"

"Now."

Archie looked at this watch. It was ten-thirty. "Okay," he said. "Where?"

"Chinatown. Fan Tan Alley."

"How will I know you?"

"You will."

The line went dead.

Archie looked at the phone in his hand. This day will never end, he thought. He peered out the hotel window. The night was thick with pea-soup fog. Archie stood and put a fleece coat on and pulled his raincoat over it. He found a pair of gloves, slipped his keys in his pocket, and left the hotel to walk downtown.

Mystery man said he had something for him, something he would want. Well, let's see, thought Archie.

It was just few blocks from the Traveller's Inn to the corner of Douglas and Fisgard, and from there he turned right and made his way toward the small, historic Chinatown. Oldest in the continent, he knew. The Chinese and the province's First Nations shared a common historical thread, both having been exploited and demoralized, their resources stolen from them. The First Nations had been imprisoned and abused in residential schools, had their culture and language stolen, their fish, trees, and minerals taken without compensation. The Chinese had been forced to pay a head tax, and toiled in near slavery in the gold mines and later on the railroad.

He crossed Government Street, passed under the Gates of Harmonious Interest — the ornate archway adorned with lions and colourful scrolled woodwork — and walked down the nearly deserted street. The air had grown cold, and the heavy fog that had formed on the inner harbour rolled in sheets through the downtown core of the city. The streetlamps were haloed in mist, and Archie couldn't see the far end of the street. He walked briskly, feeling the chill through his clothes. He passed an open restaurant that served won ton noodles, and walked past two people sleeping in a doorway to a green grocer. Then he was at the mouth of Fan Tan Alley. He stopped and looked around him. A few people strolled up from Store Street toward Government. He watched them go. He peered into the alley, so narrow that in many places a man could reach across and touch both sides. It was dark, except for the light from a hooded lamp in the doorway of one of the alley's shops, which cast a pale glow into the gloom of the night.

Archie stood for another minute, waiting to be approached, then walked down the narrow alley, taking his hands from his pockets. It was a gamble. It had occurred to him that he was being set up. But then Fan Tan was a game of chance. He was taking his.

He got halfway down the darkened passage, to a place where corridors led to courtyards, and wooden doors indicated where opium dens once operated, replaced today by a music store, a new age shop, and a traditional barber shop. He heard footsteps behind him. He turned and saw a man moving toward him through the misty night.

The man passed under a dim light, but Archie couldn't make out his face. He spoke, and Archie couldn't place the voice. "Thanks for coming, Mr. Ravenwing. I've got something that I think you're going to find very interesting."

19 Nancy Webber always sat next to the window when she flew, especially if she was flying over the Rocky Mountains. She watched below her as the foothills disappeared beneath the airplane's fuselage. It was late afternoon, and the sun was sinking into the western horizon, casting long, liquid shadows across the convoluted earth below her. She moved her face to the window and looked south, toward the horizon of bumps where just that morning she had walked. She could not discern the dark shapes of the Porcupine Hills from any of the other windrows of earth in the distance, but she knew they were there. Was it just this morning, at dawn, that she and Walter Blackwater had stood on the hilltop looking west toward the mountains painted by the rising sun? Now, as the sun faded, casting long, creeping shadows over the dales, Nancy Webber wondered what exactly she had gotten herself into.

Every decision she had made in her life had been proceeded by what she thought of now as "a moment of truth." An instant of clarity that provided her with a choice. In that moment — really just a split second of insight — she could choose which direction to follow. She could make a choice to pursue a thought, an idea, a story, a person, or not. Sometimes she chose well, and other times, not so much. Of course, the trick was choosing in the absence of knowledge of outcomes. Who knew? Who knew what the choice might lead to? If she knew, would she choose differently? It was a false argument. She couldn't know.

But she could guess. Thirty-six years of choices had provided her with a pretty solid grounding on the consequences of her decisions.

Her most recent moment of truth had come about five hours before the wheels-up of the airliner in which she was now seated.

■ She hung up the phone. She had been parked on the side of the road, pulled off into somebody's gravel driveway. The trucks that raced by on Highway 22 rocked her car. She put the phone down on the passenger seat and let her hands fall lightly onto her lap.

Now what? she wondered.

Cole Blackwater was in trouble. Again. He believed that Archie Ravenwing had been murdered: his death at sea had been no accident. Cole had asked Nancy to come to Port Lostcoast — about as near to the end of the earth that you can get in Canada — and help him figure out what was going on.

Why? Why had he asked her?

"I'm a reporter, Cole. Is that what you want? A reporter helping you? You know what that means, right? We've been through this before."

Cole had been silent on the phone for a long time. Finally he had told her that he knew that she was a reporter, and he knew what that meant. He didn't know where else to turn.

He sounded lost. Adrift.

She sat in her car and tried to think her way through this. Cole had told her that Archie Ravenwing's boat had been found, and that there was a red, tacky substance that Cole thought must be traces of blood found where no blood should have been. If Archie had in fact been swept over the side of the boat and into the sea, why was there so much blood so far from where his body should have been swept overboard? Then Cole had said something about a marine chart with blue and red Xs on it, notes to call something called the SOS coalition, the RCMP, the media, and himself. What did the Xs mean? she asked. He said that the red Xs were fish farms. The blue Xs were a mystery.

Cole then told her about the package that he had received at his office in Vancouver just days after he had flown to Lostcoast, and the letter and cheque. And finally he told her about his suspicions about the fish farms doing genetic engineering, though to what end he didn't know.

Could she help him? he wanted to know.

She had said she would think about it and call him back.

He had sounded weary. Worn thin.

There was so much about him she didn't know. She shook her head, trying to shake off the conversations with Walter and Dorothy Blackwater, and with Sergeant Reimer.

As she sat there, a thought occurred to her. Was Cole Blackwater aware that she had been to the Blackwater ranch? Had Walter

Blackwater called him the moment she had left the Porcupine Hills and told him some ex-girlfriend, the same one who had ruined his marriage and destroyed his career, was now snooping around their old man's death? If that was the case, what was Cole Blackwater's motivation for pleading with her to come to Port Lostcoast?

She shook her head, her raven-black hair falling across her face. Another truck passed her on the highway and her car shook.

She opened her phone and speed dialled a number.

"You were supposed to be back in Edmonton this morning. Where are you?"

"I'm about an hour south of Calgary."

"You better have broken down or been accosted by cowboys, Nancy."

"I wish," she said. "No, it's more complex than that. I just got a call from a source about a story that is unfolding. I want to pursue it."

"Is this the same story that has had my star reporter creeping around the foothills for the last four days?"

"Sorta."

"Explain sorta."

"I don't know that I can."

"But you want me to let you follow this source's information without being able to make my own evaluation of it, is that right?"

"Pretty much."

"Where?"

"Well, that's the rub," she said. "It's on the north end of Vancouver Island."

"That's a joke, right? You're joking."

"No joke. My source is onto a cover up of a big environmental story out there that might involve murder. Nobody else has this yet."

"You know that you write for the *Edmonton Journal*, right?"

"Yeah, I know."

"And that we don't sell many papers on Vancouver Island, right? I mean, I could check with circulation if you want, but it's likely very, very few. You know that, right?"

"Get off of it, okay. We're part of a national chain. Bump this story up to the *Post*."

"What should I tell them?"

"Tell them to trust me. The last time I followed my nose we won a National Newspaper Award."

The line was silent. Then he said, "I'll see what I can do."

■ It was easy, thought Nancy Webber, face pressed to the window, to ask others to trust her. But did she trust herself? Why take such a risk for Cole Blackwater? Why take such a risk *on* Cole Blackwater?

The flight attendant offered her something to drink; she chose coffee. She sipped from the tiny cup and witnessed the final moments of day, the last brilliant fire of sunlight disappearing from the tips of the mountains below, as if the rosy light was being sucked from the peaks by the approaching darkness.

She finished her coffee. Again she asked herself the question: why take such a risk on Cole Blackwater? She was fairly certain he wouldn't lie to her again. He'd learned his lesson the hard way. But what Nancy Webber couldn't reconcile was this: was she on this plane because of the *story*, or because of Cole Blackwater *himself?* And if it *was* the latter, was it because of what Cole Blackwater had once meant to her, and might mean again, or because of the unanswered questions she had about his father's death? Was it Nancy Webber, reporter, on the plane, or Nancy Webber, once and possible future lover of Cole Blackwater, who watched the darkness consume the light far below?

She made her living asking hard questions, and now found herself in the awkward place of not being able to answer her own troublesome inquiries.

■ In the morning she awoke and wondered where the hell she was. It took her almost a full minute to remember that she was in a hotel within sight of the Vancouver airport and not in one of several places she had slept in Alberta during the last week. She rose and walked naked to the shower. She had forgotten what it felt like to wake up on the coast after having been in Alberta.

Her skin didn't crawl, her eyes didn't itch. Her nose wasn't raw and dry. She felt as though her body was sucking in the moisture from the air around her rather than exhaling it into the parched air of the prairies.

She looked at herself in the mirror. Her hair was messed from sleep and there were dark circles under her eyes, the result of not enough sleep the last few nights. She pressed her hands to her face and ran them through her hair. Then she let her hands trail down her body, over her breasts and across her hips. She straightened and sucked in a breath of air. There was no denying that she was getting older. But everything still held its shape. She still felt good about her body. No issues there. The running helped. She let out the breath and turned the water on in the shower. She smiled at her reflection in the mirror, then caught herself thinking about Cole. About the way they used to make love. She astride him, her hair trailing over his chest. His big hands on her hips, moving her back and forth.

She shook her head.

There was no denying that she was drawn to him like a moth to a flame.

Nancy caught a flight from Vancouver to Port Hardy at ten AM. Shortly after noon she rented one of the three available cars at the Port Hardy terminal and began driving south to Port McNeill. At times she felt her breath coming fast, and she fought to control convoluted emotions. Fear was there, and anticipation. Was it anticipation of the hunt, a journalist's instincts for tracking the story? Or something else?

Nancy couldn't deny that the tingling she felt was lust.

She felt a flush of anger at herself. She was here for the story. One of the stories. Right now, any story would do.

It was late in the afternoon when she reached Port McNeill, just in time to catch the 5:10 ferry. She dialled Cole from the ferry lineup.

"Where are you?" he asked.

"Feels like the middle of nowhere."

"Actually, it's not even that central. You're on the fringes of nowhere."

"I'm in Port McNeill waiting for the ferry. Where can I meet you?"

"When you get off the ferry, turn left and come to the government docks. It's only a few hundred yards. I want to show you the boat. They've got it up and out of the water at the end of the pier."

It had been years since Nancy had been on a ferry. On the ride over, she stood at the bow of the boat and shivered, watching the shoreline pass, watching clouds scud along the ragged, clear-cut peaks of Vancouver Island. As she approached Alert Bay, a bank of fog rolled along the shore and obscured the town. When the boat docked, she climbed back into her rental car and drove up the pier; she turned left and found a place to park at the government docks.

All too soon she found herself standing where the metal ramp dropped onto the wooden wharf. The afternoon was cold, and she had only the clothing she had grabbed for her trip to High River last Sunday morning. She had put on her leather jacket for the crossing and now pulled it tightly to her body, the cool, wet air clinging to her, burrowing into her bones. Mist clung to the water. There wasn't a trace of wind, and the fog seemed to move of its own volition. Above, the sun tried to push its way into the vapour, to burn it off, but the fog held its ground, pooling low on the water and creeping like an ethereal snake across the heavy boards of the government pier, only to drop again into the pit of mist below.

She stood and breathed and wondered if a person could drown in such a heavy fog. She shivered and momentarily wondered again what she was doing there.

Then she saw the figure appear from the mist at the far end of the dock. At first it was merely the outline of a man, heavyset but moving lightly, arms swinging at his sides. Then the figure took form. Dark, curly hair. Heavy slicker pulled up around his neck. Jeans. Face emerging from the gloom of the fog. Cole Blackwater walked toward her from out of the miasma of the darkening day.

20 The long journey back to Port Hardy gave Archie Ravenwing plenty of time to think about his encounter in Fan Tan Alley the night before. He opened his battered leather briefcase and looked around the tiny airplane to see if he recognized anyone. Then he hefted the inch-thick envelope out and put the briefcase between his feet on the floor. He opened the envelope again. Of course, when he had returned from Fan Tan Alley he had briefly glanced at the stack of paper, but exhaustion overtook him and he fell asleep with the reading light on, the papers scattered across his chest and blankets.

In his dreams he revisited the encounter.

"Who are you?"

"I'm a friend. On the inside."

"Why all this deep throat stuff?"

The man laughed. "Yeah, pretty dramatic."

"Really, why?"

"You'll see when you read this." The man handed him a thick envelope.

Archie took it. "They'll be able to trace this back to you, won't they? I heard that they can trace things to photocopiers or individual printers now."

"It won't matter."

"You'll get fired."

"We've got whistleblower protection."

"Why me? Why not the media?"

"You've got the complete picture. I only have pieces. You'd never get this from Freedom of Information. This is the stuff that's always blacked out."

"How'd you get it?"

"Best that I not say."

"Stolen?"

"Liberated."

"Does this have anything to do with the First Nation's economic agreement that's going to be announced?"

The man looked around him, as if the alley had ears. "I think the minister is in the dark. I think he's walking into a trap."

"What do you mean, trap?"

"I think he's in the dark about what's going on up in the Broughton."

"Lance Grey is running the table?"

"Yeah, and he's really just a pawn in the game that Stoboltz is playing."

"And now they have Greg First Eagle."

"And others...."

"Who?"

"I don't know."

"From the North Salish?"

"I don't think so. Other bands up the coast. They're running the whole trap line."

Archie shook his head. "Can't someone get to the minister before he walks into this mess with both feet?"

"We're trying. But Lance Grey has built a wall around the minister. Nobody from the department can get in. Nobody inside that office gets out."

"What next?" asked Archie, his breath joining with the mist in the dark alley.

"You do your thing. Get all your information together. Find out what is really going on at Jeopardy Rock. The department is in the dark. Find out, and blow the lid off it. We'll try to prevent the minister from going down with the ship, but it might be too late for that."

"Thank you," said Archie, extending his hand.

"Don't mention it." The man walked quickly down the alley, into the mist, disappearing into the night.

■ He read through the pages, carefully placing them on his lap when he was done. They were deeply incriminating. They fell into two categories, as far as Archie could see. The first category was results of testing that Stoboltz Aquaculture had been accumulating over the last year about sea lice on both wild Pacific and farmed Atlantic salmon. Here was the complete data set that Archie and Cassandra Petrel had been looking for. It showed that the test site, which was only labelled as Jeopardy

Rock, had escalating concentrations of sea lice on both the wild and farmed fish. In some cases the concentrations on wild pink and coho smolts were more than one hundred times higher than the samples Cassandra and Archie had taken.

Archie put the papers down and looked out the window. On the left side of the plane the peaks of Strathcona Park rose up, the wild heart of Vancouver Island. Mount Red Pillar, Mount Rousseau, Mount McBride, and Elkhorne Mountain, all beneath a deep blanket of late winter snow. He watched the mountains slip past, watched the propeller of the turboprop aircraft whirl, watched the clouds scud across the western sky.

How was it possible that Stoboltz was finding concentrations of sea lice one hundred times higher than what he was finding? He had been up Nickol Pass toward Tribune Channel just two weeks ago, and while the number of sea lice found on the early migrators alarmed him, they had been nowhere near what Stoboltz was finding. And how was it that Stoboltz was able to send these samples to the Ministry of Agriculture without being called on the carpet before the minister? The only explanation could be that Lance Grey was keeping both the department and the minister in the dark.

The second category was equally damning. It contained a sheath of correspondence between Lance Grey, Erik Nilsson, and Darvin Thurlow. There were hard copies of dozens of emails chronicling a conspiracy of silence around the sampling of sea lice. It was almost with glee that Darvin Thurlow reported in one email that "we are nearly at the anticipated level of infection, with the sea lice occurring on 77% of the smolts sampled, and covering more than 68% of body mass. At this rate of parasitic growth, we should reach 99% by late spring of next year, in time for the main migration."

Another email, from Lance Grey to Erik Nilsson and Darvin Thurlow stated, "I am concerned with the rate of growth at this point. We had agreed to reach 99% much sooner. Continuing with this work for another year will raise suspicions. Technicians at the UVic lab will begin to question the results if we're not careful."

In a note dated late in the fall, Grey noted, "I think that you've gotten sloppy. I got a call from Ravenwing. He and Petrel got hold of some of your results. You had better speed up your work. We can't keep a lid on this forever."

A note from Erik Nilsson to Lance Grey, dated only two weeks before, said, "Our patience is running thin, Lance. We've been waiting for an injection of cash from your office to continue with our work at Jeopardy Rock for more than a month. We agreed, from the outset, that while we would undertake the salmon and sea lice development, you would bankroll some of the costs. Your announcement on the opportunities fund is long overdue."

For the duration of the flight, Archie Ravenwing pondered the succession of correspondence. The collusion between Stoboltz Aquaculture and the minister's office was occurring on multiple levels. Archie felt his heart beating. His hands were sweating. If the sea lice from the samples were now in the general population of Knight Inlet and Tribune Channel, the odds that this season or the next would be the last for wild salmon in that region were very good.

It was bad enough that Stoboltz had discovered this epidemic, but instead of trying to control the outbreak, Lance Grey seemed to be egging it on. Archie could not fathom what Grey stood to gain from this course of action. Worse still, in Archie's eyes, was Stoboltz's demand that taxpayers' money be directed to their coffers, under the guise of a First Nations Opportunity Fund, to pay for the so-called research they were undertaking at Jeopardy Rock.

The first thing he did when he landed in Port Hardy was call Cassandra Petrel.

It took Archie the rest of the day to get back to Port Lostcoast — a ride down the island with his son Jacob, and then the long boat trip into the mouth of the archipelago to Parish Island. It was well past dark when he arrived in the harbour. But before heading home, he walked to Cassandra's boat and knocked on the wooden gunwales. There were lights on inside, and he could hear her in the galley. He stepped onto the deck of the boat and knocked on the heavy wooden door at the mouth of the companionway.

Cassandra opened it and invited him in. The cabin was warm and inviting as usual. "Did you have time to eat, Archie?"

"I haven't had much since breakfast."

"I'll fix you something," she said. "Tea?"

"That would be great."

Archie stood, the briefcase in his hands.

"You sounded excited on the phone. What happened with your meeting with the minister?"

"He wasn't there. I met with Lance Grey."

"Surely that didn't get you all worked up?"

Archie grinned. "A meeting with Lance Grey gets my blood pressure up, but no, it's this, Cassandra. Look." He took the envelope from his briefcase and showed her. The kettle boiled and she poured water into the teapot.

"This is sampling data," Cassandra said. "Genetics. Survival rates. Infection rates. And lots of it. It looks similar to the material the lab sent us last fall. But it looks like the complete data set."

"It is, and it's worse. Much worse. Cassandra, there appears to be some kind of outbreak at Jeopardy Rock."

She looked at the documents spread out on the tiny counter beside the stove while she stirred salmon and scallops together with green onions, garlic, mushrooms, and leeks. The aroma was delicious in the small cabin. Archie sat down suddenly, feeling his strength give out.

"This doesn't make sense, Archie. None at all. In human terms, this would be pandemic levels. They are finding enough sea lice on these smolts to sink a submarine. Not only is the rate of infection higher than anything I've ever seen, but so is the mortality rate. These sea lice are not only more numerous, but capable of killing young adults. They are no longer just killing smolts, but fish early in the adult years. This is unbelievable. Up until now we only had to worry about sea lice killing juveniles —"

"As if that wasn't bad enough," said Archie, helping himself to tea.

"Right. But now fish that are two, three, four years old are susceptible to being taken down by these little bastards." Cassandra Petrel read while she put the fish and vegetables on a plate with some leftover rice. She handed it to Archie. "I hope this will be okay," she said.

Archie smiled at her, then picked up a fork and ate, making grateful sounds between mouthfuls. "What I don't get," he said, taking a breath, "is the sampling location. Can you make sense of that?"

Cassandra flipped through the pages. She went back to look at a few pages near the beginning. "If I didn't know better," she said, putting the pages down and looking at Archie through her reading glasses, "I'd say they weren't sampling in the open ocean at all."

Archie made a face, his cheeks bulging with food.

"Look," she said, pointing to a set of boxes at the top of one of the forms. "The only location given for all of the samples is Jeopardy Rock. That's it. No GPS reading. No longs and lats. Nothing."

"What are you saying, Cassandra?"

"I'm guessing. I'm not saying anything."

"What are you guessing then?"

"I'm guessing — no, wildly speculating — that the conditions creating these levels of infestation aren't in the open ocean at all. I'm guessing they're in the pens at Jeopardy Rock. I'm guessing they're manufactured conditions."

■ When Archie Ravenwing stepped from the deck of Cassandra Petrel's boat, the moon was up and casting its gentle light across the harbour, on the tiny town of Port Lostcoast. He was bone weary, but strangely energized at the same time. Just yesterday morning he had felt the heavy hand of defeat on his shoulder, pushing him down. He felt as though there was no place for him to get a hold of the massive beast that was both government and industry working in collusion to destroy what he loved.

Now, strangely, he felt hope. He had friends on the inside. He had growing confidence that the minister himself wasn't necessarily involved, but merely ignorant. It made the problem more manageable to know that when Archie did blow the lid off this debacle he would have backup. He walked along the dock toward the dirt road that wound its way up to the bluff house. He felt the familiar shame for his past mistakes. It would be his price to pay when he took down the cabal of crooks. Archie Ravenwing certainly had his regrets. He was sorry that the media's coverage of his own wrongdoing might diminish the pain he could inflict on his enemies. He was sorry that Grace and First Moon and other innocent bystanders would pay a heavy price for his mistakes, too. And he felt shame for the pain he would cause his people. But he knew he could not dwell on that now.

He would come clean. When he blew the lid off the Stoboltz/Jeopardy Rock conspiracy, he would turn himself over to the RCMP for fraud and throw himself at the feet of the courts. The image brought a smile to his face. He wondered if anybody actually threw themselves on the floor to beg. It would make for good TV.

He stepped lively along the dock, absorbed in his own thoughts, when he heard someone call to him. "Hey Archie, that you?" It was Darren First Moon.

Archie waved to him. Darren's little boat was moored two slips from Cassandra Petrel's boat.

"Come on over, Archie, I got a beer for you."

"Not tonight, Darren. I'm beat," he said into the night.

"I saw you come in awhile back. You've been over talking with the doc a long time. What's up, Archie?"

Archie sighed and walked over to where Darren was standing on the bow of his boat. "Do you want a beer, Archie?" Darren asked when he drew near.

"Not tonight, Moon, I'm wiped out. Just flew up from Victoria. Didn't get much shut-eye last night. I'm calling it a day."

"Okay, next time, hey? So listen, what's up for the spring?"

"What do you mean?"

"Well, are we heading out or not?"

"I guess that's up to the DFO people, isn't it?"

"Yeah, I'm just wondering. I got bills to pay and all."

"Don't we all, don't we all."

"Yeah, but you know, my kids are still at home, hey, Archie? I'm just trying to take care of the family."

"If the DFO people say the season is open, then we're going. Just like always, Darren. You can count on that."

"I'm just worried is all. I got to look out for the little ones, you know—"

"What can I say, Moon? At the very worst, there'll be a sport fishing season. We're always good for a few dozen trips with tourists."

Darren took a deep breath. "Archie, you know I got a lot of respect for you. You've been really good to me. Really good. Took a chance on me when nobody else around here would."

"You've earned my trust, Moon. You've pulled your weight. I never cut you any slack."

"I know. But you didn't have to. When I got out of the pen, not many would have given me the break you did. I mean, I'd been inside since I was sixteen." The big man laughed. "Grew up in there, pretty much. Ten years on and off. Nearly half my life, up to that point."

"That was ten years ago, Darren. It's water under the bridge. You're a good man. You have a good family. Two beautiful kids. Soon three! You're looking out for them. You're a good father."

"That's what I mean to tell you, Archie. I got to look out for the kids."

"What are you saying?"

"I got to get a permanent job. I can't live this way. It's killing me—"

"I understand. It's killing us all."

"I've got an offer, Archie."

"Hey, great, with one of the big outfits?"

"No. It's not fishing. Everybody is feeling the pinch. No—"

"You're not going to the big island are you? Taking a job in a cannery? God, Moon."

"I'm taking a job with Stoboltz."

These words hit Archie Ravenwing like a cold slap across his face. He closed his eyes and drew the cool Pacific air into him.

"I know that you hate them, Archie, but what can I do? I got debts, you know. I got bills to pay. And they offered me good work."

Archie opened his eyes. The clear night sky shone with stars. The moon, nearly full, sat fat in the sky, kissing the harbour with white light.

"Archie, come on, say something."

"There's nothing to say, Moon."

"Damn it, Archie. You got to understand, I got debts. I got bills to pay." Darren First Moon buried his hands in the pockets of his orange slicker.

"We've all got bills, Darren. We get by."

"Easy for you to say, living up on the bluff, looking out at the town. Easy for you to say with your new deck and new addition to your place. You don't have any bills for all that, do you?"

"I don't know what you're getting at."

"I've been hearing things...."

"What are you saying?"

"I've been talking to Greg White Eagle. He's told me what you done."

Archie blew a cord of mist into the night air.

"Pretty easy to be all high and mighty, Archie, when you yourself are dipping into the kitty, hey?"

"That was a mistake, and I aim to come clean on that."

"Yeah, well, don't go looking down your nose at everybody else for doing an honest day's work when you're stealing money from the band. That's fraud. So just don't do it, Archie."

Archie Ravenwing felt his heart in his throat. He said: "Stoboltz is up to no good, Darren."

"Come off it, Archie. I'm not listening to any more of your conspiracy theories."

"It's not a theory, and I don't know who else you've been listening to these days. I've got proof, Darren, that Stoboltz is up to something and the government is in on it, too. I'm going to blow the lid off their whole racket. I'm going to sink those fuckers."

"You're just doing this to get back at me, ain't you? Because you think I'm stabbing you in the back, hey?" Darren paced back and forth in front of Archie now, hands at his side, breathing hard.

"That's not true, Moon. You've been like a son to me these last ten years. I love you. I'm not doing this to hurt you. I admit that to hear you're going to work for the goddamned fish farmers feels like a knife in my back."

Darren stopped pacing. "What have you got on Stoboltz, Archie?"

"I can't say, Darren."

"Come on, Archie. Maybe it will change my mind?"

"I very much doubt that, Darren."

21 Cole stood next to the barnacle-speckled hull of the *Inlet Dancer*. The boat was resting on a series of wooden pilings and secured with heavy metal jacks. Cole could see where the boat's solid fibreglass and wooden hull had been dented where it hove up on the rocks of Protection Point. Derek Johns and Sergeant Winters stood next to him, regarding the boat. With them were half a dozen other RCMP officers. Two forensics experts dressed in their white jumpsuits were combing over the boat. Cole's cellphone rang. It was Nancy. She was just outside Port McNeill and wanted to know where she could meet him. He directed her to the docks.

Cole had been standing for an hour in the chill afternoon air watching the RCMP scour Archie's boat for further evidence of trauma. Cold air had moved in from the north that morning, butting up against a warmer air mass, and a heavy fog had fallen over the mouth of Alert Bay. The air was now utterly still.

The forensics team arrived from Campbell River via Port McNeill an hour after Cole had visited the *Inlet Dancer.* Now, it seemed, the entire detachment of Mounties from both McNeill and Alert Bay was standing on the dock watching the two-man team methodically work their way over the boat. They looked for fingerprints, scoured the boat for any suspicious objects, and spent considerable time examining and sampling the tacky red substance on the engine compartment at the boat's stern. They then used ultraviolet light to look for minute traces of blood on the gunwales, the pilothouse, and elsewhere on the boat. Cole then watched as the forensics team sprayed the boat down with Luminol, hoping to detect additional evidence of blood. Dozens of items were bagged and placed in chests for transportation back to Vancouver and the major crime unit's labs there.

Cole thought of the rope and the map that he'd removed from the boat the previous day; he began to consider the wisdom of his actions. He stood, arms crossed, and watched. From time to time he talked with one of the uniformed officers, who permitted, but did not welcome, his presence on the pier. Only Derek Johns seemed to tolerate his presence, but then again, Johns had been assigned the task of liaison with the Ravenwing family; it was his job to put up with Cole, the family's unofficial representative.

All the while he watched out of the corner of his eye for the arrival of the ferry bearing Nancy Webber. When the boat did finally arrive, cutting through the swirling fog, he didn't rush to meet her. Instead, he stayed back and watched. At last, she emerged from the fog like a ghost from his past. He saw her walk to the edge of the government pier's ramp and stop, looking for him. He strode toward her, hands swinging at his sides, his attention distracted by what was beginning to seem like incontrovertible evidence that his friend and colleague Archie Ravenwing had been murdered.

"It's good to see you," he said when he reached the end of the dock. She stepped toward him and they moved into an awkward embrace. It was always like this with Nancy. Two steps forward and one step back, he thought.

"I'm glad to be here, Cole. Thanks for arranging a warm welcome," she said, looking around her as the mist swirled off the water like dry ice on a B-grade horror movie set. "It's so cozy, it makes me want to curl up with a good book."

"Welcome to the wet coast," he said.

"I'm really sorry to hear about Archie," she said, her face becoming serious.

"You said that already. On the phone."

"I know, but we thought it was just an accident then."

Cole was silent. "Okay," he finally said. "Do you want to see the boat?" He started to walk away.

"I do, but there's something we have to clear up first."

"What's that?" he said, turning to face her.

"What capacity I'm here in."

"What do you mean?"

"Am I here as Nancy Webber, journalist, or Nancy Webber, friend?"

"You tell me."

"Well, I am here as your friend, Cole. I want to help. But I'm also here as a journalist. If there is a story here, I want it."

"I would expect nothing less," Cole said, turning to walk down the dock.

"What do you mean by that, Blackwater?"

"Nothing. Take it easy," he said, turning once again.

"I fly all the way out here, drop what I was working on, to help you out on another crazy situation, and you give me attitude?"

"I'm not, really."

She looked at him.

"Come on," he said gently. "Come."

She walked beside him through the fog to the slip where the *Inlet Dancer* was moored.

The RCMP officers turned to regard her.

"She's with me," said Cole. Cole introduced her to Derek Johns.

"Are you a friend of the family?" he asked.

"Yes. And I'm a reporter. *Edmonton Journal*."

"Okay. All press comment will have to go through our strategic communications officer in Victoria."

Nancy nodded and turned back to the boat.

Cole told her where the Coast Guard had found the boat, and showed Nancy where it had been damaged when it had run aground. "They say it's seaworthy. Jacob, Archie's son, looked it over. Says it will be fine to get back to Port Lostcoast, depending if there is an investigation, that is."

"That's still up in the air?" asked Nancy.

"Guess it depends on what those fellas make of the red sticky stuff."

"Blood?"

Cole told her.

"Jesus," she said.

"Come on, let's walk. You need to meet Grace and Jacob. And Darren First Moon."

Cole turned to Constable Johns. "Derek, will you call Grace and keep her up to date?"

"I will, Mr. Blackwater."

"Thanks," Cole said and turned back to Nancy. The other officers regarded them with taciturn silence.

"First-name basis with the coppers now, are we?" said Nancy as they walked away.

"Johns is actually a good guy. The others are a pretty serious bunch."

"They seem pretty cranky."

"No Tim Hortons in Alert Bay."

"That must have you on edge, too. Last I saw, you had a double-double in your hands and one of those apple fritters stuffed in your mouth," Nancy said.

"I can get by. I've kicked the doughnut habit. There's decent coffee at the place I'm staying."

"They got a cappuccino machine?"

"I'm sure we can find someone to put some foam on your five-dollar coffee."

"Thank God for small mercies."

"So, what were you working on in Calgary?" Cole asked, idly, as they walked along the water toward the restaurant where Grace was waiting out the day.

"Oh, God," she said, "nothing of any consequence. The *Journal* is doing a five-part series on climate change so they sent me into the eye of the storm to talk with all the big oil and gas producers. But who knows when, if ever, it's going to run."

"Is the paper getting heat?"

"Something like that."

"Most important issue of our time, the thing that will define the twenty-first century, and all the Association of Oil Producers and those mother—" He bit his tongue, remembering his promise to Sarah to curb his language. "All those fine upstanding corporate citizens can think about is their wallets."

Nancy changed the subject. "Does Grace know I'm a reporter?"

"I told her last night. I figured she needed to know. Watch what she said and all. Jacob will want to frisk you for a wire," Cole said.

She punched him the arm. "Get off it," she said.

He grinned. "This is the place," he said, pointing to a two-storey grey motel called Black Jack's.

"Charming."

"I'm staying up the road at a B&B, but it's not the sort of place where we can sit and talk, really," he said. "Grace is likely in the coffee shop. Come on."

They found Grace Ravenwing at a table by a window, drinking coffee and reading the previous day's *Times Colonist*.

"Grace, this is Nancy Webber," said Cole.

Grace stood and extended a hand.

"I was a fan of your father's," said Nancy. "I'm sorry for your loss."

"Thanks. Cole tells me you met him in Ottawa."

"At the Assembly of First Nations. When I was a reporter there."

Grace sat down. A waitress arrived and took their orders. Cole and Nancy ordered lunch, while Grace asked for more coffee.

"Can we talk here?" Nancy asked, looking around.

Grace looked, too. The place was empty. "May as well."

"Let's go over what we know," said Nancy.

"All business, this one," said Cole, nodding toward Nancy.

They discussed the facts. Archie Ravenwing had been digging into the activities of Stoboltz Aquaculture after the minister of agriculture had announced new salmon farms in the Broughton Archipelago. He had apparently been tipped off by a character who had produced a large envelope of information about Stoboltz's operations.

"Have you seen it?" asked Nancy.

"No, it arrived at my office after I left. Now it's probably sitting at Grace's place on Parish Island."

"We had better get back there to have a look," said Grace. "It could be important, now that we know what we know."

"Agreed," said Cole, continuing the recap. "Archie had apparently been zeroing in on the salmon farm at Jeopardy Rock." Cole told Nancy about the map, the Xs, and the date on the last X on the map corresponding with the night of his disappearance.

"What do you make of his writing on the map?" asked Grace.

"It looked like he was making notes to himself. 'Call Cole,

call the RCMP, call the media,'" he recited. "Sounds like a to-do list for the next day."

"He must have found what he was looking for," said Nancy. "What do you figure it was?"

"Something to do with one of two things, I think," said Cole. "Dirty tricks by Stoboltz, or dirty politics," he said, looking around.

Grace told Nancy about Archie's suspicions about Greg First Eagle and the likelihood that Greg had some dirt on her father.

"What do you think it is?" Nancy asked.

Grace looked at Cole. Cole nodded.

"I think my dad was skimming the till." She looked down at her hands.

"How?"

"I don't know for sure, but I think he was paying for work around the house and on his boat with band money. Fudging expense receipts. That sort of thing."

Nancy was silent. "It's no matter right now, unless there was some kind of double-cross or something that ended Archie up in hot water."

"That seems pretty unlikely," said Cole.

"Maybe," said Nancy. "Anyway, is there anything more?"

"Just one thing," said Cole. "I think Archie knew that someone wanted him dead. If he didn't know, then he thought that his life was at risk doing what he was doing, whatever it was. He left his will on his desk at home before he left."

"Wow," said Nancy.

"Wow is right," said Cole.

They finished their meals and ordered more coffee.

"Where to from here?" asked Nancy.

"We need to think about three things," said Cole. "Motive, method, and opportunity."

Grace looked down at her hand on the cup of coffee. Her face was ashen.

"Would it be better if we talked about this some other time?" asked Nancy.

"No, we've got to get on with this. It's been more than two

weeks since Dad disappeared, and who knows what the Mounties will come up with? We've got to get moving on this ourselves."

"Okay," said Cole, less enthusiastically. "We need to piece together those three elements. Motive, why was Archie killed." He lowered his voice and spoke flatly. "Method, how? Opportunity, or did the person who did it have a chance? Was he—"

"—or she," said Nancy.

"Or she able to get to wherever Archie was killed? Problem is, we're not entirely certain where that was."

"And then there's the boat issue," said Grace. "How did it get to where it was found?"

"Right," said Cole.

"Okay, so let's make a list," said Nancy, pulling out her notebook.

Cole shivered. "Those things give me the creeps," said Cole.

"What?"

"Those little half-sized notebooks you reporters carry around."

"Never stopped you from blabbing before," said Nancy.

"Times have changed."

"Cowboy up."

Cole drew a breath. "First, let's think about names. I'll start with Greg White Eagle. He had a clear motive. Archie knew he was on the pad to Stoboltz. That they financed the election."

"All we've got is an email Dad got through FOIPP," said Grace. "Not much to go on."

"She's right," said Nancy. "We need banking records."

"How do we get that?" asked Grace.

"Beats me," said Nancy.

"Maybe we could get some folks around Lostcoast to talk. See if Greg offered them gas money to come out and vote?" Cole said.

"Worth looking into. I'll do that," said Grace.

"Be careful," said Cole. Grace shot him a look.

"I'm just saying, if anything happens to you—"

"Let's keep going," said Nancy. "Did Greg what's-his-name have an opportunity?"

"White Eagle. That's going to be hard to figure out for anybody right now. Same as method. We don't have a body, so we don't know how he died," said Cole. Then he saw the look on Grace's face. "Sorry. I'm sorry. We don't know how Archie died," he said. "So there's no way to establish what the method was. And we don't know *where* he died."

"But we know it was likely somewhere in Knight Inlet," said Grace. "It's the only way his boat would have ended up on Protection Point, unless someone had towed him."

Cole slapped his head, and both women looked at him. "I almost forgot about the rope."

"What rope?" asked Nancy.

He reached inside his jacket and pulled out the two-foot length of rope he had taken from the cleat on the stern of the *Inlet Dancer*.

"Where did you get that?" she asked. He told her.

"The RCMP is going to be pissed if they find out."

"There was no investigation going on when I took it."

"Tell it to the judge, punk," Nancy said.

"Look, if they open a file I'll hand it over. But I think this is important. You said unless the *Inlet Dancer* had been towed —"

"Yeah, if Dad's boat had been up around Jeopardy Rock when he was, well, when he was killed, someone could have towed the boat."

"What difference does it make?" asked Nancy.

"Maybe none," said Cole. "But this was on the stern. You don't tow a boat that way, do you?"

"No, you pull it bow first. Just like you were driving it. Otherwise it doesn't tow all that well. It plows rather than cuts through the water," said Grace.

"So maybe *Archie* gave someone *else* a tow that night?"

"Maybe. But I honestly can't say that I never saw it there before."

Cole looked thoughtfully at his cup. He brushed an errant strand of hair from his forehead. "How do we find out where the rope came from?"

Grace thought about that for a moment. "What we're more

likely to learn is if someone has had to replace a bow line in the last few weeks, and even then it's going to be a stretch."

"Can you look into that, Grace?"

"Sure, Cole, there's really only one or two places here in Alert Bay. Then there's Port McNeill. And if the rope belonged to a boat from, say, Campbell River, well, I'm not sure we'll be able to track it down."

"Okay, let's get back to the list," Cole said. "So we've got Greg White Eagle. Who else?"

"What about that redneck who you beat up the other night. Dan Campbell?" asked Grace.

Nancy looked at Cole with raised eyebrows. "I thought your face was looking ruddier than usual."

Cole smirked. "He got far worse than he gave, believe me. And he had it coming. The guy is a bigot who isn't afraid to walk into a bar in Port Lostcoast with the only other white guys in town and make racist remarks about a man whose life we had just celebrated that very day! I wish I had beat him a little harder," said Cole, his fist clenched on the table.

"Still working on that anger issue, I see," said Nancy, sitting back in her chair and crossing her arms over her chest.

"Yeah, well, I guess I am. I just don't sit on my hands when someone picks on my friends." He looked at her across the linoleum tabletop.

"You two need some time alone?" asked Grace.

"No," they both said in unison, and then smiled.

"No, let's get on with it," said Cole. "Dan Campbell is definitely on the list. He's had it out for Archie for years. Once when Dan was guiding up Knight Inlet, and had just taken a party ashore to circle around on a grizzly feeding on salmon, Archie buzzed the outlet in the *Inlet Dancer*, scaring the hell out of the bear and ruining poor Dan's hunt. I think Dan and Archie's relationship went downhill after that. Remember that, Grace?"

"Oh yeah, I remember. Dad couldn't stop talking about that for a month. He and Darren First Moon were up Knight Inlet guiding a fishing party and came across Campbell and those rich Americans tying off along West Cedar Creek, about to head up on foot.

Archie told *his* boatload of rich Americans to hold on, and they powered up and swamped Dan's boat. One of the hunters lost his rifle in the drink. Dan wanted to kill Archie after that."

"Yeah, well, maybe he never forgot. So he's on the list."

"Opportunity?" asked Nancy.

"He's got a boat. We can ask around if he was in or out of port on the night Archie disappeared."

"I can do that," said Grace.

They all nodded.

"What about someone from Stoboltz?" asked Nancy. "If Archie was onto them about something they've got brewing up at — what was the place again?"

"Jeopardy Rock," Cole and Grace said in unison.

"Right, if Archie was onto something going on at Jeopardy Rock, well, maybe it was serious enough to warrant somebody at the company taking aim at him."

"Man, that would have to be something pretty serious. I mean, Archie has been hard-balling Stoboltz for what, ten years now?" said Cole. "He was a gadfly in every project they've put on the table in the Broughton. And for two years he sat with them at the negotiating table, too. I think they came to respect each other during that time. You know, got to see one another as human beings and all that. I don't know —"

"My bet would be on Thurlow," said Grace. "He gives me the creeps."

"Well, that's good enough for me," said Cole.

"No, really, have you ever met him?"

"Just the once," said Cole, "but I only shook his hand."

"He's a total cold fish. Which I guess is perfect for his line of work. He has a PhD in genetics, and another one in zoology. He's some kind of genius. But when you talk with him it's like he expresses no emotion whatsoever. It's like nobody is home."

"Okay, he sounds pretty creepy. What say you call him up for an interview, Webber?"

Nancy smiled at Cole. "Sounds like the company had a motive, but in Canada, companies generally don't go around whacking people who disagree with them. That's Central America stuff."

"Don't think of it as the company," said Grace, looking out the window. The fog had started to clear, and she could see across the road to the harbour. "It's a personal thing."

"Did Thurlow have it out for Archie?"

"I don't know. I only met him a few times. Dad didn't talk about him. But if Thurlow was head of research at Stoboltz, and we know they were doing some work at Jeopardy Rock —"

"We just don't know what," said Cole.

"— then maybe Thurlow had reason to want Dad dead."

"Can't hurt to call him and suss him out on this whole sordid mess," said Nancy, jotting a note on her pad.

"I want Lance Grey on that list, too," said Cole.

"The minister's SA?" said Grace.

"SA?" asked Nancy.

Cole looked at Nancy. "Special assistant. He's the minister of agriculture's point man on aquaculture. He's an upwardly mobile politico. He's, like, thirteen years old. Totally ruthless. And from what we've seen, he's in thick with Stoboltz. They may be greasing his palms in return for favours and trinkets from the ministry, for all we know."

"Did he have motive?" asked Nancy.

"Same as Thurlow. His fate seems tied to theirs."

"But what about opportunity? Was he even in the area? Can he drive a boat?"

"Call him up and ask him?"

"I have some self-respect left, Cole."

"You gave that up when you got on a plane in Calgary, Webber."

"Right. I forgot which crowd I was running with again."

"Okay," said Grace. "That about does it, right?"

Cole closed his eyes. "Greg, Dan, Lance, and Thurlow. Four. Are we sure there's nobody else? Did Archie piss anybody else off?"

"Is there anybody he didn't?"

"Bad enough to want him dead?"

Now it was Grace's turn to look thoughtful. A shadow passed over her face, and was gone.

"What is it?" asked Nancy.

"Nothing. Nope, I think we've got them all. Let's get to work, and huddle again tonight."

"Did you want to call Darren?" asked Cole. "See if he can join us tonight. He must be wanting to get back to Parish Island pretty soon."

Grace's face remained grey. "Yeah, I'll call him. If the RCMP want to hold onto the *Inlet Dancer*, Jacob can take us all back to Port Lostcoast when we're ready."

"Okay," said Cole. "I'm going to start by looking in on the Mounties. See if they got their man yet."

■ Cole walked along Alert Bay's picturesque waterfront, looking toward the mouth of the Nimpkish River across the opening to Johnstone Strait. Hands in his pockets, he walked past the ferry terminal, and, when he reached the government docks, kept on going. There was no point in stopping; he could see that the RCMP was still busy with the boat. Two police patrol vessels were moored nearby, and two Suburbans were parked at the dock. Instead of going to stand with his reticent friends, he continued walking. He didn't know where he was going until he passed the Anglican church. After another five minutes of walking, he passed the ageing cannery and could see his destination. Now called Namgis House, the deteriorating four-storey brick building was once St. Michael's Indian Residential School. Opened in 1929, the school housed upward of two hundred boys and girls taken from many of the First Nations on northern Vancouver Island and across the scattering of islands in the Broughton Archipelago.

Cole passed a totem pole lying in the grass at the side of the road; it was a work in progress. Beyond it were the native docks, where Jacob's boat, the *Salmon Pride,* was moored. Cole could see the U'mista Cultural Centre adjacent to the school, its long, low cedar construction culminating in a Big House where more than a hundred potlatch masks had been repatriated and carefully presented to the public. Cole walked past the leafless trees in the yard of Namgis House and stood, hands in his pockets, looking up at the structure. A sign attached to a fence on one side of the building read "Watch for Falling Bricks."

He drew a deep breath of sea air and exhaled.

Murdered. Though the RCMP hadn't yet finished their investigation, Cole knew in his gut that Archie Ravenwing had been murdered. He just knew. And so did Grace. And now, so did Nancy. He shook his head. The undeniable truth was jarring. For a man to die at sea, doing what he loved, was one thing. But to be killed, in what must have been such a brutal fashion, was another altogether. Cole was both shocked by and strangely accepting of Archie Ravenwing's unnatural death. He didn't know which upset him more.

So much pain, he thought. Standing in front of a place where children had been taken from their families and subjected to myriad of cruelties — from the loss of their families, culture, and language to physical and sexual abuse — Cole felt the culmination of that pain, now born out of Archie's demise. He felt hot tears welling in him and turned away from the building, embarrassed and ashamed. Weeping doesn't help a damn thing, his father had once told him when he had jammed his hand in the barn door bringing in the horses. He had been eight. His father had flown into a rage at the sight of Cole's tears, and Cole had never again cried in front of his father. He had never again cried, period. Not until recently.

Cole walked across the lawn of the band office toward the water, his eyes red. He rubbed them with his knuckles to banish the tears. Tears wouldn't bring Archie Ravenwing back from the dead, and tears wouldn't erase the century of abuse and cultural genocide inflicted on the First Nations people who lived on these remote islands. Instead, Cole did what he always did: he got angry. He let the sorrow for the loss of his friend and the agony of a people who now, after more than one hundred years, were reclaiming their own culture, dissolve into rage. Rage was acceptable to his father. Rage his father could understand.

Cole stood on the pebbled shore, watching the boats return at the end of the day, watching the sun sink low through the jumble of clouds over Vancouver Island. The tears were gone; now he had fuel for the work that needed to be done, to find the man who had killed his friend. Cole Blackwater's fuel was anger.

22 By the end of the following day, they had returned to Parish Island. Darren First Moon, Grace, and Jacob Ravenwing, along with Cole and Nancy, sat in the *Salmon Pride's* cabin for the journey through Cormorant Channel, across the southern end of Queen Charlotte Strait, and into the mouth of the Broughton Archipelago. Nancy watched the islands pass by as Jacob threaded his boat through the twists and turns of the passage.

"It is so beautiful here," she said, smiling, watching the cedar- and fir-draped domes of tiny islands pass to the port and starboard of the *Salmon Pride.*

Cole watched Nancy. There is no doubt, he thought, that having her here is going to help us get to the bottom of this. She's got a sharp mind, a keen intellect, and is, without a doubt, a good investigative reporter. Cole watched her observe the clutch of tiny islets between Fold and Parish Island on the starboard side of the boat.

"Eagles," she said, pointing. Cole peered through the windows of the boat and saw a half dozen bald eagles perched in the tops of trees on an island no bigger than a soccer field.

Cole told himself that he had involved Nancy because she could help Archie's family in clearing up Archie's death. But he knew there was more to it than that. How much more, he just wasn't prepared to deal with. He did know that from the second she had arrived the day before, he had felt lighter somehow. Now it seemed that the weight of the world was evenly distributed between *two* sets of shoulders. But there was more to it than that.

They reached the harbour at Port Lostcoast near dark, unloaded themselves and their gear, and agreed to meet at the bluff house after supper.

"I'll see if the old lady will let me out of her sight again," said Darren First Moon, a big smile on his broad face. "I think I can talk her into it." He set off, lugging his duffle bag homeward.

They went their separate ways, with Grace, Cole, and Nancy walking up the hill toward the house. Cole filled Nancy in on Port Lostcoast's demographics as they went.

"I find it hard to believe that a man like Dan Campbell would live here, given that the town is three-quarters First Nations."

"It's the closest settlement to Knight Inlet. It's the best point of access for all the salmon farms on the southern part of the archipelago. They all use this harbour as a re-supply point. People like Dan come here because of the economic opportunity," said Grace Ravenwing.

"*White* people like Dan?" asked Nancy.

"Not just white," said Cole.

She looked over the ramshackle houses that made up most of the town of Port Lostcoast. "Doesn't really seem like that economic opportunity is evenly distributed."

"It's taken my people some time," said Grace, "to adopt the mindset of capitalism. I'm not saying that we were a perfect people before George Vancouver, just different. We had plenty of commerce, we even had slavery, but we also had the potlatch, where we gave away much of our wealth to one another. It's taken a real shift for us to view the ocean and the forests as resources to be exploited. For ten thousand years we were stewards. More than that, really. We were completely dependent on a living ocean for our very lives. Our lives were inextricably linked. To a raven, from above, we were just another animal living in harmony with the ocean, with the woods.

"Now, for the last hundred years, we've been told to steal. Many of our people have resisted this lesson. Some haven't. It's very difficult when you're surrounded by exploitation, and you watch everything you believe in taken from you for shortsighted profit, not to want to be a part of that."

Cole and Nancy were silent the rest of the way up the hill.

They reached the house and went inside. Grace showed Nancy to the spare bedroom. Cole moved his things into Archie's office and would sleep on the hideaway couch in the living room.

"This is very gracious of you," said Nancy.

"Just trying to curry favour is all," said Grace, smiling.

Grace made a fish stew and they ate it with defrosted bread. They opened a bottle of wine.

"Has anybody talked to Cassandra Petrel?" asked Grace after they had finished supper.

Cole thought about it. Finally he said, "I can't believe I haven't yet."

"Who's Cassandra Petrel again?" asked Nancy.

"Dr. Cassandra Petrel. She's one of the world's leading experts on sea lice. She lives on a boat in the harbour here. She and Dad have been like two peas in a pod this winter," said Grace. "Dad would help Cassandra with sampling, and Cassandra would prepare the materials and send them off for analysis. She's the brains of that outfit."

"I'll talk with her in the morning," said Cole, fidgeting.

"Let's make some coffee. Darren and Jacob will be here soon."

They sat around the kitchen table, the lights low, the moon fat on the horizon. Darren was the last to arrive, begging forgiveness. "Nearly got skinned alive," he cracked, coming in the door. They offered him coffee and he joined them.

"Okay, let's review what we've learned," said Cole, assuming the position of chairperson. "Grace?"

"I looked into the rope before we left Alert Bay," she said. "First I cruised the docks, just on the off chance that I might find a rope that matched the one we found on the *Dancer*. No luck. So then I went to Tagarts and Barry's Marine and asked about recent purchases of rope of any kind. At Tagarts they told me that they don't keep track. At Barry's an old high-school friend was behind the counter and he said that he'd try to get the records and call me. I think that the rope thing is a dead end, though. I mean, everybody has enough rope on their boats to replace a bow line when it breaks. It's unlikely that we're going to find Dad's killer that way."

"Worth a shot," said Cole.

"And I'll be checking in with the harbour master tomorrow about the comings and goings on the day of Dad's disappearance," added Grace.

"Will you talk with folks around town about any money that might have crossed hands?"

"That's going to be a harder nut to crack," said Grace. "If

people took gas money to get to the polls, they're not going to want to admit it, are they?"

"Likely not," said Cole.

"I can do that," said Darren First Moon.

Cole looked at him. "You sure? You won't be making any friends. Maybe I should."

"Like an Indian is going to tell a white guy that he took cash to vote."

"Fair point," said Cole. "Okay, Darren is on the bribery squad. What about you, Webber?"

Nancy smiled. "Well, I made a bunch of calls from my hotel room in Alert Bay. Tried to reach this Thurlow guy, but the best I could do was leave messages for him. The Vancouver office told me he's in the field, whatever that means. I gave him my cell number and this number like you said to, Grace, and we'll see what happens. I'll keep trying tomorrow."

"What about Grey?"

"Better luck there. I reached one Mr. Lance Grey this morning. Told him I was doing a story on fish farms for the *Post*, and he was more than happy to talk. We spent most of the time talking about the issue of whether or not fish farms were harmful to the environment. I learned a lot. I don't know what you are all so upset about. According to the government, there are really no serious impacts —"

"Come off it," said Cole.

Nancy smirked. "The guy is a mouthpiece for industry. I'm going to have to do some background checking on him, 'cause he's way too enthusiastic to merely be a proponent. He's more like a booster. I did ask him how often he got up here, and he said not often enough. He was here for the potlatch, which you all know. He said the last time he was here before that was in August."

"That figures. I guess we couldn't exactly expect him to place himself at the scene of the crime if he was involved though, could we?" said Cole.

"I'm going to put a request in for his schedule," said Nancy. "But that could take a month or more to get through Freedom of Information."

Cole exhaled. "Okay, what else have we got?" He looked around the room.

"What did the RCMP say?" asked Darren.

"Well, not a whole lot. Those guys are a reticent bunch. I spoke with Constable Johns again this morning. He says the Campbell River team have finished their work. Says they did an inch-by-inch search of the boat. As you all know, they are holding the *Inlet Dancer* until they get the results. That's why our man Jacob here is playing water taxi for us."

Jacob smiled.

"They didn't say that they were opening an official investigation?" asked Nancy.

"Just that Archie is still considered a missing person until they find conclusive evidence otherwise."

They sat around the table and sipped coffee.

"I feel like we're getting nowhere," said Grace.

"Me too," said Darren.

"We've got a lot of work to do tomorrow, folks. Maybe it's time to pack it in."

"Are we sure we're on the right track?" asked Darren.

"You mean, are we searching in the right places for a killer?"

"I mean, maybe he was swept overboard."

"It's not out of the realm of possibilities," admitted Cole.

"I think it is," said Grace. "We all saw the blood. He was on the deck of that boat long enough to leave a lot of blood behind. Waves don't pick up one-hundred-eighty-pound men and leave a thermos. This was no accident."

They sat and looked at each other.

"Okay," said Cole. "There you have it."

■ In the morning Grace walked down to the general store while Nancy and Cole drank coffee and ate toast. She came back with a heavy brown envelope, which they eagerly tore open. Cole re-read the letter from Archie and felt a knot form in his throat. He handed it to Grace to read, and tears formed in her eyes as his words sunk in. Finally, Grace gave the letter to Nancy.

Cole stood up abruptly. "I've got to talk to Cassandra Petrel," he said, grabbing his coat and heading out the door.

There was a sharp wind blowing from the north, churning the channel outside the tiny harbour into whitecaps. Cole turned up the collar of his leather coat and stepped into the wind, making his way down through the clutch of houses to the docks. He found his way onto the slip where Grace had told him he would find Petrel's Whitby. Locating the boat wasn't hard; it was the only sailboat in a harbour full of fishing rigs. Cole looked around to see if he was being observed, then knocked on the cabin of the boat above the companionway. The wooden door opened and Cassandra Petrel's grey head poked out. She smiled.

"Dr. Petrel, I'm Cole Blackwater."

"Oh, Cole, yes, Archie told me about you. Come in," she said, moving back from the door. He stepped through the portal and down half a dozen steps to the galley of the boat.

"Thanks," he said, entering the room. It was a lovely space, decked out in polished wood and fine chrome finishing.

"Can I fix you tea? Or coffee?"

"Coffee would be good. Listen, I'm sorry to come by unannounced."

"It's fine. This is Port Lostcoast. Everything happens unannounced around here. Do you want to sit?"

"Sure," he said. She pointed to a small, built-in couch by the door and he sat, looking around him. "I like your boat," he said.

"Thank you," she said. "I like it, too."

"You've sailed all your life?"

"Didn't start out that way. My father fished. I grew up on a troller. When I was an undergrad I worked as a DFO observer on a dragger. But when I finished my PhD I sort of gave up spending time on boats. I was always in the lecture hall or in the lab. I spent all my time in front of a class of undergrads, a computer, or hunched over a microscope," she said, grinding coffee. "But I missed the ocean. A few years ago events conspired to allow me to get back on a boat," she said with a sly smile. "I sold my house in Victoria and bought this ketch in San Francisco. A friend of mine and I piloted it up here. I never intended to live on it. But I kept spending so much of my time up here and in the Charlottes that I figured maybe I'd just better move. I gave up on universities and here I am."

"How long have you been here?"

"Oh, maybe six years now." She handed him a cup of coffee. "Cream or sugar?"

"Just cream, please." She handed him his coffee and he sipped it, savouring the warmth. Cole didn't know where to start. "You study sea lice?" he finally said, looking around the floating laboratory.

Petrel laughed. "Yeah, I guess I do. Didn't start out that way. I studied whales."

It was Cole's turn to laugh. "Hard to get a whale in here," he said, looking around.

"It was *National Geographic*'s fault."

Cole sipped his coffee. "Really?"

Petrel sat down opposite him. "Yeah. January 1979. You must remember the issue, Cole. It was the one where the magazine came with the little floppy 45 recording of whale songs."

Cole's eyes lit up. "Of course I remember it! It was amazing!"

"I thought so, too. The piece was called "Humpbacks: Their Mysterious Songs." It was written by a guy named Roger Payne. I was an undergrad then, and one of my roommates brought the magazine back from spring break and played it." She laughed at the memory. "She played it during a house party. We'd been listening to some disco crap, the Bee Gees or something. All of a sudden the whole house was filled with these eerie sounds. It was really wild. People just stopped dancing and stood still. After about a minute someone put an ABBA record on, but I got the whale recording and took it back to my dorm. I put it on the turntable and listened to it half a dozen times that night. I was captivated!"

"I know what you mean," said Cole. He closed his eyes. "Mr. Elliot's third-grade homeroom," he said. "That's where I heard it. This was Claresholm, Alberta, you understand. *Popular Mechanics* was the magazine of choice in most households. But Mr. Elliot brought the record in one day. He closed the door and drew the blinds. Nobody knew what was going to happen. We all thought Elliot was a bit crazy so we all just sat there, all these grade-three kids. And then he turned on the record player and turned up the volume and put on that little record. It blew us away. Some kids got pretty scared. It was a little creepy. But for a bunch of kids in the foothills of Alberta, it was astounding to hear those first recordings of whale sounds."

"*Songs of the Deep*," said Cassandra. "Well, it got me hooked. I went down a marine track in my zoology courses, and then spent the next fifteen years studying grey whales, humpback whales, and later, killer whales. It was the orca that led me to these little guys," she said, picking up a glass vial of sea lice.

"Killer whales aren't troubled by sea lice," said Cole.

"No, but their food is. I was studying orcas, and looking at their food, and then their food started to disappear, and that led me up here, and to this," she said, holding the vial.

"Bet nobody ever made a recording of sea lice to put in *National Geographic*," said Cole.

"No. But in a way, these little buggers have a way bigger impact than the biggest whale."

Cole was silent. He finished his coffee.

"So anyway, that's a roundabout way of saying that sea lice aren't very sexy, but they are at the very centre of what's happening to a dying ocean." She put down the vial and folded her hands on the table. "Now, what can I do for you, Cole?"

Cole's smile faded. "I'm afraid I have to tell you something that might upset you."

Petrel's face darkened.

"Well, Grace and I have come to believe that Archie Ravenwing was murdered."

The colour drained from Cassandra Petrel's face. The corners of her mouth dropped.

"I'm sorry to have to tell you this. We spent the last few days in Alert Bay hoping to recover the *Inlet Dancer*. But we found something that makes us think that foul play is involved in the disappearance of our friend."

"What is it?"

"We found what we think is blood congealed in the seal around the engine compartment. If it is blood, it leaves a really big question as to how so much of it was spilled on the deck of the boat, and why it's there if Archie was swept overboard." Cole briefed her on the ongoing RCMP investigation.

Cassandra placed her cup of tea on the counter that separated her tiny sitting room from the galley. She took a breath and exhaled, shaking her head.

"Dr. Petrel, I need to know what you and Archie were talking about. He wrote me a letter and said he thought that Stoboltz was up to no good. He said that you knew about some kind of genetic engineering going on at Jeopardy Rock. Something that involved Atlantic salmon. Archie said he suspected that they were working on sea lice, too. Can you help me understand this?"

"I'm not a geneticist, Cole. My degrees are in biology and zoology."

"But you know a little about this field, don't you?" he pleaded.

"Enough to fill in some gaps," she said. "What Archie and I know for sure is that Stoboltz was spending a lot of time and money trying to breed Atlantic salmon to be more resistant to disease and to parasites like sea lice. No big surprise. If you have millions and millions of dollars invested in fish, and a little critter the size of your pinky nail could take them down, you'd want to find ways of strengthening that fish's defenses. Of course, we've always believed that the best way to protect both farmed fish and wild salmon is to have contained pens on dry land. That way, the Atlantic salmon don't pass on disease to wild salmon, and they don't pick up sea lice from the surrounding ocean. But it's expensive, and if the government won't push the companies to do it, they sure aren't going to do it on their own.

"So no big surprise that they were doing genetic work on salmon. But what we didn't realize until Archie came back from Victoria with the packet of information someone passed on to him was that Stoboltz was engineering sea lice as well. They were, in effect, creating a more potent breed of sea lice. Smaller — so that more of them could attach themselves to a salmon smolt — and more aggressive, so that the rate of mortality among the smolts would be higher."

Cole drew a sharp breath and looked down at the floor. He sat forward. "Why? Why in God's name would they want to do that?"

"I don't know."

"No idea?"

"Oh, I've got lots of ideas. But no proof."

"Can you guess?"

Petrel smiled. "Archie asked me to guess the last time he was here."

Cole locked his fingers and looked intently at Dr. Petrel. "I think that whatever you and Archie were guessing at must have been pretty much bang on, Doctor. I think that Archie went out to Jeopardy Rock to try and get proof, and my guess is that's what got him killed."

Cassandra reached for her cup of tea, now cold. She took a sip. Her hands shook. Cole could see the anguish on her face.

"Dr. Petrel," he insisted.

"It's just Cassandra out here, Cole."

"Please."

"I think that Stoboltz plans to release those engineered sea lice into the Broughton Archipelago."

Cole sat back, his hands falling to his sides. His face twisted into a question.

"Think about it this way," said Petrel. "You're in a fight with the bleeding-hearted environmentalists over the future of salmon farms. You've paid off the local politicians, in this case a band councillor. You've got the provincial government in your pocket. But you still can't seem to convince the public that farmed Atlantic salmon is good for you. There's these nagging concerns that they have higher levels of disease. And then there's the question of what the Atlantic salmon are doing to the native stocks. People start saying, hey, fish is good food, but we prefer the wild stuff. Hell, we'll even pay more for it. *That's what's happening.* Carrie Bright's campaign has been working.

"But the salmon farms and the pests that they bring, namely

our little friends there —" she nodded at the plastic baggies filled with sea lice on her table in the galley — "are driving the wild fish toward a painful, almost certain, extinction. Why not speed it up? Why not give the native stocks the push they need? Get it over and done with fast. So you breed your Atlantic salmon to be more resistant to sea lice. Because it's only smolts and juveniles that succumb to sea lice, the adult Atlantics in the open pens are pretty safe as it is. But, to be sure, you beef up their resistance so that young fish can withstand higher levels of infestation. And then you breed sea lice that are more aggressive, and you release them into the general population. I'd do it by infesting a bunch of Atlantic salmon with the lice and engineering a massive escape. It's not uncommon for farmed fish to escape into the wild population. It happens all the time. But now you'd have thousands, maybe tens of thousands, of fish covered with this new super breed of sea lice escaping just as the migration begins. The native salmon wouldn't know what hit them. Within a few years, the entire populations in the Broughton could be wiped out. The rest of the coast wouldn't be far behind. And these little guys are travellers. So the sea lice could spread all up and down the coast. And then there is Asia and Europe. What Stoboltz is up to, if my theory is correct, could be the end of wild salmon forever."

■ Grace met Cole on the road outside the general store, where he was walking with determination up the dock, the look on his face dark as a bruise.

"Hey, Cole," Grace said.

He looked up, his face clearing a little. "Hey, Grace."

"You look pretty angry."

"Just talked with Doc Petrel."

"What gives?"

He looked around him. They were alone on the dirt street. "She thinks — well, guesses, actually — that Stoboltz was doing genetic engineering on both penned salmon and sea lice. She hypothesizes that Stoboltz is planning to wipe out wild salmon."

"You're kidding. You think that's what Dad discovered at Jeopardy Rock?"

"I think so." Cole looked out at the harbour. The chill wind pushed at his face, his hair flew in the wind.

Grace took a deep breath of the cold air. "Okay," she said. Cole reached his hand out and took her arm.

"Your father would be so proud of you, Grace," he said. "You are being so brave."

She pushed a tear aside, looked up at him, and smiled. "I've got to go check on the whereabouts of some boats," she said.

"Okay," said Cole. "I'm going to follow up with Nancy on this." He let go of her arm and walked toward the bluff house.

Grace watched him go. She took another deep breath and let it out. When Cole Blackwater had come to Parish Island several years before, Grace was a new teacher at the school in the Port Lostcoast Community Centre. Fresh from community college with a teacher's certificate, Grace had returned to her home to help other young people find meaning in their lives. Too many of her friends had dropped out of school and, finding only seasonal work on the fishing boats, had turned to alcohol to fill their days. Depression was like a dark cloud hanging over her community. Several young people tried, and one succeeded, in killing themselves the year Grace came home to teach. She thought if she could give them a glimpse of their potential, they might move off Parish Island and attend school in Alert Bay after eighth grade. Families there took young people in and helped them complete high school. Who knows, they might go to a trade school, community college, or even university. Then if they wanted to return to the islands, they could. That was what she had chosen for herself.

Archie had introduced Cole to Grace as their great hope in the fight to bring down the salmon farmers. Grace sat in on their strategy sessions. A number of white activists from Victoria had come to Parish Island for the weekend; they, along with Archie, Darren, and half a dozen other members of the North Salish First Nation, sat in the living room of the bluff house to plot strategy. Cole had led them through the day, and by the end they had a working plan to stop the expansion of salmon farming. By the end of the day, Grace Ravenwing was quite smitten with Cole Blackwater. His brooding good looks, crooked nose, shaggy mop of dark curls, and his slightly softening, but still able, body stirred her.

Grace walked along the pier to the harbour master's office. She looked at her watch. The office opened at eleven AM. She was right on time.

Grace had found Cole aloof. It was hard to read his intentions. She wasn't entirely unaccustomed to white men's lack of emotional maturity, but with Cole it was tinged with something else. Fear? Anger? It was hard to say. In the end, Grace knew it would never work. They had kissed one night at the end of the docks, the moon spilling ribbons of silver across the rolling water. But Cole had pulled away, explaining that it wasn't right. That Archie was his client. And that he wasn't ready for this.

"Okay," she had said.

They had walked back to the bluff house arm in arm.

Cole Blackwater was, *is*, a good man, thought Grace, but he's got something to work out of his system, she mused. Some kind of poison. Everybody could see it. Except the great Cole Blackwater himself, she thought.

She knocked on the harbour master's door, then stepped inside.

"Hi, Grace, how you holding out?" said Rupert Wright from behind a small desk.

"I'm doing okay," said Grace, closing the door to the small room behind her. She gave him a weak smile. The room smelled of pipe smoke and coffee.

"Can I offer you something to drink?"

"No, thanks, Rupert." Grace looked around her.

"Something I can help you with?"

"Well, I'm curious about what records you have for the night my father disappeared. I want to see which other boats came and went that day."

Rupert Wright looked at her. He was in his seventies, long retired from the Coast Guard. Port Lostcoast was his retirement posting. He maintained the part-time position of harbour master, and in exchange lived in the back of the tiny office and had free mooring on the government dock.

"I can have a look," he said. He turned in his seat and clicked the mouse a few times, waking up his computer. "What's on your mind, Grace?" he asked, his back to her as he found the correct file.

"Oh, not much. I guess I'm just wondering if anybody might have seen my dad that day."

"Lots of boats out in the inlet. Not all of them would have started here," he said. "I don't have access to other harbour logs," he said, still looking at the computer.

"It's okay, I'm just curious is all."

"Can't blame you. Here you go. It's not complete, you understand. Just a head count at noon and at sunset. Though there wasn't much of a sunset that day, you'll recall. Hell of a blow."

"Yes," she said, stepping behind him. "Hell of a blow."

He pointed to a screen and she read the names.

"Is that Greg White Eagle's boat?" she said, pointing to an entry.

"Yup. He calls it *First Eagle*."

She read the list.

"What about this one?" She pointed to an entry.

"It was out all day," said Wright.

"Can I look at the previous day's entries?"

"Sure." He called them up.

She scanned the page. A shadow darkened her complexion.

"Whose boat is that?"

"That one is a Stoboltz boat. It came in around eleven in the morning. Left a few hours later. Find what you were looking for?"

"I found more than that," she said, the smile now gone from her face.

■ Nancy Webber sat in Archie Ravenwing's office. What she was doing was dangerous, she knew it. She sipped a coffee and twisted in Archie's swivel chair. Coming to Port Lostcoast had been a mistake. She shouldn't have left Alberta. But here she was, sleeping under the same roof as Cole Blackwater. Cole had seemed somehow lighter since she had arrived. She guessed that the distractions of trying to unravel the mystery surrounding the disappearance of Archie Ravenwing had kept him from descending into the dark, brooding place where he sometimes fell. He seemed more alive. More vital.

But she couldn't help dwelling on her suspicions — of Cole himself. While she, Grace, Cole, and Darren worked through the various motives, means, and opportunities of the people who might have wanted Archie Ravenwing dead, Nancy reviewed what she knew of *Cole's* motive, means, and opportunity to want his *own* father six feet under.

She doodled in her notebook as she thought, slowly twisting back and forth in the chair. She wrote the word motive. Under it she wrote, "abuse, beatings," and then she wrote "humiliation." She tapped her pencil on the page. She drew a question mark and wrote "mother?" Cole knew. His mother had told him. Could that have pushed him over the edge?

She drank her coffee. Clear motive. No question about it.

Means. That seemed pretty easy. She wrote down "shotgun."

Opportunity. She wrote, "Cole on the farm. First time in twenty years. Father dies."

She drew a barn. Could Cole have entered the barn with a shotgun, walked right up to his old man, and blown his head off? Would the old man have seen him coming or not? Reimer had told her the blast was from below and into the face. Point blank. The sort of rage necessary to do that was beyond Nancy's comprehension. But then she hadn't been beaten as a child. And Cole certainly possessed a rage that at times made Nancy uncomfortable. That rage had seemed to fester since Oracle.

Sometimes those powerful emotions in Cole became passion, and it was that passion that had attracted Nancy to Cole in the first place. That continued to draw her to him.

She drew a drop of blood dripping from the barn.

The phone rang on Archie's desk and she jumped, almost knocking over her coffee.

"Ravenwing residence," she answered.

"Who's this?"

"It's Nancy Webber."

"Just the person I was looking for," said the unfamiliar voice on the other end of the line.

■ Cole Blackwater stepped into The Strait and crossed the plank floor to the bar, his boots making a heavy sound as he walked. Half a dozen tables were occupied, mostly by men eating a midday meal. The room was hot, and that warmth felt oppressive to Cole coming in from the cool of the harbour. He scanned the room and immediately recognized Dan Campbell sitting at a table with three other men. The conversation in the room grew quiet for a moment, and Cole could see out of the corner of his eye that his every step was being watched by the four men at Campbell's table.

The same bartender was there, placing a plate of food in front of a customer who sat on a stool. He looked at Cole. "Don't want any trouble from you today. We clear? You white boys want to mix it up, you go out in the street."

Cole grinned. "You got it. What's the lunch special?"

Cole ordered food and a pint of Kokanee and sat at the bar, his back to Campbell. He took a long pull on the beer, his mind thumbing through the information that Cassandra Petrel had just given him about Stoboltz. But while he was thinking, his attention never left the table of men just twenty feet behind him.

If Petrel's suspicions were true, and Archie Ravenwing had found out, then there was a very clear motive for keeping Archie silent. But killing the man? Cole hadn't had more than a casual introduction to anybody at Stoboltz, but he did have a hard time imagining anybody at one of the world's largest aquaculture companies killing someone, even if that someone was an irritating First Nations activist like Archie. Then again, Cassandra Petrel's hunch was very serious. Businesses did hire people to take care of irritating problems, but in the western world? Here? Cole Blackwater assumed that sort of thing was reserved for Central America, South America, the darker corners of southeast Asia. And usually the businesses themselves weren't on the up and up to start with. Could that be the case with Stoboltz? What might they be hiding?

His food arrived. Cole hazarded a glance around the room as

he slipped off his coat. Dan Campbell and his friends were still at their table.

He took a long drink of his beer and began to eat his sandwich and fries. Cole was halfway through his lunch when he heard a chair scrape back from Dan Campbell's table. He took a deep breath and focused on his surroundings. He turned slightly and watched from the corner of his eye as all four men at the table stood, wiping their mouths and hands on paper napkins. Three of the men scowled at Cole as they made their way toward the door, but Dan Campbell wasn't among them. Instead he pushed his chair in and walked to the bar where Cole sat. Cole looked straight ahead and drank from his beer.

"Had to get me some stitches the other night," said Dan, pointing to his chin.

Cole turned to look at him. "Yup," he said. "That doesn't look too comfortable," he said.

"I could press charges, you know. You started it."

Cole shrugged. "Go ahead," he said.

Dan looked around him. "Yeah, well," he said, "that's not the way we do it out here."

"If you're saying that you want to settle a score, then let's get it over with," said Cole.

"Whoa, take it easy there badass," said Dan.

"What do you want then?"

"I'm told it's *you* that was asking around for me."

"Word travels fast."

"It's a pretty small town."

"It is that."

"What do *you* want then?"

"Let's take a walk," said Cole, fishing a wad of money, gas receipts, elastic bands, and paperclips from his pocket. He found a five and a ten and left them on the bar. He threw back the rest of his pint and put on his coat. The two men left together. The rest of the people in the bar watched them go.

They stepped into the grey afternoon, the chill air feeling good against Cole's face and in his lungs. Cole had steadied himself for an attack once he had stepped outside, but none came.

"Let's walk down by the harbour," said Cole. "You got a boat here?"

Dan pointed toward a slip at the far end of the harbour. "The last slip that way. The *Queen Mary Two*," he said.

"Let's go have a look," said Cole.

They walked along the harbour and onto the dock.

"What's this all about?" asked Dan.

"You and Archie weren't very good friends, were you?" asked Cole.

Campbell laughed. "You can say that again."

"And it wasn't just because he was an Indian, was it?"

"Look," said Campbell, "this is a free country. A man's got a right to his opinions."

"True," said Cole, "but part of living in a free country means that a man doesn't have the right to promote hatred."

"What the fuck are you talking about?"

"You're a bigoted prick," said Cole without looking at him. "You hate these people. What I can't figure out is why you live here with them. Why not live in Port McNeill or Port Hardy, or up the coast?"

"Hunting is good along the coast. Hunting is what I do. And I don't see where you get off calling a man a bigot. I don't hate the Indians. But I think they're lazy sons of bitches that would rather sit on their asses than work, and I'm sick and tired of my hard-earned money getting taken by the government to pay these people to sit around and carve masks."

Cole drew a breath. "Archie worked hard."

"Archie Ravenwing was a pompous jackass," said Dan.

Cole began to think that this had been a bad idea. They stepped onto the pier in silence and made their way toward the *Queen Mary Two*.

"But he worked hard. What did you have against him?"

"Same thing I have against you, Blackwater. He was a meddler, just like you. Sticking his nose in where it don't belong. Fucking bleeding-heart liberal faggots always trying to tell other people how to live their lives. Don't do this, don't do that. Save the bears, save the trees. Look around you, Blackwater. Do you see any shortage of trees?" Campbell opened his arms and made a complete turn on the dock. "There is no fucking shortage of trees. And the bears are stumbling over one another to get at the salmon. I'm doing them a favour shooting them. Makes more room. But Archie was always sticking his nose in where it don't belong. It finally did him in."

"What do you mean by that?"

"Silly bastard was out in that storm is what I mean. Out dipping his nets for that bitch Petrel. And for what? What did it get him? Got the stupid bastard killed is what it got him."

Cole looked up. "Nice boat."

"It was my father's. He passed it on."

"Mind if I look around?"

Dan Campbell looked at him from under his ball cap. "What for?"

"Maybe I want to go hunting."

Campbell laughed. "Right. Go ahead. Don't make no difference to me."

Cole stepped onto the boat. It was a forty-foot steel-sided troller that had been converted for fishing trips and passengers. Cole walked around the cabin looking at the gunwales and at the cleats. Ropes were neatly stacked and coiled on the deck. Cole slipped from his pocket the length of rope he had taken from the stern of the *Inlet Dancer* and examined it. He looked at Dan Campbell's ropes. Rats, he thought. Weathered and worn and all of the same sort. He couldn't find any that had recently been cut, or looked new enough to have been replaced.

"You about done?" asked Campbell, spitting on the dock.

Cole stepped down. "Got any other boats?"

"Sure," said Campbell, "but I don't see how this is any of your business. What are you up to, Blackwater?"

Cole stood sideways to the man. "Here's the thing, Dan," he said. "I think that Archie Ravenwing was murdered."

Dan Campbell choked on a laugh. He sounded like a dog barking. "Oh, you really crack me up, Blackwater," he said when he had stopped laughing. "That's rich. Archie goes out in a storm and gets himself washed overboard and you come around here telling people that he was murdered. That's fucking rich. Next thing you're going to tell me is that you think I did it."

"Did you?"

"You are really something, Blackwater. I read about you in the newspaper. I read about you in Alberta and your little games. I read all about that mine manager and how you helped solve his murder. Now you're looking for a killer under every rock, is that it? Want to make yourself famous?"

"Dan, it's no secret that you hated Archie. Hated his race, and hated what he stood for."

"I got to get some work done this afternoon, Blackwater. It's been nice talkin' with you." He put a foot up on the gunwale of the boat and was about to step onto it. Cole grabbed his arm. Dan wrenched it from Cole's grasp, his hat flying off as he did. "Get your fucking hands off me, you environmentalist fuck. If you put your Indian-loving hand on me again I'm going to break your neck."

"Is that how you killed Archie Ravenwing?"

Cole could see Dan's face turn red, his eyes bulge. His thin hair stood on end, and he looked like a madman. Cole readied himself for violence.

"You better get your ass out of Port Lostcoast, and take that piece of pussy you brought here along with you. If I see you again, I'm going to knock every one of your goddamned teeth right down your throat."

"You'll see me again," said Cole, fighting to control his breath and avoid choking on his words. "I guarantee it." He turned his back to Dan and walked back toward town.

23 They met at Greg White Eagle's home. It was almost noon when Nancy arrived, and the house was filled with the smell of food. Nancy was greeted at the door by a middle-aged woman in a long, blue dress and printed apron. "Come in," the woman said. "You must be the reporter." Nancy smiled and stepped into the house, directly into the kitchen. A square table was in the middle of the room, and the aroma of cooking fish filled the air.

"Can I offer you coffee? Greg is on the phone right now. He'll be right out."

"Coffee would be nice," said Nancy.

"I'm Martha. Greg's wife." She offered a hand.

"Pleased to meet you."

Nancy took a seat at the table and sipped her coffee. The room was bright, the cupboard painted white and the linoleum floor polished to a shine. But the house felt small and a little damp, and Nancy thought maybe the floor listed to one side a little.

She sat a moment in silence, watching Martha put the finishing touches on a fish chowder. As she placed slices of bread into a pan, the room filled with the sizzle and smell of frying.

Greg White Eagle entered the room like a storm. "You must be Nancy. I see you've got a cup of coffee. Have you eaten? Let's have a quick lunch and then talk. Martha, can you set Ms. Webber up?"

Nancy didn't have time to protest before a bowl of soup was set in front of her, and she had to admit that she was famished. They ate a lunch of chowder with grilled cheese sandwiches on the side. "I'm a simple man," said White Eagle, a few crumbs falling from the corner of this mouth onto the plate. "I have simple tastes."

They finished their food, and Martha cleared the table. "Can I get you anything else?"

"No, thank you. That was really delicious."

"More coffee?"

"No, thanks. I'm fully caffeinated."

Greg White Eagle laughed. "Come, let's sit in my office."

Nancy followed the big man to the back of the house. The

hallway was dark, the wood panelling stained with water in a few places.

"This place belonged to my father," said White Eagle, noticing Nancy's gaze. "He built it himself after World War II. He was stationed overseas. Used up his soldier pay building this place for my mama. It's hard to keep anything from rotting in this climate." Greg smiled, pointing to a stiff-backed chair for Nancy to sit in. His office was a tiny room off the back of the house. His desk was piled with papers and clippings and file folders, his computer nearly buried in folders and stacks of assorted reading material.

"Thanks for coming by," he said, sitting just a few feet from her.

"Thanks for returning my call."

"Not every day we get a reporter like you in Port Lostcoast. Are you here for the announcement?"

Nancy felt a flash of heat in her face. She held his gaze. "That's right."

"Good news, you know. Good news. We've been working on this for years. It's good news for the people of Port Lostcoast and for First Nations all up and down the coast."

"Good news?" Nancy said, sounding quizzical.

"Good news," repeated White Eagle. "The First Nations Opportunity Fund is just the sort of thing that coastal communities need to turn themselves around. It's the sort of investment that will allow our communities to prosper." His words sounded rehearsed to Nancy, and she flipped open her notebook as encouragement.

"Tell me more about that."

"Well, what the fund will do is put money into communities like Port Lostcoast to help us train our people to meet today's employment needs. The idea is to help our people train for work in resource-based economies. So folks in the interior will be trained in forest management. Folks in the north, mining. Here on the coast, fisheries and aquaculture."

"Haven't we seen this sort of program before?"

"I guess so. I'm new to this politics thing, so I don't have all the history. But I've been working with Victoria on this now for about a year, and I feel this will be a real boon for our nation."

"Can you say what makes this one different?"

"Well, industry is on board with it. That's going to make all the difference."

"What do they get?"

"Cash. Cash for training. Cash to subsidize on-the-job instruction. Businesses can apply to the fund to work with communities like Port Lostcoast to put people to work. Did you know that at certain times of the year our unemployment hovers around seventy percent! Nearly everybody in this town is out of work. Nearly everybody in this town depends on welfare at some point in the year. These people are dirt poor. It's time somebody did something about it. That's my job. I take it pretty seriously. And I'm sorry to say that my predecessor did not."

Nancy made some notes on her pad.

"Look, I know that you must have some kind of connection there. That's obvious. But I got to tell you, Archie Ravenwing didn't do much to lift this community out of poverty. He was too busy trying to shut down the employers, like salmon farms and grizzly hunting guide outfitters. The man was obsessed."

"Didn't sport fishing and the native fishery keep people employed?"

"To an extent, yes, but it was seasonal. The native salmon fishery has been in decline for more than a decade. If there are no fish, there are no jobs."

"I think that was the point," said Webber. "I think that was Archie's point, wasn't it?"

"You can stand around waving your arms all you like about the disappearing salmon, or you can do something to help your people adapt to the new reality. I'm choosing to help my people react to the new reality. Archie was stuck in the old days."

Nancy tapped her pencil. She looked around the humble office. "Some people would say that by working with Stoboltz and other salmon farming companies you're colluding with the enemy. You're working with the very people who are responsible for the demise of the wild salmon."

"Sea lice are natural—"

"But not in the numbers that we see today," said Nancy, finding herself on shaky ground. She'd only just read some material that morning, and was searching her memory for arguments.

"Look, whether we like it or not, Stoboltz is here to stay. They have two dozen operations in the Broughton alone. If we play our cards right, people around here might have a shot at good paying jobs that last nearly year round. Imagine that, year-round employment! People stand to make a lot of money if we play our cards right."

"What about you?" said Nancy, reaching for her trump card.

"What about me?" said Greg, tilting his head to the side.

"What do you stand to gain?"

"If I do my job right, my people will re-elect me. That will be gain enough."

Nancy steadied herself and said, "I have information that suggests Stoboltz provided you with money during the election. Money that went above and beyond a campaign contribution."

Greg looked as if he had been punched in the stomach. "What are you accusing me of?"

"Nothing, Mr. White Eagle. But I have seen this information, and it reflects very poorly on you, on Stoboltz, and on certain members of the provincial government."

"That's horseshit, and you know it." Greg White Eagle sat back in his chair and looked out the tiny window.

"Did you accept a bribe from Stoboltz Aquaculture that you then passed onto others in this community in return for votes?"

"Where do you get off coming in here and making accusations like that?"

"Did you? Did Stoboltz give you money in return for your support for expanded salmon farming in the archipelago?"

Greg White Eagle shifted his bulk in the chair. Nancy watched him, saying nothing. Let him play out the rope, she thought.

He turned to look at her. "I think you're in with that Cole Blackwater character, aren't you?" he asked. "I think you and he are working together. I know that he and Archie were pals.

I know all about Archie, see. Archie, the white knight. Archie, the noble savage, protecting his people's traditions and culture. Archie, salmon king. Well, Archie Ravenwing was a bold-faced crook. Bet your Cole Blackwater didn't tell you that, did he? Bet he didn't tell you that Archie Ravenwing had been stealing money from his own people for personal gain."

"I know about it. Grace told me," said Nancy, trying to remain calm. "But I'm not asking about Archie Ravenwing, Councillor. I'm asking about you."

"I've got all the financial records," said White Eagle, ignoring her. "Looks like old Archie Ravenwing was even skimming money from his friends. Invoices sent by a company called Blackwater Strategies were to be paid in cash, according to Archie. I wonder if that money ever made it to your friend?" White Eagle smiled a smug grin. "You start writing about corruption, Ms. Webber, I'll see to it that all sorts of stories get told."

Nancy smiled. "Where were you on the night Archie disappeared, Mr. White Eagle?"

"Right here at home."

"You didn't go out that night? Or maybe in the afternoon?"

"I was in Alert Bay for a band council meeting in the morning, and I got home around suppertime."

"Were you seen?"

"What do you mean, was I seen? Of course I was seen. My kids saw me, my wife saw me. Maybe even my neighbours saw me! What are you suggesting?" he yelled.

"Nothing. Nothing at all. I want to write a story about Port Lostcoast on the day Archie went missing is all."

Greg White Eagle took a deep breath and let it out. "You got a particular way of asking things, Ms. Webber, that gets a man pretty riled up. You know that?"

"It's my specialty," said Nancy Webber, standing and extending her hand.

■ Grace Ravenwing heard the phone ringing as she walked up the pathway that cut through the windblown grasses from the dirt road. She ran the last twenty feet and burst through the unlocked door in time to catch the phone on the fifth and final ring.

"Hello?" she said, catching her breath.

"Is this Grace Ravenwing?"

"This is she."

"It's Detective Sergeant Alan Bates calling. Constable Derek Johns of the Alert Bay detachment has briefed me on this incident. I'm with the Integrated Major Crimes unit based in Victoria. We're made up of officers from the RCMP, Victoria PD, and the Oak Bay PD. I'm with the RCMP, myself. Do you have a few minutes to chat, Ms. Ravenwing?"

"I do. Go ahead." She sat down at the kitchen table and looked out the windows at the ocean.

"We're going to open a case file on the disappearance of your father. At this time we're not willing to call it a murder investigation. It will officially be a missing person file, and his disappearance will be treated as suspicious. The Integrated Major Crimes unit is called in to investigate all such suspicious activities. Do you understand, Ms. Ravenwing?"

"I do." She touched her cheek with her free hand and let the fingers rest there. "Does that mean you found something? Something on the boat? Was it blood?"

"The substance you discovered around the seals of the engine compartment was human blood. There was quite a lot of it. Using Luminol, we also picked up minute traces of it around the wheelhouse, around the bottom of the seat, and in a pool that extended from the wheelhouse to the engine compartment. It appears to have been significantly diluted with salt water by the time it got to the engine hatch, but that seems consistent with what we are told were the weather conditions that night.

"What we haven't found is any indication that your father hit his head on anything other than the deck of the boat. There is no evidence of blood on the wheel, for example. Nothing on the control panel. Nothing on the sides of the wheelhouse walls. Nothing to suggest that the *Inlet Dancer* was hit with a particularly powerful wave that caused him to pitch forward or sideways and hit his head in a fashion that would produce such a volume of blood."

Grace was silent. Her hand rested on her cheek. A flock of glaucous-winged gulls circled over the harbour, pitching and diving.

"Ms. Ravenwing, I'm sorry. I know this is difficult."

"It's okay. Go on."

"Well, the fact is, ma'am, we're not sure what to make of this situation. Without having recovered your father's body, it's next to impossible for us to speculate on what might have happened to him. So, our plan now is to come to Port Lostcoast and do some further work. We'll want to have a look around your home, the docks, any other place your father may have spent his time over the last few weeks before he disappeared. We'll also collect some DNA samples from you at that time. If you would please not disturb any of your father's things from this point on, we'd appreciate that."

"We've been in his office a fair amount, Sergeant."

"That's okay, but please, don't disturb anything from this point on. And please don't touch his toothbrush or hairbrush at this point." The sergeant drew a long breath. "I'll be leading a team that will come to Port Lostcoast to chat with a few folks about Mr. Ravenwing. Constable Johns will accompany me, as well as our forensics experts. We'll have a few questions for you and others. You know, did he have any enemies. That sort of thing."

"When will you be here?"

"We should be in Port Lostcoast by tomorrow evening. We're going to wrap things up in Alert Bay tomorrow morning. Will you be able to meet with us then?"

"Yes," she said. She lowered her hand and looked at it, as if surprised to find it next to her face. "And you should meet with Cole Blackwater then, too."

"I have his name here from Constable Johns. What's his involvement?"

"I guess you should know, Sergeant, that we have suspected my father was murdered since seeing the blood in the seal of the engine compartment several days ago now. We've been, well, doing our own investigation."

"Who is we? Are there more people other than you and Mr. Blackwater involved?"

"Yes," she said, looking down. "A friend of Cole's named Nancy Webber has been helping. She's a reporter. And my brother Jacob, though he's just been taxiing us around. And Darren First Moon, Archie's employee on the *Inlet Dancer*. He and Archie were also close friends."

She heard the detective sergeant take a long breath on the other end of the phone. "I need to repeat that we're not declaring this a murder investigation. It's a missing person's case. And I also have to ask that you leave the investigation to the Major Crimes unit from this point on. Any interference from civilians could compromise both the investigation and, should we determine that this *is* a case of murder and apprehend a suspect, any contamination of evidence will limit the possibility of a conviction. It's important, Ms. Ravenwing, that you leave the investigation to the professionals at this point. Am I clear?"

"Yes, sir," she said.

"Good then. I'll call you from Alert Bay tomorrow if I think we won't be able to make it to Port Lostcoast by evening."

"Thank you, Sergeant."

"Yes, ma'am. I'm sorry for your loss."

"Thank you." She broke the connection.

The gulls were gone. The ocean outside the harbour had picked up some chop. Whitecaps formed and broke on three-foot swells. Overhead the sky had darkened again, threatening more storms.

■ Cole walked through town toward the bluff house. The wind was hard at his back, the afternoon having turned tempestuous. When he stepped inside the house, he went straight to Archie's office, picked up the phone, and dialled the number for Stoboltz in Vancouver.

"Can I have a number for your research facility at Jeopardy Rock?" he asked the receptionist.

"We don't have phone lines there. There's a satellite phone on station. I can give you that number. Is it an emergency?"

"Not really," said Cole, unable to come up with a convincing lie. He was learning his lessons. "I'm trying to reach Dr. Thurlow is all."

She gave him the satellite phone number and he dialled it. The strange ring echoed in his ear and finally he heard a distant voice. "Jeopardy Rock."

"Dr. Thurlow, please."

"A minute."

A minute passed. Cole fiddled with a piece of paper. "Thurlow," came a crackling voice.

"Dr. Thurlow, it's Cole Blackwater calling. We met at Archie Ravenwing's potlatch."

"How are you, Mr. Blackwater?"

"Fine, sir. Listen, I know that this is an expensive call —"

"It's fine. Don't worry about it. What can I do for you?"

"Well, sir, I'm trying to close up some of Archie's files, you know, for the family, and I came across something that has me puzzled."

"What's that?"

"Well, it's about some work that you seem to be doing at Jeopardy Rock. It has to do with sea lice. It seems that Archie had some evidence that you are finding sea lice on both farmed Atlantic and wild Pacific salmon that are hundreds of times higher than other samples taken from the area. Can you explain that to me?"

"We're breeding them here."

"Sorry, say again?"

"We're breeding them. All above board, I assure you. We're trying to understand what impact they have on both farmed and wild fish. If we can understand this, maybe we can put a stop to it."

"I'm not really following that, sir. How would that work?"

"Well," he laughed, his voice sharp over the line. "We haven't got that far yet."

"Seems to me like it's a big risk to take."

"I assure you, Mr. Blackwater, it isn't. These lice are being bred in the onshore facility here. We had it renovated, and we updated the old DFO station. It's a state-of-the-art facility now. Really something to see."

Cole was silent. He hadn't been prepared for Thurlow's admission and explanation.

"Would you like to see it for yourself, Mr. Blackwater?"

Cole took a breath. "Sure."

"Do you have a boat?"

"No, but I can have someone give me a lift."

"Why don't you come out this way tomorrow? I should be here, though I have to get back to Vancouver in the next few days. I'd love to show you around."

"I'll see what I can arrange."

"Good, then. We'll see you."

Cole hung up. Once more into the lion's den, he thought.

24 They all started talking at once. Cole Blackwater, Grace Ravenwing, Nancy Webber, and Darren First Moon were huddled around the kitchen table. Grace had served a simple meal of poached salmon, green beans she'd found in the freezer, and roasted potatoes. Cole had bought a couple of six packs at off-sales at The Strait, and they all sat drinking bottles of cold Race Rocks.

"Okay, okay," said Cole, smiling and taking a pull from his beer. "One at a time. Grace, first tell us what Carrie Bright told you on the phone this afternoon. Let's see if it fits into this at all."

"Who's Carrie Bright again?" asked Nancy.

"She's the executive director of the Save Our Seas coalition," said Grace. "They're based in Sointula, on Malcolm Island. They work with some environmental groups across the province trying to shut down salmon farms—"

"Among other things...." added Cole.

Nancy nodded her understanding. Grace continued. "I can't believe the timing of this, but the minister of agriculture is coming here the day after tomorrow to make an announcement on the First Nations Opportunity Fund. Picked Port Lostcoast because it's a symbol of the sort of community the fund will help. According to Bright, the ministry thinks that the fund will put nearly everybody in Port Lostcoast to work on salmon farms."

"On Stoboltz-owned salmon farms," said Cole.

"I got something similar out of Greg First Eagle today, too," added Nancy.

"The band chief will be here, and the minister of labour," said Grace.

"It's going to be a media circus around here," said Webber.

"It's an opportunity for us," said Cole.

"How?" asked Grace.

"Spotlight," Nancy answered for him.

Cole swigged his beer. "If we wanted to, we could blow this whole thing wide open. We could turn this media event into a feeding frenzy." Nancy could see a familiar light in Cole's eyes. She'd seen it many times in Ottawa when he was pursuing, with the single-minded determination of a dog chasing a rabbit, an environmental issue close to his heart. It was the smell of blood, thought Nancy, plain and simple. Cole Blackwater could sense that the kill was near at hand.

"I don't get it," said Grace. "Doesn't Lance Grey know what we've got?"

"Sure he does," said Nancy. "Or at least he strongly suspects."

"So why have a media event here?"

"I'll admit it seems pretty brazen," said Cole, standing to get another beer from the fridge. "The only thing I can think of is that Lance Grey is so far out on a limb that he doesn't care at this point what happens to the minister."

"There would be no way to protect the minister if this were to get out. He'd be tarred with the same brush."

"If what got out?" asked Darren First Moon. He'd been sitting quietly up until this point.

"The fact that Stoboltz is genetically engineering sea lice at their Jeopardy Rock research station," said Cole. "And the likelihood that they plan on introducing those sea lice into the inlet."

"Do we know that for sure?" asked First Moon.

"Pretty sure," said Cole. He told them about his conversation with Cassandra Petrel. "She thinks that the only reason they *could* be producing such a virulent strain of sea lice is to somehow infect the wild salmon. That's why they've been doing genetic work on their own farmed Atlantic salmon. To strengthen their own resistance to sea lice so that they don't lose their own stock."

"I don't know," said First Moon, shaking his head, looking down.

"What's the matter?" asked Grace.

"I just don't trust Cassandra. She's a nice lady, but sometimes she and Archie could really get themselves all worked up."

"I called Dr. Thurlow at Jeopardy Rock. He admitted that they are doing the research. He came out and admitted that. Of course, he just said it was to try and prevent outbreaks."

"And you think he's a liar?" asked First Moon.

"Pretty sure. But I need some proof."

"How you going to get it?"

"I'm going to go to Jeopardy Rock."

"Really? I want to come too!" exclaimed Nancy.

Cole smiled. "Let's discuss the rest of what we know here first," he said.

"Okay. I had lunch with Greg White Eagle today," said Nancy. "What an unbearable blow hard. I confronted him with the evidence we have that he's on the pad with Stoboltz, and, of course, he nearly went through the roof, a pretty good sign that he's guilty. I think if we ask around we'll find that Greg provided some incentives for people to vote for him."

"That makes me sick," said Grace, her face twisted into a knot. "Not just that he was taking the money and bribing others with it, but that people would be conned by such a thing. Makes me sick."

"Darren, you were going to ask around?" said Cole.

"I've been talking with some people and haven't come up with anything yet. No — what do you call it — smoking gun?" Darren cracked a wide smile.

Nancy took a deep breath. "Greg didn't have any love for Archie. He pretty much spit every time he said his name. He said some pretty awful things."

"Like what?" asked Cole.

Nancy looked at Grace, and then scornfully back at Cole.

"It's okay," said Grace. "I've heard it all before."

"Well, he said that Archie had been stealing from band coffers, and not just what we talked about the other day. Greg said that Archie used labour paid for by the band to build the addition to this house and do repairs on the *Inlet Dancer*. He also told me that he was paying you in cash, Cole."

Cole looked down at this beer. "I never got paid by Archie."

Grace was silent. The others looked down at the table, at their hands. Cole picked at the label on his bottle of beer. He reached out and took Grace's small hand in his big paw.

"Anyway, Greg knew that Archie knew about him being in Stoboltz's pocket."

"Could that be enough motive to kill a man?" asked Cole.

"How should I know? The only person I've ever wanted to kill was you," said Nancy.

"But you got over that, didn't you?"

"Mostly," she said, truthfully.

"Well, we can keep Greg on the list," said Cole.

"He told me he was at a band council meeting that day. The day Archie disappeared. That his boat was not in the harbour because he was in Alert Bay."

Grace looked up and said, "That's what the harbour registry shows. Not that he was in Alert Bay, but that his boat was *not* in Port Lostcoast."

"Can we check and see if there was a band council meeting that day?" asked Cole. He looked at Grace.

"I'll call tomorrow," she said.

"You said you checked in with the harbour registry?" said Cole, still holding Grace's hand.

"I did," Grace said, freeing her hand and wiping some tears from her cheeks. "There were a lot of boats out. I don't know if that's going to help us."

"Was the *Queen Mary Two* in port?" asked Cole.

"No. It was out. I checked on it."

"That's Dan Campbell's boat?" asked Nancy.

"I braced him today," said Cole, smiling at the memory. "I tracked him down at The Strait, and invited him to go for a walk to the harbour. I confronted him about Archie, basically accusing him of the killing. You should have heard this guy go off," said Cole, still grinning. "I thought he was going to deck me. Or try. He pretty much told me if he saw me again, he'd kill me."

"You have such a way with people, don't you?" said Nancy.

"Listen, this guy hates First Nations people," said Cole, looking from Darren to Grace. "How does a guy like that live here?"

Neither of them answered. Cole continued. "Anyway, he had a special hatred for Archie. Seems like he and Archie never saw eye to eye on anything."

"Was it a personal sort of hate, or just the sort of hate that rednecks have for enviros?"

"It was pretty personal. Archie could really get in people's face about things. I think Dan Campbell *could* have killed him."

"What about opportunity?" asked Nancy.

"Well, Grace tells us the *Queen Mary Two* wasn't in the harbour that day."

"Lots of boats weren't," she said again.

"Is he the kind of man who would brave a spring storm to motor up the inlet to confront Archie?" Cole looked from Grace back to Darren.

"You'd have to be extremely determined to have been out that day," said Darren. "The sea was pretty big."

"Did you case his boat?" asked Nancy.

"Sure I did. All his lines were intact."

"What kind of rope did he have?"

"Seen one, you seen 'em all," said Cole. "Some of the lines could have matched the length of rope on Archie's stern, but I can't say for sure."

"The RCMP is going to want that rope," said Grace. "They're going to be here tomorrow."

"Are they opening a file?" asked Nancy excitedly.

"A missing person's file."

"Figures," said Cole. "The Mounties couldn't find their own horses in a barn," he said.

"Cole's got a bit of an issue with the cops," said Nancy. "Don't mind him."

"I'm just saying that we can't leave this up to them, is all."

Grace said, "The detective sergeant I spoke with seemed pretty adamant that we not interfere."

"Where have I heard that before?" said Cole, rising.

"I'm not saying I agree," said Grace.

"Good. I have no intention of sitting on my hands while they poke around the islands, and while whoever killed Archie gets off scot-free."

"What do you propose, Dalgliesh?" asked Nancy, remembering a P.D. James novel she'd just read.

"Well, first we have to decide what to do about this news conference. I think we ought to line up our evidence and blow the lid off this whole thing," said Cole, pacing back and forth behind the dining room table.

"Isn't the fund a good thing?" asked Darren, face blank.

"It's putting money into the hands of Stoboltz Aquaculture so that they can build more salmon farms, kill more wild salmon, and make themselves seem like heroes to the public because a few First Nations people get jobs," ranted Blackwater.

"We need jobs," said Darren.

"You need wild salmon so you can have a long-term sustainable fishery," said Cole.

Darren looked down at his hands.

"Be nice to have both," said Grace, making peace.

Cole said, "What we've got on Lance Grey, and his connection to Greg White Eagle, is just too good not to use. And they are coming here. How perfect is that?"

"It seems too perfect," said Nancy.

Grace agreed. "It does seem a little crazy, knowing what we know. Could it be a set up?"

Cole shook his head. "Jesus Christ," he chided. "You guys are wimping out on me? What do you think is happening here?"

"I don't know, Cole," said Nancy, growing impatient. "But speaking as a reporter, I think I'd like not to get fucked if the minister or this Lance Grey guy has got something up his sleeve. I've lost one good job by not doing my homework. I'm not going to lose another." Her face was flushed, a sharp contrast to her raven-black hair.

Cole looked at Grace. "Can you call Carrie Bright in the morning and see if we can't figure out what this is really all about? Fill her in on what we know about Greg White Eagle being on the pad, and see if she can learn why Lance Grey is walking into what almost certainly will be a mess."

"But no reporters," said Nancy. "This story is mine. I get to break it."

Cole looked sideways at her.

"I didn't fly all the way out here, put my job on the line, to have the *North Island Standard* break this clusterfuck," she said.

Cole looked down at his hands then back at Grace. "Can Jacob take me to Jeopardy Rock in the morning? Where is he, anyway?" Cole looked around, as if Jacob Ravenwing might be concealed somewhere in the kitchen.

"He got a call this afternoon. Said he had to go back home."

"Rats," said Cole.

"I can take you," said Darren.

"Really?" Cole looked at him with surprise.

"Why not?"

"Well, I thought maybe you believed we were barking up the wrong tree."

"Maybe you are, maybe you aren't. But if I can help find whoever did this to Archie, then count me in."

"Okay, well, what time do we leave?"

"Meet me on the docks at seven AM."

"I'm coming too," said Nancy.

"I don't think so," said Cole.

"Oh really, Blackwater? Who's going to stop me?"

"Certainly not me," Cole said, "But you might."

"How's that?"

"Only that while Darren and I are out freezing our butts off in Knight Inlet, you and Grace are going to be cracking the minister's nuts back here."

Nancy was silent. She looked at Grace then back at Cole.

Cole said, "Once Carrie Bright fills us in on what she knows about the announcement, I suggest you get your story set up to file, so it hits the web as the minister is coming across Blackfish Sound. It will be the perfect hit."

Nancy regarded Cole coolly. "Sounds like you just don't want me along."

"And miss your charming company?" Cole quipped.

The truth was, Cole Blackwater didn't want Nancy along, and not because she could be a pain in the rump. Jeopardy Rock's secret had already claimed the life of one person he loved. He wasn't willing to risk another.

"So where does that leave us?" asked Nancy.

"Two steps forward, one step back," said Cole. "Greg is still on the list. So is Dan. This Thurlow character is an unknown to me. I guess we'll know by the end of the day tomorrow."

"And Lance?" asked Nancy.

"Motive, but opportunity seems a stretch."

"Down to three," said Nancy.

"Down to three," said Cole.

■ They cleared away the dishes and tidied the kitchen. Darren had gone home and Cole, Nancy, and Grace were in the kitchen, a kettle on the stove. It was half past eight when the phone rang and Grace picked it up.

Cole heard her say, "Yes, he's here."

She handed Cole the phone. "It's your brother."

"Walt, is everything okay?" Cole walked into the office. His back was turned to Nancy so he didn't see her eyes following him as he left the room.

"Everything is fine," said Walter Blackwater.

"Mom's okay?"

"She's fine. Fit as a fiddle. She'll outlive us both."

"It's just that you never call, so ..."

"Yeah, well, you know how it is. Things get busy. I forget."

"Must run in the family," said Cole, remembering that he hadn't called Sarah in three days.

"So listen, I had meant to call you the other day, but I got caught up in a search and rescue, some kids skiing in the backcountry got pinned down by a spring storm and one of them got pretty serious frostbite. I had to ski in and get them. Anyway, I had meant to give you a heads-up."

"What's up, Walt?"

"I was out at the ranch the other day to see to the cattle, check in on Mom. There was a reporter there."

"A reporter?" Cole recalled a reporter he had butted heads with in Oracle last year, a crude, bloodless man who had nearly upset the entire apple cart.

"Yeah, poking around the place, asking Mom all sorts of questions. She was really nice about it all, but when she and I talked I got the feeling like she was after something about the old man."

Cole heard the "she", and his train of thought changed tracks. "Who was it, Walt?" said Cole, his own reflection staring back at him from the window in Archie's office.

"You know her. That woman from Ottawa, you know. Nancy Webber."

25

Cole sat for ten minutes in Archie Ravenwing's office, looking through the ill-gotten windows into the darkness of the archipelago beyond. Finally he picked up the phone and called Denman Scott. But Denman wasn't home, so he left a message and sat for another five minutes. At last he stood and walked into the kitchen. Nancy and Grace were sitting at the table drinking tea. Cole could see Nancy's eyes following him as he entered the room, wondering what he knew.

"Everything okay at home?" asked Grace.

"Yeah," he said, still holding Nancy's gaze. "Yeah, fine."

"You want some tea?"

"No, I don't think so. I think I'd like to get some air. Clear my head. Nancy, would you like to go for a little walk with me?" Cole did everything in his power to keep his voice even and his tone soft, but he realized that he was gritting his teeth as he spoke.

Grace looked at Nancy. Nancy put down her cup. "Sure, it's a nice night."

Nancy put on her coat and followed Cole out the door. The moon was rising over the distant mountains of Vancouver Island and the night was cool, but not cold.

"Cole," Nancy began as they started down the road to the harbour.

"Just don't say anything right now, Nancy. Not a word."

They walked away, Cole a step ahead of her. They passed through the clutch of houses and storefronts that constituted town. Cole could hear the din from The Strait and felt his body reach out toward that sound in search of strong drink. They made their way to the docks.

"I should have told you I had been to the ranch," Nancy said. Cole had stopped and was looking west at the rising moon. His hands were in his pockets and the collar of his leather coat was turned up against the chill.

"It was wrong, Cole. I'm sorry."

Cole exhaled a stream of breath into the night through his lips, blowing hard.

"Cole—"

"Just shut up," he said, his teeth pressed together.

"Cole, I—"

"Shut up and listen."

He turned and she could see his eyes, the light of the moon glistening off the whites. His eyes were wide open, wild, full of rage. "You think you can come here and get into these people's lives and homes and pretend to be helping us solve the mystery, a good man, a man who spent his life serving his people, and then betray us. Betray them. Betray me." He spoke quietly, his teeth clenched, as if he were holding back his rage with them. As if they were the only thing keeping that dark beast trapped inside of him from spilling out and running wild.

"That wasn't my intention. You called *me*, Cole. I came to help. I want to solve this murder too," she said.

"You want the story is all you want. It's all you ever want. The story. It's all about the story." He spat the words at her.

"It's more."

"So why go to the ranch? Why harass my mother? My brother? What are you hoping to find? What are you trying to dig up?"

"I didn't harass anybody," she said. "I had dinner with your mother. I had a walk with your brother. I wanted to get to know them. To get to know you."

"That's a crock of shit and you know it, Webber. You want to get to know me, talk to me."

She laughed and turned in a circle, her hands slapping her sides. "Talk to you? To Cole Blackwater, mister I don't want to get into it, I'm too busy brooding. I'm too busy with my own shit, so don't ask about it? You want me to talk to you? I've been talking to you for years and you're like a closed door in my face."

"What are you trying to do? What do you want?"

"I want to know what is tearing you apart, Cole. I want to know what is eating you from the inside out."

"Nothing is eating me," he said, turning back to the moon.

"See! This is what I mean. *Nothing* is eating you? Look at you, Cole! You're seething. Every goddamned day you are seething. Everybody can see it. Grace sees it. Denman sees it. Sarah sees it. You're so angry at yourself, and the world, at your father, at everything, you're the only one who can't see it. You can hardly look at yourself. But no, nothing is eating *you*," she mocked.

"So I'm an angry guy, so what? It makes me good at what I do."

"You've been using that line for so long, Cole, I think you must *almost* believe it. Your anger doesn't make you good at what you do. It's an excuse for what you do. Beating the shit out of people. Getting the shit beaten out of you. You're so angry at yourself that you're trying to get yourself killed and you don't even know it."

"That's just wrong, Nancy."

"You're so angry that you're looking to kill someone, or get yourself killed."

Cole turned on her. "You don't know what the fuck you're talking about!" he roared, and she took half a step back. "You just talk and talk and talk but you don't know a thing about me. Not a goddamned thing."

"Then tell me."

He took a sharp breath.

"Tell me what happened to make you so angry."

He twisted back toward the rising moon.

"What happened in the barn?"

"Nothing. Go back to the house."

"What happened to your father in the barn, Cole?"

"Nancy, you don't know what you're talking about."

"Cole, what happened to your father there?"

"Nancy, you're digging a hole you can't get out of...."

"Cole, I want the truth from you. What happened?"

"Why, why do you want the truth? So you can write another story. Win another award?"

It was Nancy's turn to look at her feet. She stamped them to warm her toes. "I'm not doing this as a journalist."

"Then what, Nancy? What?"

"As a friend, Cole. I'm doing it as a friend."

"It's a funny way of showing it."

"Cole, what happened to your father?"

"He was a sick man, Nancy. He was sick in the head. He

shouldn't have come back from Europe after World War II. He should have died on Juno Beach. The world would have been a better place for it."

"You and Walter would never have been."

"The world would have missed Walt, but I don't know about me."

"Sarah. The world would have missed her."

"Leave Sarah out of this, Nancy."

"What happened to your father in the barn?"

"He was such a mean bastard, Nancy. He hit my mother. Did she tell you that?"

"No. But I heard."

"Heard? Heard where? Don't tell me. I don't want to know." Cole shook his head. "Reporters, digging into your life ... digging into your life. So you know that he beat me, too."

"Yeah, I figured that out some time ago. I just didn't know how badly."

"Badly," said Cole.

"I'm sorry —"

"Save it."

"For what?"

"For someone who cares, Nancy."

She took a breath. "You must have hated him."

"I hated him more than anything in this world," Cole said. "I was just a boy, and he took all of that rage, all of that hate, out on me."

"It's not your fault."

"I know. I've talked to the shrinks. When I was at university in Toronto I went to see someone. They told me all that crap. Not my fault. Got to forgive. Move on. But I didn't want to forgive. I didn't want to move on." His fists were clenched, his back still to her. She could hear his voice waver and imagined tears trickling over the scars on his cheeks.

"Cole, when you came back to Alberta four years ago, after everything fell apart in Ottawa, what happened?"

"It was like I had never been away. It was like the twenty years had never happened. He didn't hit me. He was an old man.

He knew better. But he didn't need to. All he needed to say was a few words. He knew how to stick the knife in and turn it."

"Cole," Nancy took a deep breath. "Did you kill him?"

Cole was silent. She watched his shoulders rise and fall as he drew in deep breaths of sea air. The moon was creeping across the sky now, reflecting off the water in the harbour.

▬ It was the spring of 2002, and Cole Blackwater was at the nadir of his existence. He had been fired from his dream job in Ottawa, caused a train wreck of immeasurable proportions in Nancy Webber's journalism career, and lost his four-year-old daughter Sarah as his estranged wife, Jennifer Polson, moved across the country to Vancouver. The last thing in the world that Cole Blackwater had to hold onto was Sarah, and so with nothing to lose, he packed a few things in the back of his aging Toyota SR5 and drove west from Ottawa. It wasn't until he crossed the Saskatchewan–Alberta line that it even dawned on him that when he drove through Calgary, he'd be less than two hours from the Blackwater Ranch in Alberta's Porcupine Hills.

Cole slipped a tape of Ian Tyson songs in the deck and sang along. "Bald eagles back in the cottonwood trees, the old brown hills are just about bare. Spring time lying all along the creek, magpies ganging up everywhere...."

When he passed through Calgary he jerked the wheel and piloted the truck onto Deerfoot Trail, and drove it hard through rush-hour traffic to the southern end of the city where the Deerfoot shot south like an arrow toward Fort Macleod. He followed the highway to High River, where he stopped for gas and a can of pop, and then pressed on to Charleston. From there he headed west again, up into the brown Porcupine Hills, their backs clear of snow as a chinook barrelled down from the Rockies.

I'll just spend the night, see Mom, avoid the old man, and be on my way in the morning, he thought.

But Cole Blackwater found that the old place was good for him, and he stayed longer. The old man kept almost entirely out of sight. Sometimes Cole would see him walk from the barn to one of the sheds, or they might pass each other at the breakfast table, but otherwise, Cole spent the time with his mother, or riding Blue, the old quarter horse, or talking late into the night when his brother would drive up from Waterton Lakes.

At the end of the second week, Cole was out riding Blue when his father suddenly rode up beside him. Seeing him then, Cole thought Henry Blackwater looked every bit the cowboy, with his tight, checkered, pearl-button shirt under a felt-lined tan vest and dark blue Wranglers. Henry Blackwater's sweat-stained Stetson was probably the same hat he'd been wearing for two decades, and at that peculiar angle.

Cole could smell the booze on his breath. He knew the old man was drunk by the way he held the reins so lightly, sitting as if the horse and he shared a secret about the world that made Henry Blackwater immune to injury. Cole thought to himself, if this old fucker were to fall off his horse and hit his head on the rocks below, that would be just fine with me. The world would not miss Henry Blackwater.

"Your mother's pretty glad you're here." The old man slurred a little as he spoke.

"It's good to see her," said Cole, his eyes held straight ahead, gazing at the horizon of blue peaks above the bristled Porcupine Hills.

"Got yourself in a bit of trouble back in Ottawa, did you?"

Cole was silent. Had his father been waiting for Cole to let his guard down before striking?

His father spat. "Got yourself in a little too deep, didn't you, boy?"

Cole shifted his weight and the saddle creaked.

"You don't have to answer me, Cole. We both know you fucked up good this time, if you take my meaning." The old man laughed harshly. "I should have made sure you knew right from wrong better. Should have taught you your lessons better. Should have made sure you knew how to take care of your family right."

Cole had been holding his breath, and he let it out with a low whistle.

"Ain't you going to say anything?"

"Not to you," said Cole, and he turned his horse around.

The old man trotted his horse to catch up. "What the fuck were you thinking, Cole? Fucking around on your wife? Making a mess of your job? Bringing shame on your daughter? What the fuck were you thinking?"

Cole pressed his heels into Blue and she stepped up her gait.

"You can't outride me, city boy. I live in the saddle. You're just a fucking tourist here."

Cole looked over. The old man was grinning at Cole.

"What made you such a hateful bastard, I wonder?" Cole finally asked.

"Having to put up with good-for-nothing pricks like you all my life," his father growled.

"If we're lucky," said Cole ruefully, "we won't have to put up with *you* for too much longer."

"I'm going to outlive you all," his father said. He spat again and turned his horse away from Cole. It was Cole's turn to catch up to his father. His vision blurred, and his hands trembled on the reins. From a distance it might appear as though father and son were out for a ride together.

Suddenly overcome with the rage he had been holding at bay these past two weeks, Cole spoke: "The best thing you could do for the world is to just go on living your hateful life. Grow old and suffer. The longer you suffer, the better." Cole's words came out in an enraged growl. "And then, when you finally die, I'm going to stand over you and spit down your fucking throat."

Cole turned away and galloped back to the barn. He unsaddled Blue and gave her a handful of alfalfa cubes and brushed her down. He saw his father sitting on his horse in the pasture, waiting for Cole to leave the barn before bringing in his own mount. Cole's heart was still beating hard when he entered the house. His face was stitched with anger, his hands trembled.

"What is it, dear?" his mother asked as he stepped from the mud room into the kitchen.

"It's nothing."

"You were out riding. Is something wrong?"

"Nope, everything is okay." He stepped to her and bent to kiss her on the forehead.

"Did you have words with your father? I saw him bring in the bay after you left the barn."

Cole exhaled. "Why is he so goddamned angry, Mom?"

His mother said quickly, "It's the war, dear."

"That was fifty years ago. It's time to move on!"

"Truth is, dear, he was like that before he went overseas. That just made it worse."

Cole shook his head and poured himself a glass of water. He drank it, his hands still unsteady.

"He doesn't mean anything by it. He's just an angry old man. He doesn't mean to hurt any of us."

Cole looked up from his water. His mother turned away.

"What do you mean, hurt any of *us?*"

"Nothing at all. Let's have a cup of tea, and I have a pie just out of the oven."

"Does he hurt you, Mom?"

"Come, dear, let's forget all this talk. It's just fine."

"Does he hit *you?*"

Dorothy Blackwater dried her hands on her apron. "It's really nothing."

Cole felt his vision begin to narrow, the rush of anger flowing through him like acid in his veins. He caught his breath. "Does Walter know?"

"Oh, good heavens, no. Please, Cole. It's nothing. He just gets all worked up sometimes and forgets himself."

"He used to beat me, Mom."

Dorothy Blackwater looked down at her shoes.

"For years. Did you know that?"

Cole could see the tears running down her face.

"And now he's beating you."

"It's not that bad. It's nothing really. I do things that upset him is all." She moved toward him, but Cole Blackwater could no longer see her. His world had collapsed around him and his vision narrowed so that all he could see was a path through the mud room and out the back door into the yard.

He crossed the yard walking hard and fast, his hands balled into fists at his sides. He tore open the gate and kicked open the wooden door to the stables beneath the barn with his foot. The door splintered and broke at the hinges, crashing against the wall.

The room was dark. He heard the horses breathing.

Cole walked the length of the stables but his father wasn't there. He stood in the darkness of the room, the only light coming from a small window that was so dirty it was opaque. Then he heard booted feet above him.

He ran the length of the stables and out the door. He tore open the gate again, wrenching it back against its hinges. He half-walked, half-ran to the front of the barn where the double doors stood at the top of a gentle grade. He was breathing hard. He reached for the latch and threw open the door, and the light of day fell across the floor of the barn, sending dust motes dancing in the pale light.

His father was standing at the centre of the boxing ring. He held a shotgun in his hands.

"Looking for me, son?" His voice sounded hollow in the barn.

Cole stood in the open door, backlit and exposed. All other sounds seemed to disappear — the birds that chattered in the bushes around the barn, the sound of the wind, the barking of the two border collies on the back step — and all Cole Blackwater could hear was his own furious heart thumping in his ears.

"What do you say, son, want to go a round?" The old man stooped and picked something up from the floor.

Cole stepped forward.

The old man moved the shotgun to his left hand, holding it midway down the barrel.

Cole prepared himself for the blast, felt his body tense. He wondered if he would be able to dive for cover like they did in the movies, and tried to see if the old man had his old single-shot 12-gauge or the newer Remington model that held five shells and could be fired quickly. It might make the difference.

Cole moved reflexively as his father raised the barrel of the gun, but the old man held it awkwardly in his left hand. Cole watched as he pressed the barrel to his own chin and, with his right hand, swung a long piece of metal down — Cole could see now that it was a branding iron — and put the hook on the end of it in the trigger hard. It suddenly dawned on Cole what was going on.

"Wait!" Cole yelled. The sound of his voice, and the choice of his words, surprised both men. "Wait," he said again, more quietly.

His father just stood at the centre of the boxing ring, motionless, the barrel of the gun still pressed against his chin.

Cole took a deep breath. A moment ago he had been prepared to kill this man. To kill his own father, for what he had done to him, and for what he had done to his mother. Now he lacked certainty. His head was flooded with emotion, and Cole fought to see what he should do next. "Just wait," he said a third time.

"Wait for what?" Henry Blackwater said, his own voice suddenly lacking conviction. He sounded small in the open barn.

"Just stop," Cole said, and stepped forward.

"For what? To grow old? Give you that satisfaction?" The old man shifted awkwardly in the ring.

"Put the gun down."

Henry Blackwater's arms tensed.

"Pop, wait."

Henry Blackwater stood, his hands tightening and untightening, the shotgun pressing into his chin.

"It doesn't have to end like this."

"How's it going to end, then? Hey?"

Cole felt a bead of sweat trickle down his chest. He was breathing hard in the close air of the barn. The light that spilled from the front doors and across the boxing ring was flecked with dust motes. "You've done some pretty awful things." He saw the old man's hand tighten on the branding iron. "But you can come clean, Pop."

"You fixing to get religious on me, son?"

"I was just a boy...."

Cole watched the emotions sweep over his father's face like the shadows of clouds passing over the foothills. "I never knew what to do with you," he finally said. Cole could see his father trembling, and wondered at the sensitivity of the trigger. Sensitive enough, he thought.

Cole felt the bile rising in his throat. "Why were you so angry?" he stammered. The old man tensed, but Cole now saw doubt in Henry Blackwater's grim expression. Cole took a step forward. The sagging ropes of the ring still stood between his father and himself, and he would have to step up onto the mat to get to his father. And Cole was still far from certain that the gun wouldn't be turned on him if he did.

"I done some terrible things. And your mother —"

"We can work it out. Put down the gun."

"I'm done with this shit," Henry said, shaking his head, pressing his eyes shut.

"Pop, we all make mistakes. We can walk back from them. We can —"

"I never could seem to make you learn, boy." Henry Blackwater closed his eyes.

"I did learn, Pop, I did. Look at Sarah."

"Sarah doesn't even know who I am."

"She does."

"She doesn't. And it doesn't matter," his father said, lost in his own thoughts.

"It does matter."

Henry Blackwater opened his eyes. Cole could not see them in the dim light, but he imagined them ringed with redness and cast with regret. Henry shook his head and emitted a half-laugh through a clenched jaw. "Fuck, you was a disappointment to me, boy."

"I'm sorry, Pop. I messed up."

The blast was deafening. Cole's body recoiled at the roar. His face turned away, but not before watching the old man's head jerk back as if on a chain, his face disappearing, a Jackson Pollock spray of blood leaping from where his grinning jaw used to be and raining down on the canvas floor, splattering across the hay behind the boxing ring.

The shotgun and branding iron clattered to the mat.

The body collapsed to the canvas with a final thud.

Overhead a dozen mourning doves exploded into flight from the eves of the barn.

■ Cole stood at the end of the dock, the moon above him, his hands still clenched at his sides.

"Cole, there was nothing you could have done."

He turned to her. There were no tears staining his face. His eyes burned. "It's not so simple, Nancy. Part of me was trying to stop him, and the other part of me was so pissed off that I didn't get to pull that trigger myself! When I went into that barn, I was going to kill him with my own two hands." Cole held them up in front of his face as if seeing them in a new light. "I don't know what makes me angrier: that I couldn't save him, or that I couldn't kill him."

Nancy stood next to him. She looked at him, but he didn't turn toward her. "You're going to need some help, Cole."

Finally he looked down at her. The moonlight caught the sheen of her jet black hair. Her eyes were luminous. "It's a little late for that," he said.

"No, it's not."

He turned away. "I need some time here," he said.

"Okay. I'm going to walk back up to the bluff house."

"I'll be up a little later."

"Cole, don't do anything stupid."

He said nothing.

"Okay, well, I'll see you."

He didn't turn to watch her go.

Cole Blackwater stood on the dock under the gaze of the moon, the quiet waters of the protected harbour gently lapping against the pilings. He gave Nancy five minutes, then he walked directly to The Strait. The magnetic pull of the bar was unavoidable. As he walked into the crowded room, he felt his body relax, the promise of a warming glass of Irish whiskey only moments away. He was not so distracted by its lure, however, that he forgot his precautionary scan. A bar full of men, he thought. How dull. But there was no sign of Dan Campbell, for which he was almost sorry. Cole shouldered his way to the bar and ordered a Jameson, neat. He pulled a wad of bills and detritus from his pocket, extracted a twenty from the mess, and flattened it on the table. He drank the first shot by throwing it against the back of his throat, his eyes burning, his gut accepting the hard liquor with no choice. He pushed his glass back to the bartender, who poured him another shot, and Cole asked for a beer back.

Cole did not see the man rise from the table in the far right hand corner, away from the bar, and walk down a long, dark hallway to the pay phone near the washrooms.

Feeling the heat of the booze in his belly and the commotion of the busy bar around him, Cole sank into a slouch. All the fire within him slowly leached into the plank floor below. All at once he felt wordlessly tired. He thought maybe he'd just drink himself asleep right then and there. He drank the second Jameson and started in on the beer, his fifth of the night. It felt cool and light on his whiskey-burned throat, and he drank half of it before putting the glass down. He looked around him, the faces and voices of strangers floating lightly in and out of focus. He raised the glass again and turned from the scene. Thoughts started to rise in his addled brain and he pushed them back, sequestering them, with years of dedicated practice, to a room securely barred and bolted.

Cole finished the beer and ordered another whiskey and another beer. The bartender poured, took his money, and attended to another customer.

Time passed in a slow-motion arc, then Cole's pockets were empty, save for the lint and a small wrench used for bicycles. When he asked if he could start a tab, the bartender told him he didn't give anybody credit. Bad policy in a place like Port Lostcoast, he explained. Cole straightened up and looked for a clock. It was past midnight now. He staggered down the corridor to the washroom, stood at the urinal, splashed piss on his shoes, caught his shirt in his zipper, and staggered out the back door.

That was what saved his life.

Cole was halfway from The Strait to the gravel road that wound up the hillside to the bluff house when he heard a voice behind him. His senses jarred to life. He managed to turn slightly and get an arm up as the fish club struck the side of his face. He felt his cheek explode, felt the hot flush of blood across his face, and the moonlit night momentarily brightened like day. He stumbled backwards, tripping on a rock and falling hard on his side, the wind sucked from his lungs.

"Get the fuck up," he heard Dan Campbell growl. Cole managed to put his hands down to protect his belly as Campbell kicked him hard with a booted foot. The air was pushed from his lungs again as his diaphragm contracted in self-defense, and he thought he might pass out then and there. Cole could hear at least two other men laugh. The blood ran down his cheek and onto the dirt. Cole shook his head and gasped for breath. Campbell tried to kick him again, but Cole managed to lurch and tackle his leg as it connected with his gut, and Campbell went down hard on his back. Cole punched him as hard as he could in the groin, and Dan Campbell roared, "You motherfucker!" Campbell swung the fish club down but Cole blocked it with his left forearm and, lying on Campbell's legs, drove his fist as hard as he could into Dan's groin a second time. Campbell gasped for breath and turned sideways to vomit in the dirt.

Now the other men were on him. Cole got to his feet and staggered sideways, his hands in front of his face, when the first man stepped into him with an axe handle, swinging wildly for his head. Cole turned and took the blow on the side of his arms and threw his forehead into the man's face, breaking his nose, spraying blood across his own face. The second man stumbled back, dropping the axe handle and clutching at his face, cursing. Cole saw the third and fourth men hesitate before stepping toward him. Not waiting for them to seize the upper-hand their numbers gave them, Cole bolted toward the man on the right, striking him in the face with his right fist, using his bulk to send the man wheeling backwards. Cole went crashing down on top of him, kicking and punching him as he landed on the man.

Cole was on top of him, wild-eyed, face covered in his own and another man's blood, and the assailant looked suddenly fearful for his own life. Cole punched the man twice in the side of his head, connecting with his ear and temple, and the man appeared to black out. The final attacker kicked at Cole, knocking him off the unconscious man, and Cole rolled in the dirt, clutching at his ribs.

"You're one crazy motherfucker, aren't you?" the fourth man said. Cole rolled and stumbled backwards, skidding in the gravel on the road. "Come here, I'm going to fuck you up." The man charged him. Dan Campbell had staggered to his feet and stepped toward Cole, the fish club held loosely in his hand.

"You're going to wish you were never born, Blackwater," Campbell said, spitting blood. Cole had risen to his feet, staggering, his vision blurred by blood and pain and booze.

Dan stepped into him, swinging the club at Cole's head. Cole ducked and drove his head into Dan's solar plexus, driving him backwards. Dan tried to bring his knee up into Cole's body but tripped as he did, and both men were in the dirt again. Cole drove his head into Dan's gut, and he gasped for air, spitting his vomit onto Cole. The fourth man kicked Cole in the side and sent him spinning into the moonlit road. The assailant picked up the axe handle and started toward Cole, grinning. Campbell staggered to his feet, club in hand.

Cole stood, hands up, his hair a mess of blood and vomit and dirt, his eyes nailed to his two remaining opponents. They both came at him at once. Stepping lightly, feeling the glide he had once known in the ring, Cole managed to deliver a solid left cross to Dan Campbell's face, knocking the man off his feet for the second time that week. Campbell spun sideways and careened into the dirt road again. The second man delivered a vicious blow to Cole's back as this happened, and Cole dropped to his knees, blinded by the pain. The man raised the club above his head as Cole knelt before him.

"Hold it!" came a voice from behind them. "Hold it right now!"

Campbell staggered up and turned to look back toward the voice. A silhouette of a man was rushing toward them, his hulking features backlit by the moon. "Take one more step and I'll cut your goddamned heads off."

Cole saw the shape moving toward them, could see the glint of moonlight off metal.

"He's got a fucking hatchet," said the man to Campbell.

"You crazy fucking Indian," said Campbell, his face a red

smear, as he started to walk away. He watched the man with the axe. "This isn't finished, Blackwater. Get out of Lostcoast before you end up like your friend, at the bottom of the channel." Then Campbell and other man were gone into the night, helping their beaten colleagues as they went.

The man with the axe reached Cole and knelt down beside him. First Moon.

"Nancy called. She was worried when you didn't come home," said Darren. Cole tried to stand but collapsed to his knees and spat blood onto the ground.

Darren First Moon took him under the arm and helped him to his feet. "Wish those dudes had stuck around," he said, fiddling with the axe. "Always wanted to use this thing on one of those bastards."

26

Archie Ravenwing sat in his office and watched two ravens chase a bald eagle across the western sky. Despite his anger, he couldn't help but smile. "Me an' Grace should be chasing that peckerhead White Eagle just like that," he said, grinning.

Grace would be disappointed in him. That was what hurt the most.

He didn't care about his own reputation. Didn't even mind if he went to jail, though he thought that was pretty unlikely. He'd have to repay what he took from the band council coffers. About ten thousand dollars. Maybe a fine on top of that. Do some community time. Talk to school kids about fraud. He laughed again. That would be a real barnburner, he thought.

Cole would be disappointed, too. That hurt almost as much as hurting Grace. Cole had never come around asking for his money, even though he needed it worse than Archie did. Archie looked around him at the office his skullduggery had built. He had justified it by telling himself that he needed the space to undertake his one-man war against the salmon farmers. But the truth was, it was pride and hubris, plain and simple. It was ego, always Archie Ravenwing's downfall.

The ravens had harried the eagle until it fled, flying west toward the inlet. That was where he would go tomorrow. Tomorrow he would rise before dawn and make for Jeopardy Rock, get the final proof he would need to blow the lid off this debacle. What would he be looking for? Records of some sort? A signed confession from Thurlow?

He'd know it when he found it, Archie Ravenwing thought to himself.

Archie rose from his chair and went to the kitchen, flipping on a light as he did. He turned on the marine radio to listen for the next day's forecast. He opened the fridge, took out a plate of cockles he'd collected that morning, and turned on the range, placing a heavy frying pan over the flame. He cut onions and smashed garlic and sautéed them in a pad of butter.

Something else saddened him. With his reputation in shatters, it would damage the effort to protect wild salmon. He'd have to turn the evidence over to someone like Carrie Bright in order to make his case. Or Cole. That's what he would do. While the butter and onions and garlic browned in the pan, he went back into the office and turned on his ancient fax/photocopier to let it warm up.

He returned to the kitchen and cut up some leeks, and set them aside in a small bowl. Then he dumped the oysters into the pan and listened to them sizzle. He poured some ginger marinade over them, and a heavy dose of tamari soy, and stirred them around in the pan. Then he added the leeks. When the oysters were lightly cooked, he removed them from the heat and went back into the office and started to feed pages from the brown envelope he'd received in Fan Tan Alley into the machine, slowly copying the entire package.

When he was done he sat down at this computer and typed out a note to Cole, printed it, and signed it. Just before he sealed it, he opened his wallet and took out a blank cheque. He made it out for one thousand dollars and enclosed it in the envelope. It was a fraction of what he owed Cole, but it was a start.

He sealed the envelope, put stamps on it, and placed it next to the front door to be dropped in the post box at the general store before he left in the morning.

"Grace, you want some dinner?" he called to her bedroom.

He knocked on the door, and nobody answered. "Grace, you there?"

"Hmm," he said, and turned back to the kitchen, where he made a plate of food for himself.

A knock at the door stopped him from seating himself. He opened it.

"Hi, Archie," It was Darren First Moon.

Archie stepped back without saying a word and walked back to the kitchen.

"Listen, I was pretty heated up down there before," said First Moon. "I'm sorry for some of what I said."

Archie looked at him long and hard.

"Aren't you going to say anything?"

"There's nothing to say," said Archie.

"You're not going to say I forgive you? You're not going to say you're sorry, too?"

"Is that what you came up here for? For forgiveness and to ask me to apologize?"

Darren shuffled awkwardly in the entrance. "What's wrong with that?"

Archie shook his head. "You know, Darren, when I agreed to hire you, your probation officer told me that you were a little thick. I never believed it. I always gave you the benefit of the doubt. But now I'm not so sure."

Darren looked away from him. "Grace isn't here, is she?"

"No, nobody's here."

"Look, Archie, what Stoboltz is doing is real important. We need the jobs."

"That's Greg White Eagle talking."

"It's me talking. I can see what's happening here, Archie. I can see people out of work. Drinking. Doing crazy stuff. Kids are trying to kill themselves, Archie."

"And you think that Stoboltz is going to save us? That fish farms are our salvation?"

"The government is going to help, too."

"I heard all about it when I was in Victoria. A big announcement. Lots of money for the company to hire Indians and give them trinkets."

"Don't talk like that. It's not like that, Archie."

"Come on, Darren," Archie said, exasperated. "Open your eyes. The government gives Stoboltz a bunch of money, and sure, they train some of our people to work on fish farms, but I guarantee that some of that money is going into the funny business up at Jeopardy Rock. I know it in my bones! That cold bastard Thurlow is using the money to bankroll his work with the sea lice. And I have no doubt that Lance Grey is in on it. And I'm going to get the proof tomorrow."

"What do you mean, Archie?"

"I'm going to Jeopardy Rock first thing tomorrow. I'm going to sample around the area, and have a look at that old DFO research station that Stoboltz took over. I'll find out what they are up to and then I'm going to blow them out of the water."

"Don't do that, Archie."

"Why not?"

"You do that and Stoboltz won't get the money. They won't be able to hire folks."

"It all comes down to that, doesn't it?"

"What?"

"Money."

"I got kids, Archie. I work what, ten, twelve, maybe fourteen weeks a year with you. What else have I got? Nothing. I own a beater of a boat. I live in a shack that leaks and is cold in the winter and hot as hell in the summer. What have I got?"

"You've got pride, Darren. Pride. And a history. Our people have been fishing in the Broughton for ten thousand years. Longer than history. For as long as there has been a Broughton, our people have been here."

"I can't feed my kids on that, Archie."

"The world loves salmon. They'll pay a premium for wild salmon. If Stoboltz gets away with what they are planning on doing, there won't be wild salmon left. They get to control the market. Do you really think they are doing what they are doing to help your sorry ass?"

"Don't go to Jeopardy Rock tomorrow, Archie."

"I'm going. If I don't, they will be getting away with murder."

"I'm sorry," said Darren looking down.

"For what?"

"For all of this. This isn't how it was supposed to turn out."

"Still time left to tell Thurlow and Greg White Eagle and Lance Grey to shove it."

"I don't think so, Archie."

"Well, then, so long old friend."

"So long, Archie." And he was gone.

■ Archie couldn't sleep that night. He sat up, his office dark, and looked out over the harbour. The night was clear and cold, the moon past full. A pale circle of haze ringed its alabaster orb. Far off to the east and to the north he could make out the dim glow of lights that shone from one of Stoblotz' salmon farms. Recently they had started installing underwater lights that confused the Atlantic salmon, upsetting their diurnal rhythms and tricking them into faster growth. The lights also attracted food to the farmed fish: a free lunch.

He heard Grace come in around midnight. He rose to say hi, calling to her, "Hey ya, Grace."

"Hi, Dad."

"Where you been?"

"I was over at Doreen's place. What are you still doin' up?"

"Just thinking."

"Everything okay?"

"Yeah, yeah, it's good. I'm going to head up the inlet tomorrow, do some more sampling."

"Okay, be safe. Hey?"

"I will. I love you." They were both standing in the dark. He could see her silhouette in the moonlight that shone through the windows.

"Love you too, Dad."

Around three AM he stood and walked on stiff legs to his filing cabinet and found his will. He'd had it made up three years before. He thumbed to the third page, past all the legal jargon, and found the section that itemized his belongings. He read down to the *Inlet Dancer*. He circled the name next to it — Darren First Moon — and wrote in the margin "replace with Cole Blackwater." He dated and signed it. When he could he'd go into Port McNeill and have a lawyer make it official.

Should anything happen to him, at least Cole would get something as long-overdue back pay. Did he think the business at Jeopardy Rock was that serious? Who knew? But he knew that Darren First Moon had crossed over to the dark side, and that it would be a cold day in hell before he gave a Stoboltz man his boat.

He put the will back in its folder and placed it on his desk.

He slept fitfully in his chair and woke before dawn, cold and stiff.

He walked into the kitchen, brewed coffee for his thermos,

packed a lunch, took his heavy rain gear from the closet, and, taking the envelope, headed out into the morning. He walked briskly through the town, dropped the envelope in the red mailbox outside the general store, and made for the docks.

He stepped onto the pier and walked toward the *Inlet Dancer*. In the last gleam of moonlight that hung like a tapestry over the harbour, Archie Ravenwing thought she looked like the most beautiful thing he had ever seen. He stopped and walked back along the dock and looked down at a small, ageing pleasure boat. A ratty canopy covered the open hatch at the back. The boat's running lights were broken. She hardly looked seaworthy, though Archie knew the boat could stand a storm. And Darren was a good mariner. The *Rising Moon* still had a few years left in her.

27 "They'll take your children away from you, you know that, don't you?" said Darvin Thurlow, his voice icy. "They won't let them stay there with your wife. She's not fit. They'll take them away and put them with a white family. You'll never see them again. They'll tell your children that you are a bad man, and they won't want to see you when you get out. If you get out."

Darren First Moon listened. "You told me to take care of it."

"I told you to shut Archie Ravenwing up. I didn't tell you to kill him."

First Moon looked down at his feet. "You said—"

"Listen, Darren. You messed up. You lost your cool. You took it personally. You made a big mistake, my friend."

"What should I do?"

"I don't know. You've got to keep your cool."

"Cole is going there tomorrow. I'm taking him in my boat."

"I know. I invited him."

"Why? Why did you do that? He's going to ruin everything."

"Darren, he's onto us. Him and that woman. The reporter. They know we're up to something out here. So, I invited him out. To show him around. He's going to come and look and see that there is no conspiracy. No evil plot. I'm not a mad scientist. In fact, I'm not even going to be here."

"Where are you going?"

"I told him I had to go to Vancouver day after next. You know that there's going to be an announcement. It's going to be in Lostcoast."

"They know about that."

"I figured they would. Lance Grey can't keep a lid on things. That punk can't keep his mouth shut."

"Are you really going to Vancouver?"

"No, Darren. While you and Cole are coming to Jeopardy Rock, I'll be paying a visit to our lady friend in Lostcoast."

Darren looked around his kitchen. His house was dark and quiet. "Don't hurt Grace," Darren said.

"Your affection is touching, Darren. It's not her that I'm concerned about."

"What do you want me to do?"

"You dug your own grave, Darren. Now you're going to have to lie in it."

"What does that mean?"

"It means that Cole Blackwater is going to have to find out that nothing sinister is happening at Jeopardy Rock."

"But what if he does? They think that the First Nations Opportunity Fund is financing your sea lice work. They're going to put it all together."

"Darren, you brought Cole into this by getting carried away. It's your fault he's here. You're going to have to figure out how to put an end to this."

"This was all a big mistake," said Darren, his voice small.

"It's not a mistake, my friend. You're doing the right thing. And never forget, Darren, that you came to us. You asked for work. It was you who was tired of living in poverty, living like a dog at your master's feet. You need year-round work, and the First Nations Opportunity Fund will provide it. We need money to conduct our research, and with the fund in place to hire good people like yourself, we can direct our resources to more fruitful pursuits."

"I'm not going to have a job if I'm in jail."

"Then clean up your mess."

Darren sighed. "And what about you? When will you be leaving Jeopardy Rock?"

"Like I said, while you're tying up ᴏ ιe loose end here, I'll be taking care of another in Lostcoast. I'l ɡet away around ten. So don't show your face in Tribune Chann el before then."

"And what about the minister? They're saying he's coming to Port Lostcoast."

"We can't take a chance that he connects the dots until after the announcement. My business in Lostcoast will look like an accident. You're just going to have to stay out of sight for a few days. Tell the wife you're taking Cole fishing."

Darren blew hard through his lips, his cheeks puffing out like a blowfish. "I don't know."

"You don't take care of this, Darren, and you'll never see your kids again. You know that."

"I know it."

"Then finish what you started."

"Okay, I will." Darren hung up the phone. He sat at the kitchen table in the dark. Dr. Thurlow's words made sense. He had to make sure Cole didn't get in the way. But kill him? It had made him sick when Archie had died. When he had killed him. Darren First Moon put his head in his hands as he thought about it. The feeling of the gaff in his hand as it pierced the soft spot above the temple. The blood. He had barely been able to hold himself together when they had found it on the *Inlet Dancer* in Alert Bay. He had vomited off the deck when no one was looking.

And now Cole. Darren First Moon was smart enough to know that Darvin Thurlow was playing him. He just couldn't think of any way out now. He couldn't think of any way to climb out of the grave he had dug for himself. Would he lose his kids? He had heard terrible stories of what white families did to First Nations children when they were taken from their parents. No doubt that with Darren gone, his children would be taken away. Betty was a good mom, he thought, but she wouldn't be able to raise the kids on her own. She liked to drink a little too much. Like his own parents. And both of her folks were gone. The community wasn't what it once was, he reasoned. The government would take his children and they would end up much the way he had. On his own, on the street, angry, violent. He didn't want that to happen.

Then Darren First Moon had an idea.

He sat in the dark for half an hour considering it.

And then the phone rang. He jumped up to get it.

"Hello?"

"Darren, it's Nancy. I'm so sorry to call so late —"

"What time is it?"

"It's midnight. Listen, Cole hasn't come home yet."

"You think he's getting into trouble?"

"Likely. When I saw him tonight he was pretty pissed about, well, about something."

"He's likely gone to The Strait. If he ran into Dan Campbell, that could be bad news."

"Can you go and look in on him?"

"Sure thing."

"Thanks, Darren."

Darren hung up the phone. He hit the front door at a run and made for the docks. He had to stop by his boat before looking for Cole. Suddenly, keeping Cole Blackwater alive was very important to his future.

28

"Daddy, who's that?"

Cole Blackwater pushed his eyes open.

"He looks awful."

Mouths of babes, Cole thought.

"That's a friend of Daddy's, sport. Go play outside, okay? And take your sister."

Cole heard the laughter of two children, the slamming of a door. Felt the cool air waft over him from the draught.

"How you doing, bruiser?"

Cole opened his eyes and strained to focus on the face of Darren First Moon.

"We at your place?" Cole asked.

"Yup. Those are my rugrats."

Cole pushed himself up and took inventory. He looked around the tiny living room. The floor was bare plywood. An assortment of ratty-looking chairs were scattered around the room. He was lying on a sagging couch covered in a moth-eaten wool blanket.

He felt for breaks. He could move his arms and legs, though his left arm hurt when he extended it. He rolled up the sleeve of his shirt and saw that it was purple from the midpoint of his forearm up to his triceps. He flexed it again. Not broken, but darn near.

"Got a mirror?" he asked.

"Bathroom."

Cole stood, his body feeling as if he'd been stuffed in an industrial dryer set on tumble. He worked to straighten his back and felt his stomach heave. Long night. Long, dark tea time of the soul. He shuffled to the bathroom and flicked on the lights. A dim glow came from a bare, overhead bulb. The bathroom was clean but run down. The tiles on the floor were cracked. The shower curtain hung by a long stick rather than a rod. He looked at himself in the foggy mirror.

"Good fucking grief," he said, and then wondered if Darren's kids were within earshot.

"Looking pretty handsome this morning, bud," came Darren First Moon's voice from the other room.

His left cheek, where the scar from a previous brawl was just starting to fade, was taped shut with six strips of first-aid tape. Under the tape was a gash nearly two inches long, running from the top of his cheek down to the edge of his mouth. He pressed it gently and felt the bone beneath it ache. Lucky not to have cracked anything. Some x-rays wouldn't hurt. But his head felt okay, with the exception of the hangover, which was monumental.

He had several other bruises on his face, but they all paled in comparison to the gash on his left cheek. He pushed his hair up and saw that his forehead wore a long, jagged cut that had been patched with bandages and gauze. The head-butt, he recalled. He looked down at his hands. His knuckles were red and raw. He felt his left side. "I think I cracked some ribs," he said aloud.

"Those guys were going to kill you," said Darren from the other room. Cole could hear toast pop.

"Only if I didn't kill them first," mumbled Cole.

"What was that?" Darren stuck his head into the washroom.

"I said I guess I have you to thank."

"No thanks to me. Thank Nancy. She called me when you didn't come home right away. Guessed that you'd gone looking for trouble. I talked to a few folks in The Strait and they said they had seen Dan Campbell waiting outside the bar with his buddies. As I understand it, you took the back door. That likely saved your skin, such as it is."

"I guess it's a good thing you showed up when you did."

Darren shrugged. "Nothing to it."

"You're going to have to watch your back now."

"I don't think so. I think Dan Campbell is through here."

"What makes you say that?"

"He went too far."

Cole pressed on his cheek again.

"You want some toast before we go?"

"Go?"

"Jeopardy Rock. Remember?"

"Good Christ," said Cole, and Darren laughed. Cole grinned.

"Do I have time to go back to the bluff house and change? Make sure Grace and Nancy know I'm okay?"

"Not if we're going to get there and back today," said Darren, feeling some impatience. "We're not taking the *Inlet Dancer*. My little boat has got some guts, but not much."

"Can I call?"

"Phone's on the table there. I put some of my warm clothes out for you."

"Thanks." Cole found the phone among a clutch of dirty plates and coffee cups on the dining table in the kitchen.

"Nancy, it's me," he said when got through to the bluff house.

"Cole—!"

"I'm okay. Got jumped coming home from the bar. Dan Campbell. Listen, I think he's dangerous. Likely our man. Can you call Constable Johns and let them know?"

"I will, of course. How bad, Cole?"

"Superficial," he said. "Nothing new. I gave worse than I got," he bragged again.

He heard Nancy take a breath. "The RCMP are already heading this way today, remember?"

"I remember. Tell them to get a move on, would you? And you guys stay put today. Is Jacob back?"

"No, I haven't heard if he'll be around today."

"I'm worried is all."

"How does Dan tie in with Stoboltz? You think they asked him to take Archie out?"

"I have no idea. The RCMP will have to get that piece of the puzzle. But you stay clear of him. I mean it."

"We'll be fine. Look, Cole—"

"Nancy, I don't want to talk about it now. Darren says if we're going to get to Jeopardy Rock and back today, we'd better get going. You need to get ready to file a story on this."

"You still want me to write it?"

"Of course. And make sure you talk with Bright about the connection between the leaked memos and the First Nations Opportunity Fund."

"Who else should I talk to?"

"Don't tip the minister's office off. God, I wish we knew who the deep throat was. Maybe you could track him down. Otherwise,

I think the best we can do is interview some of the enviros working on the salmon file."

"What about Greg?"

"You do that and he'll call the event off. He's in with Lance Grey and Stoboltz."

"So what if they call the event off? Isn't that what we want?"

"I don't know. I don't know what we want. Can you put Grace on?"

"Sure, Cole," she said, and then added, "Be careful."

"I will."

Grace picked up the phone. "Cole, are you all right?"

"Never better," he laughed. "Listen," he said, "you need to call Carrie Bright. Tell her everything we know about the funny business linking Stoboltz, the sea lice engineering, and the First Nations Opportunity Fund. Get her to come to Port Lostcoast for the announcement."

"And do what?"

"Upend the apple cart. I don't know. We'll think of something today."

"Okay, Cole...." Grace sounded skeptical.

"Look," he said, "the way I see it, Lance Grey knows we're onto this whole thing. He knows we have a bunch of the pieces. He knew Archie did. But the minister has said, 'Let's go to that nice little port town, you know, out in the islands, to make this announcement.'" Cole mimicked the minister's voice. "And Lance hasn't been able to come up with a good enough excuse not to, so he's going to string this along as best he can and hope like hell he can protect his own ass." Cole was in his bull-in-a-china-shop mode.

"What if the minister is in on this, too?"

"I can't see it."

"Okay, I'll call Carrie and set this up."

"And Grace, I told Nancy to go ahead and file."

"Yeah...."

"I still think that if we're going to bag these guys, she ought to get the story, don't you think?"

"I guess it's just sinking in that there is going to be a story on my father being murdered."

"I know. I'm sorry, look, I've got to go. Darren is jumping up and down. The *Rising Moon* sails with the rising sun!" Cole hung up and turned to Darren. "Okay, let's hit it."

■ Grace hung up the phone and turned to Nancy, who was in the kitchen making coffee. "Guess you'll want a quote."

Nancy put two cups on the counter. "I know that this is awkward."

"It's okay. The story needs to get told. So let's have some breakfast and then do this right."

Nancy smiled. "Okay."

They ate breakfast at the table as they watched the sun paint the eastern horizon crimson red. "Red sky at morning, sailors take warning," Grace singsonged.

"Is that really true?"

"Who knows? Around here we listen to the marine forecast."

"Shall we start?" asked Nancy.

"Let me get some of my papers and stuff together. That way we'll have everything at our fingertips."

Grace went into Archie's office and began to collect her own notes, the brown envelope of materials that had travelled from Victoria to Port Lostcoast to Vancouver and back in the last month. As she rummaged through the files on Archie's desk, making sure she didn't overlook anything germane to the story, she came across the will. She sat down on the chair. She hadn't opened it after Archie had disappeared, refusing to believe that her father wasn't coming back. But now she knew he was gone. Grace unfolded the papers and scanned them. She made it as far as page three, then stopped reading, turned, and looked out the window at the red eastern sky.

■ Cole sat next to Darren in the cabin of the *Rising Moon*, wrapped in a heavy overcoat with an orange life jacket and a musty woollen blanket over his shoulders. The boat skipped lightly over the water as they powered eastward. They made the wide waters of the channel near Tribune in good time, and were rewarded with an extraordinary view of the Coast Mountains backlit by the rising sun. Cole turned in his seat and saw the constellation of islands at the mouth of the inlet light up, and, behind them, the mountains of the north end of Vancouver Island glowing in the day's first light. He took a deep breath of the salty air and let the events of yesterday drain from his aching body.

Darren was silent. He stared straight ahead as the *Rising Moon* cut swiftly across the calm waters, bearing for Tribune Channel.

Cole considered his decision to make for Jeopardy Rock, knowing that Dan Campbell was walking around Port Lostcoast a free man. He yelled to Darren, "Do you think we made the right decision leaving, what with Dan and his friends at large in Lostcoast?"

Darren continued to look straight ahead, but yelled, "You mean, are the girls okay?"

"Yeah. What if Dan tries to get at something from Archie's records?"

"Like what?"

"I don't know. Something that might tie him to Archie's death."

"I thought you said there wasn't any connection between Dan and the salmon farms."

"I'm just guessing. I don't know."

"I don't think there is," said Darren. Then he said, "You think he killed Archie?"

"Seems like our best bet right now. You think we should go back?"

"I think Nancy and Grace are fine," Darren said, still focusing on the water ahead.

Cole pulled the blanket tighter. He drew a deep breath and tried to piece together what could have transpired between Archie and Dan that would move the man to commit murder. It wouldn't have taken much, Cole thought, given Dan's volatility.

For years Archie and Dan had been beating each other up in the media. When conservation groups began working to protect the mid-coast of British Columbia's ancient rainforest from clear-cutting, Archie Ravenwing was a freshman band councillor and had worked to secure the support of his people for the proposed agreements. Dan Campbell had lobbied strenuously against it, siding with logging companies in their fight against First Nations and environmentalists.

When many of those same environmentalists waged a bitter battle to ban the hunting of grizzly bears across the province, Archie had been their champion on the coast. He made the economic argument that a portion of his living was made taking American tourists up Knight Inlet to view grizzly bears feeding on spawning salmon each fall. Dan Campbell's main business was outfitting and guiding similarly rich Americans in the pursuit of grizzly trophies.

That the two men had lived side by side in the town for a decade was a wonder to Cole. What could have pushed Campbell over the edge? Salmon farming?

Cole guessed that Campbell's support of salmon farming was ideologically driven. He didn't seem to be directly linked to the practice. Like many men of Campbell's stripe, Cole figured that he simply supported industry of all kinds, believing one of two things: either God had given man dominion over all of earth's creatures, and thus the right to gobble them up; or nature simply knew no bounds, and the supposed decline in wild salmon was part of a natural cycle that would correct itself in time, as it always did.

Cole found himself wishing he knew more about Campbell's involvement in the Aquaculture Advisory Task Force. What role had he played? And what was his connection to Greg White Eagle, Darvin Thurlow, and Lance Grey? Cole exhaled heavily. In none of the packages of information he'd seen so far did there seem to be any connection. Was Archie Ravenwing's murder completely unrelated? Had Dan simply had enough of Archie Ravenwing's proselytizing and followed him out to Jeopardy Rock that morning? Confronted him? Killed him? How?

Maybe the answer would become evident when they reached the former DFO station and got a look at the lay of the land.

There were so many unanswered questions. What had Campbell

done with the boat? Cole closed his eyes to visualize the day unfolding. He pictured the *Inlet Dancer* making its way toward Jeopardy Rock. Then he imagined the *Queen Mary Two* do the same. Maybe Dan had landed at the DFO station and snuck up on Archie when Archie himself was sneaking around, clubbed him on the head with the fish club he had used on Cole the previous evening, and dragged his body back to the *Inlet Dancer*.

Dan had seemed pretty handy with that club. Cole felt his cheek. He'd need to go for x-rays. But Cole had gotten the better of him, hadn't he? That wouldn't have happened a year ago, thought Cole. The last eight months of nearly nightly workouts had helped. His reflexes were much sharper, his fists faster. His punch much more solid. But there was something else. Something that hadn't been there a year ago. Something that hadn't been there before his last trip to the ranch after the Oracle debacle. The anger that had lain dormant after his father's suicide had exploded to the surface while in Alberta, drawn from him like a poisoned magma, but never fully purged from his system.

That anger had fuelled him, burned in him, and had eaten at him as a poison does. And now he couldn't ignore it. Nancy Webber knew. She knew the truth about his father's death. Would she write about it? Cole shook his head, which he immediately regretted. Who cared if she did? He had no reputation left to protect. But he felt a wave of sickness and knew intuitively that more was at stake than his ego. Nancy Webber was at stake. His anger the previous evening had been in part fuelled by the flood of memories around his father's last act of anger and futility. It had also been fed by the bitter sense of loss he felt knowing finally that Nancy Webber *really was* in it just for the story.

Time would tell, he guessed. Bylines didn't lie.

Cole opened his eyes and watched the water pass by, watched the shores of distant islands draw near and recede. If Dan had killed Archie at Jeopardy Rock, how had Archie's boat ended up at Protection Point? Twenty miles or more away? Could Dan have towed the boat that far, and then abandoned it to make it appear as though Archie had been lost at sea? The *Queen Mary Two* was a big enough boat to have towed the *Inlet Dancer*, but not very fast. Cole guessed — and it was complete guesswork, being such a landlubber — that it would have taken the better part of a day to make that passage pulling the *Inlet Dancer.*

And that didn't explain the severed rope on the *stern* cleat of the *Inlet Dancer.* It seemed more likely that she had been the one doing the towing.

Had Archie given Dan a tow? The *Queen Mary* was too stout. At best the *Inlet Dancer* might have been able to pull her a few hundred yards, maybe a mile, into a sheltered cove. Had Archie let Dan onto his boat only to be killed by him? That was possible. Cole contemplated this thought. The code of the sea suggested, as far as Cole could surmise, that if someone was in distress, another mariner would come to his or her aid. No questions asked. Cole had even heard of a case where a Greenpeace boat, in distress, had been rescued by the whaling ships it was trying to stop.

If that was the case, Dan might have sought Archie's assistance with a distress call in the storm, and when Archie had towed him into a sheltered spot along Protection Point, come aboard, offering his gratitude, maybe even going so far as to propose amends. Then he could have clubbed him to death on the deck of the *Inlet Dancer*, thus producing the blood Cole had found on the *Dancer*'s deck.

And then what? Cut the rope? Why? Why not just untie it? Cole couldn't square that circle.

Cole tried to imagine Archie inviting Dan Campbell onto the *Inlet Dancer*. Would he have been suspicious? Likely not. Archie Ravenwing could be a pompous prick, but he was generous and open hearted. He wouldn't have suspected Dan of murderous intent. Not unless something had transpired between the two in the last few days, and even then, Archie wouldn't have left a man to face his fate at sea.

Cole watched as the peaks of the Coast Range hove into view. A spectacular jagged pair of mountains rose above the fjord. All of this beauty, thought Cole, all of this majesty. Archie had spent his life on these waters, marvelling at these mountains, and his eyes would never again see their grace. Cole looked at Darren piloting the boat, playing the wheel lightly in his knotted hands.

Maybe Darren would take over where Archie left off, fishing these waters and plying his trade as a guide to tourists.

Traffic was light on the water this morning. The *Rising Moon* had passed only half a dozen other boats, none of which Cole had really noticed. They passed another — a powerboat bearing out of the channel at high speed — as they prepared to make the turn. Darren First Moon watched it race past. Cole saw him look at his watch, and then look up again.

"Someone you know?" Cole shouted.

"What? Oh, no. Nobody." First Moon was silent a moment, then said, "You sure you want to go through with this?"

"Yeah, why not?"

"Just asking."

They were nearing the mouth of McNichol Channel, the gateway to Tribune Channel and Jeopardy Rock. Cole could see by Darren's watch that it was almost ten. Cole felt his hunger growing. He hadn't packed a lunch and wasn't sure that Darren First Moon had either. Hungover and beaten half senseless, Cole hadn't been thinking straight that morning. By the look of Darren First Moon's house and boat, Cole guessed that he didn't have a fully stocked larder. The contrast between First Moon and Ravenwing was pretty stark.

How much Archie had been skimming, and how much he had been earning, would be a matter for the lawyers to decide. Whatever the case, Darren First Moon hadn't been getting a share, Cole guessed. Blackwater felt his stomach turn, partly with hunger but mostly from nausea. Cole had read somewhere that when seasick, one should stare at the horizon and keep steady, and the nausea would pass. But in the confines of Knight Inlet, and the narrowing margins of McNichol Strait, there was no horizon, so Cole Blackwater stared at the bow of the *Rising Moon*. He focused his gaze on the rusty safety rail that ran along both port and starboard sides of the boat. He thought about Dan Campbell, and about his friend, Archie Ravenwing, and about the faces of the people that Cole Blackwater would never again see. He was only thirty-eight, but it seemed to Cole that the collection of faces that had come into his life and gone was too great. People come into our lives, he thought, and go, and before we are able to pause long enough to get to know them — to really know them — they are gone. It was clear to Cole that he hadn't really known Archie Ravenwing well. And now, he never would.

All of this passed through the miasma of Cole's hungover and beaten brain as he stared directly at the bow of Darren First Moon's junker of a boat. Somewhere amid the tattered thoughts about time's swift passage and self-slaughter, a warning light began to blink. Cole focused his eyes — tied off to a D ring on the nose of the boat was a coil of new line. The rope's newness stood in sharp contrast to the rest of the ageing pleasure craft. Cole focused on his horizon line, trying to keep his breakfast of toast down, trying to keep his growing hunger at bay.

■ Grace sat in front of Nancy at the dining-room table, a stack of papers in her hands.

"You okay?"

"Yup, okay," said Grace.

"You don't sound it. You look like you've just seen a ghost."

Grace looked up.

"Sorry," said Nancy. "Not very sensitive."

"It's all right." Grace handed Nancy the will. "What do you make of page three?"

Nancy opened the will. "You sure I should be reading this?"

Grace nodded and Nancy read. When she was through she looked up. "You don't think that Cole could have —?"

"No!"

"Of course, of course he couldn't have. He was in Vancouver."

"What makes you even think that?"

"Bad habit," said Nancy. "Journalist," she said, nodding her head. "Always looking for the worst in everyone."

"No, it's not Cole's name that troubles me. It's that Darren's name has been scratched out."

"Why do you think Archie did that?"

"I don't know. They knew each other for more than ten years."

"How did they meet?"

"Archie had just been elected to the band council. He was

doing a lot of work with young offenders, with young people who hadn't gotten off to a good start. Darren was born in Alert Bay, got into trouble in McNeill and up the coast. Fighting, alcohol, drugs. He got into a mix up one night with a logger and damn near killed the guy. Hit him with a fish gaff...."

"A what?"

"A fish gaff. They're on most fishing boats. About three feet long with a heavy metal hook on one end. Used for pinning down a fish that's putting up a fight, but most guys use them for everything from pulling a boat into the dock to opening a can of beer."

"So Archie took Darren on when he made parole?"

"That's right. Darren was in prison for six years. Maximum security for half of that. Four years of juvie on and off before that. He was pretty messed up when he got out. His parole conditions said that he needed to work with an elder for five years. Dad agreed to take him on, and they worked together ever since."

"Has he been in any trouble since?"

"No! Darren is really sweet. He was just a messed up kid. Typical. Both parents were alcoholics. Eight kids. Half of them never made it through grade six. No work. No sense of their history. They just drifted around the north island, as far down as Duncan at one point. I think Darren was on his own at fourteen, maybe fifteen. He's a good man. He loved Archie, and Archie loved him. He would never have hurt him...."

"Grace, you don't sound so sure."

"No, Archie loved Darren, but you know how Archie was. He could be pretty hard on people. I think they'd been having a bit of a fight. Nothing serious, but I heard them getting on each other's backs once or twice. Dad held people to a standard that he couldn't meet himself. I think he wanted Darren to stop acting like a dumb kid and start taking some responsibility."

"Hardly seems like the stuff of premeditated murder."

"I wouldn't really know."

"Me neither."

Grace stood and poured more coffee. "We should call Carrie Bright before we begin, don't you think?"

Nancy nodded. Grace was reaching for the phone when it rang. She pulled her hand back as though it were hot, and then picked it up and answered.

"This is she," she said. Nancy only heard one side of the conversation.

"Oh, hi, Ben. I didn't expect to hear back from you — "

"Are you sure you can tell me that?"

"Okay, I get it. Right." Then Grace listened, jotting down notes.

"Say that again?"

"That was the day I came in to ask you about the rope. Are you sure?" Grace was silent a moment, listening. Then: "Oh my God."

■ Cole closed his eyes and tried to clear his mind as they grew steadily closer to Jeopardy Rock. What were they looking for? Cole had told Grace that he would know it when he saw it, but he wasn't so sure. A bathtub full of sea lice, with an evil scientist cackling in the shadows, mumbling about the end of the world? Not likely. Cole knew almost nothing about Darvin Thurlow. He was a Doctor of something, but of what, Cole had no idea. Something about genetics? With no access to the internet he couldn't Google the good doctor and find out. It hadn't occurred to him to call Mary Patterson and find out. He was flying blind, deep into enemy territory, and he didn't have the foggiest idea how he was going to come up with "a smoking gun," as Darren had called it. He only hoped that Thurlow didn't pull one on him before he and Darren could get what they'd come for.

And the mystery of Jeopardy Rock wasn't the only territory into which he was flying blind. He felt emotionally empty after his confrontation with Nancy Webber last night. More so than getting beaten with a fish club, his bout with Nancy had drained him of all his emotional defenses. He felt naked. His most closely held secret had been exposed. And not to the world. To himself. No way to hide from this now, Denman Scott would tell him. Now he had to face it. He couldn't keep hitting the heavy bag and just hope to God it went away.

He was lost in the darkness of his own thoughts when the radio crackled and startled both him and Darren First Moon.

"*Rising Moon*, this is Port Lostcoast, do you copy?" It was a man, likely old Rupert Wright, the part-time harbour master.

Darren picked it up. "Go ahead, Lostcoast, this is the *Rising Moon*."

"*Rising Moon*, is Cole Blackwater with you?"

Darren looked at Cole. "He hasn't lost his cookies yet, if that's what you mean."

"Can you put him on the mic?"

Darren handed Cole the mic. "This is Cole Blackwater."

"Cole, it's Nancy. I've got some news for you."

■ "Nancy, I think I've made a terrible mistake."

"What are you talking about, Grace?"

"That was my friend from high school, the one I told you about in Alert Bay. He works at the marine supply store. I had asked him to check his records to see if they could say who had bought rope that was solid enough to pass for bow line. He said that he had looked through the credit card transactions and didn't come up with anything. Same for debit. Said he would get in a pile of dog shit if anybody found out what he was doing. But he still came up with nothing. Then he said he asked the other clerks if they had sold any rope that morning. He had started at two PM, just a few hours before I had come in. He told me that a guy who only works one or two shifts a week sold a few things to a 'big Indian' the very morning I was asking around. A rope, a heavy flashlight, and...."

"What?"

"A fish gaff."

"Jesus. Who?"

"Darren."

"Good Christ. Do you think —?"

Grace's face was ash-white. "Nancy, I have a terrible feeling about this. Cole is out at Jeopardy Rock with him, Nancy. What do we do?"

"Do you really think...?"

"Oh, Nancy, I just couldn't face the idea of it. But yes, it's possible. Like I told you, Darren has a history of violence. And he and Dad had been at each other's throats these last months. I just couldn't see it. Everybody was pissed at Dad for one reason or another. He could get at people like that, but—"

"We've got to call the RCMP," interrupted Nancy. "They are heading here today. Maybe they can get their asses in gear."

"Should we warn Cole?"

"How?"

"Radio. Cellphones don't work."

"Yeah, but what do we say? Tell him that we think Darren is the killer?"

"Nancy, these are VHF radios. They aren't private."

"Who cares who knows?"

"Darren will be sitting right beside Cole. He'll know we know and will find out the same time Cole does."

"Fuck. This is a mess."

"We could make something up. Something that will alert Cole without tipping Darren off."

Nancy only had to think for a moment. "I've got it."

"What?"

"You got a radio here?"

"No, we'll have to use the harbour master's."

"I'll tell you on the way. I just hope Cole hasn't told Darren too much about his personal life."

■ "What is it, Nancy?" Cole asked.

"Cole, it's your father."

"Don't be cute, Nancy. I'm in the middle of something."

"Shut up and listen. It's your father, Cole. He's dead."

"What are you trying to pull, Webber?"

"For God's sake, Blackwater. Shut up and listen for once in your life. Your father died *this morning*. Your brother just called here."

"Hold on a minute." Cole put the mic down on the dashboard. He looked at the water rushing by. At the sky. Clouds. Mountainsides cloaked in spruce and fir. Gulls. Darren piloting the *Rising Moon.*

"This morning?" he said. First Moon was looking at him.

"This morning. Heart attack."

"Wow, you're kidding. That is some news. Do I need to do anything?"

"I think you should get back here soon. In one piece. Okay?"

"Did Walter say he called the RCMP?"

"Yes."

"Okay." He hung up the mic.

"Should I turn around?" asked Darren, his face showing concern.

Cole was silent. He felt the boat slowing. "No. No, we're almost there now, right? Let's just get this done and then we can get back."

"You sure?" First Moon powered the outboard back up.

"I'm sure."

"They called the RCMP about a heart attack?"

"My dad had a history."

"Tell me about it," said First Moon.

29 The *Rising Moon* powered down as they swept around a small peninsula jutting into Tribune Channel. The far shore was less than a half kilometre away from them and rose steeply into the mountains of Viscount Island, and, behind it, Mount Frederick on the mainland. As they made the turn, a series of enclosed fish pens the length of three football fields came into view.

"So that's what all the fuss is about?" said Cole. When Cole had visited Port Lostcoast to conduct the strategy session two years earlier, Archie had taken him to see several fish farms. Coming face to face with them again was sobering. But Cole was talking to buy time.

"Guess so," said Darren, cutting the engine back to dead slow.

"Don't look so bad," said Cole.

Darren was nosing the boat toward the shore. Adjacent to the open salmon pens was a pier. Several boats were tied along the slip.

"To talk with Archie you'd have thought that Satan himself was operating these things," said Darren, angling the boat into a moorage.

Cole forced a laugh. "Archie had a way of painting things in black and white." As the *Rising Moon* came to rest along the pier, Cole could see the old DFO research station on a rocky outcrop through the cluster of trees on the shore.

"Yeah, he did," said Darren. While Darren was preoccupied, Cole searched the cluttered floor of the boat's cockpit. He found what he was looking for. He slipped a heavy flashlight into the pocket of his coat. Cole was developing a penchant for Maglites. Might buy me some stock in the company, he mused, if — when — I get off this island.

"Here," said Cole. "Let me get the bow line." Before Darren could protest, he had swung himself up onto the bow of the boat and uncoiled the new line. Nice, he thought. As the boat came even with the dock, Cole jumped onto it and made the line fast around a cleat.

Darren cut the engine. "Now what?"

"We have a look around."

Darren shrugged. He stepped off the boat and stretched. Cole looked around them. Half a dozen pens sat in deep water just off the point known as Jeopardy Rock. At the end of the dock sat a small, squat building that Cole suspected served as a supply hut, likely for storing fuel and other gear. Another newer building to the west of it was probably used for handling the operations for the pens and housing workers. Food pellets, antibiotics, maybe even the chemicals used to give the lacklustre farmed Atlantic salmon their rosy hue would be found there. And beyond that, on a rocky outcrop overlooking Tribune Channel, was the old DFO research station. It was a small, sturdy building, with boxy windows facing the eastern mountains and the waters nearby.

"Shall we see if Dr. Thurlow wants to show us around like he said?"

"You sure that's such a good idea?" Darren fiddled with something in the pocket of his float coat.

"Why not?"

"Don't we suspect this guy is connected to Archie's death somehow?"

"I think Dan Campbell killed him," said Cole, looking at Darren. "But I think Thurlow is somehow tied up in it. I just don't know how."

"And we're just going to walk right up there and say hi, and ask him to show us the joint?"

"Yup. He invited us. I bet that's his boat there," said Cole pointing at a newer-looking speedboat. "Heck, Darren, it's two against one. We can take him if he pulls anything."

"Guess so," he said. "You're a bit of a mess, though."

"Think I might scare him?"

Darren just shrugged.

"Lead on," said Cole, pointing to the research station with his chin. "I'm so scary to look at, he better see you first or he'll soil his pants." Cole laughed.

Darren trudged up the hill, hands in the deep pockets of his orange float coat. The silence of the woods was broken by the croaking of the occasional raven. The lightly used path was festooned with pine needles and hedged with thick tangles of salal. The cool air held the tang of fish and salt water. The forest was sprayed with a light gossamer sheen of mist. Cole became acutely aware of his surroundings, his senses heightened with adrenalin. They made the top of the rocks in a few minutes, both men breathing hard, the wound on Cole's face pulsing.

"Think this place has got a doorbell?" Cole joked.

"Don't know," said Darren.

"Come on, lighten up, Darren. This will be fun. Take a look around here for a way in," said Cole, "and I'll see where this pathway leads." Cole disappeared around the back of the building.

"If you say so," said Darren, fidgeting with his pockets. He looked back and forth across the windows.

"Found a door here," said Cole from the back of the building. "It's open."

"Great...."

Darren turned the corner to see the door close in front of him. He took his left hand from his pocket to open the door, his right hand still buried in his coat. He opened the door and stepped through.

Cole was waiting for him on the other side. Blackwater swung from behind the door, the heavy flashlight coming down hard on the back of Darren's head. Darren stumbled forward, his hands splayed before him, the hatchet he held in his right pocket clattering across the concrete floor and out of reach. Cole stepped in and kicked him in the ribs, and First Moon rolled onto his side. "Stop," he coughed. "Enough!"

Cole reared back with his right foot and began to swing it toward the man's face.

"Please, please, I got kids."

Cole skidded to a halt, almost tripping over the prone man. Cole was sweating. His hands trembled. He held the flashlight so tightly that his knuckles were white.

Darren lay on the floor and coughed. He curled into the fetal position, tucking his knees into his chest, his hand holding the place on the back of his head where Cole had hit him. He began to cry. Not gentle tears, but great sobs that came hard and fast.

Cole looked down at him. His hand relaxed. He drew a breath. He felt a wave of nausea sweep over him and he forced himself to breathe so he wouldn't vomit.

Cole stepped back from Darren and looked around the room. Upon entering he'd had time enough only to confirm that he was alone. Now he took in the details of the space. He had stepped directly into the laboratory. There were two dozen cement ponds in the room, each ten feet long, their walls rising two and a half feet off the floor. Cole walked to where Darren First Moon's hatchet lay and picked it up, using the sleeve of his coat to protect any record of fingerprints. He cast a disgusted backwards glance at Darren as he did, and saw the sobbing man still curled on the floor.

Each pen contained salmon at various stages of development, many of them encrusted with sea lice.

Cole continued to walk around the room. Near the windows that overlooked the eastern slopes of Tribune Channel were aquariums packed with sea lice.

On the southern wall was a door. Cole checked to see if it was locked. It was. He stepped back and with his booted foot kicked it at handle-height, and it splintered into a hundred pieces, the wooden jam collapsing as it did. Cole looked into the room. It was a makeshift office that included tables with hundreds upon hundreds of vials. Cole could only imagine what was contained there.

He walked back and crouched before the trembling body of Darren First Moon. He still held the hatchet and heavy flashlight in his hand. He poked Darren with the light.

"Darren, get a hold of yourself."

Darren tried to draw a deep breath but could not.

"Darren, where's Thurlow?"

Darren's eyes seemed to come into focus.

"Darren, where's Thurlow?"

First Moon sucked in a breath and let it out. His eyes zeroed in on Cole's.

"Where is he?"

"He's gone to Port Lostcoast."

30

The radio crackled in the harbour master's cabin. Rupert Wright stood up from his desk and walked to the table on which it sat and listened carefully.

"Port Lostcoast ... Blackwater ... read me?"

"I read you four by two, party radioing Port Lostcoast."

"... trouble ... Can you reach ... Ravenwing?"

"Party radioing Port Lostcoast, I read you four by two ... loud but not very clear. Say again?"

"Grace Ravenwing ... trouble ... Warn her...."

"Party radioing Port Lostcoast. I am hearing Grace Ravenwing is in trouble and needs to be warned. Am I reading you correctly?"

"Correct...."

"Can I tell her the nature of the threat, over?"

"Dr. Thurlow ... on his way...."

"Are you saying Dr. Thurlow is on his way to Port Lostcoast and Grace Ravenwing has reason to be concerned?"

"Yes!"

"Should I alert the authorities? Is it that serious?"

"Yes!"

"Five by five," said the harbour master. "I'll alert the RCMP and will try to find Grace Ravenwing. Port Lostcoast out."

■ Cole put down the mic and looked at Darren behind the wheel of the *Rising Moon*. "You had better pray to God that Grace Ravenwing and Nancy Webber are fine. If Thurlow harms one hair on either of their heads, I'm going to take it out on you," said Cole, his eyes boring into Darren First Moon.

The boat skipped over the light chop of Tribune Channel, full throttle, heading for the bigger waters of Knight Inlet. The wind had picked up since that morning, pushing the swell to three feet.

"Can I raise the RCMP on this thing?" Cole had his hand on the radio again.

"Should be able to. They monitor channel fourteen."

Cole turned the dial and pressed the button.

"RCMP dispatch, this is Cole Blackwater on the *Rising Moon*, do you copy?" He waited a moment. "RCMP, this is the *Rising Moon*, do you copy?"

"This is Alert Bay. We copy four by four," came a voice over the radio. "What is the nature of your message?"

"This is an emergency. I have reason to believe that two women in Port Lostcoast on Parish Island are in danger."

"What are their names?"

"Nancy Webber and Grace Ravenwing. They are staying at Archie Ravenwing's home, the bluff house. I don't think the place has an address...."

"Hold a minute, *Rising Moon*."

Cole watched the forest whir past as Darren guided the boat around the turn at McNichol Pass into Knight Inlet.

"*Rising Moon*, we have a boat on the way to Port Lostcoast. Detective Sergeant Alan Bates is heading there on the Ravenwing missing person's file. Your information has been forwarded to them. They're on the way."

"A Dr. Darvin Thurlow is either in Lostcoast now, or on his way, and is likely trying to get his hands on information that connects him to the murder of Archie Ravenwing," said Cole, shielding the mic with his hand.

"I'll pass that on, *Rising Moon*. Alert Bay out."

Cole put down the microphone. Now all he could do was sit tight and pray.

▬ Darvin Thurlow sat quietly at the galley table, his long, lean hands folded before him, his legs crossed. The tiny room was dark, the sound of the ocean resonating in his ears. He breathed slowly, taking air in through his nose and letting it out through his mouth, the way he had learned to do in a meditation class many years before. He felt a sense of abiding peace. He felt certain that nothing could go wrong for him today.

It hadn't always been like that for Darvin Thurlow. His time at UVic had been unfulfilling. The school was a haven for ideologically driven zealots masquerading as scientists. Saving the salmon, stopping sewage from being diffused in the Strait of

Juan de Fuca, protecting spotted owls — Darvin Thurlow had no beef with conservation. His father had been a farmer whose livelihood depended on sound stewardship of a resource. Darvin Thurlow believed that for the greater good to prevail, some sacrifices had to be made.

It was almost by accident that Thurlow stumbled upon work that developed the resistance among farmed Atlantic salmon to sea lice. It was thanks to another researcher's efforts that he came to appreciate how he might counter this breakthrough with one of his own. Humanity would not prevail, might not even survive, if it clung to outdated modes of feeding itself. There were too many people now. Scale had become the dominant issue in food production. Sacrifices had to be made for the greater good of humanity. And so while other researchers at the university sought ways of protecting wild salmon from decline at the hands of a fingernail-sized parasite, Dr. Darvin Thurlow fostered other ambitions.

Thurlow heard boots on the dock and drew a breath, letting it slip soundlessly from his mouth in the darkened room. He sat still in the darkened galley.

Three years ago he found a perfect partner willing to finance his inquiry and not ask too many questions, as long as what he learned helped build more salmon farms along the remote BC coast, feed more people, and create more profit. Thurlow could care less about profit. The approval he sought had nothing to do with money. How far might he go? There really were no limits. He was on the verge of unleashing a pestilence on the world that people would talk about for a generation, and in the end, he would be thanked. A decade-long confrontation would end, and humanity would triumph. And like his father, who had spent his life finding ways of growing more apples on a small farm in the BC interior, Darvin Thurlow would finally succeed in winning the sanction he had sought all his life.

But there were loose ends.

The boots stopped and he felt the boat dip as someone stepped onto it. He closed his eyes and steadied himself.

The door from the companionway opened and light flooded in, but he remained in shadow. The woman entered the room and went into the tiny galley only a few feet from where he was sitting. She lit the stove and poured water in a kettle for tea.

"Hello, Cassandra," he said from the darkness.

She screamed and dropped the kettle on the floor. It clattered across the polished wood and spilled its contents.

He was on her in a second, his hands locked on her arms, forcing her into the seat opposite from where he had been sitting, pushing her against the wall and quickly tying her arms to her side with a length of rope. She tried to scream again, but he put his hand on her chin and snapped her jaw shut.

"Don't make this worse than it needs to be, Cassandra," he hissed in her ear.

She looked at him, her eyes wild, her hair falling in errant strands over her face.

"I've got a roll of duct tape here, which I will use to tape your mouth if you even think of screaming again," he said slowly, quietly. "Got it?"

Cassandra Petrel nodded.

"Good," he said, taking a deep breath. "Now, let's have tea, shall we?"

■ "I wasn't going to kill you," yelled Darren, his eyes forward, the *Rising Moon* going top speed toward Parish Island and Port Lostcoast.

Cole yelled back, "Look, I'm not a cop, but I've got to tell you that not only do you have the right to silence, I highly recommend it."

"I just want you to know—"

"Darren, I'm going to hit you on the head with this flashlight again if you don't shut up."

First Moon looked into the distance, his face a knot of worry. The adrenalin rush that had propelled Cole for the last hour was nearly used up, and he felt weak and dizzy. He sat hunched forward in the chair as the world whipped by.

"Why the axe?" Cole finally yelled at Darren.

"What?"

"Why did you have the axe with you?"

Darren stared ahead. He could see Parish Island hove in view. Another ten minutes and they would be there.

"Darren, why?"

"For Thurlow."

■ Grace Ravenwing jumped from the chair at her father's desk when she heard the pounding on the door. She tripped over a stack of papers as she ran to the door and peered through the glass. Nancy was right behind her.

"It's Rupert Wright."

"Who?"

"The harbour master." She opened the door.

"Grace," he said, a little out of breath. "You okay?"

"Fine, why?"

"I got a radio call from your friend, Blackwater—"

"Cole Blackwater," said Nancy.

"I got a radio call from him. He said that Dr. Thurlow, you know, the scientist from Jeopardy Rock, was on his way here. He said to warn you."

"Thurlow is coming here?"

"That's what Cole said."

"Well, he isn't here now," said Grace, looking around.

"Did you call the RCMP?" asked Nancy.

"Placed the call before coming here. They have a boat about fifteen minutes away. What's going on?"

"Can you come in, sit down? We'll fill you in," said Grace.

"I should get back to the docks. The RCMP will need some direction."

"We'll stay here," said Grace.

"Lock your door," he said, running back down the path.

"I don't think it has a lock," said Grace, looking at Nancy. Then she asked, "You think he's coming here? Why?"

Nancy looked around the house. "Maybe he wants to get his hands on that brown envelope. It's pretty incriminating."

"He's got to know it's just a copy of electronic government files. The deep-throat guy has the originals. Thurlow couldn't hope to accomplish anything by coming here to get them."

Nancy shook her head. "He's a smart man. I think you're right. He knows he has nothing to gain by doing that."

"Then what?"

Nancy was silent. Then she opened her eyes wide. "Grace, who else did Archie confide in?"

■ "I think we should shed a little light on what you think you know about sea lice, Cassandra. What do you say?"

Thurlow opened the kerosene lantern that hung over Cassandra Petrel's tiny dining table. He took a package of matches from his pocket and struck one. He carefully lit the wick. "I've always loved the light these old lamps put out, don't you? It's so, I don't know, nostalgic."

He sat down across from Cassandra. Her face was composed, but there was fear in her eyes. Thurlow had tightly bound her arms with rope. A piece of heavy duct tape hung loosely from her cheek across the side of her face. Her mouth was free, but Thurlow could tape it shut in a second.

"So, you and Archie figured out that I was preparing a little evolutionary surprise for the salmon. It was only a matter of time, you know, before the sea lice did it themselves. I was only helping them along. They're such active little creatures."

"What do you want, Darvin?" said Petrel.

"Cassandra, Cassandra, Cassandra," he said, shaking his head. "You were always the greatest pain in the ass to me. Always the one who was pandering to the environmentalists. Always the one who was talking to the press. The great Dr. Cassandra Petrel, the caring, personable scientist, the face of scientific reason to the public. But it was such a load of bullshit, Cassandra. It was just you inflating your own ego. I was happy when you finally left. When you decided that the university had become too confining for your personal vendetta against businesses who are just trying to feed hungry people. But then ..." Thurlow shook his head. "But then you had to go and stick your nose into my work again."

"Darvin," she said, watching his face in the dim light of the lantern. "I don't know what you think I know, but I can assure you, if I've figured it out, lots of other people will, too."

"It's not so much what you know, Cassandra, as what you'll be willing to say. When this whole thing becomes public." He shook his head. "Which seems likely now. Cassandra Petrel, friend of the environment, will once again triumph over the evil Dr. Thurlow, proponent of big agri-business. I'm tired of it, Cassandra. That's not going to be the story this time."

She looked at him. A bead of sweat rolled down her forehead, over her eyebrow and into her eye. "So now what?" she said.

He smiled. "Lights out."

■ Darren First Moon kept the boat at full throttle as he approached the breakwater. Cole was standing now, his fingers curled tightly over the windshield, his eyes focused on the bluff where Archie Ravenwing's house stood. He wasn't certain what he hoped to see, but he looked nevertheless.

"Hold on!" said Darren as he powered back and turned the wheel to cut into the breakwater. Cole bent his knees but kept his face turned toward town. Movement caught his eye where the dirt road from the bluff met the street where the general store and The Strait sat squat against the harbour. He saw two figures running. Toward the dock.

"That's Nancy and Grace!" he shouted and pointed. He could see both women running hard along the dock. "Move it!" he yelled, and Darren throttled up, ploughing a dangerous wake toward the moored boats. They still had five hundred metres to travel to reach the docks, and Cole could see Nancy and Grace bearing straight for the end of the pier, running hard away from, or maybe toward, something unseen.

■ Grace yelled, "Last boat on the centre pier!"

Nancy didn't reply. She had no breath to waste on words. God, how she wished she had got that last workout in. Her legs felt like rubber, her lungs screamed. But the adrenalin that coursed through every cell in her body kept her moving. Just another hundred feet. Eighty feet. Sixty feet. Almost there. What she would do when she reached the boat, she had no idea.

■ "I won't say a thing, I swear it," said Petrel.

"No, you won't," said Darvin Thurlow. "Because you won't have a chance, after a very unfortunate accident," he said, standing.

She screamed and he reached across the table and hit her in the mouth. Petrel's head bounced off the wood-panelled backing to the galley booth. Her eyes glazed over momentarily, and then he was beside her, taping her mouth and, grabbing the roll from the bench seat, adding another layer over the one already there.

Thurlow bent and reached under the Force 10 stove and found what he was looking for. He watched Petrel while he fiddled with something beneath the stove. "Looks like you forgot to hook up the gas when you did some work on the stove, Cassandra. That's very unfortunate. Such a tragedy."

He stood and said, "Nice working with you, Dr. Petrel." He reached over the table to take the lamp, and Cassandra saw her opening; she lurched toward him. Arms still tied at her sides, she drove her head into his ribs. He stumbled backwards into the stove and managed to bring his right knee up, driving it into her chest, knocking Petrel to the ground. The smell of gas was thick in the room. She lay on the floor, sucking air and gas through her nose, and blacked out. Thurlow regained his composure, straightened his coat, and stepped to the door. He put a hand on the railing that led to the companionway and the centre cockpit of the boat and raised the lit lantern over his head.

■ Nancy heard a scream from Cassandra Petrel's boat, muffled by the sound of the harbour, the whine of an inboard motor revved to capacity, and her own heart pounding in her ears.

Petrel's boat was twenty feet away. Nancy's legs pounded on the planks of the dock. She was aware of Grace somewhere behind her. She reached the centre cockpit of the boat and slowed and jumped onto the deck, landing hard, skidding on her side and colliding with the hatch to the rear state room. She righted herself and made for the companionway hatch behind the cockpit seat. As she did, the hatch flew open, smashing her arm against her chest and knocking her backwards. A blast of heat jumped from the hatch. A man, backlit by flames, stood in the companionway. She stumbled to her feet and without thinking leaped at him. She connected with his body at the chest, both of them careening off the narrow hatch and landing side by side on the hard floor of the cabin.

"Who the fuck are *you?*" Nancy heard him hiss as he punched and kicked at her. She locked her arms around him as tightly as she could to restrict his movement. She looked wildly around. A woman was tied up on the floor a few feet away. The space was hot and smelled like gas, and a lantern was smashed on the floor just a few feet from her face and was burning, the flames fuelled by the air that was being sucked into the cabin through the open gangway hatch.

Thurlow connected a jab to her stomach and Nancy gasped for air. It tasted like gas. Then she bit down on any part of him she could reach, his nose as it turned out. He hollered and thrashed his head, but she didn't let go. Nancy Webber tasted hot, salty blood on her tongue. Finally he ripped himself free, blood splashing on Nancy's face, and drove his fist into the side of her head. The world went dark.

▬ The boat hadn't stopped when Cole jumped, life jacket still snug on his body, onto the foot of the pier adjacent to Cassandra Petrel's boat. He stumbled and almost ran off the side of the dock and into the harbour, but managed to right himself in time to see Darvin Thurlow burst from the cabin of the boat, knocking a bewildered Grace Ravenwing to the deck. The distance between them was no more than thirty feet, and Cole lunged at Thurlow as he made the dock and started to run for the village.

"Cole, Nancy!" came Grace Ravenwing's desperate cry from where she lay on the deck of the boat.

Cole skidded to a stop. "Where is she?"

"In the boat!"

He watched as Thurlow made for the end of the dock. He felt Darren First Moon running past him, too. Both men about to escape, Cole jumped onto the boat and ripped the companionway door open. A billow of smoke and heat flashed in Cole's face.

He put his nose and mouth in the crook of his arm and jumped down the stairs into the dark belly of the burning boat. He nearly tripped over Nancy, who was coughing on the floor. He grabbed her under her arms and hoisted her up the steep steps to the deck of the boat. A stabbing pain ripped through his body where his ribs were cracked. He managed to push Nancy up and out of the galley and onto the deck, where Grace took over, dragging Nancy over the gunwales and onto the dock.

"Where's Cassandra?" he shouted at Nancy. Her face was red and her mouth had blood running from the corner. Her eyes were bleary, but she managed to point toward the hatch.

"Below."

"Jesus Christ," he mumbled. Then he yelled, "Get her out of here," to Grace, and plunged back into the darkness.

The cabin was filled with blue-black smoke and he could taste the gas. He pressed his face into the crook of his arm and tried not to breathe. Seconds, he thought. Mere seconds. That's all I've got. In a couple of seconds the bell will ring and the final round will end.

He went down on his hands and knees, remembering fire safety lessons from first grade, and made his way through the galley and toward the hall that connected with the head and the state room. Dark-coloured flames licked at the walls and surged back toward the stove with its ruptured gas line. He could see better from the floor but gagged on the smoke. He found her on the floor that led to the sleeping quarters, her hands tied, her mouth taped shut. She was unconscious. He took her arms and hoisted her onto his back. Stumbling to his knees, he made for the direction of the hatch. The heat of the flames and the noxious smoke made his ears burn and he thought he might collapse from lack of air.

The faint glow of daylight through the dark press of the toxic smoke guided him. "*That's how the light gets in.*" He remembered Leonard Cohen once again, as he had in Oracle: "*There is a crack in everything....*" Then he thought how funny it was what came to mind just before you died. He passed the stove where the reek of gas was powerful and the crackle of flames was right behind him. With a roar he hoisted Cassandra Petrel upward and reached for the companionway. The darkness engulfed him and, in the final step before the ladder, he tripped and fell forward, Petrel's weight coming down hard on him, his chest colliding with the heavy wooden steps. He cried out in pain—the ribs he had cracked the night before shot daggers into his central nervous system. He cursed and stumbled forward, making the companionway and up into the cool air. He could hear the shouts of other men from the village. He was in daylight now, surrounded by billowing smoke, confused and striving to get Petrel over the gunwales and onto the dock. He stood on the bench of the cockpit and was about to make the final step from the boat onto the dock when the *Queen Charlotte Challenger* exploded.

31 It was like being born. The cold rush around him. The heat surging past, the whistle of air, the sharp spasm of relief as he hit the water. He couldn't hold onto her, and he felt her body slip away.

Time slowed as he hurtled through the air. The force of the explosion jettisoned him over the stern of the boat and into the water behind it. The harbour was dark and cold and, as Cole plunged under the surface, the salt water stung his eyes and burned in the fresh wounds he bore from his confrontation the night before. But his life jacket gave him buoyancy, and he bobbed to the surface like a cork. He gasped for air and did not see Petrel. Her hands were bound. He struggled to press himself below the frigid water, but his life jacket prevented it. He tore at the zipper and managed, despite the spasm of pain in his chest, to shake it free and plunged down into the darkness. He swam down fifteen feet, following the starfish-studded pilings of the dock, and reached her before she touched the bottom. She was conscious, her mouth still taped shut, eyes wide, nose leaking bubbles. Pulling her by a wad of clothing at her shoulder, Cole swam awkwardly for the surface. When he broke through into the air above, he gasped for breath and she sputtered salt water through her nose. With his free hand he tore the tape from her mouth and she sucked air greedily into her lungs.

He heard the commotion of police sirens and wondered where a cop car might be coming from. He saw men on the dock spraying water on Petrel's boat. His eyes stung and his entire body burned, but he clung to Cassandra Petrel. From above, like angels, two men climbed down the ladder at the end of the pier to fish them from the sea.

■ They sat on the dock, heavy blankets around them, the scent of the sea air tinged with the must of the wool. Cassandra Petrel shivered, her face between her knees. Cole sat next to her, an arm around her back, rubbing in slow, absent-minded circles. Constable Derek Johns hunched over Cole, administered first aid to Cole's injuries, dabbing at the jagged gash on his face, questioning him about its origin. Cole looked around. Ten feet away Nancy Webber sat sucking air from an oxygen bottle, her face black with soot. Grace Ravenwing was beside her, a small, strong hand resting on Nancy's forearm. An RCMP officer with a life jacket still tied to him was talking with Nancy, inquiring, no doubt, about how she came to be on the floor of Cassandra Petrel's boat, unconscious, and about Darvin Thurlow.

Cole watched the activity on the pier. Half a dozen men from the village had finished dousing Cassandra's boat with water from a hose that ran from a pump at the harbour master's station. They stood around smoking and talking about the excitement. The harbour master was making an inspection of the boat, taking notes in a spiral-bound notebook. There was very little left of the ketch to make notes about.

Glaucous-winged gulls wheeled overhead. A raven croaked from a thermal-air mass rising along the bluff.

"Where's Darren First Moon?" Cole said aloud, to no one in particular. Constable Johns didn't say anything. He put a clean set of steri-stips on the wound and said, "You're going to need to get into Port McNeill as soon as possible, Cole. We can take you back when we're through here. You're going to need stitches, which is going to hurt like hell given how old this wound is."

"Something to look forward to," said Cole. He stopped rubbing Cassandra Petrel's back, squeezed her arm, and looked at her. "You okay?"

She nodded and forced a weak smile. Her face was white. Cole stood and paused as a sharp pain shot through his body. "And you'll need some x-rays," the constable said helpfully. Cole smiled. He walked to where Nancy and Grace were talking with Detective Alan Bates. Cole held his arm close to his side, protecting his ribs.

"Nancy, how are you?"

She looked up at him, the mask still on her face. He thought he could see a faint smile through its plastic. He raised his eyebrows, and she took the mask off. "I'm okay. Just sucking at the oxygen here. Happy as a clam."

Cole hunched down next to the officer. "Where is Darren First Moon?"

Alan Bates nodded down the dock. Cole got up and walked its length, past the clutch of men beside Petrel's boat. He nodded to them and clasped a few hands as he made his way down the pier. There was another group of men there, standing around, talking, smoking. Cole eased through them and saw Darren First Moon standing next to a lamp post, his hands shackled to the pole, his face down. A second uniformed RCMP officer stood next to him. Darren looked up as Cole approached, and their eyes met. Cole held Darren's gaze a moment, then Darren turned his eyes away and looked toward the tiny town. Fifty feet from where he was shackled was a tan-coloured tarp in the middle of the road, with the unmistakable outline of a man beneath it. There was a shape protruding from the body beneath the tarp, creating a bulge about where the corpse's back would be. Cole could guess what the object was. The hatchet intended for Darvin Thurlow had found its mark.

32 "This is the first time I've ever owned a boat," said Cole. He was seated on the fish box on the deck of the *Inlet Dancer* with a beer in his hand.

"Does that make you a captain?" asked Denman Scott.

"If you put a dinghy on the back of this, you could call yourself admiral," said Sarah. Her nose was sunburnt and her face freckled.

Cole laughed. "Admiral Blackwater. Got a nice ring to it."

"Don't get him going," said Nancy. "Next thing you know I'll have to identify him as admiral in any stories I write about him.

Cole looked at her across the table. "I think a little respect would be nice," he said, but he was smiling. He lifted his can of Race Rocks to his lips and drank.

"It's too bad you're only captain for a day," said Nancy.

"I don't think so," said Cole.

Grace Ravenwing was seated on a blue Coleman cooler next to the fish box. "Got those papers, Grace?" asked Cole.

She smiled and fished an envelope from her jacket. She handed it to him.

Cole found a pen and flipped through the pages, signing next to the yellow Sign Here stickies. He grinned as he signed.

"You know the paperwork wasn't really necessary. The lawyers don't think so, anyway," she said.

"*I* think it is," said Cole. "I don't want anybody ever questioning this. I don't want there to be any suggestion that I contested the will. This way there is clarity around who owns the *Inlet Dancer*." Cole handed the papers to Nancy to witness. When she was done he put the pen back in his jacket pocket. He folded the papers and handed them to Grace. "She's all yours."

"We'll call you first mate from here on in," Grace smiled.

It was late June. The sun was hot overhead, but the breeze that slipped down from the coast range and trailed over the convoluted cluster of islands at the mouth of Knight Inlet gave a reprieve from the heat.

"What's happening with Darren?" Cole asked.

Grace looked at the open water. "He's still in the psych ward in Vancouver General. The judge has ordered another sixty-day assessment period."

"Archie was like a father to him," said Cole.

"I think Darren is sick," said Grace. "He just doesn't seem to understand what he's done. He doesn't seem to see the consequences."

"Is it FASD?" asked Denman. He'd seen the dire consequences of alcohol in the bloodstream of pregnant women in his years in Vancouver's downtown eastside.

"Maybe," said Grace.

"You think he'll walk?" asked Nancy.

"Hard to know," said Grace. "The Crown has him on both homicides. There were half a dozen witnesses to the killing of Thurlow. Threw that axe from thirty feet. Hard to say what will happen with Dad's case."

"How you holding up?" asked Denman.

"About as good as could be expected. This community has been great. You know, everybody loved Dad, even when he got in their faces about stuff. But family comes first for my people, and everybody on Parish Island is like a family. We have to be."

Nancy looked at Cole. "Did you know —?"

"Know what?"

"Know what Darren was going to do to Thurlow?"

"No. No idea. When we got to Jeopardy Rock, I only had a second to slip that new flashlight of his into my pocket. I thought that he was going to try and get me," said Cole, aware of Sarah nearby. "He told me on the ride back to Lostcoast that he was really going to try and take Thurlow out."

"You believed him?" asked Grace.

"He didn't have any reason to lie at that point. The way I see it," said Cole, "is that Darren figured if he showed up with me at the Jeopardy Rock research lab before Thurlow left, then maybe Thurlow would try something, and then Darren could kill him in self-defense." Cole looked at Sarah and added, "Big person talk, sweetie. Cover your ears."

"Dad, I'm nine. I've seen, like, ten thousand murders on TV."

Cole grinned. "That's great," he said. "Remind me to talk to your mom about our parenting plan, will you?"

Sarah grinned back.

"But Thurlow left early," said Grace.

"That's right. When I think back on it now, it must have been his boat that we saw as we made the turn into McNichol Pass. Darren seemed to just fall apart at that point. He had been all gung-ho up until then. After we saw that boat, he just seemed to lose his steam."

"So you think he wanted to get there before Darvin Thurlow left, and use you as bait? Then do a little bait and switch, as it were?" asked Grace.

"I think so."

"How's *that* make you feel?" asked Nancy.

"All in one piece," Cole said, holding out his arms, being careful not to spill his beer. "Not much else to say."

They sat on the large fish box of the *Dancer*, legs stretched out or hanging over the gunwales. Gulls wheeled overhead. Denman, Cole, Nancy, and Sarah had made the journey from Vancouver to Port McNeill in a rental car in one day, rising early the day before to catch the first ferry from Horseshoe Bay to Nanaimo, then motoring north along the eastside of Vancouver Island. Jacob Ravenwing had picked them up that morning and now they were all gathered on the *Inlet Dancer*.

"What are you going to do next, Grace?" Denman Scott asked, his bald head covered with a flat cap perched at a rather acute angle.

"I think I'm going to work with Cassandra. We'll use the *Inlet Dancer* for research. The government just announced that not only will they be adding fish farms to the Broughton, but they are going to allow Stoboltz to double its capacity at its existing farms. I only found out about this from a source in government. Brown envelope."

"You sound like a chip off the old block," said Denman.

"My father taught me a lot."

"He was a good man," said Denman.

Grace was silent a moment. Everybody was. "I miss him," she

finally said. "I miss him a lot." She wiped the tears from her eyes. "Anyway," she said. "I'll work with Cassandra. And then, if there's anything left to fish for, I'll crew with Jacob or one of the locals from Lostcoast to keep the tradition alive each spring."

"I can't believe the government is letting Stoboltz continue to operate after what Darvin Thurlow was up to," said Cole, looking down at his hands wrapped around his can of beer.

"There's no proof," said Grace. "We never could prove that they were planning on playing God and releasing the super sea lice. They covered those tracks pretty well."

"Too bad Lance Grey couldn't say the same," said Cole.

Nancy grinned. "That story I did for the *National Post* was like an atomic bomb dropped on Lance Grey's head."

"Yeah, and the minister's office was ground zero," said Cole.

"I expect there will be charges. The RCMP are opening an investigation. I got a source to go on the record. It was in Friday's *Post*."

"Has the minister managed to avoid the fallout?" asked Grace.

"So far, but I doubt he'll survive the next cabinet shuffle," said Cole.

They sat and watched the birds circle overhead, the boat gently rocking in its slip.

"I'm curious, Grace. What happed with Archie's debt to the band?" Nancy asked.

Grace smiled. "They forgave it. I told them that I'd sell the house and pay it off, but they said no. You know, I was surprised — even Greg said that it wouldn't really serve the community to have the bluff house sold. I think he's just trying to play nice so we don't run him off the island for his dirty tricks with Stoboltz. What do you hippies call it? Good karma?"

"Don't look at me," said Cole. "I'm from Alberta. We eat hippies. Ask Denman. He's the one who meditates."

"Guilty," said Denman, then he took off his cap and ran a hand over his bald head. "But no dreadlocks here." Everybody laughed.

Cole stood and stepped to the cooler. Grace stood up so he could open it, and he pulled another can of beer from the ice, sluicing the water from the can before opening it. "Anybody else?"

He passed beers to Darren and Nancy. "Sarah, want a pop?"

She smiled and nodded, and he handed her a root beer. She pushed the film of icy water from it and opened it, drinking the foam from the top of the can. She sat on her father's lap, and he put his arms around her — for a moment everything in the world seemed perfect to Cole Blackwater.

"Seems like most of the loose ends are wrapping up," said Nancy. "Hey, Cole, when is *your* day in court?"

"Not until mid July."

"What is Dan Campbell pleading?"

"Crown says he's pleading not guilty to assault with a weapon."

"You just going to show the judge that beautiful face of yours as evidence?" asked Nancy.

Cole grinned and felt the jagged scar that criss-crossed the other marks already there. Sarah turned around and gave him a kiss. Cole said nothing. Nancy smiled at the two of them. He was a different man when he was with Sarah.

"When do you start at the *Sun*?" Grace changed the subject.

"First of July," said Nancy. "I've already filed my last story for the *Journal*." She glanced at Cole, but he seemed lost in a different world.

■ When the party on the boat broke up, Cole and Nancy walked up the winding hill to the bluff house. Cole and Nancy lingered on the deck while the others prepared dinner in the kitchen. As the sun set on one of the year's longest days, the waters of Knight Inlet danced with a thousand shades of blue.

"God, it's beautiful here," Nancy said, looking east toward the coast range and then back to the narrow waters of the inlet.

"It's a great place," said Cole. "Archie did a good job making sure it stayed that way."

"Listen," said Nancy, which is what she always said when she was about to breach a difficult subject. "Listen...." she sighed.

"Don't," Cole said.

"Cole, I'm sorry."

"It's okay. You're right."

"I am?"

"Don't let it go to your head. It doesn't happen very often." Nancy punched him in the arm. "What am I right about?"

"Guess."

"That sounds dangerous. Just tell me, wise ass."

"That I'm rotten at talking about things. About my father."

"You can't keep it bottled up inside."

"I know that."

"It's eating you alive. All your friends can see it."

"Don't get all Dr. Phil on me, Webber."

She shot him a look. The evening sun coloured his face golden. "Denman says he's got something that's going to help."

"What is it?"

"He won't tell me. Says I have to trust him."

"That sounds interesting. Can I watch?"

"As long as it doesn't involve needles, crystals, or someone playing a didgeridoo over my naked ass, sure, I don't see why not."

"Can I write about it? I've got to make a good impression on the people of Vancouver."

He shot her a look and she laughed.

"Thank you," he said, turning to look at her.

"For what?"

"For *not* writing about it."

She looked at him a moment, her dark eyes meeting his. "You're welcome."

He looked away, out at the harbour. "I thought you were just in this for the story."

"I wasn't sure myself what I was in it for."

"And now?"

"Now I'm sure," she said.

Epilogue The sun blazed like a white scream. It was the first of July. The dark, rain-cloaked days of spring had yielded to summer's persistent tug; there hadn't been a storm cloud since the beginning of June. The sky had been blue for three weeks. Only over the mountains on Vancouver Island, and in the highest reaches of the coast ranges on the mainland, did a few cottony clouds form each afternoon. At midday the sun baked the high ranges, melting the remaining glaciers, creating mirages that danced above the serrated horizon.

At the ocean's edge it was cooler. The tide of air that flowed in rhythm with the lunar surge, up and down Knight Inlet, took the bite out of the heat. That atabatic breath of air — moving up the mountain slopes during the day and down each evening with katabatic wind — created convection currents, swirls of warm air that rose up the edges of the forests and cliffs where they met the sea.

U'melth, a solitary black raven, rose on the atabatic curl, rose up with the churning current into the sky. The bird hove above the calm waters of Knight Inlet and then drifted west, out toward the fjord's mouth and the dappled constellation of islands beyond. In the sunlight, the bird's beak glistened like polished obsidian while the bird's eyes remained opaque, inscrutable. The raven drifted, not spending an ounce of energy in flight, gliding from air pocket to air pocket, hovering over the margins where the dark forest slipped down the sides of hills to meet the sea below.

U'melth had seen more than thirty summers come and go. He was old, even for his kind. A few white feathers over the raven's dark eye gave him a patriarchal stature.

Motion caught U'melth's interest. Far in the distance, toward a point of land that fingered the inlet, an unkindness of ravens was gathering at the ocean's edge. The patriarch tucked his wings to his body and sped toward the assembly. Within a few minutes the solitary bird had joined the council numbering more than fifty. Some were perched on the branches of fir and spruce while others hopped along the shore from rock to rock. Others still turned overhead, rising up and sliding down air pockets the way children might play on a slide. While they appeared to do so at leisure, they were intent in their focus. All were absorbed by the dark mass wedged between two barnacle-encrusted boulders at the water's edge.

At high tide this place was five feet beneath the sea, but now, near the tide's ebb, the dark human form was a foot above the high water mark. A dozen birds were perched on the corpse while others moved about at the side of the clot of tattered clothing. The grandfather raven tucked its wings to its side and dropped from the sky to investigate. Landing on a rock with a bounce, he opened his mouth and tilted his head to one side. The others gave him no credence. Raven hopped twice and peered down on the mass to inspect the find.

An unmoving arm protruded from sodden clothing. The hand was fat and white, the bloated fingers the size of Sitka spruce cones, the skin torn and hanging like rags.

U'melth flapped three times and landed on top of the body. With his beak he pulled at the dark clothing. Other birds joined, and some feathers were ruffled in the effort to get access to the rest of the meat. In a moment the raven was able to find a place to peck and soon slipped away with a mouthful to eat. Finishing, it swooped back in for more. Two more mouthfuls were thrown back into the open throat before a harsh cry pierced the air, and the raven flapped safely out of reach of a bald eagle returning to pillage. Soon half a dozen eagles were standing on the rocks, challenging the ravens. The ravens took to the trees and croaked and jabbered and waited. U'melth watched the sun on its summer parabola.

The life of the man passed into the life of the raven.

U'melth feasted for two days, and when there was little left to eat, he flew east into the setting sun, up Knight Inlet, its waters shimmering like the scales of a snake resting between the backs of rising mountains. That night, Grandfather Raven rested in the top of a giant Sitka spruce and, in the morning, glided on the gently moving air currents to the headwaters of the inlet. There U'melth played along a cliff wall with ravens half his age, all of them riding thermal air masses to the top of the bluff, then tucking their wings tight to their bodies and plunging down, down, toward the forest below.

That night U'melth died in his sleep. He fell from the Sitka spruce in which he was perched and landed on thick moss and a mass of spruce needles at the tree's base.

By the next morning, a dozen species of carnivorous beetles and two massive banana slugs had taken up residence on U'melth's body. Ants had begun to colonize the bird's wings and the length of his abdomen. The following day, centipedes burrowed into the raven's fat belly.

After two weeks all that remained of the raven were its wings, skull, and beak. A mouse gnawed at the calcium in the raven's bones. In a month there was nothing left to mark U'melth's passing.

The life of the man passed from the raven into the lives of insects and creatures too numerous to number.

Summer became autumn. Rain fell nearly every day. The insects that had made a feast of U'melth's corpse fled their subterranean tunnels for the forest floor, seeking shelter from the flood. They drowned by the hundreds, and when the waters drained back into the earth and the dendridic arms of the creeks that laced the woods, their bodies became part of the humus. Their bodies' energy and nutrients passed into the living skin of soil that covered the stone skeleton of the coast ranges, the same soil that nourished the giant Sitka spruce that rose pillar like toward the sky from which U'melth had fallen.

The life of the man passed from raven to insect and from insect to earth.

Like a giant straw, the Sitka spruce sucked life from the soil. A microscopic slurry of nutrients and water rushed up the xylem and down the phloem of the massive tree. The soil's nutrients became the tree's blood, its life force, and built bark and limbs and leaves and heartwood.

From man to raven to insect to earth to tree.

Fall slipped into winter and winter into spring. The earth completed another circuit around the sun. Salmon pushed their way up into the headwaters arm of Knight Inlet. Born there years before, the pink salmon found their way into the tiny tributary stream over which the Sitka spruce stood like a centurion. The salmon had ranged across the Pacific ocean, survived countless perils, and had charted their way back to the very place of their creation.

Grizzly bears followed them. Called by the thrashing of the fish, the bears came down the mountain sides like drunken sailors, pushing each other aside and swatting at the salmon, carrying them into the woods, sometimes only eating the brains and leaving the rest of the fish to rot into the roots of fir and spruce along with the detritus of the forest floor.

Winter came. The bears retreated into the mountains. The eagles moved up the inlet, threading their way into the headwater tributaries. The dying salmon lay in spent and stinking heaps along the banks of the creeks for the eagles to gorge on. They were followed by the ravens. And the ravens by the gulls.

By midwinter's day, little could be seen of the great orgy of feasting that had followed the arrival of that season's salmon run.

The giant Sitka spruce towered over the creek. Snow fell on the earth and clung to the tree's branches.

Spring arrived with a vernal aurora of colour and life. Salmon smolts pushed their way from under rock gardens and the cooling shade of mossy stream banks and swam west, following the primordial urge to join with the sea. Many were eaten by predators before they could taste salt water.

Summer again, then fall, then winter. Summer.

Twenty cycles came and went. Twenty trips around the sun. The giant spruce survived seasonal storms, the pleading of logging companies for access to the ancient forests along the coast, and lightning in the summer, gale-force winds in the fall, snow in the winter.

It was in December, twenty-one years since man became U'melth and U'melth became insect and tree, that a winter storm surged up the valley like a runaway train, tearing at the sides of the mountains, toppling lesser trees and piling them like matchsticks along the banks of the inlet.

The giant spruce, five hundred years old, was toppled. The earth shuddered when it crashed to the forest floor. A dozen other smaller trees — spruce, fir and cedar — fell with it. The Sitka spruce bridged the tiny headwaters tributary, its trunk not more than a foot above the water when the creek was in spring flood, its moss-draped branches stuck like daggers into the creek's surge, creating a natural seine.

Seasons came and passed. The giant spruce slowly sank into the earth. Its bark melted away in winter storms, the stout, mossy arms that punctured the creek became skeletal limbs. A dozen spruce and fir saplings grew along the great nurse log's bulk. Bears crossed the river on its back, stepping around the forest of its spine.

Twelve spring floods raged and fell, and the giant spruce sagged until its branches finally sank under the creek's seasonal surges. The water pooled behind it and pushed at the tree's deteriorating skin, and slowly the demarcation between tree and creek became imperceptible. Branches broke from the trunk during floods and jetted downstream. The pulpy centre of the tree gave in to water's patient tug, and soon it began to decay from within.

Seven more autumns came to pass. As if by some miracle, salmon continued to arrive. Spawned. Died. Their carcasses caught in the crooks and hollows of the great tree's decomposing. Bears ate the salmon. Eagles pillaged as they wished. Ravens chided each other, sitting on the back of the sunken log.

The flesh of the tree passed into the water. Salmon swam into it, breathing it in, mouths agape with exhaustion and the final spasm of life that was their mission — procreation. Then they died and drifted into a quiet eddy. The life-giving waters passed over the fry as they were born, the great tree's nutrients became the water, then the salmon, and also their spawn. It was their breath of life as they slipped from the shelter of the giant spruce and raced for the sea.

The life that was man, raven, insect, earth, and tree became salmon.

From the narrow banks of the headwaters' tributary, the salmon fry surged out into the open inlet. Waters so vast, the tiny smolts were like motes of dust in a galaxy of swirling dark water. As if programmed, the pink salmon pushed en masse westward, and those that survived the gauntlet of predators made the turn from the inlet into Tribune Channel and threaded their way toward the opening where the knot of islands ended and the Queen Charlotte Strait opened, its vastness startling to the pinks born into such tranquil waters.

Most didn't survive, but those that did could not know the perilous fate their ancestors faced, their journeys roughly punctuated by fish farms, now long gone. Where once disease, pollution, and the curse of sea lice sucked the life from their tiny bodies, now open water welcomed them.

Soon the coursing salmon broke the grip of the mainland cluster of islands, and the ocean surged and moved around them, the waters bottomless, the edges of the world dark green memories far beyond the reach of their growing bodies.

Past Cape Scott, the western tip of Vancouver Island, and then the Scott Islands, and then out into the vastness of the great open ocean, the life that was man, raven, insect, tree, and finally salmon, became, at last, the sea.

THE DARKENING ARCHIPELAGO
Stephen Legault on the evolution of a series

Back to the beginning

The Cole Blackwater mysteries were conceived during a rain-soaked trip to Costa Rica in the fall of 2003. Before the metaphorical ink for the plot of the first book had dried, I began to think about what other kinds of trouble Cole might find himself in.

Cole Blackwater is, in the words of his drinking buddy, Dusty Stevens, an environmental crusader — a champion of lost causes. But the greatest compliment anybody gave me after *The Cardinal Divide* was released was that the environmental message was "subtle." Because, first and foremost for me when writing the Cole Blackwater series is the plot. If the book is to be just a thinly disguised polemic on environmental and social justice issues, then I may as well just write essays. That said, the Cole Blackwater mysteries are an avenue for bringing important issues facing the future of our society, and our planet, to a new audience. As I continue to develop this series, I find no shortage of subjects to choose from.

In 2003, when I first pieced together *The Cardinal Divide*, I was working for a small national conservation organization called Wildcanada.net. One of the campaigns we championed was called "Farmed and Dangerous." On behalf of the Living Oceans Society we helped people take action to ensure a future for wild salmon and stop massive new salmon farming operations from being developed along the BC coast. I began to wonder what the illustrious/altruistic Cole Blackwater might have to say about salmon farming, and how he could get involved in the effort to rid the province's coastal waters of these death traps for wild salmon.

Before I even had a plot, I knew the title: *The Darkening Archipelago*. The archipelago in question is the Broughton — ground zero for the explosive growth of salmon farming in BC. From the very beginning, I knew that this book would relate an ominous story indeed. *The Darkening Archipelago* maps out a race against time and overwhelming odds to keep both human souls and wild ecosystems from falling into unending darkness. But it is also a story about redemption. The three protagonists in the story — Cole, Nancy, and Archie Ravenwing — all contemplate their belief at some point in the power of redemption. None of them reach any conclusions.

That is the "what" of the story process. Here is the "how": during the summer of 2006 I received the gift of time from my friend Joel Solomon. He helped me spend a week at the Hollyhock Retreat Centre on Cortes Island, away from ringing phones and petty distractions, like the need to feed myself. There I sequestered myself in the tiny upstairs library. On massive sheets of butcher paper I drew out a twenty foot long storyboard for *The Darkening Archipelago*. In the afternoons I would sit on the beach and review what I had written, and work on character development and narrative. The whole story took shape before my eyes. The three converging plot lines featuring Cole, Archie and Nancy formed separate chapter "bubbles" which, two thirds of the way through the book, coalesced into one narrative arc.

Because of this preparation, I was able to sit down and pen the first draft of *The Darkening Archipelago* in January and February of 2007. During a paroxysmal period of scribbling I wrote 310 pages and 90,000 words in 28 days. As winter slowly ebbed on the "wet coast," I took advantage of the pivot towards spring and the burst of energy it brought, and sometimes rose as early as 4 AM to write.

There are many factors that contribute to such voluminous outbursts. It would be another six months before I heard from NeWest Press that the first book in the series, *The Cardinal Divide*, would be published. The creation of a second book in a series that was yet to have its first volume accepted for publication was an act of pure faith.

But having just received some excellent feedback on *The Cardinal Divide* from Victoria bookseller Frances Thorsen, I spent the first couple of weeks of the new year editing for the eight or ninth time the entire manuscript. That got me pretty excited about the characters — Cole and Nancy in particular — and I wanted to see what might happen to them in the second book of the series.

While the first draft of *The Darkening Archipelago* took shape very quickly, it took two more years to finish it. The version I finally submitted to NeWest for publication was draft number nine or ten — I lost track. But every single time I sat down to work on the manuscript was a pure joy.

From writing procedures to police procedurals

One of the highlights of writing *The Darkening Archipelago* came towards the end of the process. I met with Corporal Darren A. Lagan, Strategic Communications Officer for the Royal Canadian Mounted Police Island District. I wanted to learn more about police procedure to provide additional realism to the investigation of the disappearance of Archie Ravenwing.

During our discussions Corporal Lagan would say things like, "Well, Cole would likely have to do this..." and I found myself thinking, wow, he's referring to a character in one of my books as if he were real! And while I have taken some liberties with those police procedures, it was a great experience, and I think it makes *The Darkening Archipelago* a more credible novel. My thanks go out to Corporal Lagan for his generous assistance. I take full responsibility for any errors and divergence from actual procedure in the book.

Mysteries in multiples

As I mentioned above, I'd always imagined the Blackwater books as a series. Once I had settled on the theme for the second one — salmon farming — and worked through the who dunnit aspect of the plot, I spent some time considering the broader narrative arc of the books. I began to reflect on the various sub-plot possibilities for three novels, because as I was jotting down the initial notes for *The Darkening Archipelago*, I was also considering a third book called *The Lucky Strike Manifesto*.

Mystery novels should come in threes. One book is just long

enough to resolve a murder mystery, but it takes three to really explore the intricacies of a character's neurosis. I'm not saying that Cole Blackwater is doomed at the end of *The Lucky Strike Manifesto*, but there should be some resolution to the broader themes in the novel in order to make the series satisfying. I'm just not promising what shape Cole will be in after that resolution.

That Cole Blackwater had a less than cheery relationship with his father was made clear in *The Cardinal Divide*. In the epilogue of that book, I tried to make it apparent, without being overtly explicit, that Cole was somehow entangled in his father's violent death. My intent was to leave the reader guessing as to the cause of Henry Blackwater's death, and what role Cole played in it.

In *The Darkening Archipelago*, Cole's unfortunate part in this tragic event becomes clear, and with it we begin to glimpse the depth to which Cole has been damaged. His violence, his rage, his myopic drive to prove himself to the world and to those around him, start to make sense in the face of his abusive relationship with his father.

There are other elements to the narrative arc of the Blackwater series. Cole's relationship with the *Edmonton Journal* reporter Nancy Webber is crucial to the development of his character. The mistakes he made that lead to their mutual exodus from Ottawa, and the tentative steps they took in *The Cardinal Divide* to rebuild the trust between them, nearly come undone in *The Darkening Archipelago*.

These sub-plots, of course, become intertwined as Nancy pursues her insatiable curiosity about Cole's past and begins to openly ask, "did Cole Blackwater kill his father?" If you take Cole Blackwater for his word, *The Darkening Archipelago* answers this question. However, two significant elements of the plot remain to be resolved: first, how will Cole deal with the reawakened trauma born from reliving the final moments of his father's angry life, and second, will Nancy's role in rehashing that suffering impact their relationship? *The Lucky Strike Manifesto*, in addition to introducing readers to an antagonist that frightens even me, will address these loose story threads.

A critical point in history: the end of wild salmon

This book has been published at the best and worst possible time.

The Darkening Archipelago arrives in the spring of 2010 — at a critical juncture for the wild salmon of British Columbia. In the fall of 2009, a judicial inquiry was called into one of the worst disasters in fisheries management in Canada, if not the world. The vast schools of sockeye salmon that return annually to BC's Fraser River have disappeared. Of the projected 10,000,000 fish that were expected to swim up the Fraser River in 2009, only 600,000 returned. That's six percent.

As the Fraser sockeye disappear, so also do hundreds of other salmon populations from Alaska to California. After more than a decade of the salmon's decimation, the Canadian federal government, charged with protecting this international miracle of life, has finally acted on their behalf.

The inquiry will take two years. In that time, many more salmon runs could vanish.

As a reader, what can you do? Get involved. Sign a petition. Send a letter to or call your Member of Parliament. Talk about this with friends. Attend the hearings. Follow up. Don't take no for an answer. As my friend and mentor Brock Evans of the US Endangered Species Coalition says, only "constant pressure, constantly applied" will ensure that the wild creatures we love, and the wild places they need to survive, will be protected.

Thank you for reading this book, and thanks also for anything you can do to protect wild salmon and the wild oceans that are needed for them to survive.

Acknowledgements

My wife, Jenn Hoffman, for her support and love, which makes all things possible.

NeWest Press, and in particular Lou Morin, Natalie Olsen, Tiffany Foster, and Don Kerr, for their faith in me, and in Cole Blackwater.

Alexandra Morton, who has brought the issue of salmon farming and the real-life disaster of sea lice to life for me. I thank Alex for taking the time to review early drafts of this book to ensure I got the facts straight. Also, to Kate Dugas, who years ago introduced me to the issue of salmon farming and captured my attention and imagination with her passion. Her work with Jennifer Lash and Oonagh O'Connor at Living Oceans Society to protect wild salmon inspired the plot of *The Darkening Archipelago*.

Dr. Josh Slatkoff, my best friend and running companion, who has spent countless hours with me on the trail discussing Cole Blackwater's many problems.

Kathleen Wiebe, for her ongoing effort to make some sense of my sometimes incomprehensible writing.

Thanks to Corporal Darren Lagan of the Royal Canadian Mounted Police Island District, and Dan Batton of Fisheries and Oceans Canada, Canadian Coast Guard agency, for explaining the procedural nature of a search at sea.

Thank you to Frances Thorsen of Chronicles of Crime in Victoria, BC for her ongoing counsel on the development of my writing career.

And my thanks to Joel Solomon and Hollyhock, who many years ago provided me with the time and space needed to work on the very first outline of this book.

Stephen Legault has been a social and political activist for twenty years. In July 2005 he launched Highwater Mark Strategy and Communications, an environmental consulting company that advises social-profit companies and ethically driven businesses on their business practices. His first book, *Carry Tiger to Mountain: The Tao of Activism and Leadership,* was published in April 2006. *The Cardinal Divide*, Legault's first Cole Blackwater mystery, was released in October 2008. For more information, visit www.coleblackwater.com.

Legault is the adoring father of two boys, Rio Bergen and Silas Morgen, and loving husband to wife Jenn. They live in Victoria, BC.